In the Echo
of this
Ghost Town

Don't
wish
you were
here.
Sorry.
not sorry.

TO:
Griffin Nichols
123 45th Street NE
The Town, USA 67890

Also by CL Walters

The Stories Stars Tell
When the Echo Answers

The Cantos Chronicles:
Swimming Sideways
The Ugly Truth
The Bones of Who We Are

The Letters She Left Behind

To:
The Reader

In the Echo
of this
Ghost Town

by cl walters

mixed plate press
honolulu, hi

First edition: 2021

Cover Art: Sara Oliver Designs

Library of Congress Cataloging-in-Publication Data

Names: Walters, CL, 1973 – author
Title: In the Echo of this Ghost Town: Novel / CL Walters
Description: First edition / Honolulu: Mixed Plate Press, 2021
Identifiers: LCCN 2021907801 / ISBN 9781735070230
(hardcover) / ISBN 9781735070254 (paperback) / ISBN
9781735070247 (ebook)
Subjects: CYAC Realistic – Fiction / Contemporary – Fiction /
Coming-of-Age – Fiction / Male Culture - Fiction

DEDICATION

To Lavinia, who inspired Griffin's story into existence; your curiosity pushed me to open the door and peek inside.

To all the amazing readers like her for sharing their love of characters and stories. This is for you.

a note from the author...

TRIGGER WARNING (but spoilers)

Dear Reader,

Sometimes in the course of writing a story, the characters take us into places we don't anticipate. Just like life, I suppose. Because of that, sometimes those moments hurt, make us relive our own trauma. Griffin's story does this. This warning contains spoilers—**please turn the page now if you want the story to unfold without them**—but it felt only right to provide readers an option to know what's ahead.

In this story, Griffin makes some ill-advised decisions, one of which is having unprotected sex. The young woman becomes pregnant and decides to have the baby. Unfortunately, she and the baby face a medical emergency during the pregnancy in which their lives are in peril. The baby dies. These scenes are emotionally difficult and those who have experienced this trauma will face it again with these characters.

As a writer, I try to approach these narrative moments with reflective grace and care for the characters (and my readers). My heart goes out to all who may have experienced, endured and continue to process this kind of heartrending grief.

With love,

Cami

JULY

Remember when we were little and played cowboys and bandits? You always wanted to be a bandit. I did too. Why was that? My theory: the bandit was our father. I fucking idolized him. Remember when he was arrested? Held down by police, cuffed and led him from the house? I keep asking myself: is that what I thought it meant to be a man? Did that idea chase me? What does it mean to be a man? Do you know? Now, I'm not so sure.

To: Griffin Nichols
123 45th Street NE
The Town, USA 67890

1.

The cruel asphalt underneath me feels like the truth. Everything about me is a lie. I hurt. Tanner, my best friend, is on the asphalt next to me. We've been in a fight. He says something I don't catch. I'm drunk as fuck. His voice sounds distant as though I'm covering my ears even though he's just an arm's length away. I think I said something about him being pussy-whipped—definitely thought it. He bit back with sharp words, drawing blood, though I'm not exactly sure what kind of weapons they were or where they cut. I'm just bleeding internally. Angry, we sort of collided—two drunks— and rolled across the parking lot outside a convenience store, unable to keep our feet under us. We added blows with our hands to the ones with our words.

I break myself into parts to avoid the feelings—or the hurtful truth of them. There's the Griffin who wants to accept the stark reality of tiny painful pebbles pressing my skin. He wants to find a way to bandage up what's bleeding. That Griffin is the optimist, but he also feels the wounds. So, there's the Griff who adds scar tissue to protect the softer parts. This tougher Griff is filled with so much rage there aren't defenses strong enough to damn the vitriol ready to ooze from my mouth. He's the one who will cauterize the weakness to protect all of me, because gentle Griffin is an infection. Unyielding Griff won't accept heartache; this Griff is all about the lies I tell to keep the tender fragments of myself hidden.

Now, breathing like my lungs might spew from my mouth, I'm trying to remember why this battle was so important. I turn my head to look at Tanner on the ground next to me, disoriented by the movement of the world around me. I wonder why—of all the people in my life—I'm fighting with Tanner. He's my brother—or the closest thing I have to one since my older brother, Phoenix, left me—and right now, I feel like my gut is bruised from the rocks I've been carrying around inside of it. My throat is on fire with the need to cry, or maybe I just need to puke.

Tanner is on his back, like me, drunk, like me, and looking up at a black sky. But I'm looking at him, my best friend since we were fourteen. I'm always looking at Tanner.

"You were my brother, Griff," Tanner mutters up at the sky.

Were.

Were.

Were.

I get stuck in the past tense.

Angry, insulated, scar-tissue Griff tags into the match instead, hops around the ring looking for the next opening to hurt him back. Fury as a default setting.

Everyone leaves.

I recall Phoenix's back as I watched him walk away. He didn't turn around, and I think that's what hurt the most. In my imagination, I've created a version of him stopping at the end of the sidewalk, turning, and looking over his shoulder at me to smile. It's the kind of smile that says: *I see you, baby brother. Don't worry. You've always got me.* He didn't though. He just turned and kept walking toward the bus stop.

I'd looked at my mom, waited for her to change her kicked-out-of-the-house sentencing, unable to register the tears in her eyes for my own anguish. She hadn't. She shored up her defenses, her mouth thinning into a barbed-wire fence, and she waited for me to yell. I just didn't. All that feeling was stuck in my throat. The blame for making Phoenix leave dumped concrete mix down my gullet, filled me up with bitterness, and hardened my insides into stone. I stomped past her, disappeared into my room, and slammed the door but didn't scream. I couldn't. I just went silent. Flopped on my bed and stared at the hot-girls-hot-cars poster Phoenix had given me for my thirteenth birthday. Now, he was gone. First dad. Now him. What did that mean for me?

So, fury is a friend.

I roll away from Tanner. "Fuck you. You're leaving," I say. I know the feeling of being left behind better than anyone, except maybe Tanner whose brother died and whose parents' marriage exploded.

"Where am I going?"

I struggle onto my hands and knees, the loose pebbles of the parking lot biting at my palms. I don't know why I think about the sting of rocks when there's a boulder sitting inside my chest. I need to puke it up, but it's lodged there.

Tanner might be right; he isn't leaving in a physical sense. We both made sure we didn't have options after high school—too much party, not enough school—but that doesn't mean he isn't digging out.

"You left a long time ago." I spit. I do feel like I need to puke. Sick. Somehow, I get to my feet. "Everybody fucking leaves."

Tanner sits up. "I didn't. I tried to talk to you; you wouldn't listen."

I don't want to listen now. Nothing he might say will sway pissed-off Griff. Tanner violated our pact. He broke the Bro Code, and it isn't the part about fucking bitches. Tanner broke what was real between all of us, and that was the promise to always be there for one another. Tanner is choosing to walk away. Phoenix left and never came back; he just sends stupid postcards that don't make any sense. Brother by postcard proxy. Tanner isn't going to come back either.

"We aren't friends anymore," I mutter.

6

"Guys. This is dumb." Danny's voice punctuates our mutterings with the clarity of his sobriety.

I swing around toward our other friend, swaying as I do. My feet scratch over the scree of the lot as I walk away from Tanner to Danny standing near his tan car. Danny—his arms crossed over his chest and his hands tucked up under his arms—watches us. His brow has collapsed over his dark eyes with irritation which makes me hesitate. I'm not sure I've ever seen Danny mad. Then again, I can't be sure of anything since I'm wasted.

There's a shuffle in the gravel behind me which I assume means Tanner has gotten to his feet. He says, "You're right. We haven't been friends for a long time." His words add weight to the boulder that's holding down my heart.

I glance around for Josh—the fourth of our gang—but remember he isn't there. He's wherever kids with intact families who love each other go.

Lately, I feel like I've been trying to hold our brotherhood together, trying so hard to keep things the way they've always been.

I thought it would always be Tanner and me. Tanner, me, Danny and Josh.

Tanner says something about walking home.

Danny's arms collapse to his sides, and he takes a step past me. "That's pretty far, Tanner. I can take you."

I shake my head. "No. He isn't our friend."

Danny looks at me, dark eyes narrowed. "He's mine." He calls after Tanner, "I can take you home, bro."

Tanner's voice is farther away. "No."

I hear the slide of his steps across the gravel as he walks away, but I don't turn to look at my former friend. Turning around might tear open the exposed underbelly of weak Griffin. That Griffin wants to reach for when we—Tanner and me—were fourteen and walking down the school hallway, laughing after getting kicked out of homeroom together. Or when we played the prank at the end of freshman year with the fire alarm. All the times we traipsed around town before we could drive, looking for fun and usually making it. The quiet talks when life felt too heavy, so it didn't feel like we had to hold it up alone. That's been a long time ago. After months of trying to bind Bro Code together, I'm not begging Tanner to stay. Instead, I climb into Danny's car and sink down as low as I can in the passenger seat.

Danny gets behind the wheel, but he doesn't start the car. "That was messed up, Griff. What you said about Rory." I hear the disappointment and displeasure in his voice, in the punctuation of his words and the way they run together as if he's speaking Spanish.

"What are you talking about? I didn't say anything about Rory." I shake my head to deny it, but my brain is cement. Why would I say anything about Tanner's dead brother? "Tanner broke the code," I mumble and lean my head against the window, wondering how we'd gone from laughing and drinking a little while ago—Tanner, the prodigal son, returned to the fold after his misguided relationship detour with the Matthews chick—to what had just happened.

"No. He didn't." Danny starts the car; his hands slip from the key because he does it with so much force. "You're the one who broke it."

"How's this my fault?" I stare out at the overflowing dumpster at the edge of the parking lot. I turn to look at him. "Tanner's the one acting like a bitch."

Danny makes a disgusted sound. "He's tried to talk to you for months." He looks over his shoulder as he reverses the car. The staccato of the gear shift moving into first gear adds emphasis to the tension. "And Josh and I tried to tell you. You're so stubborn. That's not how friends treat one another."

"We're going the wrong way. Bella's is the other way."

He swears, and I'm taken aback by it. I've known Danny for three years. Of all of us, he hasn't been the one to let loose with his mouth. That's usually me.

"I'm taking your ass home."

"Whoa, dude. Tanner's the one who broke the code."

Danny goes silent, his hand gripping the steering wheel so tight his knuckles are white. Then he sort of unleashes, slamming the wheel with his hand and yelling, "This isn't about the fucking, stupid-ass code!"

I'm not sure what to say. Of course it's about the code! All of who we have been together has always been about our crew; why else would I be fighting for it? For the last three years, our code has been our navigational system. First Tanner (Josh has always been a ride-along) and now Danny is disabling our operating procedures. That party at Bella's was my endgame. That's the rules of Bro Code: to help one another freaking get laid. My anger collects, so when he parks in front of my house refusing to go to Bella's, I'm not only shocked by his defiance and disregard of our rules, but I'm also fuming.

"Get out." Danny won't look at me, the last of our gang. The dependable one. The one who is always there. "You're drunk, and I'm going home."

"I'm always drunk."

Danny's face turns toward me then, the shape of his usually kind features sharp and jagged like unfinished granite. "Yeah. Maybe that's the fucking problem." He reaches across me, and the door groans as it opens. "It's time to grow up, Griff. Get out."

The seat belt latch pops and releases, but I can't seem to get my feet under me and roll out of the car instead. When I finally stand, the earth tilts under me, and I sway to correct. "Well, fuck you then." I slam the door and fall with the momentum into the grass outside my house.

Danny drives away, the car huffing and puffing exhaust as if it, too, were angry.

I roll onto my back as the sound of Danny's car disappears in the distance and lay in my front yard gazing at the spinning dark sky. The expanse above me taunts me with my smallness and isolation. I'm alone and shake out my memories to find the last time that was so. They are thin and breakable.

"Fuck!" Angry Griff rages at feeling so small and reinforces his fury by lying about our victimhood.

Softhearted Griffin—who might be able to reinforce the truth if he weren't so small—makes himself smaller to stay safe.

I don't cry even if I feel the sharp points of tears crawling up my throat. Then again, maybe I just need to puke.

2.

"Phoenix?" My young voice echoes through the emptiness of the ghost town. Wooden structures rise around me, and the road stretches ahead as a brown swath of dust. Shades of yellow, tan, red, grays—muted colors of the earth—fade the world around me, making it dry and lifeless.

"Phoenix?" I call out, searching for my brother. My voice sounds like tin and bounces back to me unable to escape the prison of the crumbling, wooden buildings.

A hot wind whips through, and I shiver.

With a glance at my booted feet, scuffed with remnants of the road, I check the boardwalk before stepping up. I know to pay attention to my steps because they always get me into trouble. I've been here before, looking for Phoenix, and ignored the dangers. I always get caught. The graying wood appears solid, so, I step onto the walkway, eyes forward. Another step. "Phoenix?" I yell. Then, a few steps later, my torso jerks forward but my feet remain where they are. I'm stuck. My boots submerged in the wood as if the walkway were built around them. Struggle isn't going to get me free despite my best intentions. Getting caught here was inevitable.

I hear his mocking laugh before I see him.

That sound clicks through the empty town, bouncing from building to building until it hits me.

I turn my head and look over my shoulder for him, my heart

amplifying its fearful beat in my ears.

He's at the end of the wide, main street of the town, dressed head to toe in black, his cowboy hat pulled low. His guns on his hips suck up all the light, and his spurs ring as he walks toward me.

"I'm not the good guy," I yell out into the dry air. "I'm not." I need him to know it. I need him to approve. There's a bright, gold star gleaming on my chest. "I'm not the good guy!" I pull the star from my chest and throw it out into the street, but it doesn't land. I look at my chest. The star gleams there once again. I pull it again. Throw. It's still gleaming on my chest. "I'm the bad guy, too."

I hear the jingle of his spurs with his steps. Closer. "A bad guy, huh?"

I raise my eyes to look at him. Even though I'd been looking for him and here he is, I'm afraid.

He puts a single, black boot on the edge of the boardwalk next to me, slightly behind so I have to turn awkwardly in my wooden prison to see him. He leans forward, a forearm against a knee, casual and deliberate. With a thumb, he pushes up his hat. The face isn't Phoenix's anymore, it's my dad's. The angles are similar, but older, harsher, and smirking with derision. He reaches out and taps the gold star on my chest. "That says otherwise, son."

His blue eyes are bright like the sky on a summer day—which I know isn't right. We have the same eyes, hazel. He smiles, his teeth shining like the star on my chest.

"Are you here to kill me?" My voice shakes.

He laughs, a big one with gusto so that it bounces around between the buildings that I know will echo forever. "Looks like you're doing that well enough on your own."

I cover my face with my hands and cry.

He laughs louder. "You're a bitch."

My eyes open. The ceiling of my bedroom looms like the top of a closed box. My blue bedspread is the packing material holding me hostage. I kick at it to free myself, my heart racing with the residual emotion left over from the dream. I hate dreaming about Phoenix and my dad, but it happens with more frequency than I care to admit.

Rolling to my side, I face the wall and groan because my stomach feels like it's about to rupture. I smack my lips, my mouth full of cotton, and my head pounds with a hangover. I squint at the hot-girls-hot-cars poster and think about drinking water. Turquoise bikini blond is draped over a yellow Charger and orange bikini brunette, a blue Mustang. "Nothing like a pretty piece of ass to wake up next to in the morning, baby bro," Phoenix had said and laughed as he helped me hang it. I sort of understood what he meant. Then found it a good source of inspiration as I learned how my dick worked.

My brother.

My hero.

I'm the same age he was when he left—eighteen.

I hated mom for kicking him out and hated him for going. It had been Phoenix and me after our dad went to prison. The brother-musketeers. Maybe I've romanticized our relationship. He was a dick when he was in high school, especially his senior year. That's when the fighting with mom started. I haven't seen him in four years, and he hasn't even visited. Occasionally, he'll send a random postcard to let me know he's alive, but they're weird like he's walking down memory lane, and not in a good way. He writes random shit. The messages make me worry about him, but I don't know what the fuck for. He left. Besides, I can't write him back since he hasn't included a stupid, return address.

I sit up on the edge of my bed and rub my face with my hands. There's a haze of a shadowy figure in my mind I'm supposed to remember. Something important. I squeeze my eyes shut and try to recall it. It has to do with Tanner.

Images from the night before solidify like pixels blending on a computer screen as my brain slogs through the hangover:

Sitting in the living room getting trashed.

Danny driving us to Bella's but stopping at the minimart first.

Tanner and I getting into a scrap.

I hold up my hands. They're scratched up from the asphalt where we'd fallen during the fight.

We aren't friends anymore.

He said it.

Or I did.

I don't remember exactly. I'd broken my rules, which I seem to be doing more often lately. I'd been too drunk.

The truth of it hits me like a hammer, and my gut rolls. I rush from the room into the bathroom where there's already vomit all over the toilet and floor. I puke in it again, and shame rushes through me like the fetid regret spewing from my mouth. My eyes sting with tears, filling, but I refuse them. Griffin Nichols doesn't fucking cry.

When I'm done, I flush the toilet and move away from the mess left the night before. Sitting on the floor, my back against the cabinet door, the hardware pokes my back. It's uncomfortable, but I sit there anyway, my head in my hands.

The door squeaks open and thumps against the bathroom counter. "Goddammit, Griffin."

Mom.

"What?" I croak and look up.

Dressed in her second-job, convenience-store attire, she stands in the doorway with her arms crossed over her chest. Her light eyes are shaped with anger. "What the hell?" Her irritation is typical. She points at me. "I'm so fucking over this shit, Griffin. This has got to stop." She covers her mouth and nose.

"Can we please not do this now?" I ask and continue fighting the tears climbing up my throat. With my elbows on my knees, I fist my hands in my hair to tug and feel the sting there instead.

I'll give you something to cry about.

"Why? Because you're hung over?"

It's the truth, and I wonder what she would say if she knew I couldn't remember getting in the house, or puking and leaving it, or making it into my bed? I don't feel like elaborating, not that I've ever spent much time telling my mom about anything. How can I? She's always working.

She huffs with frustration, and then gags, disappearing from the doorway. "I'm charging you rent!" The volume of her words follows her down the hallway. "You want to party like a fucking rockstar, you can pay me for the fucking trouble!"

"Are you kidding me?" I get to my feet.

"No. I'm not." Her voice is muted by the walls between us.

I step around the mess and walk down the hallway, holding the wall to keep my feet under me. "Just like you did to Phoenix?"

"Yes."

"You kicked him out!"

There's a pause and then she yells, "He wasn't paying his rent! And I'll kick your ass out too. I don't need another good-for-nothing, sack-of-lazy shit lounging around here doing nothing with his life. I'm not busting my ass for that!" Her words leave marks, but it's Mom, and she's always worked up about something, so they heal.

"Why the fuck are you so mad all of the sudden?"

She grabs her purse from the counter in the kitchen. "Really?" She looks down the hallway and then back at me, her gaze sharp and focused. "You have to ask?"

I hear the rattle of her keys as she digs through her purse.

"Because I puked?"

She stalls and hangs her head. When she looks up, I can see she has tears in her eyes, but instead of feeling bad, it just makes me angry. Her pain is a horrible accusation against me. I feel those tears like knives in my gut. They accuse me and find me lacking. They hurt worse than the words because those are real. I want to flail my arms, come out hitting and screaming. I don't need more guilt to add to the anger.

"Your dad is getting out." Her bluster is gone, and now the truth of her emotion hits.

15

Thoughts of my father feel like a gut punch and make me want to puke again, but instead I walk past her to the sink to rinse out my mouth.

"So."

I don't want to think about the fuck-up that is my father; the man, who despite being locked up, I can't seem to get out from under. He's a mountain, and I'm sunken in a dank cave somewhere in the recesses of that mass.

She sniffs. I know she's crying. I slam the cup into the sink and retreat into the living room so I can ignore it. After flopping onto the couch, I turn on my video game. From the corner of my eye, I see her turn and face me from her spot in the kitchen at the end of the counter. She reaches up and wipes her eyes with her fingertips.

"What?"

"You're like him. Both you and Phoenix are."

I turn my head to square up my line of sight with hers, and the bomb inside me initiates its countdown. Ten. Like him. "You think I want to hear that shit?"

She walks a few steps into the room. "You need to hear it."

I don't respond.

Nine.

"Griffin." She sighs. "This can't keep happening." She waves her hands at me sitting on the couch. "This is what gets you into trouble." She points at the bathroom.

I grind my teeth together.

Eight.

"Look, I don't talk about your dad because Lord knows you don't have many good memories of him, but you need to know he did the same shit. And look where it got him."

Seven.

"I'm not him," I say through my clenched jaw.

"Then prove it. Be different." She waits. "Do something with your life. A legitimate job. I want you to be more than him."

Six.

16

"I'm not him." If I say it enough, then that will make it true.

She walks into the living room and blocks the TV.

Five.

"Mom." I try looking through her.

"Griffin. Look at me."

Four.

My eyes bounce up to hers with as much insolence as I can muster.

Three.

She crosses her arms over her chest. Her brown hair is pulled back in a ponytail, and her mouth is drawn tight with tension and disappointment. "I can want more for you, but you need to want it for yourself."

Two.

I roll my eyes. "I'll get a frickin' job. Happy?"

One

She nods. "It's a start." She leaves the room.

I hear the garage door close behind her.

Zero.

I throw the video game controller across the room where it crashes against the wall and explodes. Then I yell and collapse against the couch. Sucking breaths and feelings like a fish out of water, I think I might be suffocating. I close my eyes, willing things back into place, rearranging things into deep mind crevices where I don't have to look at them. Eventually, I drift to sleep, and when I wake up sometime later, the sun is curling into the afternoon.

Dad is locked up.

Phoenix left and never came back.

Mom is pissed.

Tanner is a traitor.

Danny left me.

Josh is MIA.

I sigh, unable to change any of that.

The smell wafting from the bathroom reminds me of the mess

that's in there. I curl my lip, disgusted at the idea of it, but I go to the door of the bathroom, where I stand looking at it. Feels like much of the same, only I've left a trail of messes from here to everywhere. I consider ignoring it, closing the door, and leaving it, but I know I can't. The carnage isn't going to go away, and while I can't fix anything else, at least I can fix this. Besides, Mom will come home, and I don't want to hear her ceaseless bitching about my failures.

I clean the disgusting remains of my failure, cursing everyone and everything while I do. Despite nearly puking again, I get it scrubbed, and the smell mostly gone. I have the fleeting thought that I wish it were that simple to fix everything else in my life.

When I'm done cleaning, I take a shower and then text Danny:

> What are we doing tonight?

He doesn't answer.

> Dan, the man. Yo…

As I dress—jeans and a t-shirt—my phone alerts me. I pick it up.

> I'm done, G. Can't do this anymore w/ u. Danny

> What? The? Actual? Fuck?

> Exactly

> Bro…

> I wish that felt true, G. It's all uneven.

> Why r u acting like a bitch? ☺

But he doesn't answer back.

I'm confused. I knew he was mad the night before, but Danny's always been there, even when I'm at my worst. He's helped me, taken care of me, gotten me home. I reread his message: *I'm done.*

I text him back: *Danny? Bro?*

But he remains silent and leaves me on read. No reply.

Like my dream self, I'm standing in a ghost town, stuck. All my friends have abandoned me, and all I was trying to do was hold us together. Now, I'm being punished for it.

With a profane shout, I throw my phone across the room. It crunches against the wall, falls to the floor, screen cracked, and the light seizes.

Ruined. Everything I thought I had is ruined.

I shove my wallet into my pocket—not that there's much in it— slam out the front door, and disappear into the night looking for something else to ruin.

3.

Turns out trouble isn't easy to find on a Monday night, especially without my friends, which adds fuel to the anger already burning me to ash. Each name on my list is kindling thrown into the flames as I walk from my house and out into the night. A lonely and messy business, really, refining all that anger.

At first, the sidewalk rises up to meet me with each step, punching my bones. I take the steps faster, until I'm running through the night. My neighborhood of squat tract homes gives way to another neighborhood and then another until they thin out. Still, I run. The pain of being hungover reverberates through my insides and threatens to turn me inside out, but I don't stop. I run until I think my chest will come out through my mouth.

I gasp for air.

Out of shape.

Out of breath.

Out of time.

When I can't run another step, I slow to a stop. Bent forward, hands to my knees, I heave like I've only got moments left to live. Turns out I'm being a dramatic bitch because I'm gulping oxygen to keep me upright. Everything slows, including my mind. I straighten.

Still alive.

And walk.

Forward.

The bright glow of Custer's Convenience emerges on the horizon. I head toward the light.

Breathing is easier now that I've slammed the energy of the anger against the concrete. Seems kind of perfect, actually: the concrete of me against the concrete of the road. You'd think I would have crumbled into dust, but I just feel more pliable. The punishment of the concrete jarring my bones seems sort of counterproductive to the nature of anger, but then I wonder if perhaps it's a little like the idea of rocks getting ground down in the water because they're bumping up against other rocks. Maybe it doesn't make a lot of sense to be angry, but it's the easiest emotion to allow myself the space to feel. What other feelings are there but the kinds that only serve to make me feel small.

Besides, it wasn't me who broke everything.

A little voice materializes inside me that wants to argue the point. I silence it and frown.

I can hear my mother: *Griffin, fix your fucking face.*

I walk into the store with my face as impassive as I can get it, and with the few bucks in my wallet spring for some water even though I really want a Slurpee. I take it outside and sit at one of the three picnic benches in front of the store not ready to walk home, yet.

Sitting alone is strange and uncomfortable, but I'm not a stranger to the feeling. There was a time when I was younger and can recall carrying a pastel plastic lunch tray across my elementary school cafeteria to sit at a table where no one joined me. Before friends. A target to teasing and taunts. I was weak then.

At home, it was just me and Phoenix (Mom was working). My older brother was all knowing and wise, but he couldn't protect me from the incessant teasing about dad's arrest and imprisonment. When I whined about the kids at school, Phoenix told me to *man up* and find a way to deal with it. He taught me how to throw a punch, but my greatest weapon was the way I could use words to tear someone else down. I'd look for their weakness and exploit it to protect my own. I went on the offensive, took matters into my own hands until I was known as Griff Nichols, son of the convicted murderer (it was a perfect cover since my dad wasn't arrested for murder). No one challenged the persona.

After Phoenix left, and my world was just me, being alone didn't have any appeal. Tanner and I became friends. Then Josh. Eventually Danny. My world revolved around them. If I wasn't sleeping or playing video games, I was with my bros. We became kings, the party crew who everyone wanted at their parties. The ones who brought the fun. The ones girls wanted to hook up with. Now I'm alone again. The quiet of alone haunts me. I've allowed angry Griff the room to keep the rest of me safe from all those haunting thoughts.

The sound of steps on gravel draws my attention from the water bottle label I've been pinching.

A girl materializes from the dark and crosses the lot. I notice she's tall. She glances at me and then disappears into the store.

My friendships rescued me from being locked in, and maybe that's why I've been fighting so hard to keep them. I was our group's social director, and Tanner the social butterfly who gave us the social capital. Josh was our entertainer and peacekeeper, while Danny was our keeper and conscience.

I frown at my water bottle and continue plucking at the label.

I decide I can't reminisce about what we were because the idea of Danny being right reveals the possibility that Tanner could be too. Which would mean I might be—

Nope. Not going there.

"Hey."

I look up at the sound of a voice, grateful to be jerked from the train of my thoughts.

The girl. She's standing on the other side of the table in her dark t-shirt and cutoff shorts, her back to the gas pumps and road. The light from the store illuminates her, and I think she's cute, but obviously not all there if she's talking to a stranger.

"Yeah?"

She sits down with a Slurpee, and I look at it longingly but also wish I had some vodka to spike it with. I conjure Danny's words from the night before. I'd told him I'm always drunk. What had he said back? "Yeah. Maybe that's the fucking problem. It's time to grow up, Griff." What if I do have a problem? Then I'm annoyed by the stupid thought—of course, I don't. What the fuck? Can't this weird girl tell I'm busy sulking?

My face must screw up because she says, "I'm not carrying any diseases."

I take a sip of my water, not sure what to do about this stranger who's sat with me at a table outside of Custer's. I glance to check if someone is playing a joke on me, but all my friends have abandoned me. So yeah, there's that. I look at her. She's got a round face, but it's smooth and pleasant looking. Brownish hair, I think, because it's pulled back in a bun or something off her face. Black eyeliner. Black T-shirt with the words Def Leppard inside a Union Jack.

She pinches the straw and moves it around the slushy. It squeaks. "Decide I'm not a serial killer?" She smirks, and my eyes are drawn to her blunt black nails at the end of her long fingers holding the red straw.

"Jury's out." I look away and take a sip of my water, annoyed but kind of curious.

"Why's that?"

I shrug. "What if I'm the serial killer?" I can't look at her, though I'm not sure why. It isn't like I'm nervous, even if she's a little unnerving. Why have I said that? The idea of being compared to a killer takes me backward. Griff Nichols, son of a murderer, when I'd been alone, but I'd shed that persona with my crew. I shove the reminder aside.

"It's a distinct possibility."

My eyes connect with hers, the curiosity revving up a notch. "Why's that?"

"Guy sitting outside of a convenience store on a Monday night looking all moody. Definitely sending shady vibes. You spike that unassuming water bottle? Use the innocence of water to lure in your victims but in reality, you're just setting the trap?" She smiles, and I see that she's joking around even though I don't know her; it's the squint of her eyes.

"You're weird."

"I get that a lot." She pauses and leans forward to take a sip of her drink and looks over at me. Her eyes sparkle with mirth, but it's hard to tell what color they are even in the light. Lightish. "So, what do you do in this town for fun?"

"Get drunk. You new?"

"Yes. Why aren't you doing that?"

"It's Monday."

"So, a drunk six days a week? You have standards, I see. So that must be real water." She pauses and raises a single eyebrow—which bugs me for some reason. "You don't look much like the type with standards."

I'm not, but I don't say it. "Neither do you."

"Touché, serial killer. So, you don't drink on Monday for other reasons, then?"

"I didn't say I don't drink on Monday. I just said it was Monday. You made the assumption."

She laughs, but it's mostly air. "Fair enough."

This conversation could die. I could stand and walk away. I don't. I blame it on my lack of being alone, which I'm going to have to reestablish. "So, you're new here?"

"Yep. Just moved. Only here for the summer."

"Why's that?"

"Why what?" She takes another sip of her slushy.

I watch her swallow it. Then I look back at my water bottle to resume plucking the plastic label. "Only for the summer?"

"The band I play with is going on tour."

"Really?"

She laughs. "No."

"You're weird."

"So you've said." She stands. "Well. Thanks for sharing the table."

"There were two other ones you could have chosen."

She glances at the other two and then leans forward. "But then I wouldn't have gotten to talk to a serial killer." She smiles, offers me a nod, and with her hand wrapped around her cup, she walks away. She's wearing jean cutoffs, tight, and the strings of the cut denim hang against her long and shapely legs.

I scoff, looking away because I don't want to notice her. A serial killer. Stupid.

As I watch her—the nameless, weird girl—walk away, I realize I forgot what I was sulking about.

4.

The unforgiveness of the pavement the night before is the second thing I think about when I wake up. The first thing is Weird Girl—whose name I didn't get—and her antagonizing smirk. This is unnerving; I'd rather focus on the fact my legs feel as though I've stripped them of muscle and then tried to hand stitch it back to the bones. I attempt to roll over to go back to sleep, muscles screaming, but my brain won't stop spinning with images of Weird Girl and Slurpees. Then I start thinking about Phoenix and Tanner and my friends, about drinking and partying and wishing things were the same. Then I'm angry about how shitty things are, so I get up before the sun peeks out from behind the plumber's ass-crack horizon and slip into shoes—old ones that I'll probably regret using because my shins are on fire—to find the pain of the pavement again.

The blue of the pre-dawn morning is cool and quiet. Peaceful. Antithetical to everything going on inside of me.

I run.

I pay attention to the jarring punch of the road every time my feet hit the pavement. The pain wakes me up, though I'm not exactly sure what I'm supposed to be waking up from. Sure, there's the literal waking up from sleep, but I've already done that. I feel like there's more to that idea working its way through me, but instead of pondering it, I focus on the pressure against my lungs, stripping away the emotional hurt. My concentration fixated on breathing to stay alive.

When I get home, I fill a glass of water and sit at the counter to cool off.

My mom walks into the room and freezes. Her surprise isn't surprising. I'm not usually up until noon, long after she's gone to work. I'm suddenly sorry for being an ass to her the day before; my shit friends aren't her fault.

"What's this?"

"Went for a run."

"Why?"

I shrug and take another sip of my water.

She slaps something in front of me as she walks past. "Here. And you're welcome."

I follow her across the kitchen with my gaze. Then I glance at the flattened white paper in front of me that was once curled up into a tube. "What is it? A receipt?" I take another sip.

"Stop slurping." She scoops coffee from a tin into the filter of the automatic coffee pot.

"Are you just planning on being on my ass all day?" I take another drink and slurp loudly just to irritate her.

"Yes. If you don't have a job by the end of the week, that's exactly what I will be, like a fucking fly on shit." She snaps the filter into place and presses the button to start the coffee, then points at the paper. "It's a job. A guy runs a construction company or something, I didn't catch all the details. He's looking for help." She goes to the sink to wash the remnants of a dinner I ate. "How many times do I have to ask you to do the dishes? Come on, Griff."

"Sorry. I forgot." But that's a lie. I was too lazy. "Leave them," I say, feeling guilty. "I'll do it." I set the water glass down on the counter, pick up the strand of receipt paper, and read the scrawled note. *CAL WALLACE* written neat, in all caps. There's a phone number and the word *JOB* underneath. "A stranger? You talk to this guy? How do you know he's not a serial killer?" I picture Weird Girl, her smirk, and shake her face from my thoughts.

"Who can know? But he came into the store yesterday asking to post a notice. Seems nice. Cute." She sets the dishes to dry in the plastic strainer doing them anyway and moves to the refrigerator. She's always moving, always busy.

I groan. I don't want to hear about "cute" from my mom. "Why don't you sit down a minute, Ma?" I ask her.

"There isn't time to sit on my ass." She's bent over into the fridge. "I have to get down to the restaurant to prep for opening. Then I'm at the hospital for a swing shift, so I won't be home until late." She withdraws some bread and a few other items that look like she's going to make a sandwich. "You need a job. He's got one."

I stand up and pour her a cup of coffee which I set down at the kitchen bar counter next to where I'd been sitting. Then I take the ingredients from her. "Sit and tell me what to make."

She looks at me, narrows her eyes but does as I ask. "Who are you and what do you want? I don't have any money for you."

I scoff. "Nothing. If this is what I get for helping, why do it?"

She takes a sip of her coffee.

I heard her come in the night before around two in the morning, which means she probably only slept three or four hours. Her schedule has been like this, well, since my dad went to prison.

"Mayonnaise?"

She nods, still watching me with an unwavering gaze over the rim of her cup. "The guy said he'd be home today. You could go by."

"I don't have a car."

She sets down her cup. "Griffin." She sighs like my name weighs a ton. "Use public transportation. You're a high school graduate, and not incapable."

She's right, even if I'd rather sit around feeling sorry for myself. I slather the bread with the mayonnaise, annoyed because she's called me out on making excuses. I hate when she does that.

She clears her throat. "Look, if you land a job," she says and takes another sip of her coffee, "I will release some of Grand Pop's money he left you so you can get a car. Especially if you're still thinking about community college. The rest will be for that."

I look up from the sliced cheese I've just laid on the bread. "Really?"

She offers a smile. "It isn't like you'll be able to get a Corvette. But a used beater to get you from point A to point B. Yeah." She smiles wider into her cup.

I finish making her sandwich with some turkey followed by some lettuce before smashing it together and slipping it into a container. "A car. Cool."

"Job first." She sets down her coffee on the counter. "You have to buy everything for it, so it's useless without all the other stuff." Then using her fingers, she counts off everything. "Insurance, gas, registration, maintenance. Everything costs money."

"I got it." I put the sandwich in a baggie and set it in front of her.

"Yeah, yeah." She nods. "Thanks for the sandwich." She pauses. "We should talk about your dad."

My shoulders tighten. I wrap a hand around the back of my neck and lean against the counter. "You think he'll come around?"

She shrugs and stares into her coffee. "If it were me, then there wouldn't be anything to keep me from you."

She looks up, and for the first time I see my mom as someone different, as a woman who has done everything she can to keep life together for her kids. For me. Of course, I knew it on one level, but I'm not sure I understood her sacrifices, so stuck in my own self-centered universe. The awareness makes me wonder about Phoenix and kicking him out. I don't ask though. I like this with her, as rare as it is. I wonder if my father even cares about us? If he ever did? Knowing he has another family out in the world makes me question it. Maybe Mom would do anything she could to see me and Phoenix, but maybe he'd do anything he could to see his other family, instead.

She stands, comes around to wash her coffee cup and sets it in the drainer, then leans against the counter next to me. "I just think we should probably prepare ourselves for it."

I glance down at her and nod.

She bumps me with her shoulder, then she rises up on tiptoes to kiss my cheek. I can't remember the last time she did that. That realization moves through me like fingernails on one of those old, green chalkboards. Jarring and uncomfortable. It's easier to be pissed at everyone, but maybe I could reevaluate the way I am with Mom. I've been mad about her kicking out Phoenix, but what if there are things about the situation I don't know. *If it were me, then there wouldn't be anything to keep me from you.* That doesn't sound like a mom who wants to kick out her kid.

If I've been wrong about that, what else am I wrong about?

The thought is uncomfortable.

So I think on more pleasant things: the image of a car. It gets me moving.

After calling the number of the Cal guy, setting up a meeting time and getting his address, I figure out the bus schedule. When the bus stops, I get off and use my busted-up phone to find the guy's place. The spiderweb screen makes it a little difficult to see the map. Eventually, the app's disembodied robot voice leads me to a farmhouse.

The building looks like a piece of shit, everything sagging and old, the paint gone or peeling away. It belongs in a ghost town because it's definitely haunted. There's a porch in the front curled around one of the sides. The other side is stark and rises two stories with old shutters, a few of which are missing or hanging from lazy fasteners who are letting go. I have the impression that a deep breath might push the house over. What was my mother thinking to send me to the house of some horrible horror story about to come to life. It's a fucking dump.

I climb the porch anyway, hopeful I won't fall through, because there's the promise of a car, and knock on the closed door, hopeful it won't come off the hinges.

Inside, I hear steps.

The door opens.

On the other side of the threshold: Weird Girl.

Her eyes—which I see now are light grayish—widen. "Serial Killer?" Her hair, which I thought was light brown, is the color of sparkling honey in a jar with the sun shining through it. It's in a thick braid draped over a shoulder. She steps out onto the porch, pulling the door shut behind her. She's built like a linebacker, tall and strong, because our eyes are almost level, but she's rounded in all the places a dude isn't. In this light and that tank top, nice and very noticeable.

I take a step back to keep some distance between us.

"What are you doing here? How did you find me?"

"What?" I shove my hands into my pockets.

She crosses her arms and frowns. "Well?"

"I'm looking for Cal Wallace."

Her arms relax and fall to her sides. "Oh, shit." The door creaks as it opens, and she turns. "Hey, Dad."

A man steps out, tall—like me—with ashy brown hair laced with silver strands. He smiles. "Hi. You must be Griffin."

I hold out my hand toward him as Weird Girl steps to the side. The porch creaks. "Hi."

Cal shakes my hand. It's sturdy, but he doesn't try to crush my bones like he's a caveman or something. "I see you've met Max."

Max. Her name is Max.

She looks down and crosses her arms again.

Her manner makes me think that perhaps she's worried I might mention last night so I say, "Yeah."

Her head snaps up, and her gaze crashes into mine. I don't like the way the base of my spine does this strange electric thing when that happens.

"Come on in," Cal says, "but it's a mess. We're still unpacking." He turns and disappears into the dark of the house.

The condition of the house inside isn't much better than the outside. I notice, however, that in its prime, it must have been beautiful. There's all this natural wood; some of it looks insect ridden, but then there are these spots where the wood looks like it's worth gold or something. There's a pretty, stained glass inset in a doorframe. Boxes in different stages of unpacking litter the floor throughout the house.

"This is—" I stop, because I can't freaking lie.

"A shithole," Max says as she walks past me.

Cal rolls his eyes and smiles. "Nice, Max. Language."

"Sorry, Dad. Not sorry. Water?" she asks me.

I don't want to say that I'm scared of what might come out of these pipes. "No. Thanks." I follow them into a dilapidated kitchen where patches of linoleum are peeling, and exposed wood is dry and graying. "Is this place safe?"

Cal offers me a chair which I'm pretty sure goes with a missing dining table. He sits in another. "Livable. This is what I do. Fix up old houses and then resell them."

"Why?" I ask because I can't imagine wanting to live somewhere like this. Sure, my house isn't all that awesome, but there aren't holes in the walls. The carpet might be worn, but at least it stretches across the room. The tile might be cracked in places, but not missing.

Max leans against the kitchen sink and crosses her arms.

Cal glances at her before looking at me. "Got to make a living. Allows us to live, me to work my business, and then to make some cash once the place is fixed up."

I can see the rationale, but I'm not sure I trust the floor, afraid to sit. When I glance at Max, her frown, added to Cal's earlier look, tells me she might not be as into this whole fixer-upper thing as her dad.

"And that's where you'd come in." Cal's voice draws my attention back. "It's okay to sit. I promise." He waits for me.

I ease down onto the chair. The floor holds.

"I'm going to need an extra set of hands with Max headed to

college; we need to get this place turned over quickly." He glances at Max again, who's looking at her feet. At the stretch of silence, she stands.

"Nice to meet you, Griffin." She disappears from the room, and I can hear every groan of the house with each of her steps.

"Honestly, Mr. Wallace," I start.

"Cal."

"Cal. I've never had a job. And I don't know much about construction or anything. My mom just said I should check in with you."

"Your mom. The convenience store clerk?" He offers a quick smile and a nod; then he runs his hands down his denim covered thighs and glances at where Max disappeared. He sighs. "It would be helpful if you did have experience–" he clears his throat, thinking, and then he looks at me again. I can see the doubt work across his features—Max has his eyes—and I'm pretty sure he's going to say, "Thanks but no thanks." Then he clears his throat and says, "I can teach you what you need; I just really need someone who's willing to work hard."

I must look surprised because he offers a short laugh. "Really?"

"Are you?"

"Yeah." I don't know if it's true, but I think it is. It could be.

Cal stands and extends his hand. "Great. Can you start tomorrow?"

"Yeah."

"Bring some tools."

"I don't–"

"Hammer, screwdriver. Gloves. Whatever you might have. Tool belt."

I nod but don't tell him I have no idea what he's talking about. If Tanner and I were still friends, I could ask him. The thought makes me feel like an empty road.

Cal gives me a tour of the place, the house—which is as bad as I thought—and the outbuilding: a combination garage and workshop. He shares his plans for the place and details all the work we'll be doing. I try to listen, try to understand what he's talking about, but really, all I feel is overwhelm because I have no idea what he's talking about. What the fuck are trusses? I try to stay engaged by nodding, but I'm terrified, and sure he'll fire me after my first day when he realizes what a fraud I am.

Cal offers me a ride home, and then asks Weird Girl—Max—to take me because he gets a call he has to take for a potential job. I'm not one to pass up a car ride over the bus, so I follow her out of the house and get into a white truck that's seen better days.

"So," Max says when she drives out onto the main road, "thanks for not saying anything about last night to my dad."

"Sure."

"How come you didn't?"

"Not my business."

"I snuck out."

"You still have to do that?"

She doesn't answer, just drives, and I don't press. I don't really want to know her weird shit. I have my own to deal with.

We pass Custer's, and I think about sitting there with her last night. I'm curious. "You sneak out a lot?" I don't know why I'm asking.

"Not a lot. My dad—he's cool and all, and he probably would have given me the keys—but he worries. I also don't like to leave him alone on the first night in a new house."

"How many houses have you lived in?"

"This makes—" she pauses, then— "ten."

"Shit. That's a lot. Ten different houses?" The thought shocks me. The thought of moving ten times—well, I can't fathom it since I've never done it once. I glance at her. "Not all here?"

I see her grip adjust on the wheel and then she leans against the door, holding the wheel with one hand. "Nope. All over."

This makes me swallow. Ten houses. Different towns.

"What about you?"

34

I tell her where to turn. "I've been here my whole life."

"That must be nice. You must have lots of friends—the same ones."

I wish I could say yes, but it would be a lie. I don't say anything. "You too? Friends in lots of places."

She gives me a tight smile before looking back at the road. "You'd think. It's hard to make friends when you're just passing through."

I hadn't thought of it like that. "Next right," I say and point out my house. "Thanks, Max." I tell her to test out her name. "Is it short for something? Maxine?"

She scoffs. "Not that. Maxwell."

"Maxwell." I hum on it. "That must have a story."

"Yeah." But she doesn't elaborate.

"Well, thanks for the ride." I slide from the passenger's seat out onto the sidewalk.

She offers me a polite smile, then drives away after I close the door. I wait a moment and watch the truck as it chugs down my street before going back into my house, thinking about what it really means to be alone.

5.

The dilapidated porch is hidden under shadows when I climb the perilous steps the next morning. Cal asked me to get to the house early. When Cal opens the door, a warm golden glow reaches for me. He's smiling, and I wonder how at this hour of the day. I can barely keep my eyes open. I'd considered skipping the run when that alarm hit but hadn't been able to go back to sleep, afraid I'd miss the bus. So I'd forced myself to get up, forced myself to face the retribution on the road again. It sands down my edges.

He turns from the open door. "I got coffee on."

"And electricity," I say, the grain of sleep still in my throat, and trail him into the kitchen.

"It will be a real house by the time we're done."

I have my doubts, but I'm willing to go on this ride for a paycheck. Besides, ten houses. Cal must know.

There's a table with a light green Formica top set up in the kitchen with four gleaming chrome chairs with green vinyl seats.

"You got a table." I put a hand on the back of one the chairs.

"Yes. Max and I unloaded more of our stuff yesterday after you left. Still lots to do." He steps around boxes in the kitchen. "We'll just unpack necessities. Figured a table fit that category. We're going to have to tear all this out and start from scratch." He pours some coffee into a plastic mug.

"Max still sleeping?"

"She's out for a run."

Running? I find the information thought provoking. Something we have in common, not that it matters.

"Cream and sugar?" Cal asks.

I shrug.

"I drink mine black, but Max likes hers with both."

"I'll try it black."

Cal smiles and slaps the lid on the second mug. "Let's go out, and I'll show you what I need you to do today."

I take the offered mug with a "thanks" and follow him from the house, taking a sip.

"You got your tools?" Cal asks and skirts around the side of the house.

"I couldn't really find any at home." I hadn't looked. Well, I had, but what we had consisted of a small kit under the sink to do minor stuff around the house. The hammer hadn't been much bigger than my hand.

He looks over his shoulder, still walking. "No tools? Nothing?" He faces forward again. "What's your dad use around your place?"

I know his question is innocent. Cal couldn't know about my dad, but the question still makes my chest burn. Anger isn't the current fire however, because I can give Cal some leeway, but his honest assumption drudges up those feelings I like to keep locked up. "He's not around."

Cal stops and turns toward me, hand on his hip, the other holding his coffee. His brows are drawn together. I don't think it's what I've told him that's stopped him, but perhaps the way I've said it. I feel his eyes assess me. He takes a sip of his coffee then resumes walking. "I think I can scrounge up some stuff for you to use."

"Thanks." Having to offer this gratitude bugs me because it feels like I owe Cal something. Then again, I kind of do; he's taken a chance on me.

We turn another corner to the back of the house where an old porch looks worse than the front. It's a mouth, missing teeth with the remaining ones discolored, broken or loose.

"You're going to take this down today. Demolition." He turns and looks at me with a grin. "I love demolition."

"Okay." By the looks of it, I could probably just give it a push and watch it collapse.

I took woods at school with Mr. Henry. I learned some shit about building stuff. Measuring, sawing, fitting stuff together, gluing, nailing. I mean, I didn't try too hard. I wouldn't have wanted to look like a try-hard or anything, but I kind of liked that class. I liked the way you could take a slab of wood and make something with it. We didn't demolish things though, but taking shit apart seems like something I might have a talent for.

"I've already dealt with the electrical, so that won't be an issue," he says like I know what he's talking about. He points to the skeleton of a light fixture. I nod like I have a clue. "Start on the top and work your way down so you don't hurt yourself."

I look up at the dilapidated roof.

"I don't want you up there—"

I breathe a sigh of relief.

"—so, we'll set up a ladder and a scaffold before I leave." He turns away and heads toward his rust dappled truck. "Taking it down will be the easiest part. When you're done, if there's any salvageable wood, pile that up in its own pile. Be sure to use gloves—I've probably got an extra pair around here. I'm not sure you'll find much usable wood on that porch. Separate the rest of what you can into trash or salvage. You know the difference?"

I don't and force myself to ask the question. "How do you know if the wood is salvageable?"

He glances at the porch. "Most of that's going to be in the recycling pile." With the hand holding his coffee mug, he points at

38

the porch. "See the dark spots? The way it looks like it's splintering?" After I nod, he says, "That's all rot. When wood is soft like that, weak, spongy, and broken, you can't use it for building anymore. If you find any pieces that look–" he turns back to the truck and presses a finger to a smooth board– "closer to this. See how the grain of this is compact?" He knocks on it with a knuckle. "No give. We're using this for your scaffold. It's strong and sturdy. That's what we want."

I nod again because it's all I know to do. I feel like an idiot and hate that I do. I wonder if Tanner would know all this stuff. Probably. I want to ask more questions but don't. Afraid to look stupid.

After I assist Cal with the setup of the scaffold, Cal glances at his watch. "I've got to get out of here. Don't want to be late for that job." He walks back to the truck. "Oh." The door creaks as he opens it. "Max should be rolling in at any moment, would you ask her to text me when she gets back so I know she's home? She'll be around, so if you need anything, she can help." He climbs into the truck and slams the door shut.

The truck rumbles and drives away.

I'm left staring up at a porch ready to topple. I use my spider-web screened phone to look up *how to remove a porch*. My data plan sucks, but after a while a video pops up. While I'm waiting for it to load, I hear the rustle of gravel and turn to see Max running up the drive. She's got on shorts, short shorts. Her legs are full, and she's glistening with sweat—golden in the fresh sunshine. She's got this fitted top that hugs her body. I look back at my phone and try to concentrate on the video taking a lifetime to load.

"So, Serial Killer," she calls. "You're just gonna stare at your phone instead of work?"

I glance at her, not really wanting to for some reason. She looks kind of...alluring. And I'm a dude. I notice shapes of stuff. "You my supervisor?"

She smiles. "You can be sure as shit that I will let my dad know if you're spending all day on the phone." She stops a few feet from me. Her skin glows from the exertion, and though her hair has been slicked back into a ponytail, lots of little hairs explode around her head. Her eyes, this pretty shade of gray with swirls of other colors I noticed yesterday, but can't see this far away, are vibrant. She's still breathing hard from the exercise, which makes me feel heated, which is stupid. She's not my type.

But that isn't true.

I haven't been all that discerning.

I look away, ignoring that fact. "Don't worry," I tell her. "I'm making a plan." I wave my phone at her. "Your dad wants you to text him."

She turns and walks away. "Got it."

I can't help it. I look at her ass, then I'm irritated with myself for doing it. New boss's daughter. Terrible idea. Besides, she's... never mind. Too much time spent thinking about her. I shut it down.

Trusses.

She calls over her shoulder. "That shouldn't be too difficult. Swing the hammer and back away." Her laughter skitters over the space between us, then she's gone.

I press my teeth together. That's it. She's aggravating. I return to the video, which I use to help me get started.

A while later, I've got the shingles and the plywood of the roof off, and my hands are blistered even inside the gloves I've borrowed from Cal. I'm pounding at the wooden trusses of the roof with the hammer (trusses are those triangles that connect the walls to the roof—I can learn). The porch shudders under the pressure and begins leaning as if it's possible to lean any further than it is already. Something cracks, and I locate the source of the sound to the edge of the truss fastened to the siding of the house. I realize Max was right: *swing the hammer and back away.* I climb down from the scaffold and hit the weak spot of the wood, grateful it isn't taking the siding with it. The porch shudders again, and with a monster's yelp, collapses into a heap.

A moment later, I hear, "You okay?"

I spin, the dust and debris settling around me.

Max is standing at the corner, no longer in her running attire, arms crossed over a tie-dyed t-shirt. Her hair looks darker, damp, and hangs in loose waves around her face.

"Yeah."

She nods. "Hungry? I've got some breakfast sandwiches if you're game."

My stomach growls. I follow her, my stomach, the ruler of most things. My dick is a close second.

When I walk into the house, I see she's unboxed a bunch more stuff, the kitchen starting to look like a kitchen and less like a run-down storage unit. There are two plates, each with a muffin sandwich layered with meat and egg and dripping cheese and insignificant vegetables. My mouth waters. She pours herself a coffee into a mug sitting in front of one of the plates and then lifts the pot with a silent question.

"Water?" I ask.

She returns the pot to the coffee maker and fills a glass of water from a filtering pitcher in the fridge. "Not sure about the pipes yet," she says, echoing my sentiment from the day before and places the glass in front of me. She turns as though to return to the fridge, but then spins and puts the water pitcher in front of me. "You're probably thirsty."

"Thanks," I tell her and watch her, like I'm trying to decipher a new puzzle. I like puzzles, though I've never told anyone that. There's something fun about having a problem and finding the solution or even better, the work around. It's probably why I like video games. They're fun to solve. Max is a puzzle. She makes me curious, but I've never actually spent time with girls who incite my curiosity. Truthfully, I haven't taken the opportunity to get to know any girl outside of physically messing around.

I frown at the direction of my thoughts and stare at the stacked sandwich.

"I don't think it's going to hurt you," she says as she slides into the seat across from me.

I shake my head to come back to the real world and nod, offering her a partial smile of gratitude. "Thanks. For this."

She nods. "Sure. I was hungry. Thought I'd make extra in case." She doesn't look up at me, dressing her coffee in cream and sugar.

I take a bite and force myself not to react. The food tastes amazing. "That's really good," I say around the bite.

"Well, most things taste good to a caveman."

I'm not sure what that's supposed to mean, but she looks at me pointedly and takes a bite.

I swallow and study her as she chews. She swallows, and I notice the movement of her throat. "Are you saying I'm a caveman?"

She sets down her sandwich and wipes her mouth. "I might be insinuating that. Yes." Then she smiles. "Serial killer and caveman. Not a great combination."

"I'm neither of those things," I say and take another bite.

She watches me, and I notice her eyes have swirls of blue and green with flecks of gold in combination with gray, swirling like the colors in her shirt. She nods as though bestowing approval and takes another bite of her sandwich.

"Where's your mom?" I ask after I've finished my bite.

She sets down her sandwich again, and I can see I've hit a nerve. She's frowning, which I've only seen her do once when I showed up on the porch after seeing her at Custer's. She takes a sip of her coffee.

"Sorry," I tell her, though I'm not sure I'm sorry about asking, more about maybe bothering her with it. I think about how Cal mentioned my dad earlier and how tripped up I felt by it.

She shakes her head. "I don't really like to talk about her."

I nod. *That* I understand.

"How about your mom?"

"She's around."

She gives me a quizzical look, her eyebrows shifting

asymmetrically over her eyes. "Cryptic much?"

I offer her another partial grin. "She's always working. Got three jobs. I don't see her much."

"Three?" This time she looks astounded with eyes wide and her eyebrows high.

I never realized how many different looks a girl can express in a matter of moments. My mom is usually just annoyed. This girl's got like a billion expressions. "Yeah. After my dad–" I clear my throat. Shit. I try to recover from the accident of mentioning him. "She's just trying to make ends meet."

"And your dad?"

I look up at her.

She's got her hands wrapped around her coffee mug, her eyes focused on me, and her attention makes me feel fidgety. "Or is that a little like how I feel about my mom?"

I nod.

She glances down at her coffee cup and contemplates it.

I take another bite of the sandwich.

"She left us," Max says after a few more seconds.

I stop midchew, surprised that she's offered this information, trusted me with it. This trust—which may or may not be misplaced—allows imprisoned Griffin the opportunity to peek at the feeling. Angry Griff swoops back in, however, and makes me hesitant and kind of resentful at what I figure is meant to be a bridge.

She keeps her eyes locked on her coffee mug. "I was five. I don't remember much about it. I mean, I do, but it's like I'm not sure what's real or made up anymore, you know?"

I don't say anything. I understand though, sort of, thinking about my dreams and how they are a mixture of my memory and my subconscious. Sometimes, a remembering of my dad's arrest. The memory makes my chest ache. I hate it. I hate it. I hate it.

"I better get back to work," I say and stand. The chair flops backward and slams with a thud against the floor in my rush. I turn, hoping it didn't bust through the floor and grateful the chair is

43

splayed out on top of the linoleum.

She looks up at me, surprised, then she nods. "Yeah." She stands, too.

I grab the plate and take it to the sink. "Thanks for the sandwich."

"No problem."

I set the dish in the sink and can't get out of the room fast enough, away from her eyes measuring me. There's a reason she's not my type.

6.

I'm alone at home, and my brain splinters with the solitude. There's the trail that leads to Tanner, Danny, and Josh. There's the trail that leads to my dad and his release from prison. There's the trail that takes me to Phoenix. I consider taking out his postcards and rereading them again, but I'm too tired to get up from the couch. Then I think about reaching out to my former friends, but the last time I did, Danny brushed me off. So I play video games with strangers online instead.

After two hours of killing shit—I feel antsy.

My phone pings. Hopeful that maybe it's one of my boys, I pick it up and open the message. It's Bella Noble. Now, there's a girl who's my type. She's hot, and we've spent a lot of time dancing around one another at parties. Lots of innuendo. I think she was interested in Tanner first, but he brushed her off, which I think is crazy, but whatever. If I can capitalize on that, I will.

I picture Max and frown.

Hey, Griff. Bella

I smile, even if a text from Bella feels strange. It's been a while.

I'm not sure what to make of it, but I don't think too hard either, craving the distraction of a party, a deep cup of alcohol and the curves of her body against my hands. I text her back:

Hey

What r u doing?

Not much.

Feel like a party? ☺

A missing bit of my confidence returns, pushing my heart into a higher speed. I text her back:

When & where?

2Nite. Carson's house.

I don't want to tell her I don't have a way there. Mom and I haven't gone to get the car yet. With a sigh, I text her back:

Kind of tied up.

Oh!

The three dots pop up on my phone.

I was hoping u could come get tied up with me. ;)

I swallow at her innuendo and text her back:

Want to pick me up?

I didn't drive.

Too bad, I reply, salty and run though anyone I possibly know who could get me to Carson's. *Maybe next time,* I text and toss my phone to the couch, annoyed by the circumstances with no intention of contacting my old crew. None of them have reached out, so why should I?

Annoyed and exhausted, I power down the console and walk into the kitchen to see if I can find something to stuff my face with before I go to sleep. The refrigerator is full of stuff, but nothing that doesn't require effort; I consider a sandwich when I hear the automatic garage door open. Mom's home. I glance at the clock and realize it's later than I thought.

I open the door to the garage and step out onto the top step in case she needs help with anything.

There's someone in the car with her.

The shadow emerges from the passenger side. Stands. My heart jumps into my throat and beats loudly in my ears. I blink to clear the hallucination.

"Hey, baby bro," Phoenix says. He gives me a smile I don't recognize, somehow muted from the vivacious smile I remember from before.

Tears fill my eyes, unprovoked, and I press my teeth together, refusing to allow them an opportunity to hit. I search for words and can't find any.

Phoenix. My brother. Standing there.

He closes the door to Mom's car and then waits, slinging a cheap black duffle bag onto his shoulder. I think he's smaller, but that wouldn't be right. I'm bigger, but I don't feel bigger suddenly. He's got tattoos on his arms; his golden hair is longer than I remember ever seeing it, the top of it pulled back out of his face. I look at him until I can't, and then shift my gaze to Mom, who's standing on the other side of the car.

"Where have you been?" I ask but look down at my feet.

"Around."

"He's home."

I look up at Mom, again. She smiles. I notice the tears in her eyes, her longing even as much as she tries to hide it. "The rest doesn't matter." She walks around the front of the car toward me, climbs the stairs, stops, and grasps my forearm. "He's home." This is said like a wish, quietly chanted and just for me. Then she passes me into the house.

I turn my back on my brother and follow her. I have so many questions.

She drops her stuff on the counter. "Let's talk tomorrow. It's late, and I'm tired." She turns to look at me—mouth thin with tension—and then looks past me.

I turn, and Phoenix is in the doorway. I'm not unhappy to see him. I'm afraid. Not of him, but of what it means. Afraid that I might find the joy of his return and insecure of that same joy.

"Let's get you settled," Mom tells him.

Phoenix passes me, avoids eye contact, and follows Mom into the hallway where they both disappear.

I grab my phone from the countertop where I'd put it while rifling through the fridge and pull Tanner's name up to text him. Then I remember, we aren't friends anymore. The thought burns the back of my throat because the one person I want to tell about Phoenix being home is Tanner. I drop the phone to my side, text unwritten and stare at the dark opening of the hall. I hear their quiet voices, the footfalls as they move through the house, and the shutting of doors.

Sleep doesn't come easy. I toss and turn, needing a counterweight, but sleep does find me because I wake up with my heart racing, dreaming of the ghost town again. I was stuck, but this time Phoenix didn't turn into Dad. He kept his face and shot me.

It's dark outside still—early morning—but a noise catches my attention. Maybe Mom.

I sit up and rub sleep from my eyes and tune into the sound of kitchen cupboards opening and closing. After getting dressed to run, I step into the hallway. "Mom?" I walk down the hall and freeze, unprepared for it to be Phoenix. His return felt like a dream. My heart flops like a dying fish in my chest. I take a deep breath to get my fish heart regular again. I squeeze my teeth together and feel the bones of my jaw protrude underneath my skin.

He's frozen too, as if it would bring me consolation that maybe he's as impacted by the sight of me as I am by the sight of him.

He looks different. Older, but not quite like I imagined. Now, he looks as though he's melted into a muted version of himself, not the hero I remember.

"You look like you could be the big bro." He fills a mug on the counter with the coffee pot in his hand. "You're all grown." He raises the cup toward me. "Want a cup?"

"Are you going to put a shot of something stronger in it?" I ask and walk into the room to lean over the counter, my hands folded in front of me.

He tosses his head, swinging his long hair out of his face. I've never seen it this long. He swipes a hand through it. "Do we have any in the house?"

Up close, his face is more angular, sharper, even if the basic gist of who he has always been is still in his features. He's got the hazel eyes we share. The last time I saw him he was my age—eighteen. He's twenty-two now. I shake my head, and he slides a cup of coffee toward me.

I look up from the red mug in front of me. "What are you doing here?"

He crosses his arms tightly over his chest and steps back so that he's leaning against the counter again. He's all sinew now, more like me, but I'm taller. "Not the greeting I was hoping for."

"What did you expect?"

"Nothing. Hoped."

"For?"

"That you'd be glad to see me."

Am I glad? Yes. But perhaps relief is a better word. I don't say it. I'm hurt and angry amid all the feelings tied up with his abandonment.

"Where have you been?"

His gaze jumps to meet mine, then slips back under water. "Around."

We've already played those cards. I want an explanation. "You just disappeared. Left. Didn't call. Didn't check in. Nothing." I feel my blood pressure rise, the internal fire of my heart building steam.

"I sent postcards."

"The ones that seemed more like an identity crisis?"

He doesn't answer my question but says, "Mom's the one who kicked me out."

"You could have pulled your weight and stayed. You chose to leave."

"Ah." He nods and takes a sip of his coffee. "Baby bro understands the undercurrent now. So wise."

"Fuck you, Phoenix."

"It wasn't about you, Griffin." He turns his back to me.

"Yeah. Fuck the fact you have a little brother—one who could have used a big bro." I stand, pick up the coffee cup and throw it across the room. The ceramic shatters against the wall and the liquid slips down to make an ugly stain. "But Griffin doesn't need anyone, I guess." I walk out of the room, grab my shoes, and leave the house to run.

AUGUST

Sometimes, hell, most times I feel like I'm acting a version of myself. Remember when Dad would tell us "Don't fucking cry." when we were little? I'd staunch those tears, wipe my face with the back of my hand. I wanted him to be proud. you know?

I don't remember it fixing the feeling that caused the tears in the first place, though. Later. I picked up a forty and drowned them. soaked those inner feelings up. instead. That worked. Until it didn't.

To: Griffin Nichols
123 45th Street NE
The Town. USA 67890

1.

I push the tool in my hand through the paint that's peeling away and feel a sense of satisfaction as it flakes off the wall and flutters to the ground below. I'm standing on a ladder at Cal's place, working on my own today because he had a *fix it* elsewhere. I might be partially submerged in the dirt of my feelings about everyone and everything. Working with Cal these last few weeks, though, seems to be the only thing giving me oxygen to keep breathing as all the rest of the shit buries me.

So far, Cal and I have methodically worked around the outside of the house. From the demolition of the porches, replacing old windows with more energy efficient ones and the rotted wood of their jams, to now scraping the house's exterior siding to locate and replace the rotted pieces of siding before we repaint. As Cal said, "We've got to get it ready for winter," which is weird, because it's August. But he wants us ready to work inside before the first snow.

I asked him, why you don't just trash it all and start over? He told me that it's good to keep what's good and to replace what isn't. Simple, and somehow kind of wise too.

Another thing I've learned is about the tools. I went to the hardware store, and it felt good to buy my own. In addition to the normal stuff like screw drivers, a hammer, and a measuring tape, I got a carpenter's square that's actually a triangle, and a level. In all the years I spent in school, I can't remember ever learning so much so easily and feeling good about it.

I like Cal, and that's saying something since there aren't a lot of people that I like. I think it's because he's quiet. He weighs his words because he knows they carry meaning and serve a purpose. There's something to be said for that since I'm not sure I've lived my life that way. With meaning and purpose.

The other thing I like is swinging a hammer around and breaking stuff. Demolition. It feels satisfying to undo something. On the other hand, I haven't minded learning about how to put things back together, either. Like replacing the rotted molding around the windows. Repairing is kind of beautiful too. The ability to look at something that's broken and figure out a way to make it right like a puzzle.

The tediousness of all the measuring and methodical pulling of materials to save them in order to reuse them taxes my patience, but then sometimes it resets my brain and gets me to steady the racing of my mind. Kind of like when I run to silence the thoughts.

By the time I get home after working, I'm too tired to engage with Phoenix. Truthfully, I don't really want to, which I think is weird. For so much of the last four years I thought all I ever wanted was him home. Two years ago, I would have been happy that he'd returned. Four years ago, I'd asked him not to leave. Now, there's a gap between the wants of me then and those of me now. Maybe it's because the stories he's telling don't seem to be drawing real pictures. Instead, they're like stick figures with missing parts, so I'm wary. He won't tell me about the fucking postcards, which makes me wonder what he's been doing and where he's been. I wish I could talk to Tanner about it, but I won't.

With Phoenix home, however, Mom has a lighter step despite all her bluster. After yelling at us to do our part peppered with her colorful language, she punctuates it with, "My boys are back together" and smiles. But I play along. I don't want to steal Mom's joy.

Phoenix has moved back into his room. He's looking for a job, or so he says. Hasn't found one yet. I think that if he was really looking, wouldn't he be able to find one? I did, even if it was kind of lucky. I mentioned Tanner's dad's company, and Phoenix told me to mind my business. So I stay out of his way, and he stays out of mine. I'm out in the morning before he is, and when I get home from work, he's usually gone. He's doing his own thing, closed off and protected, and I think he has his own version of Angry Griff, only it's Angry Phoenix.

There's an undercurrent I can sense tugging us toward the deep end of a body of water I can't see but can feel is there. I want to be a good brother, to trust Phoenix and fall into the roles that we've been assigned by DNA or whatever. The thing is, I don't know him anymore to call him a brother. We've missed some important years. I want to trust that my family is just trying to figure out how to be together again, so I quiet the doubts even if I'm struggling to breathe through that unseen charge in the air around us.

"Are you awake up there?"

I glance away from the section of house I'm scraping and see Max is standing at the bottom of the ladder. "I hope so," I say and return to pushing the tool over the wood siding. "You shouldn't be around this without the gear."

I'm dressed in thin, white coveralls over my normal clothes. I look as if I'm a doctor in one of those movies where they're trying to contain a disease. I look weird, but Cal insisted. "It's an old house, which means the paint is probably filled with lead and other horrible stuff they used back in the day. Better to be safe than sorry," he'd said. Besides feeling like a clown, it's freaking hot. I'm glad I'm on the shady side of the house right now.

"I've been down here talking to you, and it's like you're somewhere else," she says.

"I'm working, Einstein. Remember when you threatened to tell your dad if I wasn't working?"

She has the nerve to laugh. "Yes."

I stop and look down on her from my vantage on the ladder. "Did you need something?"

"I was wondering if you'd help me move something in the house."

"You can't do it with all of your muscles?" I ask her.

She blushes and looks away, which is odd. Knowing her for the last several weeks, I can't remember seeing her get embarrassed about anything, and she has a lot of emotions on that face. This reaction makes me unbalanced.

"Actually, I just needed help." She isn't smiling anymore.

It makes me feel self-conscious. I hadn't been trying to upset her.

"But that's okay." She turns and disappears around the side of the house.

I scramble down the ladder and pull off the facemask. "Max! Max!" I walk after her.

She stops near the open maw of the front door that somehow looks naked now without the porch that Cal and I removed, turns, and brackets her annoyance with her hands on her hips. "You didn't need to get down."

"You said you needed help," I say, not sure how to address the fact I somehow upset her, though I'm not sure what I did. I feel breathless, my heart pounding as I slide back to the fight with Tanner. *We aren't friends anymore.* "I'm here."

She doesn't respond and uses the step ladder to climb into the house. I follow, the white overclothes whispering out loud as I do, and I wonder what to say, feeling like maybe I should turn around and climb back up the ladder where my thoughts seem easier than trying to solve the enigma who is Max. Even if I do like puzzles.

"The house is coming along. In a minimalist kind of way." I follow her through the living room. It's just boxes lining the walls under the windows. I've learned they do most of their sitting at the dining room table.

"All of this stuff will have to be moved again when you do the inside of the house."

"And what will you be doing then?"

She stops at a cabinet that has seen better days and looks at me. "I'm leaving." She swipes at something on the wood, and I hope it hasn't given her a splinter. The cabinet looks about as appealing as the house did that first day I arrived.

"Leaving?" I ask. The thought makes me feel thin, as though I'm a balloon that's lost some air, still bouncing about in a breeze but drooping now.

"College." She walks around to one side of the cabinet and grabs a hold of the sides.

Words catch in my throat until I'm able to cough out, "Oh. Yeah. That's good. Me too." I mirror her on the other side and peek around the cabinet at her.

Her eyes catch mine even though she doesn't have to chase my gaze very hard. There's something about her eyes that make it difficult to look away. "You're leaving for college?" She says it with curiosity rather than it being an impossibility which is more like I might have said it.

"No. I mean, I'm going to community college in September."

She offers me a polite smile, but it isn't her usual one. I like the other one better. "That's good."

I don't really want to talk about school. That conversation will lead to questions about why community college. Then I'd have to talk about high school and the kind of guy I was only a month ago. It feels like a lifetime because I feel stripped down to my bones. Except that past is recent history. It's a relief she doesn't have that info to judge me.

"This is huge. You want to move this?" I lean back to study the cabinet.

"Yes. It's an old china cabinet. Solid wood." She thumps on it, and I see her dad in the movement, which makes me smile on the inside even if it doesn't touch my face; it's a warmth that spreads through my chest. She doesn't notice, still looking at the cabinet. "I wanted to move it out into the workshop."

"Your dad doing something with it?" I ask.

Her eyes jump to me and narrow. I've annoyed her further. "No, Serial Killer. I am."

"You haven't called me that for a while," I say. She hasn't called me anything for a while, avoiding names altogether.

She makes a noise that comes through her nose and reiterates her annoyance. "You haven't deserved it."

"Well, I'm sorry for annoying you," I say and roll my eyes. "I can help."

After tipping the beast of the cabinet to its side, Max and I maneuver it through the house. Together, with her at one end and me at the other, we lift it. It's heavy, awkward, and requires stops along the way to regrip and regroup, all without fighting about it, which I think might be a win.

When we get to the door, we stop. The sudden chasm at the door to the ground is an obstacle.

"Any idea about how to get it out the door without steps?" she asks.

"I think we could slide it down a ramp. Like a board."

"What if the board breaks?" She looks at me, then twists to stare outside.

For some reason I want to solve this puzzle and make her smile again. A Max smile, not the fake I got earlier. "I bet the scaffold boards would work. Does your dad have one of those carts?"

She nods, and I see the start of a smile at the corner of her eyes.

I feel ten feet taller.

"Yeah. In the workshop."

"You get that, and I'll grab the boards."

A few minutes later, after reconvening and lamenting that we hadn't used the dolly earlier, we build a makeshift ramp and muscle the cabinet as gently as we can on the rollers down the incline. By the time we cart the cabinet into the workshop, we're both sweating and panting from the exertion. But she's smiling again—the real one—and for some inexplicable reason that makes the effort worth it.

The realization makes me uncomfortable, like it's too authentic or something, like the half of Griffin that would open up and be vulnerable, and I'm scared to be that Griff. I clear my throat. "I'm going. I'll grab some water and get back to scraping. Got to get that side of the house finished today."

She nods.

I turn to leave.

"Hey, Griffin?"

My name. Not some nickname she's come up with to irritate me. "Yeah?"

"Thanks for the help."

I nod and start to the door but then hesitate, thinking about Danny and his words the night of the fight: *you ruined this.* I stall, worried about ruining the tentative bridge between Max and me. I turn back around. She's standing near the cabinet looking at it, her hands on it again. The yellow light filters through the windows into the wooded workshop, filled with dust. She looks like the subject of a pretty painting. I shake my head at the dumb thought. Max is making me as weird as she is, but I follow the earlier impulse further. "You know, earlier? Did I say something that, you know, made you mad?"

Asking this question feels like unzipping my skin, opening it up, and offering her a knife to go to work on my insides. Not one for real conversations since they feel too close to the Griffin I'm trying to protect, but Danny's words have haunted me: *We've tried to talk to you for months.*

Max crosses her arms over her chest like she's protecting herself. "It's no big deal."

I know just by looking at her stance that she isn't telling the truth. "Kind of seemed like it was."

59

A short laugh flutters out of her, quiet like butterfly wings. "I used to get teased for you know–" she flaps her hands around in front of her body.

"For using your hands to talk?"

That makes her smile, and her shoulders relax as she sighs. "I got teased a lot for my size. Growing up."

I feel like a dick because I'd noticed. I never would have taken the time to get to know her because of it. Circumstances seemed to decide that was going to happen in some capacity anyway. Here we are, standing in a workshop, and I stopped to discover something that holds a mirror up to my face and says, "See what kind of dick you are?"

There isn't another girl I know who could have helped move that cabinet (my mom doesn't count because she would move it out of spite). Or another girl I know that could make a breakfast sandwich like she can. Or one who just shows up with water, just because she knows it's hot and her dad needs it. A girl who loves her dad so much that she doesn't like to leave him by himself. In the weeks I've known her, she might be a girl who's freaking weird, but I think she's pretty, damn cool.

Fuck. Vulnerable Griffin is forcing a fucking appearance.

I swipe my hand down my face, the white clown suit making noise to remind me I look like an idiot while I'm trying to be nice. "I'm sorry," I say unsure what to say in circumstances like these. I don't think I can tell her all the other shit without sounding like a moron.

"You didn't know." She flicks a hand toward me, but her protective shield drops.

"Well, I'm sorry people are assholes," I say, speaking mostly for myself.

"Thanks," she says. "I appreciate that."

I turn back to the door again but stall at the threshold once more. What the fuck is wrong with me? "My dad," I tell her before I even think about what I'm doing. "He's been in prison since I was eight, but he's getting out. People used to tease me about that." I glance at her over my shoulder and figure maybe we're kind of even.

But her eyes are huge. "I've been calling you a serial killer. Shit. I'm sorry."

This makes me grin. "He's not a murderer or anything."

She presses her hand to her chest. "Shit. Still."

"It's okay, weirdo." I laugh as I walk back to finish the scraping, and for some reason as I climb the ladder—even dressed like a stupid clown—I feel like air was added back into the balloon around my heart.

2.

I'm painting primer over the siding at the farmhouse when I get the text from Marcus letting me know there's a bonfire at the Quarry, probably the last of the summer. Even though it's a Saturday, I'm at Cal's and Max's. It's one of the only days a week where Cal can devote the whole day to the farmhouse, and since I don't have anything better going on, I come out to help him. I've got the roller on one side of the house while Cal's using the sprayer on the other; he'd like to get it done this weekend so we can paint it next week.

I need a way to get to the Quarry and put my phone back in my pocket to ponder my options. Mom needs her car, and I don't have mine yet. The bus doesn't go out there. I can't call one of my former friends. I'm stuck.

I haven't been to a party since the last one with Tanner, a few nights before our fight. We got so wasted celebrating the fact he was back in the fold. That was the night he punched Chris Keller; he'd yelled something at Chris about messing with Emma Matthews. I'd got it on camera and posted it to my stories on Insta because it was hilarious. Tanner never fought. Of all of us, I'm the punchiest. And there he was punching Keller because of some rumor the guy spread about Emma being a frigid bitch. While that's a highlight, that punch wasn't what I remembered the next day; it was the broken way Tanner had opened up. He'd slipped in comments about Emma, his feelings for her, and I'd ribbed him about them, shut his feelings down as stupid. Then he'd said—and I'll never forget it because he echoed the words bouncing around inside of me—*I'm not good enough.*

I'd been too drunk to do anything other than grab the back of his neck and shake him about in the good nature of friends, laughing to get him out of the funk. I was so happy to have Tanner back with me, and not with her, that I'd been trying to get us back to the fun of us. Then the fight happened a couple of nights later. I haven't had anything to drink since that night, which, surprisingly, has left me clearer.

We've tried to talk to you for months.

Is that what Danny was talking about? It was true that Tanner had been sharing more. I'd teased him about it.

I stop rolling primer over the surface of the wood, uneasy about how I'd responded.

I've gone down a rabbit hole and shake myself back to the problem at hand, pushing the roller again. I need a ride to the party. Then, I remember the last text message I got from Bella and wonder if she'll be there. Maybe I could get a ride with her.

I text her: | U going 2 the bonfire 2Nite? |

I put my phone back into my pocket and continue spreading painting primer on the siding of the farmhouse.

My phone buzzes. Bella has answered:

Going out w/ the girls. Tanner coming with?

I grit my teeth and shove my phone back into my pocket.

"Griffin?" Max walks around the corner, carrying a pitcher of water. "I thought you might–" she stalls when she sees my face, which I can only imagine looks like a pile of shit. Covered in flies. "Are you okay?"

I try to adjust using my mom's wisdom: *Fix your fucking face, Griffin.* "Yeah."

"You don't look it."

"So, you're saying I look like crap?"

"No. Just upset." She holds up the pitcher.

I pick up my empty reusable water bottle and hold it while she pours in cold water. "There's this party later, and I don't have a ride. Haven't got my car yet."

"I can drive." She returns the pitcher back to level. "Unless you don't want to be seen with someone like me."

"What the fuck is that supposed to mean?"

She shrugs.

"You're willing to drive?"

"Sure."

"Will your dad care. I mean–"

"Because I'd be going with you? To a party?"

I just look at her, figuring my silence is confirmation enough.

"Don't worry about him."

But I do. I like Cal and don't want him to think I'm trying to make any moves on Max. Am I? No. Absolutely not. "Why are you always bringing out water and stuff?"

Her eyes narrow. "Why? Is there a crime against being nice?"

I take a sip of the cold water, then wipe my mouth with the back of my hand. "I don't know. I just–"

"Not many people have been nice to you, SK?"

"Oh. You're back to calling me names?"

"I figure SK is an acceptable compromise. It isn't targeting the fact your dad is where he is, but I still get to tease you about the night I met you. And you've changed the subject."

I've been around her for weeks, and this is the first I've noticed she has a dimple in her cheek when she smiles deep enough. "I guess not." I grasp onto the roller extension pole and resume priming the siding.

She grunts as she turns away. "The proper response is 'thank you, Max.'"

"Thank you, Max," I echo and watch her walk away out of the corner of my eye.

She stops at the corner, hesitates, then turns back around. "I'll drive. Just tell me what time to come and pick you up." Then she disappears around the side of the house.

After I've finished priming my area of the house and check with Cal, who's almost done too, I cart all the supplies into the workshop where there's a sink to clean up the tools. Max is in there with her cabinet, which is sanded down to the naked wood.

"That looks totally different."

"I figured there was something beautiful hiding underneath all the rotted layers on top." She glances at me and then looks away, using a screwdriver on the hardware of a door. Her hand slips, and she steps away to look at the cabinet.

"What are you looking at?"

"I'm not sure if I want to leave the doors on."

"What are you going to use it for?"

"I wanted a surprise for my dad. For his books."

"Then maybe he doesn't need doors for them. Unless they're, like, worth something. Are books worth something?"

"Not the ones he has, but yeah, there are book collectors out there."

I scrunch up my face. "For real?"

She laughs and returns to the cabinet to remove the door. "I think I might have tightened it too much."

"Here." I step forward at the same time she steps back. She bumps against the front of me. I grab her upper arms to keep us upright, and I can't help noticing that she smells good, like pumpkin pie. She's so close, and my stomach does this twisty thing that makes me a little jittery.

"Sorry," she says and scrambles forward to get out from under my hands.

"My bad," I tell her and hold out my hand. "The screwdriver."

"Oh." She's blushing, and my heart kicks up into a higher gear because she's pretty, which is a weird and unwelcome thought.

She hands me the tool, then steps back to let me get to the fastener.

I make quick work of getting the door off. "There." I hand her the tool. "Anything else you need my muscles to accomplish?"

"Hah," she mocks. "No."

I retreat to the sink to wash the tools I'd used and think about texting my mom to bring home some pumpkin pie from the diner.

"The primer looks great," Cal says as he stomps into the workshop, his feet thudding against the wooden floor. "That's looking great, Max-in-a-million. You going to stain it?"

Max-in-a-million. The nickname makes me look at her again. It's fitting.

"I wasn't sure. I kind of like the nude wood," she tells him.

"Me too. Maybe just a polyurethane finish."

Max nods, and her gaze slides to me to share a secret smile.

I look away. I can't keep a grin from my face because she just played him. I wonder if he has any idea about her surprise.

"I'm going to go with Griffin tonight," Max says.

I cough and duck my head into the sink to focus on cleaning the roller which doesn't want to release all of the primer.

"Where to?" Cal asks.

The silence makes me look up from the sink. They're both staring at me.

"Where to?" Max asks.

I swallow. "The Quarry."

"That's the park with that lake out of town?" Cal asks.

"Yes, sir."

"At night?"

"There's a bonfire with people from Griffin's high school."

"Is it safe?" Cal's eyes are on me.

I feel like a deer in the headlights and can't speak. I nod.

His eyes bounce from me to Max then between us again until they land on Max. "You can take the truck."

She offers him one of those bright smiles and leans forward to kiss his cheek. "Thanks, Dad."

"Griffin, would you wash this for me?" he asks and disassembles the sprayer. He drops the pieces into the water that need to be cleaned to keep it clear of clogs. "Thanks." Then, without a word, he disappears from the shop.

I feel jumpy, like pieces of me might tear through my skin. It isn't like I'm trying to get with his daughter. We're friends, I think, but for some reason I feel nervous. Strange. I decide it's because I've never been friends with a girl before, and I'm not sure what to expect.

Max chuckles.

"What?" I ask from the sink.

"Your face." She cracks up, using the side of the cabinet to hold herself upright.

"Shut up."

She laughs harder.

Later, Max parks the truck in front of my house. I've heard it before she even parks, already walking toward the vehicle from my house when she stops. Max waits in the driver's seat. Her hair is loose, obscuring her face, her head tilted down.

I walk around the back of the pickup and open the passenger door.

She turns to face me, looking up from her phone. "You ready?" She's smiling the good smile. Dimple.

It makes me feel both hot and cold at the same time. She's wearing one of those rock-n-roll t-shirts she likes—Def Leppard, again—and she must really like it because there are holes in the black fabric with all the wear. I notice her tan skin underneath as well as the yellow swimsuit strap tied at her neck. Then she's got on these denim cut-offs that are snug. I feel like I need to both clear my throat and swallow and suck in a lungful of oxygen. "Yeah," I croak out and look at my phone, not because there's anything to see underneath the spiderweb screen, but because I need to look at something else.

"Is it weird I'm excited?" she asks.

"You're weird, so that would be normal for you."

She offers me a mocking laugh.

And I breathe a little easier now that we're back in familiar territory.

"I haven't done anything since we moved here," she says. "This will be my first time out, since the night I met you, SK. You're navigating." She drives the truck away from the curb.

I think this is the most I've ever heard her talk—chatter really. "You aren't missing much. If it makes you feel better, this is the first time I'm going out too."

She looks away from the road at me.

"I may not have a car, but I do think it entails watching the road while you drive."

"I'm surprised. You kind of seem like the party type."

"Didn't we establish that at the first meeting? Six days a week. Mondays off?"

"You're making my point. Thank you."

"Right here. Yeah. That was my MO."

"Was?"

"Things change."

"By choice?"

"Necessity." I give her directions to follow, and she steers the truck in the correct direction.

"Sounds like there's a story there."

"I'm going to skip it."

"For now." She leans to turn up the radio playing pop country, which I'm not crazy about, but it's clear the truck doesn't have a lot of options on its ancient, push-button sound system.

I look out the window when she steers the vehicle onto the highway. "Just stay on this road. The entrance we want to the Quarry will be on the right side."

"Truth: I haven't really had any friends. All the moving. Hard to hang onto any when all I did was leave."

"They're not all that they're cracked up to be." They ditched me, and I stayed in one spot.

"I'm beginning to question my choice of hanging out with you."

That makes me chuckle.

She's quiet, then eventually says, "Okay. Since you're stuck with me tonight, tell me something else."

"I'm getting a car soon."

"You are?" She sounds excited for me, her tone climbing up a notch.

"I'll only be able to afford a piece of shit, but I won't have to share with my mom anymore."

She reaches over and turns down a random song that's a little twangy. "Where's the first place you want to drive this piece-of-shit car?"

I haven't really thought about it before, but now that she's asked, I just say the first place that comes to mind. "There's this ghost town I heard about an hour or so from here that I'd like to visit."

"A ghost town? Really? Not like to your best friend's house or something?"

She's right. If I'd gotten a car when Tanner and I were still friends, that would have been the first place I drove. But we aren't friends anymore, and it makes me feel empty. "Yeah. The ghost town."

"So why there?"

"I–" I stop. I'm not sure I want to open up, but then I glance at Max who is paying attention to the road, not me. The golden hour fills the truck cab, and everything about her and the moment seems shiny and magical. Safe. "My brother and I played cowboys and bandits when we were little. Our dad used to watch those old black and white western movies when he was home. Those were his favorite. Phoenix—that's my brother—was always the villain, and I wanted to be a part of his gang, but I usually had to play the sheriff to chase after him and take him to jail. I guess, I just always wanted to see one of those old towns."

She makes a humming noise, gives me a sideways glance and a smile before refocusing on the road. "I think that would be something cool to see."

"Yeah. I think so too. Turn right up here."

She turns the big truck with ease and moves us down the entry road to the Quarry parking lot which is full of day campers who use the picnic areas near the water's edge.

"The bonfire will be in the camping area. We'll have to walk in from here," I tell her as she navigates the truck into a parking spot.

She nods and gets out, the door groaning as she opens it.

I meet her at the tailgate and notice again how much I like watching her. I look away. It isn't smart to be checking out my only friend or my boss's daughter. And besides, there's Bella. I conveniently ignore that she'd asked about Tanner even though my heart reminds my head. So maybe there isn't anyone. I wouldn't want to cross any lines with Max. She's weird-cool, and I don't want anything being awkward between us. I like her smile too much. "This way."

"So, what am I going to see?" she asks.

"A bunch of drunk people dancing around a fire. You're really nervous?"

She does this funny thing with her mouth, drawing it to the side as if she's thinking, and her brows come together. It's cute. She looks at me. "Truthfully, I haven't been to many parties. A couple. So, yeah, I'm kind of nervous."

I make a noise acknowledging that and look closer at her as I learn something new. "You act so worldly."

"Are you making fun of me?"

"No. Just making an observation."

"I may have lived in a lot of places, but I haven't really known a lot of people who invited me to stuff."

We keep walking, and I listen to the sound our shoes make on the asphalt mixed with the bright shouts of kids in the water.

She continues talking. "I went to my first party in the eighth grade. A group of kids invited me. I showed up and realized I hadn't been invited. They were just playing a joke on me. And in high school, I think I went to one party after a dance and left early because my date hooked up with someone else." She stops, and we walk a few steps before she adds, "Makes me really nervous about college."

My heart knocks about in my chest thinking about her experiences and how different they've been from mine. I recognize myself as the villain in her stories. I wonder what she'd think of me if she knew how I'd been in high school. If she'd think I was a jerk like everyone else. For some reason, the idea that she'd think worse of me feels like added weight. "Parties aren't all that great," I say. "But you should definitely walk into parties—as a girl—with smarts."

"That's sexist."

"Yeah. But there's a lot of douchey guys."

"Are you speaking from experience?"

I swallow. Tanner or Josh would play off her question with something funny, and I wish that I had the ability to do it, but my brain sort of stalls with the truth of her statement. My mom always said with her hand squeezing my face, so I was looking her in the eyes, "No matter what, Griffin, you say the words, 'do you want to have sex,' do you understand me? Don't make assumptions, you hear?" Or my favorite, "If you ever bring a girl home pregnant, I'm going to knock you into next year." Her point was to protect me, I think, from being in a situation where a girl felt like she was being coerced or worse, but I can't completely absolve myself from all my sexual encounters. I never forced a girl, but I probably talked my way into some of those experiences. Those girls agreed—they had

71

said 'yes'—but had they been honest about what they really wanted?

"Maybe," I tell her, going for what's honest rather than the lie. I'm not trying to offer her a fake version of me. A boulder of unease sits in my gut. I hate admitting it.

She walks next to me in silence for longer than is comfortable.

"It isn't like I purposefully set out to be a douchey guy," I qualify, worried that she's thinking poorly of me even though she has the right to.

Her shoulder bumps against mine as we continue walking. "And what constitutes a douchebag, coming from someone who may or may not be a douchey guy?"

I stop walking. "Max."

She continues on ahead, then stops and turns to look at me.

"I don't want you thinking bad of me." I look down at my black Converse-covered feet.

"I call you SK, remember. I already *do* think bad of you."

"Ha ha," I mock her and catch up.

"I think since you know your way around a party, you can offer me pointers."

I hum again, considering her point which has merit. "Okay. First, don't get too drunk."

"But a guy can?"

"He shouldn't either. You need to keep your decision-making functioning. If you're shit-faced, you aren't going to be clear enough to. Like if you want to hook up with someone, you should be aware of that decision so there aren't any regrets."

"You have regrets?"

"Lots of them." The words make me sick. She waits for me to elaborate. I don't.

"So, don't get too drunk in order to make proper decisions. Check. Next."

"Stay away from the guys—or girls," I look at her.

"Guys."

"Guys who are saying all the right things. Stuff you want to hear."

Her eyes narrow, which I can see looking at her from my vantage. "I'm not sure what you mean."

"Like the smooth talker who seems to be saying everything that connects with you."

"That just sounds like someone being nice."

I take a few steps to pass her and cut her off, so she has to stop. "This is really important, Max."

She looks up at me, though she doesn't have to tip her head very far since we're almost the same height. "Can you be more specific?"

I don't want to. I don't. It means I'm going to have to show her how, and then she's going to think even worse of me—which I deserve—but she also needs to know. She's going to college, which means maybe this is me doing a good deed, I reason. A favor to Cal, I decide. "First, Max, he'll just be nice, like you're saying. He might grab you a drink, find you a place to sit, maybe offer you his seat. He'll be like a new friend."

"That sounds nice."

"He isn't doing it because he wants to be your friend." I take a step closer to her. Surprisingly, she holds her ground, but then, she trusts me—I think. "He wants you to trust him so that when he takes it another step further, he can get what he wants from you. He's not being nice to you for the sake of being a good human being; he's thinking about it like a business transaction, kindness as currency. He'll compliment you." I pause, then allow my eyes to roam over her face, which is pretty. "Max, you have such a sexy smile."

Her cheeks warm, and her eyes widen. She fights a smile.

My breathing thins, and I lean forward so my mouth is closer to hers. "I bet every guy here wants to get with you."

She leans back, her eyes wider as she searches my face, and she isn't fighting the smile anymore. Her lips part, though I'm not sure it's because she wants to say something.

I stop speaking, but I don't move away from her; I'm staring at her lips which make me think about kissing. I remind myself I'm trying to show her how a douchey guy would act not really be one. So I reach out and put a hand on her waist which I rationalize is because I'm just trying to show her. I ignore the heat of her under my palm, burning through my hand all the way up to my shoulder. I dive in to fuck it up. "I bet you can do a lot with that gorgeous mouth."

She shoves at my shoulders. "That's rude."

I take another step back and look down at my feet because I don't want to see her anger or her disappointment in me. "Yeah. It is. That was perfect, Max," I tell her. I present my back as I walk away. "Stay away from those assholes." When I don't hear her behind me, I stop to look for her, finally able to meet her gaze, worried at what I might find there.

She's following and watching me with a calculating look on her face as if she's trying to measure me for my rottenness.

"You still want advice?"

"I think perhaps I've come to the right guy." She catches up.

I continue walking. "A guy like that will try and talk you into being alone with him somewhere. Then there are worse slimeballs out there who force things."

"Have you done that?"

I stop and turn to her. Of this, at least, I can absolve myself. "Fuck, no. Of course not. That's terrible and illegal. Shit. I can't believe you asked that." I run a hand through my hair. "Whatever happens between people should always be consensual and mutual, you know? But there are douchebags out there like that."

"And you'd know?"

I wave a hand around. "Did a report on it for health class." I didn't. I'd been in an assigned group at school who had. I guess I retained some stuff.

She takes a breath.

I keep walking. The music and the noise of the party can be heard in the distance. "There's also the guy that will pressure you until you give him room to keep pressuring you. He wants you to say yes, which is why he'll look for the drunkest girl in the room."

"Don't get too drunk."

I turn to her again and grab a hold of her shoulders, holding her at arm's length. "And never, ever leave your drink alone with anyone. In fact, you should only get your own drinks—don't take a drink from someone else."

She gives me that calculating look again.

I hold up my hand and shake my head. "Give me a little credit. I would never do that. I wouldn't want to get with a girl because she was so drunk, she couldn't decide. I think that's awful and would beat the shit out of someone who did, but I've heard stories though."

"You have principles then, when hooking up?"

"I guess so." I let go of her and turn back toward the party, leading her down the path. I hadn't ever considered they were principles, just Bro Code agreements.

"Like only drinking six days a week?"

"Yeah. I have some rules."

"Can I ask what they are?"

"You can." I don't elaborate.

"Will you tell me your rules?" She clarifies her question.

I sigh and stop walking, deciding she already thinks the worst. Might as well take it the rest of the way. I turn from staring at the lake between the trees and look at her. "I don't get too drunk, though I've broken that rule a lot but try to avoid getting with a girl when I do. I don't get with a girl who's too drunk either; I want her to be able to say what she wants." My cheeks heat, and I look away from Max's gaze, tabulating my character. "I want what happens with a girl to be mutual. I always use protection because I'm not about that long term stuff."

"So, you just hit it and run."

I press my teeth together. "Historically, yes."

"No girlfriend."

"No."

"How many girls have you been with?"

"A few."

"Vague." She looks at me, her gray eyes moving around my face, surveying the truth. She must come to some decision because she nods. "Okay, SK. I appreciate your candidness."

"Speak English."

"I am, SK. Honesty." She shakes her head.

My body does this weird thing where it relaxes with surprise. "You're not disgusted?"

"Want to know my rules?" she asks and walks away so that I have to turn and catch up.

"What?"

She looks at me with a dimpled grin. "Stay away from guys like Serial Killer."

I shove my hands in my pockets, look at the ground, and smile. "Smart," I tell her, but even as much as I want to strive for levity, the truth of her statement slams so hard in the chest, I rub it to catch my breath.

3.

When we break the clearing, the sun has slipped below the horizon. The bonfire glows like molten lava casting both heat and shadows of those dancing around the flames and weaving energy like magic. The last time I was at a bonfire, Tanner brought Emma. I gave him shit for it, and he punched me. To be fair, I'd hit him with a low blow with my words and got up into his face inviting it, but the interaction was more of the same of what had been breaking between us, exposing the cracks.

I wish that things were different. Now that I'm outside of things, the more I ponder Tanner's and my fight, the more I recognize my role in it. He liked Emma, and I dismissed his feelings like she was just another bang. If we could rewind time, I feel like I could hear him, be better. Except, if we rewound time, I'd have to take everything I've learned since because I was lacking awareness then. Danny had been right. Tanner had tried to tell me, and I hadn't been listening.

More things to regret.

I lead Max around the bonfire worship to the kegs set up away from the fire, though I'm not sure I want to drink. I glance at Max. "Hey, I can stay sober if you want to drink," I offer.

"Griff!" Marcus Mayhan accosts me with a bear hug, and I bump against Max.

I mumble an apology and turn to face drunk Marcus, pushing him away. "Hey, dude."

He flicks his shaggy blonde mop, grins, and wraps an arm around me. "Shit. I haven't seen you all summer. It's not the same with you and the crew missing."

"Been busy," I tell him, stepping away and avoiding Max's gaze. I shove one hand into my pocket and wrap the other around the back of my neck. The unease of facing this past version of me unwieldy. Maybe I just demonstrated it for her, but now she'll meet people who confirm that douchebag. Maybe it's futile to try to be anything different.

"I see why," he says with a smug look on his face as he assesses Max.

My stomach churns with annoyance and disgust; Max deserves more than that. I shove my other hand in my pocket.

I chance a glance at her and notice she looks annoyed, her face devoid of affect, her eyes unexpressive. The realization hits me that I could totally say the wrong thing and make her feel bad, which I don't want to do. "This girl would never fall for a shithead like me," I tell him.

Her eyes snap to mine, and I note a new expression I don't recognize. I avoid diving in to explore it, however. I don't have enough practice with things beyond the superficial. "This is Max. She just moved here."

Marcus holds out his hand. "Hey, gorgeous."

I press my teeth together, clench my fists inside my pockets, and fight rolling my eyes.

"I've heard a lot about you on the walk here," Max says as she shakes his hand.

I nearly laugh, a puff of air coming out my nose. She's a smart girl, this Max, who has so many variations of her face, smells like pumpkin pie, and calls me out for being a jerk.

78

"All good, I hope," Marcus says, and leans to look at me. "If it was from this guy, he's always got a bro's back." He grins and telegraphs a look that makes me annoyed and protective. I'm disgusted as I realize that I haven't been any better than Marcus and shift on my feet, feeling ashamed. I'm not sure what to say to that so I don't say anything. He's not wrong, after all. It was me who pressed so hard on the Bro Code.

Max threads an arm through mine. "Griffin is showing me around."

"Maybe I'll see you later," he says. "I'll get you a drink."

She waves her keys at him. "Driving. Besides, I get my own drinks." Her eyes meet mine with a smile. "But thanks anyway." She exerts pressure to get me moving.

"A quick study, I see," I tell her as we walk away, proud of her. The bare skin of her arm presses against mine, and the friction it creates shoots sparking energy at the base of my spine that climbs up my back.

"A proficient teacher," she replies and doesn't move away as we walk through the crowd. "You know where there's a restroom?"

"This way." I lead her away from the fire to one of the bathrooms. "I'll be out here."

She disappears through the doorway.

There are other female voices inside, drifting from the openings near the roof. They quiet a moment which makes me think they stopped talking when Max walked in.

I cross to the wall rather than standing out in the open and lean against it to wait.

"Did you see Josh?" one of the voices asks.

I feel my eyebrows draw together, knowing it could be any Josh, but I know the voice. Greta Mills.

"Yeah. Did you hear that Tanner isn't going to parties anymore?"

Siobhan Crawley.

"Who said?"

Bella.

"Well, Josh is here with Ginny Donnelly and Emma Matthews." They all make a scoffing sound. "When I asked them where Tanner was, they just kind of shared a look and said, 'not here.'"

"Trouble in paradise?"

"I heard they aren't together anymore."

A toilet flushes.

"That was only a matter of time. Matthews is a fuckin' prude. You all heard what Keller said about Junior Prom, right?"

They titter.

I'm not sure why this tightens my chest. I'd said the same thing to Tanner. Everyone had heard it. The rumor called Matthews a dead fish because of her lack of performance on prom night. I'd wondered about it then—Keller told a lot of stories. Tanner also wasn't one to go ballistic about a rumor; there was probably more to it since it had pissed Tanner off enough for him to throw hands. Hearing someone else say shit about someone I'm realizing Tanner really cared about makes me feel something akin to protectiveness. Like I want to jump in and defend her for my boy. I recognize it as ridiculous, though. He isn't my bro anymore, and I owe Emma nothing.

"I was hoping he'd come with Griff tonight."

Bella again, and I think about her text that pissed me off.

I notice running water.

"Is Griff here? I thought you two were getting together."

"Why would I get with Griff if I had the opportunity to get with Tanner? That's like choosing a Nissan over a Tesla."

"Jesus, Bella." They all laugh.

"It's true. What does Griff offer anyone? The only reason anyone ever put up with him is because he's Tanner's friend."

I swallow the acidic rocks in my throat, and they splash into my gut, making nauseous waves.

"He'll probably end up in jail like his old man."

They laugh, and I slip back into my elementary school body

80

when the running joke was if I was going to be a prison bitch like my dad.

The ground crunches.

I look up.

Max is standing there.

I swallow, feeling sick to my stomach, unable to push away from the wall. My body is a cemetery. I know Max has heard everything. I try to smile, to appear unaffected by what I've just heard, but I can't get my mouth to work right. I'd come out thinking that maybe I could get with Bella, that she was interested in me, not Tanner, but there's no doubt now.

I don't know what I was thinking.

I'm not good enough.

Max steps closer and leans against the wall next to me, shoulder to shoulder. "Griffin?" she asks, her voice muted.

I can't look at her. I'm embarrassed and bruised, and I don't want her to know they were talking about me, though I'm pretty sure she already knows. They mentioned my dad, and coupled with the empathy on her face, it's hard to mistake the pity.

The voices are suddenly louder as they leave the bathroom. Their steps crunching against the detritus of sticks, leaves, gravel littering the ground.

I push away from the wall, wanting to get away, but it isn't fast enough.

Someone mutters, "Oh shit."

"Griff?" Bella pulls up short when she sees me, the girls coming to an abrupt stall behind her, exchanging looks by the movement of their heads. It's too dark to really see their eyes.

I clear my throat, going for the insulated power of angry Griff to protect the vulnerable one that has somehow stepped outside of the box I chain him inside. "Hey."

Bella stutters a moment—her words starting and stopping— until she finally says, "You didn't text me back."

"I was working."

Her words get jammed up in her mouth as she tries to come up with something else to say. "I'm glad you're here," she says.

A lie.

"Too bad I'm not Tanner, though, right?"

She starts to say something as her girlfriends snicker, heads bent together behind her, but she stalls when she catches sight of Max. Her eyes narrow. "Who's your friend?"

I don't want to introduce her. Not because I don't want to introduce Max but because I don't want to introduce them. Max deserves better.

Max pushes away from the wall and steps up next to me so we make a wall. "I'm Max," she says and takes my hand, lacing our fingers together. "Babe?" She looks up at me with complete adoration, or so I catalogue that expression to be, even if it's fake. "Are you ready for that swim?"

I'm staring at Max, feeling the way she's leaning against me, noticing the supportive strength of her hand in mine, and my distress drips down from my heart toward my feet. She's trying to save me and even though there is no saving me, I'm okay with pretending, if only for a moment, this is real. "Sure."

Max looks at them. "It wasn't nice to meet you," she says, then draws me away past them back toward the water, my hand in hers. As we walk away, she says loud enough so they can hear, "Who the fuck were those bitches?" She keeps a hold of my hand all the way to the water. When our toes reach the water's edge, she lets me go. "I'm sorry," she says.

I squeeze my fingers together into a fist noting the way my skin tingles from her touch, then cross my arms over my chest, tucking my hands up into my pits. "For what?"

"For what happened back there."

"You didn't say it."

She's silent, which makes me think she's not sure what to say. I know a lot about not knowing what to say.

"Well, I'm sorry if I crossed a line." She pulls her shirt over her head.

I turn my head to look at her. Her yellow bikini top covers a lot of her skin, but it doesn't hide her shape, which, I'm realizing, is nice. She's rounded in all the right places. "You didn't." I look away, keeping my thoughts in compartments for safe keeping—looking at her feels dangerous.

She makes a sound that whooshes air through her mouth. "I'm relieved."

I can tell she's teasing me.

"I wouldn't want you to get any ideas, SK." She laughs and undoes her denim shorts, pushing them off her full hips and down her legs.

I smile despite everything else and still peek at her bikini bottoms. They cover a lot, and I think about the poster in my room that leaves very little to the imagination. I would have thought I liked that better, but Max's swimsuit, like one of those old school ones that covers her to her belly button with the top covering most of her torso but for a slice of skin, is sexy. I force my eyes away—back to the water—and scold myself, but I'm a dude after all. This is the longest stretch of time—since before graduation— I've gone without sex or some version of it in the last two years. The thought makes me apologetic; Max is my friend.

"Come on, SK. Let's swim." She moves into the liquid which sloshes around her as she disappears into deeper water. It's dark now, but the moon, the stars, and the bonfire offer slices of light—enough to see by.

"That defeats the purpose of going to a party and meeting people." I toe off my shoes, pull off my shirt, and follow her into the water. It's cold. I shiver and dunk myself all the way. When I emerge, I shake out my hair, causing Max to hold up her hands against the water droplets and giggle.

"If the rest of the people are anything like the people I've already met tonight, I'm good."

I laugh. "There are probably some good ones." Not that I know many to introduce her to.

She goes underwater, then reemerges, her hair slicked back off of her face. By now, I've made it to within an arm's reach of her. She smiles, and I imagine her dimple at the corner of her mouth. "You're 0 for 5, SK. It's not looking good."

I laugh again, drawn into our usual way of being together. "Well, as a fake serial killer, I don't have a lot to offer in terms of friendship. You should probably branch out."

"That is a huge red flag." She splashes me. "You check all the SK boxes."

I can't help that I'm grinning even if I want to stay moody. It's hard to when I'm around Max. She's easy and fun to be with. But I don't say anything, not sure what to say, and just tread water near her. But Bella's words resurface and threaten to pull me under.

What does Griff offer anyone? The only reason anyone ever put up with him was because he's Tanner's friend.

"Are you okay, Griffin?" Max asks. "What they said was really shitty."

Words hit me to deflect and talk bad about them as payback, but I realize why it hurts so much. It's the truth, or at least the one I've always believed about myself. Bella and her minions' observations just reinforced it. "Truth hurts." I figure that being upfront will reinforce the wall. Besides, I've already laid the worst parts of myself bare for Max earlier.

I glance at Max, though can't make out her details. She's a blue shadow of herself, moving her hands back and forth in front of her through the water. She makes a humming sound in response to what I've said.

"What?" I ask.

"Who's Tanner? Or is this the story you skipped earlier?"

I figure I owe her something given what she's done for me. "The same."

"Well?" she asks after I go silent.

"He was my best friend."

"Was?"

"We got in a fight. The night before I met you. Haven't talked since."

Movement of water and the muted sound of voices at the party on the shore fills the silence around us.

"What was it about? The fight?" she asks.

"Something stupid." But even as the words leave my mouth, I'm not so sure anymore. While the fight itself was probably stupid, I'm beginning to wonder if Tanner's fight wasn't for something bigger that I refused to understand, and the thought feels terrible. It makes me ashamed to consider that I was the one who broke our brotherhood and not the other way around.

"If it was stupid, how come you haven't fixed it yet?"

Anger festers in my belly with the acidic rocks from earlier still sitting there. "I don't think it's like your cabinet," I answer and cringe a bit at the bitterness in my voice, afraid I'm going to squash the one relationship I have that seems to be sort of good. I'm putting up protective walls to combat the sick feeling in my gut. Bella's observation flipped a switch and talking about Tanner reinforces my need to be stronger.

"You might be surprised."

"At what?" I turn away and swim back toward the shore. I don't want to talk anymore. Not about this.

"I just think that if a relationship has strong enough roots—trust, honesty, respect—then a fight won't damage it beyond fixing," she says, following me back to the beach.

I climb out revved up, though I'm not sure where to direct the fury. Bella and her group's words? Dredging up the fight with Tanner? My own inadequacy and failure? Max throwing truth? My skin feels extra tight, and my temper might burst out from me like a monster inside.

I tug on my t-shirt. "I'm going to get a drink."

"Griffin. Wait."

I don't listen. Instead, I force on my shoes, and stalk up the shore, into the tree line and straight for the keg. By the time Max has reached me, I've already paid the fee and thrown back two cups. I'm working on my third.

"Griffin." Max puts a hand on my forearm, and I pull away, taking another gulp of the beer.

"What? You can't fix me like a cabinet," I tell her. "No matter how much you strip away these layers."

"I didn't mean–" she steps away from me.

I drain the third beer and ask for another.

"Griffin. Stop."

"You aren't my mother," I tell her.

Her eyes narrow. "No. I'm your ride. And you're about to break your rules because it will fuck up your decision making."

I want to argue with her, but she's right. I did share the rules with her. But instead, I smirk at her and tank the rest of the beer in my cup. Then I turn and ask for another.

"Dude. I'm going to have to charge you again," the guy running the keg says.

I take out my wallet and slap another twenty down in his hand. He hands me another cup.

"This won't solve anything," Max says.

I know she's right. I know it like I know it's dark outside. Like I know the fire is hot. Like I know that I've never felt worth more than when I was friends with Tanner. I see it though, it was always because of Tanner, not me. Had I been holding the group together for all of us or just for me? Because I could see the truth? That without them I wasn't anyone worth knowing.

I chug it and hand it back to the guy running the keg. "Another."

"Dude. You should slow down. Listen to your girlfriend."

"She's not my girlfriend," I say.

"I'm not his girlfriend," Max says at the same time, our words crashing against each other.

"Griff?"

I whirl at the voice. Josh. The red-head next to him and—stop the presses—Emma Matthews. Though I was thinking about defending her earlier, seeing her now just flips the ignite switch to my resentment bomb. Rational or not, she represents the wedge that broke Tanner and me. The girl who broke up Bro Code and our brotherhood.

"Fancy meeting you here," I sneer, ugly, cornered Griff coming out of my mouth.

"Bro. What's happening?" Josh looks concerned, his brows hovering over his green eyes. He glances at Max. "Hey."

I watch Emma, deciding she is the object of all my misery, and then offer a condescending look to Josh. "You'd know if you texted."

"I've been travelling with the family. Haven't been around," he says. "You know that. What the fuck happened with Tanner?" He shakes his head, disappointed.

"I don't want to fucking talk about it," I say and punctuate it with a slug of beer.

"Hi. I'm Ginny." Red waves to Max. "And this is Emma."

"Hi," Max says but her tone lacks her usual joy.

My fault.

"That's Max." I wonder if my words are slurring, or if it's in my head. "That's one of my bros, Josh. Used to be."

Josh shakes his head. "What the hell, Griff?"

"I heard about you earlier," Max says.

Josh's eyes bounce from Max to Ginny, who shrugs, and return to Max. "I hope it wasn't bad."

"Just some girls gossiping in the bathroom about some guy named Tanner and Emma."

"Let me guess. Bella's crew." Ginny crosses her arms over her chest. She glances at Emma.

"Ding. Ding. Ding," I sing and take another drink.

"Don't worry about them." Josh pulls Red into a side hug. "You either, Emma. Can't sweat the small stuff," he says.

I scoff aloud at his positivity.

Emma's head is bowed, her gaze on her feet. She dumped Tanner, huh? Or was it the other way around?

"Or the small minds?" Ginny asks, looking like she's tasted something unsavory.

"Right." Josh presses a kiss to Red's temple.

All of it pisses me off. So domestic. "You two are together now?" The way I say it isn't nice. "Seems all of my friends are hooking up with long-term shit. Tell me Emma, how's Tanner? He hit it and leave?"

Emma's eyes narrow, but she doesn't deign to respond. The ice queen turns on her heal and walks away.

"Dick," Ginny calls me and disappears after her.

"What the fuck, Griff?" Josh snaps.

"Stop, Griffin," Max says.

I slash my gaze to her, ready to snap and snarl and bite.

Josh, who must sense I'm ready to go for blood, interrupts me. "Are you coming to Danny's swearing in?"

"I wasn't invited."

"Yeah. You were. You're just being a dick."

"I haven't talked to him either. And I've never claimed to be anything else." I hold out my arms as if presenting myself in all my craptastic glory.

"We should go." Max plucks at my t-shirt.

"Go." I shrug away from her touch.

"I'm your ride."

I scoff. "Yeah. Right." The sexual innuendo catches and hangs about us like old party decorations slumping after everyone has gone, needing to be cleaned up.

Max's forced smile slides from her face, and her eyes narrow. "Who are you?" Then, "I don't need this shit." She turns to Josh. "It was nice meeting you." She walks away.

I watch her disappear into the crowd. "I'm shit," I mutter, answering her question, and staring at the beer in my hand. The numbness is finally starting to infiltrate my system.

"What are you doing?" Josh asks. His tone of voice surprises me. He's pissed, and that isn't usual for him. Carefree Josh who diffuses tension, doesn't add to it, is angry.

I will the tears burning behind my eyes to stay hidden on the inside. "I don't–" but I stop because feral Griff won't let me say anything that might be vulnerable and crack the dam.

Josh shakes his head, frustrated. "This isn't who you are. You like to throw that around, but it isn't."

I want to yell at him, cuss at him, punch him. "What do you know?" I snarl instead.

He presses his lips together, and they thin out with anger. He nods after Max. "Was she your ride home?"

"Yeah," I reply.

"Guess you better go, or you'll be stuck." He turns and walks away.

He's right. Shit. I tank the rest of the beer and go after her, slogging through the crowd down the path we walked when we arrived, alternating between self-recrimination and self-righteousness. By the time I make it to the parking lot, she's backing the truck from the parking spot. Fortunately for me, she follows the rules despite the almost empty parking lot and drives around to get to the exit which allows me time to get into her path.

Her headlights blind me, and the brakes squeal when she stops.

"Get out of the way," she says after unrolling the window. "You don't need a ride, remember?"

"I'm sorry," I say. The words aren't tight and instead slip around in my mouth and mind. I know I'm supposed to say it, but I'm not exactly clear why. I just need a ride.

"You aren't. You're lying."

"I am," which I can say with absolute certainty. I am not sure why I'm sorry, but I follow it up with a truth: "I am sorry I am who I am."

I can only see the shadow of her outline in the cab of the truck as she sits there coming to a decision. She hasn't run me over yet, even if that might be a relief.

"Get in."

I move around the truck and climb into the passenger's seat.

She drives.

I scrunch down into the seat, head against the cool of the window, and feel sorry for myself. "Thanks."

"Don't talk. I don't want to hear your voice."

I don't say any more words, which is all right with me. My head spins with thoughts of what's just happened, then spins because I drank so fast, but I'm not so inebriated that I'm unaware. Demolition. I'm great at it.

I keep my eyes fixed on the shadows of the trees outside of the truck, the stars in the sky, and the sound of the country twang coming from the radio. Then I just try not to think or feel anything at all.

4.

My sleep is restless with images of Max, Josh, Tanner, Emma, and Bella trying to keep from being sucked into a tornado. I'm the tornado. When I open my eyes and gaze at the ceiling of my bedroom, the weight of what I did crashes down on me and makes it difficult to get out from underneath the rubble. I messed up and not being able to assign blame to someone else, even though I want to, leaves me exposed. I owe Max an apology. I owe everyone an apology. My life feels like I should be a walking apology.

When mom knocks at my door, "Griffin?" I sit up and glance at my clock. I slept through the alarm and skipped my run.

"Yeah?" I stare at the door, wishing that I could open it to different circumstances.

"Let's go get your car."

The prospect should be more exciting than it feels. I'm too filled with self-loathing and feel undeserving of the convenience. "Be right there."

With a sigh, I rub my face. Danny was right; I have a problem. I need to stop drinking. I'm worse when I do. In the month I hadn't, I hadn't fucked anything up. Running helped too, I think. The discipline meted out by the road has been a deterrent to my dickish behavior.

I need to go see Max and apologize.

Mom is waiting in the car by the time I'm dressed and ready. I slide into the passenger seat. "Ready to do this?" she asks.

I nod, and she reverses from the driveway.

"Where were you last night?"

"I went out to the Quarry."

"That crappy truck that dropped you home looked like the truck the guy you work for drives. I see him at the store every couple of days."

"Cal? Yeah. I was with his daughter, Max."

She turns her head to look at me. "Is that a good idea?"

"We aren't involved, Mom. Jeez. I'm not stupid." I say it, but then that's not true. I have been stupid.

"I never said you were, but you Nichols' men don't always make the best decisions when it comes to your dicks."

"Mom!" My cheeks heat.

"What? It's true. Look at your father."

The heat of the blush cools, and my insides slow, straining as if moving will detonate the moment into smithereens. She never says much about my father, and we've never once talked about his other family. It was Phoenix who slipped about it before he left and was the only reason I knew. I assumed Mom knew or discovered it, and that was how Phoenix had known, but she's never said a thing to me. "What about him?"

"Nothing. Forget I said anything."

"Mom?" I want her to tell me. I want her to drop the walls and rant about how much he's hurt her, but she doesn't. Instead, she closes up.

"Forget it." She offers me a half smile. "I was just trying to be funny."

We drive in silence.

I was little when dad went to prison, too little to consider what it did to my mom, and then didn't consider it at all. Sure, I've been incensed and self-righteous knowing he cheated on her—on us—but I didn't think about the impact on my mom over the last ten years. I glance at her and wonder how a guy does that to her.

But I hurt Max.

I hurt everyone.

Maybe I'm not so different from him, and I hate that thought. I'd made a promise to myself a long time ago to not be like him.

When we get to the used car lot, Mom parks, and three men descend like vultures. She asks for some guy named Bill.

"Who's Bill?" I ask her.

She puts her keys in her purse. "The manager here."

"How do you know him?" I glance at her.

She situates her purse tightly against her side. "He's a customer from the diner." She isn't look at me, and her cheeks are pink.

I grimace. I don't like the look and the assumptions I'm making.

Bill's a little short. Well, shorter than me. He's got a lot of silver hair and a ready smile. Kind of tan. A tiny bit paunchy in the midsection, but not too bad considering the guy is old. He fills out his plain, blue collared shirt with the car lot logo like he works out. His handshake is firm. He's looking at my mom with too much interest. She keeps blushing. I press my teeth together and remind myself I'm there to get a car.

Bill leads us around the car lot. He shows us different options based on what I've told him I want, and all the while he's flirting with my mom. All smiles and jokes. I don't like it. I don't like it at all. I shouldn't care, but I do. I know where this guy's mind is at. And that's my mom.

I finally pick a blue car in my price range.

"Now comes the fun part," Bill says and leads us into the dealership, where he gives us water and a granola bar. After haggling—and I'm thankful for my mom, who won't budge on a monthly payment—Bill presents me with an offer I can afford.

"Congratulations, Griffin. You have a car." Bill holds out his hand to me.

I just want to get away from Bill, so I take his hand again to get this over with.

"Maybe I'll see you again," Bill says.

I offer him a forced smile and hope to God I don't.

He says something to my mom, who smiles, and I want to shove him away from her, but I know that doesn't make any sense. Mom's a grown woman who's spent her life taking care of me, but I suddenly feel irrationally sullen.

After we finish the paperwork, I'm handed the keys to something that's mine. I drive from the car lot sort of bursting with excitement even as disgusted as I am about Bill hitting on my mom. The first place I drive is to Max's.

As I turn into the gravel driveway, I notice the house and how different it looks from that first day. Not beautiful, by any means, but stripped in a way, naked and exposed. Somehow, that's better. It's like everything that was weighing it down and threatening to topple it has been removed. When I park, Cal walks around the corner. I see him look over his shoulder, then change direction to walk toward me.

"Look who got some wheels." He's smiling and claps my shoulder when he reaches me.

I'm not sure why it makes me feel proud, but Cal's approval does. "Yeah. It gets good gas mileage and only has 35,000 miles on it."

Cal nods. "Good. Good." He walks around it like he did Max's cabinet the other day and asks about the features.

I catch sight of Max standing in the doorway of the workshop. She's dressed in oversized, denim overalls with a fitted black t-shirt and goggles hanging around her neck. A yellow handkerchief is tied around her hair keeping it off her face. Hands in her pockets, she starts across the drive toward us.

"No more bus then," Cal says.

"No more bus." The thought gives me a warm glow.

When Max gets to us, she remains distant, arms crossed over her chest.

"Looks good, Griffin. I'll see you tomorrow morning, right?

Painting this week."

"Yes sir," I say.

Cal claps me on the shoulder again as he walks away.

"Nice car," Max says but stays where she is. I don't know if she's said it for my benefit or to hold up a version of the world being normal for her dad.

"The first place I drove."

"Where? Your ghost town?"

"No. Here. To show you."

She nods, but it seems more like a rote movement without meaning. Her mouth does that sideways thing. She looks at the house.

I lean against the car and look down at the keys in my hands. "I'm sorry about last night, Max."

She hums a sound like she doesn't believe me. "Do you know what you're apologizing for or are you just saying it?"

"For being a jerk."

"I need you to be more specific, Griffin."

Griffin. I've noticed she only uses my name when she's serious. I swallow. "The drinking."

She makes a buzzing sound. "Nope. Thanks for playing. Nice car. Nice chatting." She turns to leave, the gravel scraping underneath her shoes as she does.

"Wait." I scramble toward her, and my brain jostles memories trying to figure out exactly what I've done to owe her an apology.

She stops. Waits.

I know it could be any number of things, and she's going to just get more upset if I can't identify it. I drank to numb the anger. I took it out on her because she was there, like a punching bag, only with my mouth. "Honestly, Max, I'm not very good at words."

She shakes her head. "You being terrible with words isn't an excuse to be a dick. Your words do a pretty good job of hurting people." She turns away again.

"I didn't mean it like that."

She doesn't turn back around but remains where she is.

"I meant that I know I say shitty things that hurt people; what I'm not good at is figuring out how to use them to fix things. Not a lot of practice."

She faces me, eyes narrowed, and crosses her arms. She's a force, and I'm slightly terrified.

I shove my hands into the pockets of my jeans.

Her hands go to her hips. "I don't have time or patience to teach you, Griffin. You're a man already and need to own your shit. You're old enough to know how to treat people. But since you tried to teach me some life lessons, here's one for you." She holds up her index finger. "One of the things you should do is follow your own rules about drinking and decision making." She holds up a second finger. "You shouldn't treat your friends like they're your opponent, use them like verbal punching bags, but then treat an enemy like they are somehow better than you." She holds up a third finger. "And you shouldn't make jokes at your friend's expense. It hurts."

Her skin is flushed with her hurt. I think about my mom again and wish my dad hadn't hurt her. I wish I hadn't hurt Max. I want to be better than him, even if I'm not sure how to be, but I take in Max's lesson. I wonder if my dad ever apologized to my mom.

"I'm sorry, Max. Really. I am. Let me make it up to you."

She waves a hand. "Apology accepted, SK." She turns and starts back across the driveway away from me. "But I don't want to look at you right now."

"Does that mean you don't want to go for a drive?" I call after her.

"I'm busy." She disappears into the shop.

I get back into my car and sit in the drive for a moment longer than is probably necessary. I consider going after Max and talking her into a drive but decide that might make her really angry. Since I'm forgiven, I should leave that possible hornet's nest alone. So I drive home to save gas, for some reason happier than when I woke up, lighter too, and when I get home, I go for a run.

5.

The clouds are thick and heavy when I leave the house the next morning to run, and halfway through, the sky unlocks the door to meet the earth, dumping every drop of moisture it held hostage. I wonder if Max is out running too. When I make it home, I climb into the shower to warm up. I dress for work, looking forward to driving my car, to seeing Max, to working with Cal, to focusing on something productive.

The rain is still slick sheets when I park my car in front of the farmhouse. I hurry through the swath of mud to the workshop, ducking into the doorway, soaked through. It's dark and empty. No Cal. I glance about the place, his truck isn't here either, which is weird. So I dart across the yard for the back door, which is closer than the front. I knock.

Max's face, her hair wet, appears in the glass a moment later; she opens the door. "Dad's not here. You can't paint in this."

"Yeah." I look at the water draining waterfalls from the roof of the barn and shop. "Okay."

She pushes open the screen door to let me in. "You're soaked." Her eyes linger on my shirt stuck to my body as I walk into the house, squeaking as I do. She whirls away and disappears, and like most mornings I help myself to the coffee, which I've acquired a taste for with a touch of cream.

"Did he leave me directions?" I call out not sure where she is, or if she can hear me.

"He said he texted you." She walks back into the kitchen and tosses me a towel. Then she passes me to get the cup of coffee waiting for her on the counter.

"Maybe he forgot." I flip the towel on my shoulder and pull my phone from my pocket to text him. I set it on the counter to wait for his answer and run the towel over my head. When I've wiped myself down, I pick up the coffee cup and wrap my hands around the ceramic for warmth.

"What happened to that?" she asks, indicating my phone with her eyes. Her hands are wrapped around her coffee mug, her nose perched just above the rim.

I watch her eyes fix on my hair, which I'm sure is probably standing on end, and use my fingers to tame it. "Stupid choice," I tell her.

Her eyebrows lift with her head in a knowing nod. "You're full of them."

My phone pings.

Cal's answer:

> Sorry, Griffin. Got an emergency call early this morning. A plumbing thing. No painting. I didn't prep for anything else.

"Looks like I have a day off."

I wish I didn't because I don't want to be alone. No. Not accurate. I wanted to be with Cal. And Max. Plus, now I have a car to pay for.

"Big plans?" she asks.

"No."

"Would you like to demonstrate how sorry you are for Saturday and be my chauffeur? And think very carefully before you say 'yes,' because I will not allow you to bitch after you agree.'"

"Sure."

She grins over her mug, her eyes curling up at the corners and sparkling, which makes me wonder what I've agreed to. "Remember what I've said, car-slave."

I feel the grin inside my chest but refuse to allow it on my face. "Yes, ma'am."

After I run home to change into dry clothes, I learn I've agreed to car-slave for college supplies because Max is skipping town at the end of the week. When she asks me to take her the extra thirty minutes into the city to the Triple B: Bed, Bath and Bigbox, I pretend to agree with reluctance, and Max reminds me of my agreement. The truth, however, if she were to climb into my head, is she'd know there's nothing reluctant about my agreement. An opportunity to drive. I'm down. An opportunity to spend time with Max. Yes.

I park my car, find a cart, and sail past her with my momentum. "I'll even drive the cart."

She trails behind me, studying the list she made on her phone. "Bedding first," she calls from behind me as I enter the automatic doors.

I turn and wait for her. "I'll follow you."

"I don't know where I'm going."

"Me either. We shop at the CheapMart."

We meander.

"Max, do you want one of these for your dorm room?" I ask her, holding up a giant box with a bright red mixer.

"What am I going to do with that in a dorm room?" she asks.

I put it back. "I don't know. What's it for?"

"Baking."

"Who bakes? I thought that was only in the 1950's or something."

She laughs.

I like her laugh. The joy in it makes me smile (one I don't hide), and warmth spread through my chest like my hands wrapped around a warm ceramic mug. I have this sensation that I'm filled with helium and might float away.

"You could bake."

"I don't have one of those."

"You don't need one of those."

"I don't know, Max. Triple B seems to suggest that I need one of those."

She rolls her eyes and keeps moving through the maze of the store. Eventually, we find blue signs tacked to the wall with arrows. "There." She points at one. "Bedding." I push the cart behind her until we arrive in the bedding section.

I sit on one of the many sample mattresses that isn't really a mattress at all, but a plywood box dressed up in a pink and blue bit of fluff with too many pillows.

"Griffin! Stop. Get up!"

"I'm so tired," I whine even though I'm not really. I'd never admit it, but I'm enjoying being with her. She's fun. I flop backward.

"You're going to get us kicked out!" Her voice is thin and whispery as she glances around.

I grab a strange lacey concoction of a pillow and put it under my head.

"Griffin!" She tugs at my t-shirt sleeve. "Get up. That's decorative."

"I think you should try it to see if you like it." I grasp her wrist, pull, and roll, drawing her with me. She rolls over the top of me until she's awkwardly lying next to me on a bed that's not a bed, her legs draped over my hip, and my hand on her waist.

"What are you doing?" Her eyes are huge, and she's fighting a smile.

"You should test out the product. I think it's scratchy."

We're facing one another. She laughs, her head tipped back, and her eyes squeezed shut with mirth. That pleasant floaty feeling happens in my chest again, but this time there's a little pinch to go with it, a tiny bit uncomfortable as if it's telling me, "Yo, Griffin. Take note."

When she opens her eyes, they connect with mine, her pupils dilating to swallow most of the gray. "You'd wash it first, so it wasn't so scratchy." Her words fade to black.

My smile fades to black because I'm looking at her, really looking at her. I feel hot all the sudden, finding it difficult to draw a breath—my lungs have tightened while my heart thumps around, bouncing against the inside of me. I swallow.

Her smile slips, and she moves, extricates herself from my proximity on that bed that isn't a bed. She stands.

I sit up and scratch the back of my neck. "Scratchy. Not very good." Then I stand and return to leaning against the cart, walking back through what just happened on the bed that isn't a bed. "That is why it's important to test it out," I say, but it's in my robot voice because I'm not thinking about that at all. My eyes jump up from the blue plastic plate that reads *Triple B* on the cart to Max who's across the department muttering about sheets.

I push the cart after her, quiet now, taking stock of the moment, replaying it. Her laugh. The wide look of her gray eyes lost in the moment. The way her honey hair draped about her head. The way my pulse pitched to the side because the earth began to shake—my stomach following suit. I felt a seismic shift in me, pushing my tectonic plates into a new and unfamiliar mountain range, but I refuse to hike it. I know that's a place to get lost.

After some analysis, I decide I'm not attracted to Max. Enjoyment being around her doesn't mean there are other feelings; I don't do feelings very well. She's my friend. Actually, I don't do friendship very well either. My track record is shit. Navigating the two would be a disaster.

"Are you listening?"

I shake my head at the sound of her voice as if stepping from a vacuum. "Huh?"

"Car-slave. I need you to look for the extra-long, fitted in this color. Can you do it?"

"At your service." I crouch down to look. "Where am I supposed to find the size?"

"The label. Here." She points.

We spend the next hour and half maneuvering down her shopping list and then comparing prices. I'm tired, like bored tired, but I hold to my agreement not to bitch since this is me making up for being a jerk on Saturday. It would be a lie to say I'm not relieved when we finally walk out of the store with all the packages.

I take Max to eat when we finish. While we wait, then eat, she chatters and asks me innocuous questions about myself. I answer some, avoid others, but enjoy listening to her, nonetheless. Then I drive us back to town. By the time we get there, the rain is sheer, misty, and temporary. I help Max cart in the bags. When I'm done, there's no reason for me to stay, but I'm reluctant to leave.

"Want to see the cabinet?" she asks. "It's done."

I follow her out to the workshop.

She flips on the light.

"Wow," I say. The light wood shines through the finish. "It's amazing, Max. It looks completely different. Perfect really. Brand new. Your dad is going to love it."

"He already does, he just doesn't know I did it for him." She runs her fingers across an edge. My gaze catches on her fingers and lingers. Her nails are painted pink, like cotton candy you get at the end-of-summer fair.

My phone buzzes.

I hold it up. "It's your dad," I tell her. "He says we won't be able to paint this week. Supposed to rain tomorrow, he's got the plumbing job to finish up, and because you're leaving on Sunday, he's got to help you get ready on Friday and Saturday." I look up at her. "He gave me the rest of the week off."

"Oh." She runs her hand along the side of the cabinet.

My chest tingles, and I press my fingers to my heart to massage it, afraid that this might be the last time I get to see her before she leaves. I'm grasping for reasons to be able to spend time with her. Then I remember the drive. "What are you doing tomorrow?"

"Packing."

"Can you take some time off from that activity?"

"To do what?"

"Go for a drive with me? I mean, I tried to take you on my first drive, and you refused me."

She smiles. "Your first drive was here."

"Technically, yes, but I came to get you. And I still haven't gone."

"Okay, SK. I'll go on a drive with you."

I smile—relieved—and nod. "I'll call you in the morning to check on the time. I don't have your number." I hold up spider phone, then program her number into my phone.

"What did you name me?"

"Max."

"Text me so I have yours."

I do. "What are you going to name me?"

"SK." She scrunches her nose, then laughs.

"Ha ha." My tone is sarcastic, but I smile.

Silence finds its way in between our levity, and in the acoustics of the workshop with our laughter gone, the thick silence between us makes the place feel smaller. My muscles tense and turn jittery. I squash the impulse to move toward Max and step away from her instead.

"I better go." My voice is pitched weird, awkwardly coarse. I turn to the door.

Max clears her throat and thanks me.

Then I flee. Flee from impulses I don't trust, from a girl who I'm suddenly thinking about more and more, who's awakened something like happiness in me, and I know I'll ruin it because I ruin everything.

6.

Mom is already awake with a cup of coffee in hand when I walk into the dining room the next morning. "You're up early."

"Was going to run."

"In this?" She glances outside at the steady rainfall that blankets the view of the backyard.

"Was." I detour to a cup of coffee and sit down with her. We sip our coffee in silence, content to be in one another's presence. Usually, we're moving through one another's lives like lone planets on our own revolutionary tracts.

"You working today?" I ask her.

"Always. Just a swing shift at the hospital. Feels a little like a vacation with only one place to go." She smiles and takes a sip of her coffee. "You?"

"Cal gave me the week off."

"A whole week?"

I can tell she's thinking about the money. "Yeah. Don't worry. I've been saving most of it. Max is leaving for college, so he's taking her in a few days. They're getting ready."

She sips her coffee again.

"Mom, may I ask you something?"

She sets her mug down and leans forward to give me her undivided attention. In that moment, I see her as someone with a life I don't understand. After getting the car and watching that whole thing play out with Bill, I feel like maybe I want to understand her better. I haven't done a good job of being a good son.

Her eyebrows shift with hesitation, and she's back to my mother. We aren't a family of deep conversations.

"It's about Dad."

Her features harden into rocks. "I did say we should probably talk about him."

"Did you divorce him because of prison?" I'm really asking about the other family, but not asking, in case. We aren't a family who talks directly about deep shit either; I don't want to hurt her.

She leans back in her chair, and I wonder if she'll avoid the question. She surprises me. "Partly."

"How so?"

"It was the lying, mostly. He lied about a lot of things: what he was doing, where he was, who he was with."

I look up from her coffee cup to her face. "Phoenix told me once that he has another family."

She considers, picking up her mug again, then nods. "One of the things he was lying about."

"What else?"

"His whole life really. Told me he was a mechanic—and he was at one time—but money has a way of changing people." She moves her thumb back and forth over the handle of her cup.

"So how come you didn't date anyone, after?"

She looks closely at me as though measuring my questions for their reasons but can't decipher them. "Is this about something specific?"

Yes. "No," I lie. "Just curious."

She shrugs. "I don't know. I think, at first, I was so hurt by your father's lies I didn't trust the idea of opening up to anyone else. You and Phoenix were my life, and as you grew, you were going through your own stuff. I didn't have the energy."

"Phoenix was what?"

Mom and I both turn toward the voice. Phoenix, rumpled from sleep, is standing at the opening between the hallway and the dining room. His long hair sticks up around his head, and black mesh shorts are askew on his hips. He shrugs into a green t-shirt before walking past the table.

"Just talking," Mom says. "About your dad."

Phoenix walks into the kitchen, gets his own cup of coffee, then joins us.

It feels strange to all be sitting at the dining table together. I glance at my brother and wish we were closer; wish for the ability to walk the stretch of time between us, but the bridge is so unstable.

"Did you ever see them?" I ask her. "The other family?"

"Why are you bringing that up?" Phoenix asks. He sort of spits it like the words taste nasty, and I recall when he spilled the info all those years ago. He sounded similar then.

Mom puts a hand over his arm. "It's okay. Griffin has a right to know. I'm okay." She pats him and looks at me. "I saw the woman in court once, before your dad was sentenced. That's when I found out."

I think about it, wonder how that went down, but don't really want to know that story. Imagining it just makes me upset for her, for us, and I can understand why the knowledge makes Phoenix mad. "And he has another kid?"

"I saw her once," Phoenix says, mostly to himself, the focus of his gaze somewhere else.

"How?" I ask, thinking about his postcards. I attempt to balance those two pieces of information together. "Where do they live? The city, right?" I study Phoenix, who's looking at the cup he spins around and around on the surface of the table. "You said you were traveling around."

His eyes drift to Mom, then back to me. I feel him shuffling around information in his head, trying to figure out what to say, how to say it, filtering it, making sure it lines up into the parameters he's already set. I recognize it because I've done it. "I was in the city for a while."

"And you didn't come home to see us?"

He looks down at his coffee cup, and I know he's withholding information. "I was mad, okay? I got kicked out."

"No. You left." I look between him and Mom, and she's looking at her coffee cup. They look like two sides of the same coin. "What aren't you telling me?"

"Leave it alone, Griffin," Phoenix says.

I stand up and take my coffee cup to the sink, finished with this impersonation of an actual family. "You know why this family sucks?" I turn from the sink in the kitchen and look at them, the counter bar between us. "We never talk about real shit. We just stuff it into boxes like secrets we figure will go away if we ignore them long enough." I stare at Mom. "You divorced him because he was a liar? Well, what the fuck are we then?" I ask and leave the room.

I hole up in my bedroom and listen to the low voices of Mom and Phoenix talking, unable to make out the words through the doors and walls between us but note the forceful and sometimes harsh tones. I take out Phoenix's postcards and flip through them, rereading. Mom's voice is clear when she says, "You need to tell him." Then I hear her leave.

I make Max a road trip playlist, wondering what I need to be told, rereading those stupid postcards. There's no making sense of them, so I stuff them back in the drawer of my nightstand.

"What are you doing today?" Phoenix asks, walking into my room without knocking.

"What the hell," I say without any fire. "Knock."

He glances at the open drawer next to my bed where I stashed his postcards. There's also a nearly empty box of condoms and some other junk in there.

I push the drawer shut. "Max and I are going for a drive." I don't tell him where. I don't want to offer the obligatory invitation.

"Your boss's daughter?"

"She's my friend."

He makes a humming sound. "So, what are you doing?"

"Making a music playlist."

I feel him lean over my shoulder.

"You should get that fixed," he says about my phone. "Griffin's Road Trip Playlist? Shouldn't you name it something more creative?"

"Do you need something?"

He returns to the doorway, leans against the doorframe, and taps a tube of papers against his thigh, staring off at something abstract rather than the doorjamb in front of him. He glances at me as if he wants to say something, then looks down at the paper in his hands and twists it into a tighter tube. I wonder if this has to do with his and Mom's argument.

"What's that?" I ask him just to fill the silence, nodding at the tube of paper.

He looks at it as if it's the first time he's seen it. "Possible jobs."

I want to roll my eyes because it's taking him a long time to find a freaking job. "That's good," I say instead.

He straightens and taps the doorframe with the paper tube. "Yeah." He clears his throat. "Good talk, Baby Bro." He offers a Phoenix smile as he backs away, using the tube to point over his shoulder. "I better get going." Then he disappears, having said nothing at all.

By the time I park in front of the farmhouse, I'm still in a funk about my family. Max runs through the rain, her face tucked under the hood of her yellow raincoat, and I resolve to forget them the remainder of the day.

"I made a playlist," I announce when she gets in the car.

"On that monstrosity you call a phone. Are your fingers

bandaged?" She grabs my hand to inspect it.

I wrench my hand free, disturbed by the intense shockwave that shoots up my arm. "Wow."

"Seriously, you should get that fixed." She leans to look out the window at the weather. "Is this a very good idea?"

"It's supposed to be clear at The Bend. And my phone still works." I back out of the parking spot. "Just push play."

"I'm not touching it. It's going to sliver my delicate fingertips with broken glass."

"Don't be such a baby. I can't. I'm already driving."

"Fine." She pushes play, and the opening guitar riffs of AC/DC's "Highway to Hell" play over the car's speakers. Max looks at me agape. "Oh my, Griffin! What is this? Are we headed toward the afterlife?"

"It is a ghost town." I grin at my cleverness. "The playlist is from all of the band shirts you wear."

With a serious look, she shrugs out of her raincoat and turns so I can see that her bright yellow t-shirt is sporting AC/DC in the center. "Have you been spying on me? Do I need to add *stalker* to the list, SK?"

"What? No. Completely coincidental, but if I was truly a serial killer isn't stalker inclusive?"

"You make a good point." She smiles—a good one. "Seriously, Griffin, this is the nicest thing anyone has ever done for me." She bobs her head a bit with the bass guitar rhythm.

My insides flop over with her smile but tighten toward discomfort with her words. I can't remember anyone ever using *Griffin* and *thoughtful* in the same sentence. Griff and selfish, Griff and asshole, Griff and dick, Griff and dumbass are most of the pairings. Her words do something more integral to the threads that hold me together, and I can't trust them to maintain their strength. But I smile at her, then force myself to focus on the road. I'd like to stop for some reason and just look at her. Maybe something more. I squeeze the steering wheel and shove the thought into the appropriate box for safe keeping.

"I think it's time for some better friends," I say.

"Well, since I've mostly forgiven you for the Saturday debacle–"

"Wait. Mostly? I thought that's why I was car-slave. This nicest-thing-anyone-has-ever-done-for-me playlist should have put me in the clear."

She smiles. "Almost."

"What now?" I'm worried.

"Here's the thing, SK; I have traced your emotional degradation on Saturday night to one moment."

"Would you please speak English."

"I am. Is this Def Leppard?" She reaches over and turns up the volume, then gets lost in the music. I look over; her eyes are closed, and she mouths the lyrics. My heart thuds in my chest watching her, her mouth, hypnotized.

"T-shirt."

She opens her eyes to look at me, still swaying to the music, and sings the song. Pink paints her cheeks.

"Saturday?" I prompt trying to get her back on track because I'm finding version of Max a little too erotic. I focus on the road and chant in my head: *just my friend.*

"Right. Sorry. I was thinking about it, and I think besides the obvious restroom-side chat, your mood soured when we talked about this character named Tanner."

I tighten my hands on the steering wheel, all erotic thoughts vanquished. "I don't want to talk about it."

"Which is why I think you should."

"Did you plan this?"

"What?" She puts a hand on her chest and bats her eyelashes with feigned innocence. "Me? No. How could I have known we'd be stuck in the car for–" she picks up the phone and looks at the navigation app– "an hour and fifteen-minute drive?"

"Yesterday. When I told you."

"True."

"I'm beginning to wonder if you're the serial killer."

"A serial killer of bad moods." She snickers at her joke. "Griffin, you should really talk about what bugs you."

The observation slams me back to the stilted conversation I had with my mom and brother just hours prior, and my criticism that we don't really talk. I'm just as bad.

"I already told you about him. We became friends when we were fourteen. We got in a fight." I grind my teeth together, stubborn. What had I said: *We never talk about real shit. We just stuff it into boxes like secrets we figure will go away if we ignore them long enough.*

"Superficial, SK. I want the details. The moment I mentioned the importance of the friendship, you freaked out."

"It's more involved, and I don't want to really get into it."

She faces forward, puts her stocking feet—her socks are black with yellow bees on them—on the dash because she's taken off her shoes, and rests her arms on her legs. She goes silent.

"Are you mad?"

"No."

She's turned away from me, staring out the window.

"Why are you being quiet and moody all of the sudden?"

She looks at me, chin high. "I'm doing an impersonation."

"Of–" but I know what she's going to say.

"You. Oh!" She points at the radio. "This is your song. Just listen to the lyrics."

A guy rap-yells about running being easier than facing the pain. He wants to numb it. I glance at her.

"That's what you did on Saturday when I got too close, SK."

"That isn't fair."

"Isn't it?" she asks and glances at me. "I'm not trying to be a bitch, Griffin. I'm trying to be your friend."

And I know it's fair; she's nailed me down, and I don't want to acknowledge the truth. I feel like I'm about to be dissected, but I also can't get enough of it either. Her awareness makes me mad while at the same time feel seen, and I can't remember the last time I felt understood and seen. Then again, recalling how things broke apart with Tanner, maybe that's all he'd been asking for, and I hadn't been able to do it. I hadn't been able to let him see me either, and I don't understand why. I'd been scared, but of what? Losing him? He's gone. Losing something else? I've lost everything already, so none of it really makes sense.

"Fine," I say.

I can feel her eyes on me again, and suddenly her hand is on my arm, burning my skin with her gentle touch that feels like the warm summer sun.

"Griffin?"

I turn to look at her, and my heart ricochets around inside my chest like a stray bullet looking for soft tissue to mutilate. "Yeah."

"I won't hurt you."

But I'm beginning to think it might be too late for that. "You're leaving." Just like everyone else in my life that I care about.

She doesn't remove her hand, but I have to look away, keep my eyes on the road, which is both a blessing and a curse. Despite my fear, I want to see her expression.

"Physically, maybe," she says, "but I'm not going to stop being your friend just because I'm a few hundred miles away. Especially now that I know."

"Know what?"

"What having a good friend is like."

I swallow. Another string of kind words that haven't normally been associated with me. I don't think I've been a very good friend. Tanner, Danny, and Josh could testify against me in friendship court.

She removes her hand, but her touch has left a sunburn on my skin. "You have to be willing to trust me."

I decide to open the box, look inside, and share it. "When I was fourteen and my brother left. I blamed my mom for making him go, and I blamed my brother because he left."

"Like your dad."

I nod, slowly. "I guess. I met Tanner my freshman year. Before that I was mostly alone because people were always talking shit." I pause a moment before continuing. "Tanner and I had homeroom together and this teacher—he was such an asshat—was picking on Tanner. The thing was, everyone who went to school with T, knew that his big brother had died of cancer, and he and his family hadn't ever recovered from that. So, when this teacher started giving him shit, I jumped in. We both got kicked out of class and somehow became friends."

"Like brothers."

"Yeah, I guess. We both sort of became the brother the other was missing."

"And the fight?"

I sigh.

"I can't think any worse."

"You might." I don't look at her.

"Trust."

"We had this agreement called Bro Code that we made during our sophomore year. It was me and Tanner and Josh—you met him the other night–"

"With Ginny and Emma?"

"Yeah. And Danny. My friends."

"Bro Code. That doesn't sound good."

"You can probably guess."

"Like a bros before hos thing?"

"Yeah, and some."

"So how does that lead to the fight. Tanner take your girlfriend?"

"No girlfriends in Bro Code, and Tanner would never do that. He fell for this girl at the end of senior year, like right before graduation."

"Emma?"

I sigh. "Yes. I wouldn't let up about Bro Code. I wouldn't listen to him when he tried to tell me how he felt differently about her. I just accused him of breaking the code."

"Did he?"

"In my head, I thought so, but now, I don't think so anymore."

"What do you think now?"

"That I was just…afraid." Admitting this sucks. The protective side of me threatens to make me clamp my mouth shut.

"Of what?"

Max's response surprises me. *Of what?* Just matter of fact and lacking in judgement. I suppose I thought that if I admitted my fear, an asteroid might annihilate me from the planet and leave her laughing at my weakness. She doesn't even blink, and I'm still driving down the road like nothing has happened.

"Things changing. Losing my friends. Ironic right?"

"So, that was the fight?"

"Ultimately, yeah, but it happened because we got drunk, and I said some shitty things to him about his brother. Then I told him we weren't friends anymore." I want to press my hand against my heart. My chest has tightened with the thought. I need relief, but there isn't any. I'd broken my rules. I'd broken the friendship, not Tanner because I'd put him in a box too. I don't want to look it, but now I can't unsee it.

"Do you miss him?"

"Yeah."

"You should tell him."

"I think it's more complicated than that."

"Why? It shouldn't be. You care about him. If it's a real friendship, then it shouldn't be more complicated than working it out."

"Is that what you'd do?"

"I haven't had many friends. Not like you and Tanner, anyway, but if it were someone who meant a lot to me, I would."

But I'm not sure I agree with her. "I don't know if it was a real friendship."

She doesn't say anything, just waits for me to continue.

"When Bella said what she said the other night about me—"

Max rolls her eyes and scoffs.

"—I believed it. And I think I have for a long time. Tanner's a good guy. I'm not, though. I'm not a good friend. And maybe I've always wished I could be more like him."

She doesn't say anything, just makes a humming noise. Then I feel her hand on mine. She isn't looking at me when I glance at her. She's looking out the window at the landscape of farmland sliding past. Though I feel her touch and could interpret it to mean something, I don't. It feels like comfort, like a simple way to say: *I'm here. You aren't alone.*

I choose to believe it. For now.

7.

"You ready for this?" I ask her after I've gotten us a day pass for a hike to The Bend Ghost Town Trail. I open the map of the park from the visitor center.

"I was born ready."

With our backpacks and our map, we set off down the dusty trail. It's a beautiful walk, a wide swath of dry earth outlined by tall green grass. Butterflies dance across the top. The river curls like a blue ribbon through the meadows and aspen trees. Birds chirp and flutter about, flitting from tree to tree, the leaves still summer green. The sky stretches clear overhead except for a few clouds that seem to hang suspended by invisible strings.

The day has been strange. First the conversation with my family and the realization we are all hiding from secrets and feelings. Then opening up to Max, allowing her to see the part of me I've spent most of my life protecting. The strangest part, I don't feel terrible about it, but rather closer to her somehow. And clearer headed, as if sharing it—even though I've stripped away the tape I was using to hold myself together—offered freedom to own it. I wonder if this was what Tanner meant when he asked me if I'd ever thought there as more to life than Bro Code. I'd ridiculed him for it. The thought shames me.

"So," Max says after some time.

"So what?" I ask.

"I've given some thoughts to your rules."

"Why's that?"

"Well, I feel like perhaps they are limiting you."

"They're for parties, Max."

"Right. But if those are the only rules you're living by, you know, I think maybe you need to expand. Especially because of what we talked about on the way here."

"Okay," I say, drawing out the word and trying to find a clever argument against it. My skepticism is just because all of this openness feels unnatural and frightening. But Max hasn't really steered me wrong yet, so I can't find one.

"I've decided to share my rules with you."

"I wasn't aware you had rules."

"I definitely have rules."

"Wasn't the whole purpose of me sharing my rules because you hadn't been to parties? If you have rules, I didn't need to share mine."

"Oh. These aren't for parties." She glances over her shoulder at me a moment with a sly grin.

"What are these rules for?"

"Relationships."

"Because you've had so many?"

"I beg your pardon. I've had a boyfriend. You haven't even had a girlfriend."

"You had a boyfriend? When was this?" This news upends my perspective and makes me feel like I might lose my footing, though I'm not sure why that would be so. I glance at her, thinking about this fact. A boyfriend. Someone who wanted to be with Max exclusively. Someone who kissed her. And… maybe other stuff, too. My stomach clenches and twists.

"Yes. Last year."

"How long did you have this boyfriend?" I want to put a clamp on my mouth. It's none of my business, but my brain spins on the information. I can't stop thinking about some guy who captured Max's heart.

Her head turns to look at me, and she offers a strange smile. "Six months, give or take. So, your objection is irrelevant and overruled."

"Did you just lawyer and judge me at the same time?"

Six months, I think. I want to know so much more, curiosity curling through me like car oil keeping my engine running. I wonder if she loved him, but I don't ask.

"I did." She laughs. "I'm going to school you on my rules."

We come to a fork in the trail.

"Hold onto that for a moment," I say and open the map. "Let's figure out which way we have to go." After a quick study, we veer away from the river. "It says here that resources dried up, and that's why everyone moved away," I read.

"Isn't that why most ghost towns become ghost towns?"

I shove the map pamphlet in the front pocket of my backpack without removing it. "It isn't because everyone mysteriously dies, and then the town is haunted by the remaining ghosts? I thought we were going to a massive, haunted house."

She laughs. "That sounds more imaginative."

I grin and wonder if her boyfriend loved her laugh. I sure like it. It's musical. When it's real, it comes from her belly. Plus, I've never been considered the funny one with my friends, so making her laugh sort of feels like winning something, like when she smiles that real smile, the one with the dimple.

"Okay. So, your rules," I say.

"Yes. My rules. First rule, you have to trust."

"Okay. Trust. Got it."

I wonder why they broke up.

"Do you?"

"I trust you." I say it and mean it. I've never said or thought this about a girl before.

"Because I coerced you into it."

I look down at my feet to hide my smile. "Well, I allowed myself to be coerced, by you. If I didn't trust you, I wouldn't have shared. I haven't shared it with anyone else."

Max's eyes leave my face and return to the trail. "Rule two is that you have to talk."

"I talk."

"About real stuff."

The comment hits me like another bullet, and she's full of them today. Same shit. More reality that forces me to look at myself and my own choices. I clear my throat and keep to the banter rather than slide down into a broody rabbit hole. "What isn't real about ghost towns?"

She stops, and I catch up with her. "Griffin. You know what I mean."

"Okay. Okay. Talk. Next."

"Third rule: you have to be willing to share the hard parts of yourself."

I nearly stumble and raise my eyebrows when look at her. "The hard parts, Max?" I smile and can't help but grasp onto the suggestive innuendo in her comment, even if it was unintentional.

I wonder if she and her boyfriend had sex, and this thought cinches my muscles tighter, because I'm so curious now. I know it's a dumb mind trail to follow, but I can't seem to control my thoughts about it.

"Griffin!" Her cheeks have turned, red and I discover I like it. "I didn't mean it like that." She tries to hit me.

I laugh and dodge her playful smack, so her fingertips slide over my backpack. "You said 'hard.'"

"You're a child. I meant–" she says the last words louder to get my attention. "I meant, the difficult stories, the harder things to share about ourselves."

"Hard."

"Griffin." She all but stomps her feet, her hands on her hips.

I smile and keep walking. "Fine. I get it. Be willing to share. How many more rules are there, because this seems like a lot to remember."

"Really? You had four. I'm only at three. Trust. Talk. Share."

"Trust. Talk. Hard." I dart forward to get away from her, but I don't make it.

Max's catches me and wraps me in a bear hug from behind. "Stop it."

I grin and cover her hands clamped around me with mine. "Share."

She releases me.

I ignore the part of me that misses her being so close. It's dumb to want something like that. I'm trying to be a good friend, not a jerk.

"Rule four: allow others the space to mess up."

"Huh?"

"Case in point: Saturday night."

I wrap my hand around the back my neck and rub it, feeling the heat of embarrassment. "Oh. Got it."

"And the last rule."

"Thank God. My limited brain capacity just can't take anymore. It's just too *hard*."

"Griffin! You're obnoxious."

I bark laughter as she comes after me again. "Go. Go. Sorry!"

"Rule five: forgive."

I glance at her. She forgave me for acting like an ass. Max has demonstrated every one of her rules. I stop and face her. "I think for someone who says they haven't had very many friends; you have some pretty smart rules."

She stops too and looks at me. Her eyes search my face, measuring me for something only she knows, which I hope turns out in my favor. Then she says, "Well, I've recently had the opportunity to test them on this really unruly guy I met." She smiles and walks past me, her shoes crunching on the gravel. "Plus, I have Cal."

I follow. "I bet you had a chance to practice them with this boyfriend. Was that *hard*?"

She chases after me, giggling while she does.

I stop, and she catches me then pushes. We're both laughing, and I can't remember ever having this much fun. Ever.

We keep walking, talking about normal stuff. Favorites and stuff like that. I'm still wondering about this boyfriend, but I don't consider why I'm fixated on it.

The trees thin the further we walk, the blue sky, collecting with more ominous gray clouds, a stark contrast to the faded greens, yellows, and browns into which the world around us melts. Eventually we reach a ridge that descends into a valley. From that vantage, the many weathered buildings of The Bend lay like a forgotten toy town in the distance.

"There it is," Max says.

We walk the switchback down into the valley. I'm not looking forward to hiking back up and out to the car but seeing this ghost town seems even more important than before. We take the last of the hike down the curling path in silence. I'm in my own thoughts, but I'm not sure where Max's head is. It looks different than my dreams, which seem more like the perfect movie version of the Western town I grew up watching. This town doesn't look like that at all. The closer we get, the more desolate and emptier it feels.

When we reach the first building, I stop.

Max's steps crunch along the dirt road ahead of me until she realizes I'm not following. She stops and turns. "What is it?"

"It's creepy."

She turns and looks. "Is this what you imagined?"

"I thought there would be a boardwalk." It's a dumb statement. The walkway has always been such a big part of my dreams, but there isn't one here. As I stare down the main street of this ghost town, reality looks different, but the desolation of how I've felt most of my life is accurate.

"Do you still want to go?" she asks.

I nod.

Max waits for me so we can walk side by side.

The clouds are more ominous. The wind has picked up, swirling the tall grasses and trees. A breeze howls between the buildings like an echo of a ghost.

"I don't know that we have a lot of time before the rain hits."

"We're here and walked all this way." Max shrugs. "Might as well look around."

We stop at a house and peek in a window. It's dusty inside, old, the walls peeling with damage, and the floor littered with grime. Another building is a steepled wooden church and cemetery. The wooden crosses marking graves. "They were left behind," Max says. "It's so sad."

"Couldn't exactly take them."

We walk along a wooden porch that juts out from the building like a tongue and peer into a saloon through plexiglass. The bar laid with glasses that are murky with dust, a few tables with hands of cards lying fanned out on top, an old piano, the keys warped with disuse. All of it trapped in time.

"It's so quiet," Max says.

"It's hard to believe that people are just gone, left everything like this. Abandoned."

A raindrop.

Another.

I look up at the sky as the rain begins to fall.

"There!" Max points to a building with an open doorway at the other end of the main thoroughfare. By the time we reach the opening, our t-shirts are spotted with raindrops, our hair slick with moisture; we duck into the darkened interior, a barn. It isn't comfortable, but it's dry.

"It could be a while." I stand at the doorway, looking out at the

122

gray sky that's opened, emptying on the town. I shake out my hair.

"It's okay."

I turn from the doorway as Max takes her yellow coat out of her backpack and lays it down on the ground near a wall.

"You sure? We could make a run for it. I know you had plans."

She sits down. "I don't mind waiting."

"It's going to be muddy either way." I look back outside.

"Packing isn't going anywhere. Besides, I'm an expert at it."

I turn away from the entrance and follow where she's gone deeper into the building. Leaky places are beginning to make music in the room of the barn, but Max has picked a place that is dry.

Using my own jacket, I lay it out next to her and sit down. "I packed some food."

"You did?" She smiles. "I'm impressed."

I draw the peanut butter and jelly sandwiches from my backpack. "They're smashed. Sorry."

"Still food." She thanks me when I hand her one. "Who knew you were so resourceful. I may have to change your name."

"To what?" I unwrap my smashed sandwich and take a bite.

"I'm going to be thinking about it. What does your name mean, anyway?"

"Griffin? It's a monster. You know the one with the lion body and the eagle head and wings. When I asked my mom why she named me after a monster, she said she wanted something to match my brother's name."

"What's his name again?"

"Phoenix."

"The bird that rises from the ashes?"

"She claimed something like the griffin is a revered monster."

"Well, you know the internet never lies." Max bumps my shoulder with hers.

"It says 'ferocious monster.'"

"That plus Serial Killer. Car-slave. They all kind of work. You could have a name like mine that means 'great stream' and get teased for having a strong urinary flow."

This makes me smile, draws me out of being moody about my name. "Great stream, huh?" I pause and am unable to control myself. "Is that before or after it's hard?"

She backhands my shoulder playfully, and we sit in the ghost town together, laughing.

It's funny, I think, how an echo of desolation has bounced around inside me for so long, and suddenly, sitting here with Max, her echo seems to answer mine. Now, I don't feel like a shadow but someone alive, and it took her friendship to help me begin to find myself. The realization that she's leaving in a couple of days, and I will be on my own again, alone, drifting, thins me out. I'm not sure I will ever be able to escape that echo.

8.

"What is wrong with you?" Mom asks as she moves through the living room, plucking up her things for work.

I press buttons on the remote, killing stuff, and while video games usually bring me to an even plane of emotional existence, even my first-person romp in a graphics-induced universe isn't helping my mood. It's been a couple of days since my hike with Max, and I haven't run since. I don't want to acknowledge the foulness of my mood, but it's getting more difficult not to. Max is leaving. It makes me want to break shit, but I don't know why, and I don't want to think or talk about why my mood might be related to that fact.

I change the subject, focusing on my mom instead, taking in her scrubs. "Maybe since I'm working now, you can quit one of your jobs."

She straightens. "Don't think I haven't thought about it."

"You should. I mean, you're getting rent from me, and should be from Phoenix, soon."

She stuffs her cellphone in her purse. "I'll think about it."

"You could do something you want. Maybe start dating."

She freezes. "What are you talking about?"

I shrug. "Just throwing out ideas."

She moves again. "Well, don't think too hard. You should shower. You're starting to stink."

She's right, I haven't showered since I got back from the hike. I haven't had anywhere to go or anyone to see. Didn't seem to be a point.

"I won't be home until about two."

I nod, listen to the door close behind her as she leaves, and maintain my position on the couch with my remote and escapism.

Sometime later, Phoenix wanders into the living room and flops into the chair. "Damn, you're ripe."

"Fuck off."

"Where's the other remote?"

"I broke it. But there's an old one you could plug in."

Phoenix digs through all the video game paraphernalia until he finds it, then plugs it into the console to charge. He returns to a seat and watches me play until we can program him into the next game. We play, doing something normal like laughing, pushing, ribbing one another. Acting like brothers, I suppose.

My time with Max to The Bend inspires me to keep ahold of what's real, even if it's difficult. So as Phoenix and I play, I work up the courage to try and unpack some of the boxes I've been carrying. "Why didn't you come see us if you were in the city?"

His avatar ducks behind a concrete pillar to avoid enemy fire. "I told you. I was mad."

"At me?"

Phoenix sets down the control and looks at me. His avatar gets blown up a few seconds later. "No," my brother says. "Why would you think that?"

I shrug, struggling to figure out what I'm trying to say. "I just—" I stop. I'm not sure how to articulate the feelings. I feel anger, sure, but that's my default setting. I feel... hurt. "You're my brother, and all that time, you didn't want to know how I was? To check on me?"

Anger must be Phoenix's default setting too. He stands up with

126

a frustrated noise.

I think he's going to leave, run away from the conversation because it's what I would have done, but before he disappears down the hallway, he turns and stalks back into the room.

He looks conflicted, the whole of his features frowning, his body sort of hunched over on itself. "Yes." He runs a hand through his hair. "You're my brother. There wasn't a day that went by that I didn't think about you, that I didn't wonder how you were."

My avatar is long dead, and the default settings of the game are playing on the screen. I watch them a moment, both buoyed by his acknowledgement of missing me but also crushed by it. "Then why didn't you come home?"

"I couldn't."

"Why?"

"Can't you just fucking drop it? I'm here now. I'm not going anywhere. You have my promise about that."

"Why can't you just be honest with me?"

"Why is this about honesty? I'm being honest with you. Right now!" His hands fly out to his sides.

"I'm not a fucking idiot, Phoenix. And I'm strong enough to handle whatever it is you aren't telling me."

"I'm not! Don't you fucking get it yet, Griffin? I'm not strong enough." He turns around and stalks out of the room. Part way down the hall, he yells, "Just drop it!" then slams his bedroom door. A few minutes later, he stalks through the living room. "I'm going out."

I watch him walk down the walk and turn up the sidewalk, reminding me of Tanner. Only this time I was the one trying to talk, and Phoenix is shutting me out.

My phone pings, drawing my attention back into the room. It's Max:

Would you like to come over for farewell pizza?

127

I text her back right away.

Yes. What time?

5

I look at the time on my phone. *I'll be there,* I text her.

Needing to burn off frustration before then, I go for a run. The movement spends the energy I've got pent up from what happened with Phoenix in addition to my sour mood, so when I get back home, I feel more balanced. After a shower and a trip to the store to pick up something for Max's farewell pizza (I chose a cake with flowers and a giant, shiny *Good Luck* balloon), I park the car.

Max swings open the front door, maneuvers with ease down the ladder, and hops toward the car. She looks cute in those favorite denim cutoffs that show off her legs. The t-shirt is tie-dyed a rainbow of colors, Poison written in block letters with "Nothing but a Good Time" scrawled underneath. I didn't add that song to the playlist. I'll have to remember it. She's smiling and pulls her hair back, tying it up into a loose bun as she walks toward me.

"Am I late?" I ask when I get out.

"No. Pizza hasn't arrived. You won."

"I didn't know it was a competition."

"Life is a competition, SK. Come on."

"I bought you a cake." I hand it to her.

"That's sweet, literally." She smiles, and the dimple is etched in her cheek.

"Clever."

"Kind of big for the three of us."

She starts up the short ladder to get in through the front door. I'm behind her, working to keep my eyes off her ass, but then it's a good thing I've allowed myself to admire it because she loses her balance.

128

I reach up, hands on her waist to help her. "You good?"

She hums an affirmation, which hits my gut with warmth that spreads outward.

I make sure she's all the way up the ladder before I let go, and the skin of my palms burns from touching her. I wipe them against my thighs, trying to reset my nerve endings. *Friends, Griffin. She's leaving.*

Pointing at the cake, I say, "I picked that one out because you never know. Maybe that's what your dad will eat when he gets back."

Her smile fades.

"Shit. I'm kidding, Max." I grasp her shoulder to offer her comfort and bend slightly to meet her eyes, which slide down to the ground. "I'll make sure he's eating good."

Her eyes jump up and grasp onto mine. "Promise?"

I nod. "I also got this for you." I hold out the balloon to her.

She takes it. "I'll bet you think you deserve some applause for it too."

I grin at her. "Maybe."

She snorts, shakes her head, and then leads me into the house. "Griffin's here, Dad."

Cal turns away from the counter where it looks like he's making a salad. "I'm glad you're here. This one's been moping about."

I measure her with my gaze, recognizing myself with Cal's words.

She stops next to him at the counter, her back to me. "Dad, you lie."

He wraps an arm around her, squeezes her with affection before letting her go to finish the salad.

"All packed?" I ask.

"Yes. I guess."

"Nervous?"

"Yes."

"Excited?"

"Yes."

"I'm not," Cal says.

Max hands me some plates. "Help me set the table?"

After the plates are on the table, Max is folding napkins, and I'm setting the utensils on them. "You know pizza is a finger food, right? All the water wasted washing dishes."

"But salad isn't a finger food."

"It could be." I set down a fork and go to retrieve the cups.

Cal sets the salad bowl on the table just as a knock signals the pizza guy has arrived. "I'll grab that." He disappears.

Max places her last napkin. "That makes you a caveman."

I stop next to her and set down the last fork and cup. "Is that your new name for me?" I drop my arms to my sides. "I thought I was going to get something nicer."

Max assesses the table, dropping her arms to her sides. "You think you deserve a nicer name, SK?"

We're standing close enough that the skin of our arms and the backs of our hands brush. A current sizzles from where her skin touches mine, rushing through my body and seizing up my heart so that it palpitates in an unsteady rhythm. I swallow, wanting to explore the sensations but afraid. I disconnect instead, folding my arms over my chest. *Friends.*

"I hoped."

"Here's the pie." Cal walks back in with the pizza. "Let's eat."

We settle around the table to eat, and I realize I can't remember ever doing this with my own family. Maybe when I was little, before Dad went to prison. After, Mom was always working. Phoenix and I ate in front of the TV. I mostly sit and observe Cal and Max, the way they talk and laugh. The way he watches her with a smile and his eyes shining with vibrancy I might characterize as affection, probably love. He tells me about the cabinet Max refinished for him and how beautiful it is, the pride evident in his smile and words. I offer thoughts when they invite me into the conversation, laugh when I'm supposed to, but it would be a lie to say I'm not feeling the pall of the impending departure. Tomorrow, they won't be here.

Has it only been seven or eight weeks ago that Max walked into my life?

We play cards. Eat cake. Talk more. I hear stories about Max growing up. Her spreadsheets using star stickers to keep Cal on budget, and her color-coded grocery lists.

"I think that's enough *embarrass Max* for one night." She stands, still smiling.

I will my heart to stop its weird dance when I look at her.

She carries the cake into the kitchen.

"I don't think it's embarrassing," Cal says, leaning back in his chair. He stifles a yawn.

"Dad," she looks over her shoulder, "you told Griffin I color-code the grocery list."

I stifle a smile. "I'm sure it's helpful."

"It is." Cal stretches. "Before I forget, Griffin, would you do me a favor while I'm gone?"

"Sure."

"Would you come out to check on the house every day? I'm a little worried about those doors."

"You got it."

Cal stands. "On that note, this old man is sleepy. I'm going to leave you young ones to clean up."

"We got it," Max says, standing by the table again.

Cal leans over and kisses her temple. "Night."

We both wish him a good night and watch him leave the room. I get up to help clear the rest of the table.

"Thank you, Griffin."

"Sure. No problem. I don't mind." I like helping her.

"No." She hands me a damp cloth. "I mean for being there for my dad."

I can see she's trying not to cry when I take the cloth.

"It's for the table." She turns back to the sink.

I wipe the table so it's clean. "He's going to be okay."

"I know."

I stop next to her at the sink and drop the cloth into the sudsy water. "Then what's up?"

She doesn't look at me and continues washing the salad bowl, but it looks more like she's just swirling around the water. "It's just me."

That organ in my chest keeping me alive sputters again. "What?"

She turns and looks at me, and I see her teary, gray eyes are sparkling water under a starry sky. "I'm scared to leave him." She blinks, and a tear drips down her cheeks.

I wrap an arm around her and draw her against my side. "You're going to be great. I know it."

"What if I'm not. What if I can't find any friends? What if I can't find my way around. What if I flunk out? What if I just miss Dad so bad that I sink into a horrible depression where I never shower and my roommate plots to get me removed." She smiles through her tears.

"All of those things are improbable."

Her eyebrows arch over her tear-filled eyes with a question she doesn't even need to vocalize.

"You're one of the weirdest people I know," I say.

"That doesn't help."

"Sure it does. Weird is good. You're original, and fun and kind. You care about people. I mean, if you could care about me—a fake serial killer—and get me to talk to you, then surely you can get normal people to like you. And you're one of the smartest people I know. As for the roommate and depression and stinking up the place, I'm not sure a girl who color-codes lists is bound for not showering."

Her arm wraps around me from behind, the heat of her hand imprinting my skin through my t-shirt near my hip, and her head tips to rest against my shoulder. "Want to hear something really weird," she says and sniffs.

"You mean something normal since everything you say is weird."

"I'm going to miss you."

My throat constricts. *Breathe*, I tell myself. *Breathe*. I take a breath. "I know," I say, going for our usual sarcasm since it feels safer.

She pinches my side. "I'm being serious."

I accept her words for what they mean to me—everything—and offer them back to her with honesty. "I'm going to miss you, too."

I turn my head toward her, intending to plant a kiss against her cheek. At the same moment, she turns her head. My lips brush the corner of her mouth, right where her dimple would be if she were smiling.

I freeze.

She freezes.

Her eyes jump to mine, and her fingertips press the place I've kissed.

The air contracts around us, heavy with suggestion, anticipation, tension.

My eyes drop to her fingertips. Her lips, pretty and pink, slightly parted, and my heart drops into my stomach. It shouldn't. *Shouldn't. Shouldn't*, I repeat to myself as a reminder that Max is my friend.

Max moves. Her hands frame my face, and she presses her lips to mine.

Her pumpkin pie scent swirls around me and makes me hungry for her. My first impulse is to grasp her hips, walk her backward, press her against the counter, lift her so she can wrap her legs around my hips, and taste my fill.

But it's Max. Max, who I care about. Max, who's my friend.

I pull away.

Her eyes open.

I take a step away and gulp my feelings because my impulse is to go the other direction. I don't trust my impulses. My brain is telling me that I need to preserve what I have with Max at all costs. *Don't ruin it. Don't ruin it. Don't ruin it because that's what you do, Griff.* But my heart is slamming around in my chest, trying to get my feet to close the distance between us.

"Oh. I wanted–" she starts.

"I'm sorry–" I say at the same time.

Whatever she was going to say dries up, and she looks down at her feet. "I guess I hoped–"

"Hoped?"

"That maybe you might be–" She pauses, looks away, turns away, cuts me out with her body language. "Forget it."

"Max–" I fold my arms and fist my hands to keep from reaching for her.

"It's okay. I get it."

"Get what?" I ask.

"I'm not your type."

"Max. No. That isn't–" I want her to turn and look at me.

"Please. Don't say something you don't mean."

"I'm not. It's just I care about you."

Her head shifts so she can look at me, and her eyes narrow. Then her head tilts. "What? I'm confused. You care about me. You just don't want to kiss me?"

I don't admit I do want that. I can't. It would cross a boundary, and I ruin things. I can't ruin this. "You're my friend."

Her mouth does that sideways thing I find adorable, but in that moment it's terrifying. Her eyes narrow, and I don't want her to look at me anymore. "So, let me get this straight. You have four rules about getting with nearly any girl that moves as long as she isn't drunk and is willing. Is there another rule you skipped?"

When she says it like that, I hear how terrible I sound. "No." I groan in frustration and run my hand through my hair, turning away. "I don't sleep with girls I care about." That sounds worse and isn't what I'm trying to say at all. I sigh. "I'm not saying this right."

"You think that's supposed to make me feel better? That it sounds better? And who said anything about sleeping together?"

All my thoughts feel jammed up in my head like when all the logs meet in the river and stop things up. "I just don't want–"

"Yeah. I get it," she interrupts. "Me. You don't want me. It isn't

134

you, it's me, right?" She grabs the salad bowl and lifts it, dumping the sudsy contents into the sink. I can tell by her clipped movements she's angry.

"Max—" I start, but I'm not sure what to say. How to make it better.

"Just—please, don't." She smacks the bowl into the drainer. "I think you should go." Her voice catches in her throat.

Is she crying?

I can't move toward her to check. I don't trust myself. And she's asked me to go. "Max. Please don't do this—" I say.

She twirls around, her eyes swimming again with tears. "Go! Please." The last word is barely audible as her chin quivers, and she covers her mouth with her hand.

I back away from her stunned, hurt, and filled with regret, but I listen. I do what she asks because not only is it one of my rules, but also what are friends for?

SEPTEMBER

If swallowing the feelings doesn't work, and drowning them doesn't kill them, what then? I had this coach who used to say, "Men don't cry. Suck it up, boys. Move forward." But what if you're stuck and can't move forward.

Does that make me a failure? I feel like I can't even be a man correctly.

To: Griffin Nichols
123 45th Street NE
The Town, USA 67890

1.

I miss Max and replay what happened the night before she left over and over like a scratched record. I replay it from the beginning, then skip about, dragged toward the center where white noise is the only sound.

What's the point?

2.

My breath is steel in my lungs caught, sharp, and cutting up my insides with rusty edges. I squeeze the edge of the open door with my hand. I'm not sure how I'm supposed to feel, staring at my father who I haven't seen since I was eight. He looks at me with such earnest hope I feel like I might vomit my rage.

"What are you doing here?" I keep the screen door between us.

"I got out. I thought you knew."

"Yeah. I heard. What are you doing here?" I repeat the question because he has no fucking right to be here. I'm glad Mom isn't here.

He's standing at the bottom of the concrete steps. His hands are in the pockets of his black pants. He looks down, shakes his head, then swipes one of his hands over his shorn hair. I can hear the bristles against his palm and feel them against my own like tiny needles injecting me with animosity. "I wanted to see you and Phoenix. Your mom. I'm over at a halfway house in the city."

"Your other family wouldn't take you back either?"

His eyebrows shift over his eyes first with surprise, then with what resembles regret. He draws his eyebrows together, and I'm struck with how much older he looks. I remember him—a tower over me—smiling like he held the secret of life behind his teeth, and he only had to tell it to me. Now, though, I can see the truth. The fade of his eyes, the lines in his skin. He's got a tattoo climbing up one side of his neck leaking out of the collar of his white t-shirt. I don't remember that as a kid. His body—always muscular—is now wiry with it, lean and sharp.

"I've seen them," he says. "I'd like a chance to explain." He takes the first step toward me.

"No. I don't want to hear it."

He freezes.

"Phoenix isn't home. I'm leaving."

"Your mom?"

"Moved on."

He nods with acceptance. "Yeah. I just–" he stops. His eyes assess me. "You're so grown."

"What did you expect? I'd still be a little kid playing with fucking Legos?" The memory of the cops moving through the house to arrest him, the Lego kit I'd been playing with upended into the shaggy carpet of the house comes to mind. It had been my birthday.

He looks away, his jaw sharpening into strong points.

I step back into the house. "I have to go to work."

He stops me with his voice. "Griffin. I just wondered if we could talk. Maybe meet or something. Coffee? Breakfast?"

"To what?"

"I'd like to get to know you. Catch up."

Catch up. Like he's been away on vacation in the fucking Hamptons.

Tears sharpen to points in my eyes like nails along with a great gust of anger so strong it becomes a tornado inside of me. I want to release the storm, but I can't open my mouth afraid the tears will be a torrent as much as the dangerous debris I will throw at him with my words. He sees it, takes a step backward down the sidewalk away from me.

"It doesn't have to be today. Or this week or anything. I'm just putting it out there. I'd like to–" he pauses.

And I finish his sentence in my head: *Be your dad...*

Which enrages me further even though he hasn't said that.

"—I'd like to be a part of your life," he finishes.

"Don't." I hold up a hand and step back. "Just—" I shake my head. "You need to leave."

"Please, son."

"Don't you fucking call me that!" Each word feels like a nail shooting from my mouth like Cal's nail gun.

He takes a step back to avoid them, hands up in acquiescence. He nods, eyes lowered. "Okay. Okay."

I push the fading thought of Max's relationship rules away, deciding that the rules only apply to relationships in which both parties are mutually invested. I am not invested in this man. I shut the door in his face.

I lean my forehead against it, breathing hostility, and weeping resentful pain.

He didn't write.

I didn't write or visit either.

We are built with silence.

Here's the thing about silence; it bounces around between you like an echo looking for an end, but there isn't one. The echo just keeps going, seeking a landing spot. The silence from my father is bouncing around, echoing a story that I wasn't worth the bother. I wasn't worthy of his time. His words were silence, and now, when I'm old enough to answer, it's the echo I'm giving him back.

3.

First, I think of calling Tanner to tell him about my dad. Then I think of Max. I don't reach out to either.

What's the point?

4.

Text from Josh:

> Don't forget Danny's swearing in on Tuesday.

> Griff?

> You'll be there, right?

> It will mean a lot to Danny if you're there.

Text from Max:

> Thanks for helping my dad.

Several days later, Max texts again:

> Are you alive?

> Dad says you're coming to work so, I'm making assumptions that you're still on the straight and narrow…

> no SK activities. ☺

> It's okay here. So far.

> I'm still showering.

Several days after that, Max texts again:

> Griffin?

> Are you okay?

> I'm sorry about getting mad.

> You were right, and

> I shouldn't have put pressure on you.

> I'm sorry (see! I'm following my rules).

I don't answer her, so she texts again a few days later.

If you don't answer me
back this time, I'm

going to spam your
phone with emojis.

Would you like to test me on this?

The flatlining of my heart beeps back to life, so I text her back.

5.

I can't get what Max said about relationships out of my head. The rules: trust, talk, share, accept, and forgive. The catalyst is my father showing up at my door. As much as I hate him, I can't get her voice shouting those damn rules out of my mind. I have no intention of using them with my father, but I wonder if I can try and start with my friends. I decide to go to Danny's swearing in. Truthfully, I'm terrified, knowing now that I'm the one who broke up the band.

The room is compact. A small space set up in an office over a strip mall in the middle of town, so even if I'd wanted to hang out in the back and remain unseen while Danny swears in, it isn't going to happen. The moment I walk in, Josh sees me, and it seems like relief hits his features because they relax. He offers me a grin and waves me over. That's when I notice Tanner standing next to him.

My step falters a moment, and I consider turning around. I'm not angry, but I'm shaped by shame, regret, and guilt. I haven't seen Tanner since that night when we'd both been drunk and stupidly rolling around in a parking lot fighting one another with misguided punches and mean words. I don't want to not be friends anymore, but there are so many words I'd like to say and no rules for how to carry that out.

I think of my dad and wonder if this was how he felt standing at the door the other day.

I release the thought into the void. Our crimes aren't comparable.

Tanner offers me an acknowledgement with his eyebrows and a slight rise of his chin. I slide back to one of the many times when all we had to do was look at one another and everything we needed to say was communicated by a look. Now, though, the clairvoyance isn't calibrated anymore.

I offer him the same in return.

He returns to watching Danny, who's standing with two other guys in the middle of the room, his back to us.

It isn't more than what any acquaintance might offer another, but I don't blame him.

I take up a spot next to Josh.

He leans toward me. "Glad you're here."

I've missed him and regretted the Quarry. So many things I wish I could fix, but I just offer him a nod. That's the most I can do, unsure of who I am in that moment: Pre-fight Griff or Post-Max Griffin?

There's a 99.9% chance I'm about to screw this up somehow. I don't know how to be anymore. It feels easier to just stay rooted to what's familiar even if it goes against one of Max's rules.

Flags in stands outline the opposite side of the room from where I'm leaning. A small podium is set between the guys swearing in and those flags. A man wearing fatigues faces them, and us, and leads Danny and the two other guys through the ceremony. The Air Force inductees repeat the oath, and suddenly the ceremony is ending. Danny shakes hands with the two others and the recruiting officer. Then he turns, smiling. He hugs a man—his dad—and a younger girl, who I assume is his little sister. Then his eyes slide to us, and to me. His eyebrows jump but he smiles, surprised, though joy colors all the spaces on his face.

I've missed Danny, too.

"Griff," he says, walks over, but instead of shaking my hand or offering a fist bump he wraps me in a hug.

I tense.

He draws back and says, "I'm glad you made it."

I give him a half-smile and nod again as words catch in my throat. I'm so glad, suddenly, that Josh pressed the issue, that I asked Cal for the afternoon off, that I took the risk to be here. This wasn't about me at all. It was about Danny. This awareness feels giant in my body, pressing outward, and threatening to tear me apart. I want to retreat.

I remember his anger at me. *You're the one who broke it, Griff.*

I don't know how to repair it. Cal's offered lots of lessons in building and fixing tangible things. Max has given me rules for relationships that seem to work with her. I don't know how to marry the two things. How does one repair a relationship you broke? Especially when "sorry" doesn't seem like enough.

Danny shifts to hugging Josh, then Tanner, and there is banter between them that feels familiar. The sound, the rhythm, and the laughter, but now I feel outside of it as they talk.

"What about you, Griff?"

I look up from the floor where I'd been studying the flecks in the linoleum. "Huh?"

Josh's eyebrows are high and coaxing me to participate. "Ready for school?"

"When have I ever been ready for school?"

They all laugh. Even Tanner smiles, his eyes warm with familiarity. The sound of laughter is a little forced. I have the sense none of us know how to be together anymore, though I can tell the others have moved forward together. Just not me. True to Josh form, he's trying to build a bridge between us because he takes us down memory lane about the night before the first day of school senior year when I decided to throw a party at Tanner's pool. I'd gotten so drunk I'd missed the first day of school, nursing the hangover of all hangovers.

I glance at Tanner.

He isn't smiling and is staring off at something unseeing, hands in his pockets.

I feel embarrassed, and my defenses rise like walls around me.

"Are you moving to the city?" Josh asks me, changing the subject.

I shake my head. "Commuting to school. Working."

"Tanner, isn't that what you're doing too?" Danny asks.

I glance at him.

"Yeah." Tanner isn't looking at any of us. His tone of voice is tight, and his jaw works over the words.

I notice Josh glance at Danny and recognize this for what it is, an intervention. It's so obvious they're trying to fix whatever is broken between Tanner and me. Except they can't. As much as I want things to be like they once were, I don't want the same either. I don't know how to do it. I just feel inadequate and lost and less than each of them which makes me feel broken, ugly, and wild. As soon as those insecurities creep up on me, I'm angry and defensive. I feel the cracks erode, widening, and the tension bubbles up through me.

I need to go.

"What happened with that girl?" Josh asks me.

I know he's talking about Max and the night out at the Quarry, but I play dumb. "What girl?" I don't want to talk about Max; there's too much of the real me invested in that relationship which feels tentative and dreamlike. She's gone, and I'm beginning to think the better version of me when I was around her is gone too. My edges are sharpening, and I'm worried I'm going to use them.

Tanner's eyes slide to my face, a questioning quirk of his brows as he takes measurement of me. I want to smirk back like I used to—the unspoken words passing between us like the old days—but I can't.

"From the Quarry?"

"Nothing."

Tanner doesn't look away, and I have the sense he can read me like a book since he does so much fucking reading. I don't know what my story is telling him, however. He tilts his head, curious, but I also see the wounds riding his features, a tightness in his gaze that feels like an accusation.

I set my jaw.

"She must have forgiven you since you look like you made it home." Josh laughs.

Tanner still assesses, observant and knowing. He does know me best, after all, but I'm not sure he can read between the lines of my story to the truth anymore. The Griffin I was with Max wasn't the Griff I'd ever been with him.

My defenses are jagged now, and while I logically know that Josh's comment isn't disparaging of Max, I feel the insinuation under my skin because of all the history wrapped up with my friends. It feels like he's made a joke of that night, of her, of me. They know how I was, and maybe I'm kidding myself that I can be anything different.

I push away from the wall. "Yeah. I made it home."

"For the record," Josh says, "she seemed cool."

I press my teeth together but offer him a nod.

"Still seeing her?"

"What do you think?" I say, and it comes out like bricks to build the wall I want it to.

Josh leans away, and his smile flickers.

I shake my head. "I should go." I look at Danny. "Congratulations."

"Come to lunch with us," he says, his eyes gentle and inviting. I know his invitation is earnest. "Everyone is coming."

"Yes," Josh says.

"You should," Tanner tacks on, and his eyes meet mine. I see there's an invitation, and I should know that Tanner only says what he means.

The hope in my gut feels dangerous and untrustworthy. I shake

150

my head and take a step away from him, from my friends. "I can't. I have work." I hold out my hand to Danny. "Good luck."

Danny takes it. "Thanks for being here."

I nod and chance a glance at Josh then Tanner. They are both unreadable, their facial expressions neutral. I turn away before I can see them switch to disappointment and walk away from them, sure that Max's rules aren't for rebuilding, only maintenance. If I've proven anything in my life, it's that I can't do either.

6.

I tell Max about seeing Tanner, Josh, and Danny. Her hope—
the positivity—feels like oil. I try to grab ahold, but my fingers slip
through the viscous feeling. It coats my skin but washes away
without her.

I don't tell her I was a coward; she already knows. I ran away
and failed her relationship rules. Too many feelings.

Feelings.

What's the point?

7.

My house is full of people, but the shitty realization is that of the people partying in my house, I only know a handful and none of them are my real friends. Mom is at work. Phoenix is out. Max is at school, though she sent me a *Happy Birthday* text. We'd Facetimed, and she was at a party where some guy put his arm around her. I ignore feelings about that. Josh and Danny have left town; I got texts from them too. Tanner is MIA (though to be fair I didn't invite him). No text from him. The rest are people I've partied with but don't know anything about me except the version I've offered for consumption. It's just the shitty version of me on my shitty birthday, surrounded by people but really alone.

I fucking hate my birthday, and it's always the perfect day to get completely trashed.

Marcus walks in through the front door, sees me sitting on the couch like a king on his throne, and yells, "Happy birthday, Fucker!" He smiles and greets guests as he walks across the room, then slaps my palm with his when he reaches me. He holds out a bottle of Jack. "Have a good time, bro." He winks like we're in on a private joke.

The bottle feels heavy in my hands like both a promise and a curse. "Thanks. How'd you get your hands on it?"

"A cousin. You're nineteen now?"

I nod.

"Two more years and you can buy your own. Fuck yeah."

I offer Marcus a cool smile, that's what he expects.

He glances around, looking at the meat market. "Where's that hot girl you were with at the bonfire?"

Max.

He continues talking, his eyes returning to me. "She was fine. I would have liked to hit that. I hope you did." He chum-punches my shoulder like we're brothers in arms.

I feel a little sick and disgusted that he's relegated Max to nothing more than item and ashamed that I've done the same thing to others. He sounds like a tool. "College," I tell him.

"My loss, I guess," he says and heads into the kitchen.

Your never, I think.

The front door opens.

Bella walks into the house with her friend, Greta.

I'm surprised. They probably showed up hoping Tanner would be here. Resentment churns in my gut. I twist open Marcus's gift and take a swig.

Bella's blue eyes find mine as she meanders through the room. She looks good, like she always does. Her straight blond hair is long and sleek, her body banging in a short skirt and a fitted shirt that shows off her curves as well as slices of tanned skin at her waist. She offers a tentative smile.

I don't return it, but I watch her walk across the room toward me as I take another gulp of the Jack. I'm tense and raise my shields.

"Happy birthday." She sits down on the couch next to me, so close she might as well be sitting on my lap.

Greta passes to talk to Marcus who's at the dining table now.

I look at Bella. Her eyes are rimmed with eye makeup the color of smoke. It makes her blue eyes brighter. "Tanner isn't here." I adjust myself so she isn't a layer I'm wearing and take another drink.

She looks down at her hands in her lap and swipes at the skin of her bare thigh as if there is something there. There isn't, just smooth, tan skin. "I came for *your* birthday, Griff." Her gaze jumps back up to mine, and she smiles again, this time with more convincing brightness.

I hum and take another drink.

"May I?" she asks and holds out a hand.

I give her the bottle.

She tips it up and takes a gulp, her eyes never leaving mine. Then she winces as she hands it back to me. "That burns."

I smile, and my bitterness smooths out. I take another drink. "An acquired taste."

Her eyes move across my face, as if she's taking stock. "Yes. I think it is." She leans closer, her lips moving against the skin of my ear. "I have a birthday gift for you later." She leans back slightly and smiles, the promise of what she means clear.

I'm not sure how I feel about that. A few months ago, getting with her was all I wanted, but now her words from the Quarry solidify like knives stabbing me in the gut; *choosing him would be like choosing a Nissan over a Tesla.* I take another sip, and despite the wound made by her words, my mood is smoother as the alcohol mellows me. I consider her offer, but there's something else in the shadows, something distant and lonely. My instincts suggest a hasty retreat, but I decide that can't be right. Here's a beautiful girl offering up… something. Bro Code. Guys don't feel that way, not when a hot girl expresses her interest, right? I recall telling Max my rules, though I don't want to think about Max, and decide that if Bella checks all the boxes, I should be into it. Right?

I take another drink, stretch my arm over the back of the couch, and hand her the bottle again.

She takes another sip.

We don't really talk, just exist in one another's spheres while the party happens around us. I drink. She drinks. The alcohol doing what it's supposed to, lower the inhibitions, free up the constraints of whatever ills walk alongside me, until all the emotion is numb, but the physical sensation is wide awake. Her constant touch, skin slipping against mine, kindles physical sensation, but something in the recesses of my emotional ghost town echoes that physical and emotional aren't the same thing. I dismiss it.

Phoenix walks into the house at some point during the night. I've lost track of time. He stalls at the door, taking in the scene. Sounds of the party coil around us, tightening the walls of the room. I'm still on the couch with Bella rubbing against me. Her hands haven't stopped touching me. One of her hands is in my hair at my nape. Her boob is pressed against my arm. Both of us are drunk and dumb on that bottle of whiskey we've been sharing.

Phoenix's eyes meet mine, but he doesn't smile like I expect. Hot-girls-hot-cars poster expectations. Instead, he hesitates at the door, then picks his way around the revelers. He's carrying a pink box. When he reaches me, he sets it on the coffee table littered with cups, bottles, and cans.

"I got this for you," he says over the music.

I lean forward. It's a cake with *Happy Birthday* written across the top. "Thanks, bro." I give him a loose smile. "Come have a drink with your baby brother." I hold out the partially empty bottle to him.

He glances at it and takes a step back. His eyes dance around the room and then rest on Bella, who's snuggled up against me. "I didn't know you were having a party." He has to repeat himself, leaning closer, and I lean forward to hear him.

I lean back after I do. "It's my birthday, and it sucks. Might as well party." He knows why I hate my birthday. He was there. Cops. Shouting. Tears. Father led out in handcuffs. A birthday to remember.

He shakes his head. "I can't stay."

"What?" I try to stand but flop back onto the couch, drunker than I thought. That and Bella holds onto my arm, making it impossible to move anyway.

Phoenix holds up his hands. "Don't. I just–" he stops. "Never mind. Happy birthday, Griffin." He offers me a smile that doesn't reach his eyes and disappears somewhere.

I don't think too much about it, just sit in my kingdom, feeling not much of anything at all.

The party waxes and wanes until there's only a handful of us left. Greta disappears out the front door holding Marcus's hand, and Bella's still next to me. She's drunk. I'm drunk. She leans over and trails kisses on my neck.

I stand, barely, and hold out my hand.

She takes it.

I lead her to my room using the wall for support, and then draw her into the dark when we get there. "You into this?" I ask. I'm asking her, but the question smacks me. Am I? I wrap my arms around her and kiss her jaw because I'm supposed to be into it. A little voice that sounds like Max says, "What about your rules?" I shake my head to dislodge the thought.

"Yes." She turns her face, so her lips connect with mine.

"You sure? I'm not Tanner," I say against her mouth.

She pulls away. I can't see her face clearly in the dark, but the moonlight outside my window makes her eyes shiny orbs. "I'm sorry about that."

"Sorry you said it, or sorry I heard it?"

"Both." She draws me toward the bed, sits down, leans back, then pulls me onto her. "I haven't been able to stop thinking about you since. And you were with that other girl."

I have the faint thought that this is happening because of Max. She's a giant missing piece of a puzzle I can't finish. I shake my head again. I can't think about Max right now.

My mind teeters and slips toward focusing on my body, which doesn't really care about Bella's admission, more interested in the sensation of her hands on the skin of my back under my t-shirt. Her mouth, her lips against mine wakes the necessary parts of me up as I settle in between her thighs (which is a relief that everything is in working order considering I'm drunk AF). She tilts her hips to invite me to settle deeper. The physical effects of lust run through my blood like lightning. I'm hungry. She must be too, tugging at my shirt until it's off and hers follows so we're skin to skin.

The last time I was with anyone, it had been her, and that was months ago, just after graduation. The physical connection is easy between us. The physical function of my body as it prepares to connect with hers isn't a thinking endeavor. I'm wound up, tense, and decide release is what will help me get back on track. I kiss her with all the pent-up energy inside of me.

I don't sleep with girls I care about.

I falter as the words I shared with Max slash and burn my physical response.

My mouth drifts away from Bella's, and I use my arms to push away from her. "I don't think I can do this," I say.

But Bella's response to my drifting is to turn up the physical. "I want you," she pants, pulling me back to her. She kisses me deeper, reaches into my pants and touches me. "Please."

Her skin against mine physically feels good.

She wants me.

The voices in my head reminding me about the rules recede. I grasp onto being wanted and to the physical pleasure associated with that want.

The response of her mouth is as hungry as mine, filled with heavy sighs and warm moans, sounds that add fuel to the fire. She offers reciprocal pleasure with her tongue and her touch. I give both back because the voices fade, the emotions numb in comparison to what I'm feeling in my body, which is nice and loud. My brain feels far, far away. The sensations override everything else.

"Griff?" Her voice draws me back from the alcohol pleasure numb, and she moves her hips against me. "Do you have a condom?"

"Yes." I reach into the cabinet drawer next to my bed, and she unbuttons her skirt shimmying out of it. I can't find the box and look for it. It's gone. "Fucking Phoenix," I swear and bow my head.

Bella's mouth moves on my shoulder, her hands are all over me.

"What is it?" She pushes at the waistband of my jeans. "I need this. What's taking so long" Her voice is threaded with a high note of need.

I look at her. "I'm out. Unless you have a condom."

"I'm on the pill," she says while touching me, offering, needing, drawing me back to her, and pushing me onto my back.

If I were thinking, I might take stock that the missing condoms are a sign, but I'm not. I don't believe in signs. My brain is connected to my animal needs. She doesn't seem to be thinking either because she draws my mouth back to hers. She tugs on my jeans, releasing me from the confines of the denim and my boxers and pushes everything over my hips.

She returns, straddling me. "It's okay. Please." Her mouth works magic against my skin, and she leans forward, her breasts in my face, her body rocking against mine.

I descend further into the basic need of release.

"Griff. Please."

It's against the rules, a quiet voice reminds me.

What's the point? What have any rules ever gotten me? Instead, I grasp her hips because I'm not thinking past the moment. I hear her wants, her words, *Please, Griff.* I hold myself and guide her, until all I feel is wrapped up in the sensation of her body snug around mine. I draw in a breath, and I forget where I am. I forget what I was looking for. I forget to think at all, and I just exist in the sensations. The skin of her hips against my palms. The sound of her moans. The movement and friction of our bodies working in concert and climbing toward the crescendo. Then I reach it and fall over the edge, letting go. My mind goes refreshingly blank, and I drift into the darkness of release, then sleep, not feeling so alone, not really feeling anything at all.

The thud of a door somewhere in the house wakes me up. My mom is leaving for work, I decide. The room sort of spins in the twilight of predawn, and I remember the party, the drinking, and Bella. I try to shift onto my back, but warm skin presses against my own, and I realize she's still in my bed with me.

I lift my head and see her arm draped over me.

Shit.

What have I done?

Shit.

With a sinking feeling in my gut, I know I've gotten drunk and slept with Bella, even after what happened at the Quarry.

I've fucking lost my mind.

With two fingers, I move her arm as gently as I can. Then, mustering as much finesse as I'm able, despite what I'm realizing is a massive hangover thrumming through my head and gut, I extract myself from my own bed. She rolls over, and I freeze. Then, I slink across the room to my dresser and find the first clothes available. Slipping into the black sweats and a random t-shirt, I glance at the girl in my bed.

She's as nude as I was, the blue comforter draped across her hips. She's on her side, back to me, her hands tucked under her. Her blond hair spread out around her. I have the strange awareness that seeing her this way at one time might have awakened the sexual attraction I've always felt for her, but for some reason it's regret swirling through me instead. What I thought I wanted incongruent with the road I've taken to get to this moment. I've broken so many of my rules.

I'd gotten too drunk.

I'd slept with her without a condom, even if she is on the pill.

I'd used her.

I feel used.

My stomach tightens with unease.

I sneak from my own room and use the bathroom, brush my teeth, check for life inside my house. I'm expecting to find a party mess because I didn't clean up, but there isn't one. Everything party related is gone. No cups, bottles, cans. No trash or food. No empty wrappers, or stray dishes. The couch looks perfect, the carpet vacuumed. Everything in its place.

I make coffee because I need to think, but the impending headache is making it difficult.

A noise draws my attention to the hallway.

Bella—dressed in her clothes from the night before, her hair a haphazard mess—has her shoes between the fingers of one of her hands, her phone, and keys in the other. "Shit," she mutters. It appears she's trying to sneak out.

"Coffee?" I ask.

She shakes her head. "I should get home. My mom–" she waves her phone– "needs the car. I didn't want to bother you."

I turn away and stare at the coffee pot, wishing it would brew faster so I could do something else instead of talking to her. My face and ears flood with embarrassment, and I think she's feeling it too, trying to sneak away. I don't want to be a coward though, so I turn to face her. "About last night–"

She stops her creep across the floor toward the living room and sighs. "Can we not?" She lifts her head, and I notice the dark rings around her eyes, the make-up and shadows of my own regret reflected at me. "I look like shit. I feel like shit. And I don't know if I have it in me right now to figure out what just happened between us."

"Is there an us?" I ask and realize it sounds abrupt and rude. "Did you want me to call you?" I regret the second question the moment it's drifting between us. I don't want to call her, and that makes me feel worse because if I did, it would just feel like going through weird and unnecessary motions to a predictable end. Have I ever wanted anything with her beyond sex? No.

She looks at the front door as if it's the promised land, sighs again, then turns to face me. "I don't think so, Griff."

Her words provide both insecurity because I can't figure out what's wrong with me that she wouldn't, but also relief. I don't want it any more than she does. I won't show her either of these feelings, however, and just give her a nod punctuated by no words. What's there to say?

The coffee pot beeps.

I turn around and retrieve a coffee cup. While I'm pouring the liquid into my mug, I hear the front door open, the screen door squeak, then thud closed.

Alone again. Always alone.

Only this time, it's a relief.

OCTOBER

I'm supposed to be strong. I filled my life with all the ways to prove it. My hands and knees might be in the dirt with my teeth kicked in and my mouth dripping blood but I'm a fucking man. Watch me bleed.

I'll crawl through this shit anyway, carrying that burden because this is all there is.

I think it might be a lie.

To: Griffin Nichols
123 45th Street NE
The Town, USA 67890

1.

Being on the roof of the farmhouse, the comfortable early October breeze swirling refreshing air around Cal and I, isn't bad, even if the work is hard. Over the last week we've stripped all the old shingles off, patched the damaged portions, covered, and sealed it. We're finally adding the new shingles. All the work we've done so far amazes me, considering a couple of months ago the house looked like it would topple over. Now it's painted white. The new windows are framed with shutters painted a fresh black. There are two, new porches that look like band-aids still needing paint. While I'm working in between school, commuting and weekends, we've accomplished a lot. Anytime I work with Cal, even if we don't talk, what's in me—the doubt, the fear, and the anger—settles. It feels good to do something with my body and my hands that creates rather than leaves me in purgatory.

It's been a few weeks since my birthday.

I haven't tried to call Bella.

She hasn't called me either.

What happened with her on my birthday has me second guessing myself, though the why doesn't make sense given my history with Bro Code. My doubts about being with Bella, even if the encounter fits with the code, contrasted with my fear about that kiss with Max, which had nothing to do with Bro Code, are wreaking havoc with what I've always thought about relating to someone else. All of it makes me feel insecure about the way I interpret my own thoughts.

I slam the hammer against another nail to fasten the shingle. Grab another from the box, line it up and nail the next one. Cal's nail gun thumps. He moves quicker than I do because of it, but I like the satisfaction of hitting the nail, my muscles feeling the motion and the strain. I'm tired, but it's better than feeling the awful discomfort of insecurity.

My phone buzzes in my pocket.

I set the hammer down after finishing the shingle and sit, taking a moment to check it.

I need you. Max

My heart stalls, and the refreshing breeze suddenly feels cold against my skin. I call her, unconcerned that I'm on the roof of the house with her dad. "Hey. You okay?"

She's crying. Hard. I glance at Cal over my shoulder as if he knows, afraid he does. Something keeps me from alerting him. Max has called me, not him. I slide around so my back is to him. "What is it?"

"I. Need. You." She sobs each word as if each is its own sentence.

Fear climbs up into my shoulders, which rise to meet my ears, freezing there with the breeze. "What's going on?"

She continues to cry and attempts to talk, but it's incoherent.

Now I'm terrified. "Are you safe? Shit." The hand not holding the phone to my ear grabs a fistful of hair.

Somehow, I'm able to make out a *yes*.

"I can be there in a few hours." Speeding, but I don't add that. "Do you need me to come there?"

"Yes."

166

"I'm on my way." I press end on the phone, and I notice that the thump of Cal's nail gun has stopped.

"Everything okay?" Cal asks from the opposite end of the roof.

I glance at him over my shoulder and wag the phone at him. The truth sits on my tongue, then I think about how he'd worry about her. Max didn't call him; she called me, and I don't know if it's something she wants him to know. I swallow as terror squeezes my throat and lie. "My mom. She forgot–" I stop because I can't think of a lie between Cal's concerned stare and the echo of Max's broken sobs still in my ears. "She needs me."

"Go." He nods at the ladder with his head. "It's your mom."

"Thanks." I shove the guilt down into deep places, but justify it because I know he'd be running if he knew it were Max.

When I'm in the car, I call her again. It goes to voicemail. "Fuck. Max. Do I need to call 9-1-1? I'm leaving now. Call me back." I plug the spider phone into the jack.

A text comes through:

Safe.

I drive. Town disappears behind me, and the stretch of country road, farms, livestock, lay out for me as I head toward Max's college. My heart's racing on the road next to me, apprehensive about what I'm driving toward, my imagination making up the worst-case scenarios. When I finally reach the edge of the town a little over two hours later, I check the address she texted me, and map it on my phone.

I call her. When she answers, though her voice doesn't sound like her, I say, "I'm almost there."

She tells me where to park and says she'll meet me.

I follow her directions, and by the time I park the car, Max is walking from the building, no jacket, her arms crossed tightly over a blue tie-dye shirt, as if she's holding herself together. The breeze whips her hair, and she's looking down at her feet. When she looks up at me, her eyes are red from crying.

My gut tightens with concern. This isn't the Max I've come to know. She smiles. She laughs. She cajoles and teases. Even if the last time I saw her with my own eyes—because Facetime is different—she was pissed at me. Her jaw set with hurt because I hadn't kissed her back, and I'm suddenly wondering why I didn't. I have the fleeting thought that I wished I'd been with Max on my birthday instead of Bella, but that's a stupid thought. I don't want to talk to Bella anymore, and I always want to talk to Max.

And now, Max looks undone.

I step around the door to meet her and when she reaches me, she collapses against my chest. I wrap my arms around her and press my nose into her hair. "What is it? What happened?" She smells good.

"I didn't know who else to call," she mumbles into my sweatshirt, her voice muffled.

I hug her tighter, so she knows I won't let her go. "I'll always be there for you, Max." It feels good to have her there, to see she's physically okay, but it doesn't ease my worry.

"Thanks for coming."

"What happened? I'm kind of freaking out."

She steps back. "Let's go inside. It's cold."

I take my sweatshirt off and hand it to her. "Here. Put this on."

She gives me a partial smile that doesn't reach her eyes and slips the black hoodie over her head. "You came straight from work?" She glances at my dirty clothes.

I follow her from the parking lot toward the dormitory. "Yes. We were working on the roof." I smooth the front of my t-shirt as if it will help. It doesn't. I probably stink.

"Does he know you're here?" The fear strains the edges of her eyes, confirming my suspicion that she didn't want her dad to know.

"I told him I was helping my mom."

She glances at me over her shoulder, the tension in her body relaxing a bit more. "Thank you."

I follow her through a maze of hallways and stairwells to her dorm room. Inside, the space looks like Max, well, half of it anyway. Efficient and clean but something feminine about it. She's got those fairy lights strung around her bed which is made with the pinkish bedding we picked out before she left. Her desk is clean but for the stack of textbooks on its surface. She's hung the rock posters, some of which I got her.

"What happened?" I repeat, the fear coiled up around me like a tight rope.

She walks past me and climbs onto her bed, then pats the top with her hand, inviting me to join her. She waits until I'm settled, my back against the wall. She's facing me at the head of the bed, her pillow pulled into her lap. "My mom."

I'm confused. "What about her?"

"I don't know where to even start."

"Try at the beginning."

She gives me a look with a tiny smile. "I walked out of class and there she was. I mean, I know I haven't seen her since I was five, but it was like no time had passed. She called my name and then said stuff about my dad. I didn't know what to do. What to think."

I sit forward. "Wait. What? She's here?"

Max nods. "In town."

"Why? What does she want?"

"She said she's been trying to find me. She said my dad kept me from her."

"Whoa. Like kidnapped?"

She looks like she might cry, which makes me nervous, then nods. "Not those exact words." She covers her face with her hands.

"But–" I reach and grasp her hands, pulling them away from her face, forcing her to look at me. Her tear-filled eyes break my heart. "Tell me."

"I know she had a problem, but that doesn't mean she's lying. What if what she said is true?" She stops, her chin quivering. "I just got so upset and confused."

"Not that it matters now, but your dad had custody of you,

right?"

She nods. "But what if she's right? What if that's why we were always moving because he didn't want her to find us?"

I grimace. I can imagine it, thinking about my mom saying she'd do anything for me and Phoenix. "Maybe it wasn't about keeping you from her, but instead protecting you? I'm sure your dad has a good explanation if you let him explain."

She scoots down, lays back, stretching out her legs so they are draped over mine, and stares up at the ceiling. "I don't know how to ask him. I'm afraid to hurt him or make him think I'm accusing him of something. I just know he'll be on his way here when he finds out."

"But you've got your rules," I remind her.

She raises her head to look at me.

"Why don't you just start with what you just told me?"

Her head falls back to the bed. "What if I don't like what he has to say?"

"But you love him. Trust. Talk. Share. Accept. Forgive, remember?"

"You were listening," she says. I can hear the smile in her voice.

My face heats, but it's incognito since she's staring up at the ceiling.

"My mom invited me to meet with her to talk."

"What did you say?"

"I ran away."

I look down at her legs. She's warm, and I resist resting my hands on her knees, keeping them parked on the bed next to my hips. "I essentially told my dad to 'go to hell' when he showed up."

"How come?"

I glance at her. She hasn't moved, the fabric of my black sweatshirt stretching over her torso, her honey hair draped over her shoulders. I look away. There's an awareness of her low in my gut that I wasn't expecting. "I just got so angry." I pluck a stray thread from the black fabric of her tight pants wrapped around her thigh.

"He didn't write to me. Not once. And then there he was asking me to go to breakfast. Do you think I should have listened to what my dad had to say when he showed up?" Then, because I can't keep my hands to myself, I rest my arms over her legs, toying with the thread in my fingers.

"I don't know. Maybe he wants the chance to apologize?"

"What if there's more to the story with your mom?"

She sighs and sits up. Her legs move across mine as she maneuvers herself upright. "You're right."

I grin at her. "What was that?"

She smiles. "Don't get used to it."

"Oh. I will."

She scoots until she's leaning against the wall next to me, our shoulders touching, then leans her head against me. "Thanks for being here, Griffin."

I suppress the connection I'm feeling to her and focus on the thread still in my hands. "Not SK or some other name?"

Her head moves against my shoulder. "No. Not today. Just Griffin, the hero." She takes my hand in hers and threads our fingers.

My chest tightens as I reject her words. My heart skips around looking for a place to land. I study our hands threaded together, unable to look at her, and say, "I'll always be here for you, Max."

As I say it, I think about Bella who I've avoided. I don't feel I would do the same for her, and yet I slept with her. This awareness bothers me, and I'm pretty sure that if Max knew, she wouldn't be calling me a hero. I know I'm not. Yet, everything inside of me wishes that it were true so that I could prove Max's opinion right.

She goes quiet, her thumb moving over my skin.

I try to ignore the warm message the movement sends the rest of my body and attempt to focus on something else besides the feel of her skin moving over mine.

Eventually she breaks the silence, "I feel bad you drove all this way. It seems sort of small, now."

"I'm not." And even though it could be a lie, it isn't. "And I don't think it's small."

She sits up and scoots off the bed. "I'm supposed to go to a study session—which I wouldn't have made anyway—but since you're here, maybe we could go eat?" She looks through her backpack, then wags her phone at me when she finds it.

"What about your mom?"

She texts someone. "Not today. Tomorrow"

"But—"

She shakes her head. "No. You're here. She can wait. She's waited thirteen years. I can't deal with calling her until I have some food. I'll be too hangry."

This makes me smile.

"See. Let's go eat."

"Then you'll call her?"

She nods and holds out her hands to help me from the bed.

I stand and reach out and brush a lock of her hair from her cheek, tucking the strand behind her ear. My tingling fingers snap me back into my guarded body. I pull my hand away, swipe it over my pants, and swallow the reaction sparking through me.

She reaches up and does something to wrap her hair into a knot, then secures it with a band from her wrist.

I clear my throat and look away, too aware of the way she moves, and nod. "Okay. Let me take you somewhere to eat."

2.

Max chooses a pizza place on Main Street with dark wood, red lamp accents offering low-key ambiance. The walls are covered with photos of strangers, framed newspaper prints, and other paraphernalia, meaningful to whoever owns it. There are TVs set up in corners around which people are seated, talking loudly about the sporting event being televised. I follow Max to the counter where we discuss pizza choices and compromise on something with everything. I pay. Max is annoyed about it, saying it was supposed to be her treat. I figure I haven't been a gentleman about much in my life, but I could start with this.

"I feel like I owe you," she says, slipping into a high-backed booth in a corner away from the TVs.

"That's dumb," I tell her and set down the pitcher of soda on the table before taking the seat across from her.

"Wow. Thanks, Griffin. You just called me dumb." Her face screws up.

"No. Not you. That you'd feel like you owe me. There's a difference."

She tilts her head and her eyes narrow. "Why is that dumb?"

"Because what are friends for?" As the words fall from my

mouth, it makes me think of Tanner, Josh, and Danny, and the glaring awareness of how I haven't been that friend for them. I'd expected them to be there for me. I'd thought our friendship was about being together, about what we did together, and how we supported one another to get laid, but not just for the sake of being a friend. I hadn't ever driven nearly three hours for them. Sure, circumstances were different because I had a car now and a job, but if I'm honest with myself, I've done a lot of taking. My cheeks heat with embarrassment, remembering a day a few months ago when Tanner had asked to spend time with Matthews, and I'd crashed it. A dick move. *That* had been dumb.

I grab the pitcher to pour the drinks into our empty cups. I need to do something busy to keep my mind off the truth of how little I really know about friendship. When I set it down, I look at Max and realize that what I've told her is true. For her, I would do whatever it took to be there for her. Driving for several hours is nothing. Buying dinner feels like something small to see her smile again. Taking care of the relationship with her—because having her in my life is more important than not having her there—makes me wish I'd been a better friend to Tanner, Josh, and Danny. Maybe I can't fix what happened with them, but I can do the right thing to keep Max as my friend.

"So, tell me about your dad." She draws one of the full glasses toward her and wraps her hands around it.

"We're not here because of my dad," I say, then take a sip of the sweet soda.

"Right. But let's talk about it anyway."

"Can we not?"

She shakes her head. "Friends Rule number 2. I want to hear about it."

"For you? Or because you're trying to make me work through something?"

She smiles, and takes a sip of her soda, then giggles after she's swallowed it. "For me. Yes. It's all about me."

174

I know she's lying, but relent by saying, "It's different than with your mom."

"How do you figure?"

"Because your mom left. My dad, though–" I stop. Thinking about him hurts, which then ignites the fire of anger. "He's a selfish prick."

"Why? Because he went to prison?"

I look up at her. I see her, pretty Max who's watching me with those aware eyes, but I don't really see her. Instead, I just see someone asking me to dive into the feelings I've shut away. "Yea. And he was fucking around on my mom."

Her eyebrows rise up over her eyes with surprise.

"He has another family. Married to my mom, but had another woman tucked away and shares a kid with her—a girl. She's a couple years younger than me."

"Have you met them?"

I shake my head and stare at the liquid whirlpooling in the glass.

"How do you know then?"

"Phoenix. I was around twelve or thirteen, and I was begging to go visit Dad. My brother was so pissed off. I didn't understand until he said something about Dad's secret family. Then it all kind of made sense. His absences, his indulgence, his disconnection from us. He was a liar."

"Whoa. I'm not sure what to say to that."

"There's nothing to say to that." The words sound like rocks hitting mud, ugly, messy, and final with each splat.

"Max?" A strange voice says her name.

I look up and notice a group of guys moving past the table we share, but one has remained standing at the end of the table. He's smiling at Max. His dark eyes drift to me, assessing. A good-looking guy, I guess, kind of familiar. Dark haired. On the shorter side but fit. I recognize his look. He's sizing me up as competition, but it's low key because Max isn't supposed to notice. His smile stays, but his eyes shift to me, then he widens his stance as if to demonstrate his manliness.

I shift in my seat, spreading out in my own space, and realize I've just done the same thing he did. I look to Max, confused by my own response, and adjust back to where I was.

"Hi Ben." Max smiles at him.

I look away, focusing on the TV across the room. For some reason Max offering her smile to anyone else bugs me. Her smiles have always made me feel like I've won a prize but watching her smile like that at someone else feels like bullets piercing my gut. *Fucking Ben.* Even if these feelings don't make sense. She's my friend and feeling anything else for her other than friendship is off limits. *You don't feel jealous of friends*, but the thought hits me like a spike in the brain: I'd been jealous of Tanner's shifted attention to Emma. With a jolt, I acknowledge it, but am confused by it too. Why would I be jealous about Tanner's attention? Dudes don't feel jealous of their friends. What a stupid thought.

"What are you doing here? I missed you at our study session. Renna said you were sick," Ben says to her.

I keep my eyes on the TV but press my teeth together. I don't like the way this guy is talking to Max, as if she has to answer for her whereabouts to him. I allow myself another glance, pretty sure my distaste is probably all over my face.

Fix your face, Griffin. Except, I don't want to. I want to throw a punch at this guy. That is also a stupid thought.

"I'm feeling better and needed to eat. This is my friend, Griffin." Max introduces me, which means I have to engage with this dude.

Friend. The word drags against my insides like gravel, but it's accurate. Friend.

I lift my chin. "Hey."

He answers in kind with a lift of his chin. "Hey." He also holds out his hand.

I take it.

"Nice to meet you," he says, even if his tone and grip says everything but that.

"Quite a grip, Ben." My longing to punch him intensifies.

He smiles and shifts his attention back to Max. "Are you going to that party this weekend?"

Max shrugs. "I haven't decided."

"You should. It would be cool to see you there. We could dance again." He glances at me, then says, "Maybe Griffin, here, would like to come, too."

I know why he's familiar now. The party. Facetime. His arms around Max. I fist my hands on my thighs.

Max—with an awareness I wouldn't have pegged her for—looks from him to me and then smiles. "Yeah. Maybe. And maybe not." She offers him a smile again, this time shadowed with what I know is annoyance, and it makes me feel better.

"I'll see you in class," Ben says. He gives me one more glance, then disappears from the table.

She leans forward and asks, "What was that all about?"

"You going to that party?" I ask and then want to punch myself for asking since it isn't any of my business. I rationalize that it would be okay for friend to ask what another friend is up to, even if what I'm feeling resembles jealousy. I press it down into the blackness of my being.

"I don't know. You think I should go?"

I think about the last party I was at, my birthday party. I think about drinking, about hooking up with Bella, about the regrets I've been feeling since, and instead of saying anything, I shrug.

"Well, that isn't very helpful. Maybe I will."

I nod at Ben now sitting with his friends. "That guy likes you."

Her head swivels to follow the trail Ben left with her eyes. Then she looks back at me. "How do you know?"

I move the things around on the table. I avoid bringing up Ben's territorial showcase both now and on Facetime and say, "I'm a guy. I can tell."

"Oh?" She presses a hand to her chest. "How do you know? Was it the way he looked at me?"

I answer with my eyebrows and tilt my head, "Just a feeling."

Our pizza order is called out over the sound system.

"I'll get it," I tell her, glad to get away for a moment. It isn't because of Max—not really—but rather the feelings bubbling up around my insides trying to boil out of the boxes and asking that I pay attention to them. I don't want to acknowledge the nagging awareness I'm having about Max, her pretty eyes, the dimple in her cheek when she smiles, or the fact that other guys are interested in her.

We could dance again.

Again.

I need a moment to stamp the lids on the boxes back down and lock them back up. Except they won't close.

What happened with Bella, and the uncomfortable way I've processed it—or haven't; the callous way I felt about Bella, about using her, about allowing myself to be used, all make me feel worse sitting across from Max, who I've warned away from assholes like myself. I don't deserve to be her friend and allow these strange feelings to slip into the empty crevices I haven't filled in with concrete yet. And perhaps, because I haven't allowed myself the opportunity to process what happened with Bella, to figure out what happened between a comment about me being less than Tanner to then wanting to fuck me.

By the time I return with the pizza, I've rearranged the open boxes so they aren't spilling out the contents I've put in them and can look at Max again like a friend should.

And maybe I'm not the only one who needed a minute because Max's conversation shifts too, away from things like attraction and parties to safer things about school and classes, her roommate, to asking about her dad, and then what to do about her mom. I share about working with Cal, about going over for dinner, about school, but I avoid talking about my family and that party, afraid to reinforce Max's beliefs about me and making them any worse than they already are.

I drive her back to the dorms.

"You'll wait while I call her?" she asks when I've parked the car.

"Sure." I'm starting to feel the wear of the day. Working on the roof, the long drive, and the emotional stress, but I don't say anything.

She gets out, needing privacy, and makes the call. I can see her through the window, pacing around the front of the car. It's still running because I need the heat. I worry about the fact that she's out in the cool of the night, but notice she's still got my sweatshirt. She leans against the hood of the passenger side and wraps her arms around herself as she listens, nods, speaks. I'm fighting with my eyes, suddenly heavy in the warmth of the car, and lose track somewhere between the space of looking at Max through the window, and her voice coaxing me back to awareness.

"Griffin?" Her hand is on my arm.

"Sorry." I sit up with a start. My eyes find Max's face so close to mine. I remember where I am. She was making a call. "All squared away?"

"Come on. You're not driving home right now."

"I'm good," I tell her, though I'm not sure that's true.

She shakes her head. "I'd never forgive myself if something happened to you. Come on. You got anything clean back there?" She investigates what might be in the backseat.

I think about arguing with her. I don't have toothbrush or clean clothes, but in the whole scheme of life and death, it seems a weak argument. "A workout bag." I grab that, lock up my car, and follow her into the building.

After handing me an extra toothbrush she fishes out of this miraculous box under her bed with extra stuff in it, I take a shower in the bathroom she shares with another room and change into the shorts and T-shirt from my workout bag.

"All set?" she asks when I emerge from the shower.

I nod, feeling self-conscious. It's just Max, except I'm beginning to suspect that she isn't *just Max* to me anymore. "Where's your roommate?"

She stops near me. Her head tilts, and her eyes rove over my wet hair. "Her boyfriend's." She reaches up and swipes a strand from my forehead, then drops her arm back to her side. "She won't be back tonight."

The heat of her light touch lingers on my forehead. I recall the way she'd looked after the night we'd kissed, then banish the memory by saying, "I should text my mom. Let her know I'm safe."

She escapes into the bathroom while I do.

I sit at her desk and let my mom know I'll be home the following day. There's a text from Cal asking if everything is okay, which makes me feel guilty. I text him an "all clear" with a thumbs up, and a promise to see him for work.

While I wait for Max, I scroll through Instagram. Josh has posted pictures from college: one of him and a couple of guys throwing deuces; another of a sculpture with a caption about the art at Davis tagging Ginny. New friends and places. Danny hasn't posted anything, too busy with basic training. Tanner hasn't been on since a picture he posted of him and Emma somewhere; it looks like it's from a house. He's tagged her. I click to her account. She's posted some from college: dorm room, roommate, landscapes. None of Tanner recently, but when I scroll through her feed and find a few of him, still there. I return to Tanner's account and check the picture he posted with her. It was weeks ago, and he hasn't removed it. I wonder if he still has feelings for her and think that if I was a good friend, I would reach out.

I miss my friends.

"I thought you'd be asleep already."

I look up from my phone to Max who's standing in the space between the shared bathroom and the closets framing the doorway. She's dressed in tiny shorts that show off her legs and hips and a matching top that hugs her torso. I can see the outline of her body. Her hair is wet and wavy, the ends making the fabric of her shirt wet at the swell of her boobs. She leans to the side and squeezes the ends of her hair with a towel.

My throat dries out, my dick twitches, and I look back at my phone. "I wasn't sure where to sleep. Figured you might have a blanket or something for me to set up on the floor." The moment feels so intimate and vulnerable, I'm insecure.

"I'm not making you sleep on the hard concrete floor, Griffin. Get in the bed."

I look at her again and swallow.

She smiles one of those beautiful smiles that suddenly make me want to take her face in between my hands and kiss her. A redo.

"Don't worry. I'll be a perfect lady."

I laugh, nervous. I can feel myself getting hard looking at her, thinking about her hips, the fullness of her thighs. That smile on her mouth. I clear my throat again and shake my head as I swivel the chair around and away from her so I can adjust my shorts and pinch my dick into submission. "You want the inside, or should I take it?"

She climbs into bed first, situates herself against the wall, then holds the covers open for me.

I climb in after her, reach over, shut out the light on the desk, and lay on my back. That doesn't work on the twin bed. I'd like to turn to face her, but I don't trust myself, so I roll away from her. It seems like the safest option.

The darkness in the room becomes an entity smothering me. Even though there are strange sounds in the hallway reminding me we're in a dormitory—doors shutting, stray laughter, voices talking as they walk down the hallway—I can't stop thinking about Max laying behind me. I was incredibly tired a little while ago, but I can't get my mind, or my dick, or my heart to settle down. I want to turn over and face Max, but I don't. I don't trust myself not to kiss her. I keep thinking about that kiss the night before she left, wishing it had been different.

"Griffin?" Max's voice is a whisper against my back.

"Yeah?"

She doesn't answer right away which makes me think there's

something she wants to say and is measuring her words. Then she says, "Thank you for being here."

I think she's censored herself and wonder if there was something different she wanted to say, but I don't chase it. Rather, I let it alone, more cognizant of the fact that Max isn't one to hold back. She never has been. Then I remind myself that she kissed me, and I rebuffed her. She probably wouldn't ever want to replay that even if I've been thinking about it. Besides, she deserves more than me. She deserves the Tesla not the Nissan, maybe someone like Ben, who is probably nicer.

"Of course. I'm like Batman. Just flash the bat signal, and I'll be there."

She makes a little noise that tells me she appreciates my humor.

Then it's quiet again, and despite the warmth moving across my body and the way the scent of her shampoo or body spray or whatever that sweet, spicy scent is, I can't relax. My breathing is tight and labored, and I'm fighting to keep it even. I'm working to shut off all the sensations. I try closing my eyes and thinking about putting shingles on the roof. I imagine laying the shingle, lining up the nail, and pounding the nail with the hammer. Hammering makes me think about sex. I shake my head and instead imagine stripping the roof, but shit, that makes me think about taking off clothes. *Fuck.*

"What?" Max asks from the darkness.

Did I say that out loud? "Huh?"

"You say something?"

"I don't think so," I lie. It's safer than telling her what I'm really thinking.

I picture Cal's face and his voice as he talks about how we're going to replace the roof, because that's safe. I think about climbing the ladder to the roof and the feel of the breeze. I replay talking to him about school and classes. Until somehow, I slowly fade into the darkness and find sleep.

When I'm pulled from the dark into consciousness again, I've turned over to face the wall with my face pressed into Max's shoulder, breathing her sweet scent. Her backside is pressed into my groin. Our legs are intertwined, and I've got an arm wrapped around her waist, holding her against me. I pull her closer, content, and smile. She adjusts, her hips rocking into my groin, and my eyes fly open, now completely aware of where I am and who's in my arms. Just as I wake, my dick wakes up too, and I draw my hips away from her.

She moans. "Griffin?"

I shift the covers off. "I'm here."

"It's cold."

I stand up and tuck the covers around her. "I'm going to go," I whisper.

"What time is it?" she asks, her voice heavy with sleep. It's a sexy sound.

"Early." I pick up my phone and read 4 am through the cracks in the screen.

She rolls onto her back to face me, but I can't see her features since they're obscured in the inky darkness of the room. "I don't want you to go."

Her voice and words almost make me climb back in with her, but I don't. Instead, I look for my jeans and bump the chair, so it rolls and knocks against the desk. "Shit. Sorry." I don't trust myself climbing back into that bed with her. I don't trust myself with her heart. "I have to get back. I have class in a few hours." I replace my shorts with the jeans.

She makes another sexy sound. "I'll get up and walk you down."

"No." I button the jeans and lean over the bed. "I can find my way. You sleep." I lay a hand on her shoulder. "Thanks."

She covers my hand with hers and then draws me toward her. Next thing I know I'm wrapped in her arms, and she says against the skin of my neck, "I miss you."

I turn my head and press my mouth into her hair. "I'll text you when I get there, okay?"

She nods.

I breathe deeply, drawing in the breath of Max like I can keep her there, then release the embrace to stand back up. I make sure I have my stuff and leave the dorm room. Finding my way through the maze out into the night is manageable but climbing into my cold car is lonely. I sit there while it heats up, staring at the dark windows of the dorm and thinking about Max asleep in her bed. I think about how it felt waking up next to her in contrast to Bella.

I reverse the car from the parking spot and drive away from Max with a newfound understanding that has me feeling scrambled. I'd ditched Bella in my room with no inclination to stay. Now, I've left Max's room, but almost every part of me is screaming to remain there with her. Only the part that's afraid to face the feelings I'm having, and the part of me that must keep moving forward to keep from drowning, is content to be sitting in the car driving home. I let Bella walk out of my house with relief. Leaving Max behind makes me feel like I'm being ripped in two. This split isn't like gentle Griffin and tough Griff in the name of self-preservation, though. Instead, it's like my heart—the whole of it—has been duplicated. The real heart has remained with Max. The shadow part is beating inside of my chest as I drive away.

3.

The innards of the refrigerator are sparse, and I'm holding the door open, staring inside unseeing, out of habit. Thinking about food seems better than fixating on the strange conglomeration of thoughts I've been having about Max after the other night at her dorm room. I did text her and let her know I made it home safe. She texted me and said she'd had coffee with her mom that went badly. She followed that up with a text that told me she checked in with her dad about it, which explained the text from Cal saying he was heading to see Max for the rest of the week and that we'd resume inside of the house next week. I was glad they were going to talk, but I was now ruminating on feelings I wasn't sure how to process and no one to process them with.

Mom. Nope.

Tanner. Not an option, even if I wished it were. Maybe I should text him.

Phoenix. Maybe. Haven't seen him.

Cal. Stupid idea.

My dad. Hell no.

Max. That would be weird.

I feel like one of those half-used jars of salsa surrounded by other mismatched items that don't go together. I'm beginning to see the benefit of having people to bounce ideas around with; how there are ways people complement one another—like Max—or distract like Marcus or Bella. Max is the chips to my salsa. I think maybe I was in the latter category with my friends. Understanding it makes me miss Tanner because when it was good, before I messed it up, I think we were like chips and salsa too. This awareness makes me frustrated at the same time. It reminds me that I wasn't a great friend and looking in the mirror—or at salsa without chips—sucks.

With a sigh, I shut the door and decide that going for a run will be a better use of my time. At least the thrashing from the concrete will quiet my thoughts for a while and deplete this awful energy I've got building up. It's making me think about letting off steam by doing something stupid.

"Why are you sighing like a bitch?" Phoenix walks into the dining room from the hallway. His hair is standing up in tufts all over his head, and he scratches his stomach scored with a lot of ink. He opens the refrigerator.

"There isn't much in there," I say and ignore his comment. "You cleaned up the house on my birthday?"

He glances at me, bent over into the fridge. He nods.

"Thanks."

"Happy Birthday."

"So, where here have you been?"

He closes the fridge after looking inside. "Someone ordain you our mother?" He walks past me to the coffee pot.

"Just haven't see you that's all."

"We really should stop meeting this way." He chuckles as he makes a pot of coffee. "Been busy."

"Doing what?" I ask as I walk down the hallway. I walk into my room and jerk my t-shirt over my head to change my clothes for a run.

He stops in the doorway of my room, leans against the jamb. "Again, are you my mother?"

I flop on my bed to put on socks. "Whatever. You haven't

gotten a job yet?"

"I got some prospects."

I roll my eyes.

"What?"

I look around my room for my shoes and think that maybe I should buy some new ones as much as I've been running. But I need other stuff like gas for my car, to replace the screen on my phone, and a cheap laptop for school. I can make do. "You've been home almost two months, bro."

"Stuff isn't panning out."

"And why's that? It took me less than a week."

"Well, you don't have–" he stops himself, stares at the carpet, then disappears from my doorway.

"I don't have what?" I follow him back into the living area, shoes in hand.

"Never mind. Forget it." He pours a cup of coffee before the pot has finished its cycle; it hisses at him.

"I'm not going to forget it. Mom works too hard. Today's her last day at Bob's. She needs us to step the fuck up."

He faces me. "Last day at the minimart, huh?"

I don't respond because I see what he's doing. I've done it. I did it to Tanner when he tried to talk to me about things that made me face feelings. I'd change the subject, offer sarcasm, anything to avoid talking about what was real.

I walk around into the kitchen, removing the barrier between us. "I don't have what?"

"Just forget it. I'll find a job. I got some feelers out there."

"Legit ones?"

His eyebrows come together, and he's gone from twenty-five miles-per-hour to eighty. "What the fuck, Griffin?"

"Where were you, Phoenix? The last four years?" I ask.

"Around." He walks around me into the living room.

I follow. "Around my ass. What do you have that I don't?"

"Fuck off, little bro, and go take your jog."

187

"Tell me, Phoenix. Stop being a pussy and just tell me."

He slams his coffee cup on the coffee table and comes at me. "You want to know?"

I hold my ground. "I'm not little anymore, Bro. Stop trying to protect me."

He twists away from me, runs a hand through his hair, then resumes his big man posturing even though he's smaller than I am. "That's my job."

"Since when? You aren't around. We're here right now. Different."

"You don't have to fucking remind me. I feel guilty about it."

"About what? It's always fucking secrets and lies with us. What the fuck is it?"

"You don't fucking want to know."

"Why?"

"Because I fucked up!"

I stop, wait, because I know he's going to finally tell me. I don't want to chase the truth away with something stupid I might say.

He makes a frustrated sound, then says, "I was in prison. Just like dad. Like father, like son. You happy now?"

I'm not happy. No. But I'm relieved to know the truth. I'm relieved to know that he didn't contact me for a reason. I can understand this. I wouldn't have wanted him to know if I'd been in Dad's shoes either. I don't know what makes me do it, but instead of punching his face like I wanted to do a moment ago, I wrap my arms around him. It's Max's rules running through my mind. Rules 4 and 5: accept and forgive.

Instead of pushing me away like I expect him to do, Phoenix sort of wilts against me. Then he cries. It's awkward as hell, my big brother letting his emotions loose, but I don't run away from it like I did with Tanner. Sure, Tanner didn't cry or anything. In retrospect though, I think he was trying to share his feelings, and I shut him down. Phoenix breaking down is like getting another opportunity to do it better. I hold him tighter.

He steps away eventually, depleted of his anger, but looking sheepish. "Fuck. Sorry." He wipes his face with his hands.

"I don't think you need to be sorry about that." Saying it feels right, feels like something Cal would say.

Phoenix just looks at me. "Are you a Nichols man?" He offers a teary grin and crosses his arms over his chest. His smile fades, and in that instant, I see the shadow of our father on his face.

"Yeah. And so are you."

His eyes jump to mine, then Phoenix's eyes slide away because he can't meet my gaze anymore. I get the discomfort since I've heard it before, *real men don't cry*. There's a lie in there, though, I think. I've got so many feelings wrapped around the complications of my life. Feelings coiled around Tanner and my friends, my brother, Mom, and my father, around Max and Cal, even around Bella. All these threads that are different and messy and knotted. I don't know how to unravel them, but it doesn't change the fact that there are emotions at play. I'm not looking at my brother as if he's weak because he's cried, but rather brave because he has. I don't think he sees it. I don't know how to say that though. I'm not sure he'd hear it.

He clears his throat. "You going for that run?"

"Yeah." I sit on a chair next to the door and put on my shoes. "Want to come?"

"No." He sits on the couch and reaches for his coffee which has sloshed onto the table. "Shit," he mutters and takes the sip of his coffee and uses his t-shirt to clean the mess. "Thanks though," he adds as though wanting to keep this peace we've brokered. "When did you start running."

"A couple of months ago."

He doesn't say anything.

"I was drinking too much."

His eyes fly up from the coffee mess on the table to my face.

"I didn't want to admit it to anyone, you know, but I was drinking so much, blacking out, and doing stupid shit. Lost all my friends." I almost gag when I say it, taking responsibility. Hearing it out loud sucks and being the one to admit it even worse, but then it's almost like the power of it hanging over me lessens. "I wanted a drink so bad, that I just went for a run, and it made me feel like shit, but a good kind of shit." I scoff at the reality of it. "A kind of shit that made it, so I didn't want that drink."

"You go to one of those programs?"

I shake my head.

"Want to?"

"Like AA? You do?"

"Yeah. It's a twelve-step program for recovering addicts."

"You go?"

He nods. "That's why I left your birthday. It's where I go, mostly."

I look up at him. "We must really be Nichols men."

He gives me a grin full of regret. "Yeah."

A couple of days later, I drive Phoenix to one of his meetings and stay with him. I park in a church lot and follow him up the stairs into a meeting room where there are a bunch of chairs set up in a circle on a cheap blue carpet. The meeting fills up with people, all men.

"Griffin?"

I turn at the sound of my name and come face to face with Tanner's dad.

"Hey, Mr. James."

He extends his hand. "Welcome."

I shake his hand. "I'm here with my brother." I use my thumbs to point over my shoulder at Phoenix who's talking to someone behind me.

Mr. James's eyes light up. "I didn't know Phoenix was your brother. Goodness. It's a small world."

"I didn't know you came to this—" I stop unsure what to say, not wanting to be rude.

"About a year now. The meetings and the community have

helped me in lots of ways. Not just with the drinking, but also with other things."

I shove my hands into the pockets of my jacket and look down at my shoes. I think I know what he's talking about, but I'm feeling so uncomfortable with how out in the open he is.

"That's good," I eventually say.

He smiles, and I see Tanner. "Yeah. I'm better, but you know it isn't all easy. I have to work hard at being better every day. I'm just glad I've been able to start fixing things with Tanner."

I study him, interested in this bit of information. I know a version of what he did to Tanner and Tanner's mom. I know what Tanner has had to deal with. I wouldn't have ever thought Tanner would forgive him.

"We're a work in progress. Geez. Listen to me going on and on. How have you been?"

We talk about my working for Cal. Tanner's dad offers me a place if I ever need it, so I mention Phoenix looking for work, and they talk for a bit. The meeting begins, calling us into the circle.

Phoenix and I take our seats. I look across the circle at Tanner's dad and wonder if Tanner was willing to forgive his dad for all that he did, would he be willing to forgive me?

Phoenix leans toward me, "I don't know if I can do construction."

"I didn't think I could either, but you might like it. It's like running. Besides, it's a job."

The meeting opens with a prayer, a recitation, and a reading. I suddenly feel like I'm in a church service and fight the urge to flee. It's fucking uncomfortable, and I can't put my finger on why I feel like I want to run away, but I do. I grasp my phone and think about Max who I know would tell me to calm down and be there for my brother. When people begin sharing—much like Tanner's Dad earlier—I feel the fight or flight response, afraid of all the feelings.

There are tears. Men sharing. Crying. Offering their stories that reveal their hearts. I think about how vulnerable many of them are and consider how I thought Phoenix was brave for sharing with me. I have the feeling all the ways I'd thought boxing up gentle Griffin and protecting him with defensive Griff perhaps wasn't brave at all, but because I was afraid.

Later, I'm lying on my bed trying to sleep thinking about all those boxed-up feelings, and the hot-girls-hot-cars poster leers at me from the wall. It makes me think of Bella. I've been putting off calling her for too long, but there's a bunch of snakes swirling around in my gut, hissing anxiety about doing it. I reach for vulnerable Griffin, and instead of thinking about it, I dial Bella's phone. My heart thunks around in my chest, rattling like a broken-down car as the phone rings. I'm hoping she won't answer, like she'll see my name and avoid a poor imitation to Tanner, but the next thing I know I'm hearing her voice.

"Hi Griff. This is a surprise." She sounds the same even over the phone which is a weird detail to grasp onto.

Before, I would have said something to attempt to charm her. Now, though, it's like I can't find those words anymore. The importance of being honest rears its head at me thanks to the voices of Max and those honest voices at Phoenix's meeting. "I wasn't going to," I admit.

"Then why are you?" I can hear annoyance edge her voice, a typical Bella tone.

"I felt like I owed you an apology." As I say it, I'm not sure I mean it. She'd been the one to compare me to Tanner. She'd been the one so adamant we have sex even if I'd been willing. She hadn't reached out to me either, yet here I'm calling her to apologize. For what again?

"What? Why?"

"I just wanted to say I was sorry with how things went down between us at my party, and after. I was drunk and I shouldn't have, you know–" My tongue trips over itself trying to find the words to express what it is I need to say, even if I don't really know what it is I need to say.

"No, Griff, I don't know. What are you talking about?"

I hesitate, pause to search for the truth because lying would be a lot easier. Was I sorry I slept with her? Yes. But what if she wasn't sorry about it? And why would I apologize for that. *Because I'd used her. Because I'd ignored my inner voice who'd told me not to.* But I don't say those things and instead say, "I'm sorry I didn't call you. After." It's true, but it isn't hurtful. Hurting her isn't what I want, which is new. Four months ago, I wouldn't have cared. Four months ago, I wouldn't have called.

She sighs. "It's okay. I'm sorry how I just sort of left, too, but it isn't, like, you or anything. I don't want you to get the wrong idea after—you know—what I said. It's just, after your party, I feel like maybe I wasn't making good choices for myself."

I withhold a sigh of relief but then get caught on her words and narrow my eyes. "Because I'm a bad choice."

"No. No! That's not what I mean." She sighs loudly. "It's just that I've been partying a lot, for a while, and I feel like I'm not going anywhere. I've seen where that dead end took my mom, and I just think I want more for myself, you know?"

"Yeah." I know exactly what she means.

"I started Cosmetology School."

"What's that?"

"Beauty school. Like cutting and styling hair, doing makeup and stuff."

"That's cool," I tell her.

She talks a little bit longer about it, and I'm not interested at all, but I listen anyway because I'm trying to be better. Eventually she says, "Thanks for calling."

"Yeah." There's an extended pause that stretches after my words. I'm not sure what else to say, and I just want to cut the line. "Well, I should go."

"I should go," she says at the same time.

We laugh uncomfortably.

"Thanks, Griffin."

I hang up and am simultaneously unnerved by the call and relieved, that door closed and sealed. I look up at the hot-girls-hot-cars poster and take it down. I don't want to be that Griffin Nichols anymore.

NOVEMBER

196

1.

I stand inside the doorway of a building at the community college where I'm taking classes, shrugging into my jacket, backpack between my feet on the floor, measuring the weather with my eyes, and contemplating the Chinese take-out I'm going to pick up to share with Cal. Tiny snowflakes dust the world in quiet chaos. It isn't really the kind that will stick, but it is November, so that could change.

"Griffin, right?"

I turn my head to see who's talking to me and zip up my jacket.

It's a cute girl from my writing class. She's got a puffy, blue jacket on, and her short, blond hair, framing her face, is covered with a matching yarn cap layered with greens, blues, and yellows, and one of those puffs on the top.

I pick up my backpack and sling it over my shoulder. "Hey. Yeah." I don't know her name.

"Lauren."

"Writing class."

"You finished with your next paper?" she asks.

"No." That's a huge ass no. I always wait until the night before. I hate writing.

The truth is, I don't like school. I wish I did but sitting in classes feels more like a visit to the dentist to poke around for cavities. My mind never roots in the classroom. Instead, it drifts to thinking about working with Cal. I break through the drywall and rip out the old stuff, take the innards of the house down to its skeleton. I picture the wood framing lined with treasures like wires, pipes, casing, and mistakes that need to be fixed. It's where my roots have grown.

She smiles. "I was thinking that maybe—if you're interested in some company—we could meet up at the library and work on our next paper together."

I noticed her a couple of months ago when she'd walked into class that first day. She's got this vibe I found appealing at the time. Back in September, a part of me was running from the weird kiss with Max and the awful hookup with Bella. I looked at her and thought, "Hell yeah!" But after being honest with myself about what happened with Bella added to the mixed-up ways I'm still thinking about Max, I haven't thought about her since.

"I work, so it's kind of hard to meet outside of class." I shove my hands into the pockets of my jacket.

"Oh. Right." She glances away, and I have the feeling that maybe I've misread her, that she might be disappointed. Maybe she's interested in me.

That idea feels good.

She turns and looks at me with a full-wattage smile, dimples in both cheeks. I have a thing for dimples, I decide, and picture Max's smile. I miss the opportunity of making her smile.

"Okay. Thought I'd ask."

"We could plan ahead for coffee or something," I offer, wanting to maintain the heat of the pleasant warmth in my chest of feeling worthy of someone's attention. Do I like her? I don't know her. Is she cute? Yes. Am I interested? Maybe.

Her eyes—brown—come back to mine, the edges curl with that cute smile. "That would work," she says. "I'll give you my number."

I feel lighter. After the self-confidence killer that is Bella along with my insecurities about Max, having someone interested in me is pretty, fucking fantastic. I return her smile and enter the numbers she gives me, then send her a text. "Sounds like a plan."

I pick up Chinese food, take it to the farmhouse, and eat with Cal. We talk about stuff: school, work, and Max comes up, but he's reserved about it. I don't push because I know that never works with me, unless you're Max.

The next day, I arrive at Cal's ready to work. The sound of my boots as I stomp the thin layer of mud on the mat echo like gunshots in the acoustics of the stripped farmhouse. "Cal?" I call and wait to hear his voice.

No answer.

We've spent the last weeks since his return from his visit with Max, working in companionable silence. I've heard about what happened in snippets over text from Max. I wonder if Cal's withdrawal is because of what's happened with his daughter, or about something else. The isolation in his emotional cave isn't how I know him, but I recognize it. I live there most of the time. Thing is, even recognizing it, I don't know what to do. Mostly, I feel helpless. From the outside, I can see two people who adore one another unable to find handholds against the cliff where they're both hanging.

"Cal?" I call again.

"Back here." His voice bounces against the recently installed drywall in the living room.

I stomp over naked floorboards through the empty main room until I reach the back porch. Since it's an enclosed space, he's using it as a staging ground for cutting, sawing, and storing as the winter weather sets in.

Cal glances up from the board he's cutting, and resumes running the blade across a squared-off space. He cracks the gypsum along the bladed line, and it opens, splitting cleanly along the line into two sections. "Think you can manage tearing out the rest of the kitchen?" he asks as he walks past me with his board.

I retrace my steps following him. "Yeah. I can do that."

"Try and save the cabinets. We're going to reuse them."

"In the kitchen?"

"No. Probably in the workshop. New cabinets are ordered and should be here in a week or so. I'd like to get that kitchen back online before Christmas."

"Max coming home?"

"So she says."

The way he says it is layered with the sound of what's remained unsaid. I figure it's an opening. "Everything okay?" I ask.

He holds the board up to a space by the new window. "Why wouldn't it be?" He uses his tape measure and a carpenter's pencil to make marks.

I shrug, even though he can't see me, and search for a way to open a door for him. He's been there for me, after all, and it feels like Max has saved me. "I don't know. You just seem kind of–" I stop when he glances at me. His frown and his pinched forehead with heavy eyebrows over his disconcerting gray eyes land on me. I fidget but commit– "off. Since you went to visit her."

He sighs, looks away, cuts the board, then levels it off before taking the nail gun to it. Then, instead of marching back the way he came, he leans against the unfinished wall joint. "My ex-wife showed up to visit Max at school and made claims about me as a dad."

I raise my eyebrows with a question to invite him to continue but keep my mouth shut. I don't want to say something wrong or hint I know more than I'm letting on.

Cal looks down at his hands, flips them over. "When I was your age, I was more worried about where the next party was." He stands, hesitates, then says, "You don't want to hear this drama." He walks back the way he came. "Help me with these boards."

"I don't mind listening," I tell him as we carry several back into the room.

He doesn't say anything at first, concentrating on leaning the boards to be hung against a space in the room that's easily accessible.

Then he surprises me by breaking the silence when he says, "Indigo just walked out—that's her name, my ex-wife. Max was five. I should have known that it was coming, but I was blind to her struggle. I just told myself Indigo was a free spirit. After Max was born, though, I couldn't use that excuse anymore. She'd slip into these dark places. It wouldn't matter what I did or didn't do, what I said, how I acted. I just wasn't enough."

I help him with a board, holding it up, and he uses the nail gun to fasten it in place.

"Then one day," he continues while he uses a tape measure to the next board, "she just walked out of the house with a suitcase and didn't look back. I thought she'd be back because she did it a lot, but when she didn't show up the next morning, I called her parents. We found her high in one of her usual haunts.

"I asked her if she wanted to come home with me and Max, she refused. Her parents took her and placed her in one of those ritzy in-treatment centers. I tried to visit her, but we weren't allowed. Then she hopped to a ritzy meditation retreat. An artists' commune. A whole string of ways to find herself and no intention to include Max or me in those plans. Finally, I was served with divorce papers, no contest for custody, so I signed them."

He stops and puts up another board. I help him. We put up three more, saying little more than what needs to be said.

"And she never asked to see Max?"

"No, but I didn't make it easy either. I moved us, at first, because I needed new scenery. Max was going to start school, and I thought it would be a perfect way to start over. Found us a fixer upper and off we went. I hadn't considered we'd leave there, but I got an offer on the house after I finished it that was too good to pass up, so I found another fixer upper somewhere else. And again, until we'd left a trail across the country. It worked when Max was little, but I should have known better when she reached middle school. Now, we're here."

"And your wife-"

"Ex-wife. Indigo."

"–Indigo is back? For good?"

He nails in the board we're holding. "Showed up outside of Max's class and claimed I'd kidnapped her. That I'd intentionally kept Max from her mom. I don't think she stayed, just dropped in, dropped that bomb and left."

"Shit. That's heavy. How's Max?"

"She's mad."

"At you?"

He itches his cheek with the back of his hand. "She's upset about her mom showing up because of the therapy exercise she was doing—feels used. I can understand that. She's upset at me because I moved her like an Army kid when it didn't need to be that way. And maybe—deep down— I *was* trying to keep her from her mom. I don't know." He turns and leans against the wall now covered with new drywall. "I just thought–" he swipes his hands over his face and sighs. "I don't know what I thought."

"Can't change it now."

He pushes off the wall and looks at me. "You're right. Past is the past, but I've got to try to figure out the road ahead. That might be different than what I'd had planned."

"Yeah? How's that?"

"Don't know yet." He leads the way back through the house to the porch. "Since we're gabbing away like two old ladies, help me finish the drywall, and I'll help with the kitchen after. Then I can teach you how to tape later this week."

"Got it, boss," I say.

When I get home after a day hanging drywall and some time spent pulling things out of a kitchen falling apart, my body aches. I'm hungry, and I'm ready to collapse into a dead sleep, though some time spent lounging on the couch in front of the TV sounds awesome. But when I walk in through the front door of my house, Mom is there with Bill—used-car manager Bill—and a cozy dinner for two is set out on the dining table.

I ignite from tired to volcanic but hold in the eruption and vent steam by shutting the front door, removing my shoes, and moving my toolbelt from one shoulder to the other. Mom having Bill over is a strange thing to be angry about. I was the idiot, after all, who'd suggested she start dating. I suggested she quit one of her jobs so she could have more time for herself. Now, though, seeing the idea in the flesh, I'm strangely upset about it. I also know that I have no right to have an opinion, but I fucking do.

"Hey Griffin," she says when I walk into the house.

I grunt at her.

"Would you like to join us?" she asks.

"And impose? No thanks."

Her smile fades with embarrassment, I'd imagine, and it makes me feel guilty which increases my irritation. "It's no problem, right?" She looks at Bill and then back at me. "You remember Bill?"

Her deference to Bill makes me see red. She's never asked permission to do something. Not from us. Not in her own fucking house.

"Griffin. How's the car?" Bill responds, and I can tell he wants anything but me sitting down with him and his date. It's on his face. The forced smile, the disappointed way his brow has fallen over his eyes.

She's my mom. My mom. I ignore his question. "Where's Phoenix?"

"Out."

A meeting, I guess. He probably wanted to be around this as much as I do.

I harumph a noise at her. "I'll just clean up and get out of here." I trudge down the hallway and duck into the bathroom before she can say anything. She doesn't, and that makes my mood even worse.

It's irrational.

I text Max:

My mom has a date at the house!

> Good for her.

No! Not good. The guy's a tool.

> How do you know?

I don't. I know nothing about Bill. And I don't think my mom does either.

Max texts again:

> Why does that bother you?

I want to throw my phone. Fuck! I don't know.

I look at myself in the bathroom mirror and realize I've felt like this before. With Tanner. When he pulled away from our friendship and started dating Emma. I was angry and wanted to hold onto him because he was my best friend. I'd gotten sullen and sarcastic. He'd always been there for me, and I'd become afraid of losing him as my friend. My fear had been a self-fulfilling prophecy. That is exactly what had happened. Jealousy IS the most apt description.

Max texts again:

> Relationship rules, SK. Trust your mom.

Ok

> I'm here to listen.

I look at myself in the mirror. I don't want to do the same thing to my mom as I did to Tanner. What had Cal said earlier? *Past is the past, but I've got to try to figure out the road ahead.*

By the time I'm showered, dressed, and leaving the house, Mom and Bill stand side by side at the kitchen sink, cleaning up the dishes. Still annoyed but more aware of my feelings, I sneak out the front door without saying a word. As soon as I make it to the car, I hear my mom coming out the door and down the walkway.

"Griffin. Wait."

I turn and look at her.

It's cold, and she's come out into the frigid night air without a jacket. Her arms are crossed over her chest, her hands each holding an arm.

"You don't have to go." She tilts her head like she does when she's studying me as if I'm a puzzle to be solved.

"You've got a date. I'm not staying."

"But Bill doesn't mind."

I roll my eyes. "I don't care what Bill minds, Mom. I care what you mind." I get into the car.

She knocks against the window until I unroll it. "You're annoyed."

I sigh. "I'm tired." Which is true.

"You suggested I date."

I look at the keys in my hand.

She stands in the cold at the window.

"You should go back into the house. You don't have a jacket."

She nods. "I don't know if I'll see you tomorrow, but I wanted you to invite your boss and his daughter over for Thanksgiving. You mentioned their kitchen is torn up, and I know they don't know anyone in town."

"You're doing Thanksgiving? Here?" The idea is preposterous in my mind since she's always worked. We've never actually had a real Thanksgiving.

"Yes. Shit, Griffin. Give me some credit." She turns away. "I do cook."

"Okay," I call after her. "I'll tell him."

She waves at me without looking back, hurries up the walk, and returns to the house. Back to her waiting date. I clench my teeth and back the car from the driveway, not sure where I'm even going.

2.

The past is the past; I've got to figure out the road ahead.

Cal's refrain plays through my head as I drive, and after mindlessly driving around town, I find myself in Tanner's neighborhood, which is perhaps creepy on the surface. I rationalize that I'm not a creeper and pull my car over on the side of road outside of Tanner's house, considering that maybe if he's home, I'll go apologize.

Most of the windows at Tanner's are dark, and though I can see the glow of the kitchen, Tanner's room faces the back of the house, so I can't tell if he's home. The garage doors are closed, which means I don't know if his truck is parked inside without going to check. That would definitely make me look like a creeper. I can't say I would knock on his door if I did see his truck.

I'm not angry at him anymore, just embarrassed, and insecure about my own role in the disintegration of our friendship. It's weird to think how if one were just measuring the superficial differences of us, we'd be like night and day. Like our houses, for example. They are so different and yet our experiences are similar. Divorced parents, an older brother gone—though Tanner's died and mine's the prodigal son. The two-story monstrosity of his house might seem to insulate him from the same kind of hurts, but it hasn't. When I consider the fissures between my best friend and me, I'm realizing I was the one to widen them. Tanner tried building bridges, while I just blew them up. He has every right to be angry with me, and that's what I'm afraid to face: the truth through his eyes.

I imagine walking up to the door. Knocking. Tanner opening it, seeing it's me, then slamming it in my face. That's something I would have done. I did it to him when he chose Emma. Told him not to come crawling back to me when she left him because he wasn't good enough. Thinking about it now, I cringe. I deserve a door slammed in my face, but I can't face the idea of it occurring. Pride or something like it. Knowing Tanner though, like I do, it's doubtful he would slam the door in my face. He'd sort of waved a white flag at Danny's Swearing-In Ceremony, but still, I don't take the risk. Instead, I decide to text him and take my phone out. I open my messages and press his name, but then stare at the bouncing line in the space. I start a message. Delete it. Start another one. Delete it.

With an annoyed huff, I toss my phone in the seat and drive away.

I don't want to be at home with my mom and Bill. I can't bring myself to talk to Tanner. Max is gone. I don't want to do the same stuff I used to in order to feel numb. I'm not sure where to go, but then my stomach rumbles with hunger. I can eat.

I park at a diner. The restaurant isn't full, a few patrons at the counter, and a smattering scattered throughout the joint from the tables set up along the rock wall on one side and the booths along the window of the other. I've never gone into a restaurant and sat by myself. With a sigh and a belly growling, I leave the safety net of my car and walk in, where I sit at the counter and pluck a menu from a holder.

But I'm not really looking at the menu. I'm thinking about Cal and his words. The past is the past. I get I don't have to live there, but I also know that I need to face that I've messed up too. Like they talked about at Phoenix's meeting, seeking forgiveness and shit.

I pull out my phone and text Danny:

> How's basic?

I set the phone down and resume studying the menu. The message wasn't what I should have said. I pick up the phone once more and try again:

> I wanted to say you were right, bro.

> About everything.

> Thanks, and I'm sorry for being such a tool.

I set my phone down and select something from the menu, wondering why I can text Danny but am avoiding Tanner. As clear as the picture of the hamburger and French fries on the page, I hear a voice in my head: *You have more to lose with Tanner.* Why had Phoenix hidden the truth from me? He'd been afraid. Why am I avoiding Tanner? I'm afraid he won't forgive me. I haven't hurt Danny like I hurt Tanner. Tanner is my brother, and I stomped on that trust, that bond, and cracked it like bones. Danny told me the truth and drew a line, but I didn't grind the heel of my foot into Danny's heart.

The waitress stops to take my order. As she walks away, my phone buzzes.

I look at it, hoping the message is from Danny. It isn't.

> Hi. It's Lauren from class. Ready to make a plan?   Lauren

My eyebrows arch on my forehead. A couple of days ago, I was interested in the hypothetical idea of meeting up with her. Receiving the text, however, feels more real. I may have had quite a few encounters with girls, but I have no experience outside of Bro Code. Just Max. Without the alcohol and the party, how does one interpret another's intentions?

Lauren's text blazes in my eyeballs like a foreign language. Is it a hook up text? An 'I'm interested in you' text? A friend-zone text? I feel out of my element and too deep in my own swamp to know for sure.

I need help, but I'm too embarrassed to ask my brother. My former friends aren't an option, so without thinking it through, I text Max:

> Hey. I need help.

> Yes. You do, SK. You good?

My heart bounces in my chest when her text comes through, and I smile. The waitress catches my eyes as she delivers the chocolate milkshake and my food, so I look up and wipe the smile from my face. When she's gone, I pluck a French fry from the basket with one hand, smile again at my phone and Max's text in my other. I grip the food between my teeth to free up both hands to text her back.

> All good. Eating French fries. How's Ben?

Shit. Why did I write that? I frown and set the phone down as if it's burned me, but that was all me. I've had Max on the brain, wondering about that Ben guy from the pizza place and his territorial show. I've wondered if it worked, and if Max is interested in him. I've hated that I've wondered since I know I don't have any right to.

The three dots pop up, disappear, then reappear. I wonder what she's writing, wonder if my question has freaked her out. I pick up the phone, needing to see her response more than I need to eat.

> Ben who?

A short text for all the writing and rewriting. This response makes me smile and buoyantly happy even if it's irrational to be so.

> Maybe you didn't go to that party since your dad showed up?

> Oh. THAT Ben.

That makes my smile short out like a broken neon sign.

> Why? Is there more than one Ben?

There probably is, I decide. Max is awesome, and any number of Bens would be lucky to call her a girlfriend. What the hell am I thinking? I'd texted her to ask about Lauren, and now I'm annoyed thinking about Max being any Ben's girlfriend. My stomach feels like it's in knots. I glance at the burger, unsure if I can eat it.

> Tons of them! ☺

> I'm at a party right now.

> Ben's a few feet from me probably thinking I'm weird because I'm grinning at my phone as I text you at said party.

> There's also Derek. Hank. Billy Bob. The Hulk.

A lightness floats about in my chest at her humor but also a protectiveness.

> Only I can say you're weird.

> Says who?

> Me.

The possessiveness of the statement is glaring and loud even though it's just a text. I switch gears, jumping into why I'd originally texted in order to cover it up.

> Can I ask you something?

> I need your female expertise.

> My eyes just narrowed. Are you being sarcastic?

This makes me scoff out loud. I glance around, but no one has noticed.

> LOL. No!

> I just had this girl from class text me. I'm not sure how to interpret it.

> Are you trying to make me jealous?

> No. Are you?

I wonder if this is a Max joke. My insides are outlined with a strange awareness which is trying to reorganize my organs into different places within my body. Do I want Max to be jealous? I realize I'm irritated by the idea of any number of Bens or Dereks or Hanks, and it wakes up something inside of me. Something like I felt earlier when I'd walked into my house and saw Bill sitting at the table. It's angry, but not exactly that. Am I jealous? Is she?

The phone rings; it's Max.

I smile and answer, but my voice sort of shakes even though I don't want it to. "I didn't call because I thought you might be busy." There's noise in the background, lots of voices, the bass of music. I stare at my hamburger, which I haven't touched yet.

"Hold on," she says, and then the noise lessens. "Okay. What's this about some girl calling?"

"Texting. Are you really at a party?"

"Yeah. With Renna."

I clench my jaw and press the top bun of my hamburger. So, Ben is there. "How is it?"

"A party, which for the record I don't like all that much. You're changing the subject," she says. There's a noise, then the muffled sound of Max's voice as she talks to someone. "Yeah. This is private. Thanks."

I wait a few more seconds, listening to the sound of her voice, and get lost imagining who she's talking to. Wondering who is interrupting her and vying for the attention she's giving me. This knowledge should make me feel happy, but instead it makes me feel lonely. I want to be there with her.

"Sorry about that," she says.

"We can talk later. If you need to go."

"No! No. I want to talk to you. It's just loud and someone— never mind. So, a girl texted you."

"Yeah. From class." I trace the edge of my napkin and fold the corner as I talk. "She asked me if I wanted to get together to work on class stuff, but I told her I couldn't because I work. I offered to meet her for coffee or something. She just texted me."

"Why do you need me for that?"

"I don't know what it means." The sounds of the party removed from Max's proximity stretch inside the silence. "Max? You still there?" I know she is because I can still hear the party.

"I'm here. Just thinking."

"Thinking what?"

"She's interested in more than coffee," she finally says. "The question is, are you?"

It's a fair question. Historically, Lauren is the kind of girl I've been attracted to. But the reality has been those are the girls I've pursued for sex only, and if I'm being honest with myself, I don't know enough about Lauren to know if I'd like her, even if her attention has made me feel somehow better.

"I'm not sure," I say.

"What aren't you sure about? It fits with all of your rules." The sound of her voice has changed; it's edgy and sharp.

I furrow my brow and poke the hamburger bun with my finger, leaving an indention in the bread. "My rules? This isn't partying. I've never gone out with a girl except... for you." I swallow, considering the truth of that statement.

"Your rules still apply. Willing partner and all that." Her voice sounds strange in my ears. Not Max. The levity is missing.

There's something familiar about her words, and I think about our one kiss and the aftermath. She'd said something about rules then. What had she said? I can't remember. Shit.

"I haven't been partying. I don't think that—never mind. Maybe I shouldn't have bothered you with this."

She sighs into the phone. "Coffee won't hurt, I suppose, but if you aren't interested, you shouldn't string her along."

"Wait. What? I haven't answered her yet," I clarify. "I'm not stringing her along."

"You suggested coffee. She might have hope."

I'm confused and wonder if we're still talking about Lauren. "Are you mad?"

"Why would I be mad, SK?"

"I don't know. You seem irritated. And I don't understand what you're talking about."

She sighs again like I've missed the entire point, and I guess I have. I just feel confused. "I have to go, Griffin."

"Wait!" I scramble, trying to keep her on the phone. "Are you coming home for Thanksgiving?" I rush the words out afraid she'll hang up.

"Yes. I'll be home."

"That's good. Your dad's been kind of a mess."

She makes a noise in the phone. "I'm coming home."

"My mom invited you guys over for Thanksgiving dinner. If you're interested. Your kitchen is being torn out, so you might have to take me up on it."

"Great." She sounds sarcastic.

"Are you sure you aren't mad?" I feel like there's a tenuous tightrope between us, and both of us are about to topple into a chasm of unknown territory.

"Not mad. Thanks for the invitation. I'll be sure to tell my dad."

I'm afraid to say something wrong and make it worse. "I'll see you in a week or so."

"Yep. See you." And then she's gone, and I'm looking at the phone, unsure what just changed between the beginning of the call and the end.

What I have realized, however, is I don't want to meet Lauren, not if I'm going to leave my past in the past. Lauren isn't forward for me. She's a Bella, the status quo, and besides, there is nothing about Lauren other than her attention that moves me. I know this because there are other sparkling threads that I feel tied to Max. I've spent a lot of time insisting she's just my friend, but those threads feel like they might be weaving me into something new, and I've got to figure out what the road ahead looks like.

3.

I'm fucking coming out of my skin waiting for Max—and Cal—
to arrive for Thanksgiving. Thinking about our tiny-ass ranch style
house with a tiny-ass living room and dining room, all of us packed
in like sardines in a can, makes me hot and sweaty. The discomfort
isn't the space, it's the idea of being so close to Max. Since my
misguided attempt to share what happened with Coffee Lauren, my
texts with Max have been different—not as easy as they once were.
I'm afraid I've ruined us somehow, and I just want to fix what
happened, to go back to the way things were.

I check my reflection in the bathroom one more time, to make
sure I look okay. I've changed—sort of—since graduation. I'm not
as skinny. I've got more defined muscles now from the physical
work of construction stuff, and the running. My neck is wider, my
face a little wider but sharper. I went and got a haircut because my
hair was looking shaggy. I'd been inspired by Phoenix whose hair
looks like shit—all long and ratty. I run my hands through my own
hair one more time, then smooth my dark blue shirt, as if it will ease
the ants crawling around inside my chest. I take a deep breath to
douse their fire, but they crawl down my arms and out into my
fingertips. I crack my knuckles.

"Griffin!" my mom yells from the kitchen. "Would you grab the door?"

I walk into the dining room and take an olive from a dish on the table set for six. Mom, Phoenix, and me. Bill. Cal and Max. Whatever Mom's doing has my mouth watering. Who knew she could do the whole feast? She refused my help because Phoenix was in the kitchen helping her. She said, "It's a two-butt kitchen, Griffin. You're on house-straightening duty." That took less than an hour. The rest of the unstructured time has added to the way my brain and nerves are spinning. Even the run hasn't helped today.

"Stop eating the olives and get the door."

Bill is on the other side. It's clear he's put some effort into his appearance for my mom, and I recall just looking at myself in the mirror, wondering why I went to the effort. His grayish hair is neat and trimmed. His red shirt buttoned up under his black leather bomber jacket. He's tucked the shirt into gray slacks so his belly presses against the buttons a smidge. The cologne he's wearing is strong and hovers around him like a cloud, but he offers a warm smile. He's got a bottle of wine, flowers, and something store bought in a paper bag. "Hi, Griffin."

I step back to let him in. "Hey."

"Happy Thanksgiving," he says.

I offer him a peacekeeping smile. "Yeah. You too."

He passes me, drops everything but the flowers on the counter, then disappears from my view, but I can hear my mom's pleasure and exclamation over the flowers.

Phoenix appears at the end of the hallway. He's dressed, though not with as much attention to detail. Jeans and a blue t-shirt with a Star Wars Boba Fett encircled on it. His hair is pulled back into his version of a man bun, most of the hair hovering over his shoulders. He glances at whatever is happening in the kitchen and looks away, his eyes catching mine. For a moment, our brotherly language returns crossing space and time. *That's fucking annoying*, he says without making a sound.

I roll my eyes in acknowledgement.

We smile together as he sits on the couch. I join him. He turns up the volume on the football game, so we don't have to listen to the disgusting flirting occurring in the kitchen. Side by side, we watch the game. I like that our brother language has begun functioning again.

"You hear from Dad?" Phoenix asks between an offensive and defensive series on the TV screen. The game goes to commercial.

Mom laughs in the kitchen at something Bill's low voice has said, though I can't hear what it was.

I glance at my brother, who is avoiding my gaze. His is fixed on the commercial. "No. You?" I already know the answer to this question.

Phoenix clears his throat and runs his open hands across his denim-clad thighs. "Yeah. We've been talking."

I look at the TV and watch some guy standing at the edge of a mountain cliff with his new SUV parked behind him. My heartbeat tightens in my chest, keeping things small and compact. I want to say something about it, but the feelings are first, surprise, given how much Phoenix hated our dad when we were younger, and second, insecurity, so I don't know what to say.

"He wanted me to tell you Happy Thanksgiving."

I press my teeth together and cross my arms over my chest. The words 'go to hell' surface on my tongue, but I don't voice them. I just nod to let Phoenix know I've heard him, then watch as the uniformed men pummel each other on the TV screen.

When there's a knock on our front door, my heart stalls because I know it's Cal and Max. My hands start to sweat, which is weird.

"You just going to sit there?" Phoenix asks and pushes me. "You're closer to the door."

I find a way to get my muscles moving, swipe my hands over the back pockets of my jeans, and open the door.

Cal's in front, taking up most of the real estate on the porch. He smiles, and I offer a distracted smile, more interested in seeing Max. I haven't seen her in person since my visit to her dorm a month

217

earlier, and I recall the way I hadn't wanted to leave her. My heart speeds up, and my stomach dips and rolls tying itself up into knots. I'm not sure this is how other friends feel…

Cal steps into the living room, and Max is behind him. "Hey, SK." Her honey hair is down, draped over her shoulders like a pretty waterfall. She looks up at me, and her eyes crash into mine like a wave. Feeling floods me.

…because I like Max. Oh my fucking god. I like Max, and it's definitely more than friendship. The realization makes my breath logjam in my chest, and my head spin in the thought. I have feelings—real feelings—for Maxwell Wallace.

I recall the feel of her body pressed against mine that morning, and the way I wanted to crawl back into bed with her. The wish that I hadn't had to go.

The way I feel bright and warm when she texts.

I remember laughing with her at Triple B.

I picture her working on the cabinet and the way her focus makes her lips look soft and kissable.

I feel her sly smile across the table at the pizza parlor, filling the empty deep spaces inside of me with joy.

My stomach does a dizzy dance, and I fist my hands at my sides to keep from reaching for her.

I've been so stupid.

Max is the way forward.

I don't want her to date the Bens or Dereks or Hanks. I want it to be me she chooses—and then realize she tried. I ruined it, like I always do.

I clear my throat so that I can get words that disguise what I'm feeling out. "Happy Thanksgiving."

She smiles, and her cheeks bloom roses. She swipes a lock of hair, tucks it behind her ear and looks down at her feet to navigate crossing the threshold. When she leans forward, she gives me an awkward hug with her hands on my shoulders. Unsure where to put my hands, I lean closer, breathing in cinnamon and spice, a hand on her back.

I swallow, my throat suddenly dry.

"Close the door. It's cold," Phoenix says.

I glance at him, see he's shaking Cal's hand, and close the door. "I can take that," I tell Max.

She hands me the package she's holding and removes her coat. She's wearing a blue dress and an open sweater over the top of it. I don't think I've ever seen her in a dress. She looks so pretty that it hurts, a lump in my chest that my heart can't seem to get around to function properly.

I lead her and Cal into the kitchen, where I introduce them to my mom and Bill.

"Thank you so much for your invitation," Cal says. "Our kitchen doesn't look much like a kitchen right now."

"Yes. Griffin told me," Mom says. "Would you like a glass of wine?"

They talk like grown-ups, and I tune them out in favor of focusing on Max.

Her eyes slide to mine. She smiles, and it hits my heart like a sharp dart in a bullseye of the board. I can't keep looking at her because of the weird way it hurts, and I need to reset myself. I'm acting like an idiot. I go to the table and take some olives.

I track Cal as he returns to the living room to sit with Phoenix to watch the game. They talk though I can't hear them.

Max, who's standing next to me, has put olives on the tips of her fingers. She wiggles them at me. "I love olives."

I smile. "I don't think I've done that since I was a kid."

"Then you're missing out," she says and bites one of her fingertips.

I follow her movement with my eyes, her fingertip to her lips. They close over the flesh of the olive, and it disappears. My belly constricts. When I reconnect with her eyes, she's watching me. She smiles.

I clear my throat, look away because my skin is overheating, and coax myself not to be an idiot. *Find something to say*, I tell myself. "How are things with your dad?"

"Fine." She eats another olive.

I beckon her to follow me and lead her down the hallway to my room. When I stop in the doorway, I realize I haven't thought this through. The room might be sort of neat, but there aren't a lot of places to sit.

Max doesn't seem to mind and moves past me to sit on the end of my bed. She looks around.

I follow her in and stand awkwardly in the middle of the room. "You sure you're okay?"

"It's good. Dad and I talked."

"You upset at him?"

"No. I was never really upset with him. Just the circumstances, you know. Indigo disappeared like I figured she would, and I realized that's what he'd been trying to protect me from."

I sit next to her.

She turns to face me.

I look down at my hands. It's easier than getting stuck on the pretty way she looks. "He missed you. And when he got back, whatever happened shook him up."

"Yeah. It shook me too. He's all I've got."

I can't help but look at her then. I search her face. This close in this light I can see she's got a beauty mark just under her left eye. Her eyes have these deep blue striations and a splash of green in the left one. I'm drawn to the pretty pink sheen of her lips. They're not smiling at me but downturned just a touch. Kissable. I can feel her eyes measuring me, too, and it feels a little reminiscent of that day in August, when she kissed me. Hope offers a tentative pulse inside of me. Could she still want to kiss me?

"You have me," I tell her.

She looks away, turns so she's sitting on the edge of the bed, and examines her fingers. Her nails are painted blue to match her dress. "I'm glad."

I realize even if she is still interested in me, she'd never be the one to cross the line of friendship. Not after what happened in August. I rejected her. Fear coils up like a snake inside of me, tight around the terror of ruining our friendship. Knowing me, that is exactly what I would do. I've left a trail of ruined friendships.

She stands, moves away. "So, this is SK's room." She glances over her shoulder at me with a fun smile. Dimple.

My belly responds, flopping about. I want to touch her, draw her back to the bed, kiss that dimple.

She moves about the small room with her hands clasped behind her back. "This doesn't look like a serial killer's room." Her voice is low when she says it, like she's imparting a secret.

"That's because it isn't." I lean back on my hands to watch her move. "What does a serial killer's bedroom look like?"

Her upper lip quirks with one of those sassy smiles. "Oh. Full of all the news clippings of all their nefarious activities." Her eyes sparkle as she says it.

"Nefarious? Speak English." I purposefully goad her.

"I am. Sinister. Come on, SK." She resumes looking around. "But there isn't much here. I mean, it doesn't really reflect you. Where are your posters? Trophies? Pictures of friends?"

I sit back up and glance around. She's right. There isn't much of me in this room. "I took down the one poster I had."

"Oh." Her eyes light up. "I bet I can guess what it was."

I raise my eyebrows to invite her to guess.

She returns to the bed and sits next to me. "A picture of a hot girl in a bikini."

I smile. "Close."

"And a car."

This makes me laugh. "Closer." I wish we were sitting closer.

She smiles. "Why did you take it down?"

I look around at the room, which suddenly feels like a stranger's space; I don't know who this person is, and there's nothing here to tell me. It's empty. "It just didn't feel right anymore."

She hums a response. I don't know what it means. It doesn't sound judgmental.

"Would you like me to take your sweater?" I ask her.

"Sure." She gets up.

I stand, stepping up behind her—closer—to help her.

She turns her head slightly, and I notice the way her lashes fan over her cheeks.

My fingertips graze the bare skin of her shoulder.

She stalls, and her eyes flash to mine.

I freeze.

Someone laughs in the other room.

She shivers, looks away, says something about keeping the sweater, and shrugs it back on.

I don't catch all of what she's said more cognizant of the fire burning from my fingertips straight to my center. "Max." I don't know why I say her name. I just need to. I can't find my balance without saying it. I don't reach out and touch her. I don't move. I'm in suspended animation.

She draws her hair from under the collar and turns to face me. "Yeah?" Then her eyes flick up to mine, and I know she can see all the feelings my features are telling her. While I may have been able to hide them from everyone else, I've never been very good at hiding them when it comes to her. She saw them the very first time she met me when she sat down at the table. She hadn't even known my name.

She steps closer.

When she takes a breath, I can feel the shift in my shirt, whispering a caress across my skin.

She tilts her head slightly to meet my gaze. "Griffin?"

Griffin.

Not SK.

Griffin.

My heart is in my throat, filling it with its mass rather than words because I don't know what the words are. I just know there are

222

flashes of lightning electrifying me. I notice her breathing—it's erratic, faster than a moment ago. These tiny observations make me think that maybe she wants me to kiss her. That whatever happened last August is still between us, that all the tension I felt at her dorm wasn't just me.

I'm afraid.

"Me too," she says.

"I said that out loud?"

She offers a tentative smile, nods, then leans toward me as if to tell me she's willing to meet me halfway.

I reach out and pinch a strand of her hair between my fingers, afraid to touch her, but she tilts her head so that her cheek presses against my hand holding the strand of silky hair. I release it and lay my open palm against her cheek.

"I want to kiss you," I say, but the words barely make a sound.

"Hey!"

I straighten, and Max whirls around at the sound of Phoenix's voice.

Standing in the doorway, his eyes darting between us, Phoenix smiles a toothy grin, which makes me want to punch his face. "Dinner," he says.

"Okay." I offer him a frustrated look.

He winks at me before he disappears, and I grind my teeth together.

Max, who is suddenly intent on looking at the stuff on top of my dresser, has her back to me.

"Ready?" I ask.

She turns, her cheeks pink with a blush, and nods. "Starving."

I wonder if she's talking about the meal. The thought excites me that she isn't.

4.

Thanksgiving, or rather that moment right before dinner in my room, has replayed in my mind like a fevered dream. I imagine the moment as it was. Then I rewrite it to include a kiss. I imagine more that includes hands and other body parts. I'm feverish with it, ill at ease with wondering if the moment was all my imagination and hoping it wasn't. Dinner went better than I suspected and included a prayer said by Phoenix (which surprised me but shouldn't have considering his Twelve Steps), delicious food, and easy conversation. My concentration on said conversation was shit, however. I couldn't tear my focus away from Max.

When I open the door the following morning for a run, it's cloudy, cold, and muted with coming snow. I layer on an extra sweatshirt and find solace in the heartbeat of my feet against the pavement. I'm not cognizant of my direction until I'm almost to Custer's store, the same one where I met Max for the first time. I stop in the parking lot, hands on my head, clouds of steam making me the dragon I feel like most of the time. I stare at the table where she sat down with me, asked me if I was a serial killer, then walked away with a smile. More than the fight with Tanner, more than Danny's real talk, more than Mom's appeal to me to change, it was that moment that stands out as the moment an *after* began. Max.

Brazen and brave, sitting with a jerk drinking water and sullenly pouting away his life.

I turn around and run back home.

When I get there, Phoenix is up and drinking his coffee. He looks up from the cookbook he's reading at the table when I walk in. "How was it today?"

"Cold. You should join me." I flop on the floor near him to stretch.

"Hell no." He takes a loud sip of his coffee. "There's a fresh pot."

"Thanks. I need a shower first. Mom still here?"

"Left for the hospital while you were out. She's got a date with Bill later."

"Bill."

He chuckles. "Okay. So, I don't hate the guy, but he's not what I would have expected."

"Which would be?"

He shrugs. "I don't know. Maybe someone more like dad."

"That guy is the furthest thing from our father."

"My point exactly."

"And maybe that's why she likes him. Our dad didn't offer much beyond us."

"And look at us."

Ouch, I think, but realize he isn't wrong.

Phoenix takes another sip. "I'm thinking about meeting him."

After hearing they've been talking, I expected this, though the idea pisses me off. I also recognize it isn't my place to be pissed off at what Phoenix wants to do. "Twelve Steps?" I ask instead of allowing the anger.

He nods. "Sort of. It wasn't like I wronged him."

"The other way around."

"But–" he ignores me– "maybe an origin for all of my shit."

I notice he doesn't say "hurt" and wonder about it. We sit in our own thoughts for a while. I'm contemplating the idea of hurt and why it makes me feel like I'm backed into a corner. The thoughts are like a vat of acid eating through my skin and settling into my bones.

"What if it doesn't help? Like what if the truth just hurts worse?" I worry that coming face-to-face with the man who's been the villain in my ghost town dreams might propel Phoenix into a ditch he's already been stuck in and is trying to climb from.

Phoenix makes a noise in his nose and sets his coffee cup on the table with a thud. "I've thought about it, and I think that's giving him more power over me than he deserves. Like that prayer we recite at the meetings, 'to accept the things I cannot change, to change the things I can, and the wisdom to know the difference.'" He pauses. "I think that I can see Dad as he is now—just a guy who's as fucked up as any of the rest of us."

I stand.

"And, meeting him wouldn't be for him. It would be for me," he adds.

The thought lodges in my chest. I hadn't thought of it like that before. In my mind, my father, my memories of him, of the man I see through my eight-year-old eyes, has held all the power. Phoenix's words swivel the image in my mind, change my perspective to see that perhaps I'm giving him all my power. I wonder what else I've allowed to take my power.

"He invited us to his place for Christmas Eve." My brother waits for me to say something, and when I don't offer a "fuck that" must consider it a win because he adds, "Would you go with me?"

I just look at him unsure how I feel about it. The way he's asked isn't about capitulating to my dad, but instead being there for my brother. Isn't that what I have wanted all these years? "I'll think about it," I answer.

He nods, accepting of that outcome. Then he grins. "So. The girl. Max," Phoenix says into a book.

I have to catch my balance against the wall.

He chuckles. "You've got it bad." He looks up from the book.

"She's cute. Nice."

I don't know why his observations, that he can see through me, makes me want to pound his face in. I growl at him again.

He laughs into his coffee cup.

I leave him there to shower, thinking about the possibilities of being around my dad for Christmas. An inner battle between anger and curiosity tug on my insides. When I'm done washing away the run, I dress. My phone alerts me I have a message. With a swipe on the cracked screen, I see it's a notification from Max and can't keep from smiling.

> When are you coming to get me?

She sent the message almost an hour ago, while I was on my run.

I answer her: | Now. |

I send it, hoping I'm not too late, but when the bubble appears on the screen and she writes, *dress warm*, the joy expands in my chest.

When I park in front of her house, and before I can turn off the car, Max walks down the steps. She's dressed in a bright, green, bubbly jacket, a hat and mittens, scarf, carting a backpack and a cooler.

I climb out. "What is all that?"

"Surprise. Just open the hatch."

I comply, and she sets the stuff in the back.

Then she turns toward me. "That doesn't look very warm?" She nods at my hoodie.

"I brought a jacket."

With a nod, she gets into the passenger's seat like it's hers, and maybe it is. She's the only one, besides Phoenix, who's ever ridden in it.

With my hands on the steering wheel, I wait. "Where am I driving?"

"The Bend."

I turn and look at her. "What? It's freezing. And it's supposed to snow later."

"Scared?" Her eyebrows arch up over her eyes with a challenge.

"You know you can't dare me like that. I'll bite every time."

She smiles and looks straight ahead. "Let's go then."

By the time we pull into the parking lot at the visitor center, it's deserted, and there aren't any tickets to buy since it's winter.

Wrapped in our jackets, hats, and gloves, Max carries the backpack and I lug the cooler. When we reach the switchback, the town looks like it did the last time, only in the cold of November, it appears more desolate than even in August, except more peaceful perhaps in the frozen world.

When we get to the edge of the town, intermittent snowflakes are falling.

"What made you think of this?" I ask her as we walk the main street. I know without question that we're headed to the barn.

"I woke up thinking about it."

"What about it?"

She shrugs and keeps walking. "Let's see if anything has been moved by the ghosts." She grins.

We stop and peer into the same house, then we stop to stare into the saloon once more. They all look the same. "Still frozen in time," I say. With my hand cupped around my eyes and pressed to the glass, I look for something that's different.

"Like us? Right now?" She's looking at me.

I map her features and nod.

"Did you expect it to be different?" she asks.

I draw away from the glass and see my reflection. The truth is I'm different than the last time I was here. "Yeah. No. I mean, I knew it wouldn't, but it feels like it should look different." Because I feel different. I look at her. It's started snowing more consistently now, flakes collecting on her hat and her eyelashes, melting on her cheeks. The acoustics mute my words and makes everything silent.

"I get it." Her eyes rove over my face a moment. Then she nods before turning away and continuing down the street toward the barn.

When we get there, the stillness of the space is insulated and warm. She draws a gray wool blanket from the backpack. "Here."

"What's happening?" I ask.

"A picnic."

"In November."

The shape of her look tells me I'm an idiot, which I know to be true, but then she smiles. "What did you think?"

"You probably don't want to know."

She stops moving a moment, just a fraction of a second, keeping her body busy. "Put the cooler here."

I follow her directions and sit down on the edge of the blanket.

The darkness of the barn is punctuated at both ends by light. It makes it easy to see, and the hushed snow fall illuminates things in a way that makes it feel like we're isolated in our own private, frozen universe. I turn to watch her. It's preferable but also strange to study her with this newfound awareness and longing twisted up inside me. Like that opening at the other end of the barn, my inability to function as her emotional equal is glaring and burns brightly in my mind.

When she's set out all the food—sandwiches and chips, sliced carrots and celery, oranges, apple cider in a bottle and cups—she holds out her arms and says, "Ta da."

"Wow. You put my sandwiches last time to shame."

She grins. "But those were some incredible PB&J sandwiches. Best I ever had."

"Liar."

"Never," she says with a bright smile.

I feel that smile weighted in my chest and find it difficult to get my lungs to work right. My mind slips back to the confines of my room with her silky hair between my fingers. I focus on the cups.

"I woke up thinking about this place because I woke up thinking about your name." She adjusts herself on the blanket, the food between us. "This is where you told me about it."

I look up at her.

"I mean, to answer why here," she says; the question on my face must have been obvious. She shakes her head and unzips her jacket, removing it. "Last time we were here, you told me your name meant 'monster.'" She sets her puffy jacket aside, her mittens threatening to spill from the pockets. The rainbow yarn cap and matching scarf stay on, draped over her dark green sweater.

"Yeah. That's a weird thing to think about and not particularly confidence building for me."

She laughs. "I looked it up."

"You did?"

She blushes, and it reminds me of last night.

The want to kiss her bounces around in my head, but I stay where I am.

"You know it doesn't just mean monster, right?"

I shake my head. I'm trying to focus on her words. Monster shmonster. Whatever. I'm looking at her lips.

"Did you know that a griffin was considered a majestic creature in mythology? That really, in most articles, the griffin wasn't really a monster at all, but a powerful guardian of priceless treasures?"

I quirk my eyebrows. "Really?" I didn't know this, more attuned to the monster myth. "A guardian of treasures, you say?" The thought makes me think about her and how I am ill-equipped to guard priceless treasures. Break them is more my MO, but I swivel the perspective. What if I made choices that reflected a guardian instead?

She nods and hands me a cup of cider. "Yep."

I take it, take a sip, and set it near me. "That's definitely better than a monster." I pick up a sandwich and flip the wax-papered meal over in my hands. "And that's what made you think about coming out here?"

Her hands, I realize have been moving the whole time. She's nervous, and I've never really thought of her as nervous—ever. She puts them in her lap, takes a deep breath. Then she looks at me, and that look on her face is the one I think of when I imagine Max. It's calm and serene. Honest and forthright. Brave. "I thought about how I wished I'd told you about what I'd been really thinking last time. A do over."

"And what's that?"

Her mouth opens and then closes. She glances at the food between us and says, "Let's eat."

"Scared?" I ask her with a smirk, parroting her earlier word to me.

She smiles but doesn't answer and crunches on a carrot stick she's grabbed instead.

So, we eat.

And talk. About what happened with her mom and the aftermath with Cal. About Phoenix asking me to visit my dad. About work and school.

"And the girl?" she asks. "Did you go to coffee with her?"

I take my final sip of apple cider and then fiddle with the cup. "Naw."

"How come?"

"I didn't want to." I take a breath, look at her and say, "I realized I have feelings for someone else. Wouldn't want to string her along." I can't believe I've said it. But there's no taking it back, and I don't want to.

She blushes, makes a humming noise, then moves to pack up the remnants of our picnic. I help her, placing the used items and what's left over inside the cooler. We reach into the confines of the space at the same time. Our hands bump. An electric shock drives up my arm to my elbow, but I don't retreat. She doesn't either. Instead, I release what's in my hand, take her hand in mine and run my thumb along her skin.

I don't look up at her and instead keep my eyes on the place where I'm touching her, knowing that even if I could formulate thoughts, I can't form words.

She moves, withdrawing her hand from the cooler, mine still holding on because I don't want to let her go again. She pushes the cooler aside, removing the last barrier between us. Both of us are on our knees facing one another, my hand wrapped around hers. She turns hers, so our palms connect, then threads her fingers with mine.

I can't find myself. I'm floating, even though all my physical senses are attuned to her.

"The last time we were here," she says quietly, looking at our joined hands.

I follow her gaze. We're different. Her hands are soft and smooth, pretty, and feminine. Mine are angular, sharp with veins, different now because of the work. Calloused. Then I look up at her face. "What were you thinking?"

"That if I'd been braver–" she stops and swallows– "That if I'd been braver, I would have told you that I couldn't stop thinking about you. I would have said that I like you. I would have said that every time I called you a silly name, it was because I was afraid."

"Afraid?"

"Because every time I say your name, it's a tattoo that I feel." She reaches over and presses her other hand to my chest, where my heart aches, beating with longing. "Here."

I move closer to her and reach out for her.

She shivers.

"Are you cold?" I ask and bring my hand up to her cheek.

She shakes her head and leans against my palm.

There isn't anyone to interrupt the moment this time. No Phoenix. No laughter. No calls to dinner. It's just us in the barn of this ghost town, the world silent around us. There's no breeze, no sound except for one another. Our matching breaths.

"Are you still scared?"

I caress her face, run my thumb across her dimple, and nod.

"How come?"

"I don't want to fuck this up," I say.

"Then don't," she says and leans toward me at the same time I close the distance to her. I frame her face with my hands, and when our lips meet, I think perhaps the heat melts everything else away, refining all my old fears with something vibrant and new.

DECEMBER

I didn't realize that there are people who come along willing to help carry the load. Except, letting go feels like a violation of the unwritten code I can't find to study or decipher.

To: Griffin Nichols
123 4-5th Street N.E.
The Town, USA 67890

1.

I'm stoked. I'm going to spend the weekend with Max since I'm done for the term, and she still has another week. With the music in my car turned up loud, I drive. The sun has just set when I park my car in the same spot as the last time I visited Max, and she's running from the building as I close the door of my car.

Then she's in my arms.

Her mouth is on mine. Her hands are bunched in my hair. Her tongue talks with mine. Hot. Hungry.

My stomach bottoms out. Hands on her cold cheeks, I kiss her in the middle of the parking lot like it's nothing and everything.

"I. Missed. You," she says between kisses.

I draw back and wrap my arms around her in her puffy coat. "I missed you, too." The realization of truth spreads in my chest like I'm sitting next to a fire. I haven't said a line I've practiced to get somewhere with her. She's been flowing through my blood vessels, thoughts of her running through every part of me for so long.

We separate so I can grab my stuff, and even though she's by my side, it feels colder without touching her. She takes my hand and leads me up to her room. This time her roommate is there. She's a cute girl, a Filipina with slick dark hair and dark eyes. She lifts her chin in greeting.

"This is Renna." Max introduces me.

"Hi."

Max takes my stuff and sets it on the end of her bed. "Renna is staying at her boyfriend's this weekend."

The girls share a look and a smile.

My blood hums under my skin, and I glance at Max. She's blushing.

Over her last break at Thanksgiving—after our first kiss—we've done some kissing, and some hand holding, but that's it. I've spent some pleasurable moments in the shower imagining what sex is going to be like with her. I want to feel Max's skin under my hands, feel her mouth on me, have my mouth on her. And of course, I'm okay if she's not ready, too. I just want to be with her. Near her.

"We're going with Renna to a frat party tonight. Okay?"

I haven't been to a party since my own, and I hadn't made the best choices. I also hadn't had a drink since then either. Phoenix's AA meeting surfaces like something floating to the surface from the bottom of a lake. I figure I can handle myself because I have a strong motivator standing in front of me. Besides, Max's excitement is contagious. "Yeah. Sure."

Later, when we walk into the party, Max, who looks gorgeous, glances over her shoulder at me and smiles, calming me. It's as if she knew I was wound up tight in the unfamiliar environment. My hand is in hers. Her silky hair brushes the back of the red shirt she's wearing, and when she moves, I can see glimpses of skin at her waist. She's smiling, that dimple in her cheek, her eyes aglow, and I wonder how many of these parties she's been to? How many guys have noticed how hot she looks? Ben, obviously. How many guys has she turned down? How many guys hasn't she?

I swallow. Nervous, suddenly, because what if everything about me disappoints her. She'll realize I'm that tiny, economy car with no bells and whistles to offer.

Once we've made it to the keg, she hands me a red cup filled with golden liquid and sips on her own. She leans closer and says in my ear over the noise, "You're frowning."

I shake off the pall of doubt, squeeze her hip with my hand, and pull her closer, so thankful I'm the guy she wanted to be here with.

"Nope. I'm good. I'm here with you." I smile, kiss her cheek, and then take a drink.

She leads me to the dance floor.

This girl.

The things around me slow, the movement deliberate because she is all things. The party dims, the bass of the music thumps in my muscles to match my heartbeat, but everything recedes except for her. She turns toward me, smiling, the dimple deep in her cheek.

I lean forward and kiss that dimple because I can now.

She grins and wraps her arms around my neck.

I can only use one hand to hold her, the other holding the stupid red cup. I've got a hand on her hip, one of my fingers curled through a belt loop of her jeans. Her hips move with me, and her hands find the hair at the nape of my neck. We dance, swaying, swiveling, a suggestive dance that excites me. I kiss the space just below her jaw, inhaling her.

"I'm so glad you're here," she says in my ear.

I draw back to look at her and offer her a smile with a nod.

She pulls me closer.

I don't want to be at this party. This is new. I just want to be alone with her, but I remain present. I press my nose into her neck to catch her spicy scent when I need a reminder—I'm there with her. She smiles and tucks herself in closer.

We dance some more, drink some more, take some time in the cool air of the backyard to cool off.

"You want to get out of here?" she finally asks. Her cheeks glow, but she doesn't seem drunk.

I'm feeling loose, but I haven't overdone it. I nod and take her hand, my turn to lead her from the house.

When we break out into the cold December night, it's refreshing, but not for long. We laugh, slipping over the icy concrete trying to get back to her dorm. No jackets, I wrap my arms around her. By the time we walk into her dorm, we're shivering. I'm not sure it's only because of the cold. She leads me through the maze again, strangely silent, which feels like the weight of anticipation. All I can think about is the intense need to kiss her.

She opens the door. I step inside after her, and when the door is closed, I pull her back to me. "Max," I say, but I don't wait. My hands frame her face. "I've thought about this all night." I kiss her.

She returns my kiss—her tongue tastes like the beer we've been drinking, but also like the cinnamon of her gum. "Me too."

Hands on her hips, I pull her against me. We lean on the door, and her body fits between my legs. I kiss all the parts I can: lips, jaw, neck, collar bone. The only sound in the room is our breathing, heavy with want. Then I'm walking us though the room to her bed, until we're there, stretched out with one another.

More kissing. My knee, high between her legs. I can't get close enough to her. She moans. She breathes my name, "Griffin," like it's a prayer, and it makes me hotter. My hands grasp her hips, find the skin at her waist, and run up, over her ribs, to the bottom of her bra. I trace the lace with my palms, filling my hands with her softness.

We kiss, and kiss, and kiss.

"Max." Her name is like breathing. Necessary. Life giving.

She rolls me onto my back, the waterfall of her hair cascading around us. She stops and gazes down at me.

I can't see her very well in the darkness of the room, but I grasp her hips and draw her to straddle me. I'm hard, and I know she can feel it, because she rocks her hips against me.

I groan. "I wanted to do this the last time I was in your bed," I say, but it sounds pained. What she's making me feel hurts so good, and what I've said is a terrifying admission. I feel exposed. In as many experiences as I've had, I've never cracked open the door to let anyone in to see the heart of me before.

"You did?" She leans up on her hands, hemming me into her space.

"Yeah."

"You didn't."

"I didn't want to ruin things."

"You say that a lot." She leans back down and kisses my jaw.

"What?" I'm chasing after my breath, trying to stay connected to talking. I'm awash with sensation and drowning in the physical response she's creating.

"That you ruin things." She sits up and moves her hips again, and I draw in a breath, squeeze her hips to still her.

"Max." I feel powerless, cast in a spell she's weaving.

"What?"

"You're making me crazy."

"Why do you say you'll ruin things?"

"Max. I want you." I sit up and hold her still in my lap.

She hums a noise. "Answer my question, Griffin." She flips her hair over her shoulder so I can see her neck, the outline of her jaw, her eyes shining in the dark. She tugs at my shirt, and I adjust so she can pull it from my torso.

I kiss her instead of answering. That's where my mind is, with her, needing her, wanting her.

She releases a rush of air at the feel of my tongue against the skin of her neck and my hands stroking her, then she moves her hips again. I stop her movement. I'm not going to last.

She pushes me onto my back, moving forward with me. "Tell me," she says and presses her mouth to my shoulder and trails kisses down, over my chest.

I'm up on my elbows, my eyes following her descent.

She stops, her eyes watching me at the same time she begins to unbuckle my belt.

"Oh fuck, Max." I swear because I am undone. The door to me is wide open.

"I want to know." Her tongue slides over my skin, lower still, my pants open and my body free from the confines of them. "May I kiss you? Here?"

"Yes. Yes." My head falls back, holding myself up on my hands, and I groan when her tongue finds me.

"Why do you say that Griffin?" she asks again.

My fingers are weaved in the strands of her hair as she takes me in her mouth. I can't hold myself up anymore and lay back. "I can't. I can't think. I don't say the right things. I don't do the right things." I pant the words, unable to staunch the flow of the words amidst the sensations she's creating in me both physical and emotional. "Max. I use people. I ruin things."

She's using her mouth like a truth serum, and I can't stop talking and even though she should stop with my admission, she doesn't. She keeps going, and the volcano in me is building. I keep going, the words coming like a broken song. "They leave me. I push. They leave. They leave me." And suddenly I can't contain myself because I'm lost to what she's doing and too near my ending. I grasp at her arms to pull her back up and kiss her, save her from me, but she doesn't stop. She presses me back and takes me all the way to an end. Or a new beginning.

The sensations subside, and Max moves back up my body, pausing to lick and kiss, tender and sweet. I sigh, throwing an arm over my eyes, feeling weak because I lost control. I'm afraid of what I'll see in her eyes when I look at her.

"Griffin."

When her face draws even with mine, she pauses. My eyes have adjusted to the darkness, and I can make out some of her features, filling in the rest with my memory. She's studying me but hesitates to kiss me. I interpret it as hesitation because I've revealed this weakness, but then she says, "Can I kiss you?" She sounds so unsure.

I don't have any words. They were lost in the moment I let go. I've felt pleasure before, but never like that. Never from a place where I felt like all my emotions exploded and opened up the fissures to let the darkness out. The only thing I can do is grab her face and kiss her, show her how I feel about her, how she made me feel.

She kisses me back, abandons her fears somewhere else, and moans in response.

I draw her shirt from her body and roll her onto her back, trading places. I create the same trail down her body as she did mine.

But then she stops me, her hands on my arms.

"Is this okay?" I ask.

"I'm–" she stalls, then says, "I'm a little scared. I haven't done this."

"I won't if you don't want to." I say it, and mean it, though I hate the idea—I want to show her how she matters.

"What if you don't like me. You know. After."

I rise back up onto my hands, even with her face. "That's an impossibility." I smile and kiss her lips. "How you make me feel, Max." I kiss her deeper, use my hands to show her, help her move the breath through her body like the ocean as she begins to come undone as I did. "Can I make you feel like you made me feel?"

She nods. "Yes."

I move deliberately. I retrace the trail down her body and settle between her legs to worship at her altar. I pray there until she can't string together anything but moans and pants and hands grasping for something to hold. There, I find both joy and truth, and it is powerful to give and worship that way.

Later, Max is curled against me, her head in the crook of my shoulder. It's weird, not super comfortable. I've never cuddled with a girl before, but laying like this with her, after our non-sex sex, feels really satisfying. She feels good on my skin. The silky strands of her hair sliding between my fingers feels good. Listening to her chatter feels good. We might not have crossed the full penetration sex line, but I haven't stopped grinning. It's Max. Max. Max.

She shifts her head to look at me. "What do you think?"

Shit. I lost track. "About what?"

Her eyes narrow, and she leans up on her elbow. "Have you heard a word I said?"

I could lie, but that's what old Griffin would have done. I run a finger under the stringy strap of her bra on her shoulder. "Sorry. I kind of zoned out."

She gives my shoulder a playful smack. "Griffin!"

I grab her wrist, push her until her back is on the bed, settle my hips between her legs, then lean down and nuzzle her neck. "Max. You feel good." I grind my hips against her, and her breath catches. Her eyes slip closed as she moans.

I kiss her jaw, then resume staring at her pretty face.

Her eyes open and her gaze darts to my lips, but instead of drawing me back down to kiss her, she says, "You know, before?"

I nod, licking my lips, preparing to kiss her again anyway.

She watches my tongue, then refocuses on my eyes. "I'm not going anywhere."

I stop my descent to her mouth, and my chest constricts.

"What you said, about everyone leaving."

I swallow.

"I'm not going anywhere," she repeats.

I push away from her and rise up to my knees, sitting back on my heels. "You can't say something like that. No one can."

She rises up onto her elbows. Her bra is a greenish-blue lacy confection, and I want to see her with it off. Her bare stomach, the curve of her hips, the matching panties. I feel the twitch of my dick and force myself to look at her face. She isn't smiling. Twitching dick stops.

"I can. I know myself. At least not without serious conversation. I'll follow the rules." She smiles.

I turn away from her, sit on the edge of the bed, and run a hand through my hair. It flops back into place, and I sigh before saying, "It wouldn't be because of you, though." I glance at her over my shoulder to see if she understands.

She's working her bottom lip between her teeth, staring at me, but not seeing me, thinking.

"Remember that night at the Quarry?"

Her eyes waltz to mine, and she nods.

"Most of the shit I told you about the douchey guy, everything you heard from those girls in the bathroom. It was true. I've told lies

243

to get what I wanted. I've gotten so drunk I couldn't stand up. I've used drugs. I've used girls. I've used my friends. I pushed my best friends away. I didn't want to listen to them. You see?" I look away because I don't want to see the regret on her face if it's there. "It's me."

I feel her shift on the bed until she's sitting next to me. Her thigh presses against mine. Then she's folding my hand in hers and laying her head on my shoulder. "You act like I didn't know all that beforehand. You told me, remember?"

I shrug.

"I still choose you."

I don't say anything. What's to say. The realization humbles me.

"I don't remember my mom walking away when I was five. But her return and the truth of it is really clear now."

I look at her. "She's missing out on the best thing."

"You think I did something to make her leave?"

I shake my head. "Fuck no. That was all her."

"I think you've forgotten something important."

"What's that?" I look at our joined hands.

"Your dad, your brother—you didn't cause them to leave."

I look down at her profile, and my throat tightens. She's right. I can see the truth of it even if the emotions of it don't register accurately. But them leaving doesn't change what I've done, who I am. Tanner still left. Danny still dropped me off and drove away. But I did that. The problem has always been me.

"And–" she continues as if reading my mind– "you aren't being that other guy anymore."

"You sound so sure."

She slides her head on my shoulder until she can meet my gaze. "I have a really good feeling about you." She smiles.

I offer her a tight grin in return.

She stands and keeps a hold of my hand.

I twirl her so I can look at her before drawing her in between my legs. Then I press my face in the warmth of her belly and hold

244

onto her as if she's a buoy in a stormy sea. "I don't deserve you."

She leans down and places a kiss on my head. "We deserve what we believe we deserve," she says. "Until we can both see it, we should keep things simple."

I look up at her. "Simple? I'm not sure what we just did was simple."

She moves her fingers through my hair.

I'm getting hard again.

"I just mean, we probably shouldn't have the baby-making kind of sex."

"You're the boss," I tell her.

"But I'm afraid that if I leave you to go take a shower, I'm going to miss you too much."

"Are you suggesting that I follow you into the shower and make sure you're extra clean?"

"Yes."

"Girl, I can't promise that I won't have a raging boner seeing you naked. If you're ready to see that, okay, but I'm not sure that's simple."

She laughs and then drags me toward the bathroom. "Sounds simple enough to me."

After an education in showering with a girl without actual sex, we get dressed, turn off the light and climb into her bed. This time, instead of sleeping with my back to her, she curls into my arms. And for the gazillionth time, I'm realizing how good it feels to have her there, how fortunate I feel. I'm floating with it, happy in a way that I can't ever remember feeling before. Excited because in a little over a week she'll be home. And I'll get to see her, touch her—

My optimism stalls like a car and slides over onto the shoulder smoking and in need to repair. Fuck. I'd forgotten.

Cal.

It isn't like I can just kiss Max in front of him. He'd freak out, even if he didn't say anything, inside, he'd be blindsided. I owe Cal more than that.

245

"I'm going to talk to your dad," I tell her.

"What? That's–no. He doesn't get a say in who I date."

"Not for that reason," I tell her. Of course, I know she has every right to date who she wants without permission from anyone. "He's my boss. You see how that's like a complication, right?"

She's silent for a moment. "And how do you picture that going?"

"Probably shitty." I pause and suppress a shudder thinking about doing it. Cal is awesome, and he's been a rock these last few months but coming out and telling him I want to date Max feels like crossing a line he isn't going to like. He's a guy. He knows how guys think. He'll know what I'm thinking about Max, like all the time. "I don't want to sneak around, and he deserves to hear it from me."

She's silent a while. I figure she's thinking, but then wonder if maybe she's fallen asleep until she says, "No. He deserves to hear it from us." She presses closer to me. "Okay?"

I kiss her head. "Okay. From us."

I lay there with Max in my arms, and sleep creeps up on me. I fall asleep imagining that door I've opened, how wide it is and how much light there is outside of it, wondering what if I can't keep all this light safe from the dark insecurities locked up inside of me?

2.

The guilt I'm carrying around while working with Cal is like heavy planks of drywall. In the whole of my nineteen years, I don't often recall that feeling as a driver. Anger, annoyance, rage, irritation, disengagement are the norms. Guilt and concern, not so much. The fact that I'm messing around with his daughter is a bucket of mixed concrete in my body that needs to be poured before it solidifies. Except my lungs feel like that concrete is setting. I'm finding it harder to breath around him. I think it's because I like and respect him, so sneaking around feels like past Griff, and I'm not supposed to be him anymore. Yet, here I am, being him. And if I can't shut down old Griff with something like this, how will I ever be able to do it?

We are putting the final touches on the kitchen. The room looks amazing. The painted cabinets, the matching tilework backsplash, the new appliances, the new flooring throughout the downstairs. That newness stretches from the kitchen though the dining room and entry out into the living room and the study and a half bath we ripped apart and redid. The new windows and the refurbished fireplace, the painted walls—a muted gray that Max picked out when she'd been home for Thanksgiving and painted with her dad—all speak to a house becoming a home. There's still a lot of work to be done on the second floor.

"I got a project next week, so you'll be working alone for a few days. Well, Max will be home. She'll help."

I swallow the confession. "Okay." I let the silence linger and then because it feels like he's watching me and reading my mind, I rush to cover up the insecurity and say, "Plans for Christmas?" and smear some grout over the tiles to avoid looking at him.

I hear Cal finish screwing on a new handle on a drawer. "Max and I keep it quiet. Always just the two of us. You?"

"Yeah. My mom. Brother." I don't say Bill will probably be a part of things or that my dad has asked Phoenix and me to come to his apartment. I'm still deciding.

Cal hums a response, reminding me of Max. I smile at the wall, thinking about her, and smear more grout. "It will be nice to have Max home. I've missed her chatter."

I don't say anything. What's there to say? *Yeah, sir. I've missed her too. So much so I went up to see her last weekend and we did stuff which made her chatter more.* Yeah. Probably not that.

"I'm going up to get her on Thursday, so I'll leave you a plan."

"Sounds good."

We continue working, finishing off the tile, the hardware. By that afternoon, we've finished the downstairs punch list except the back porch, so we start on the upstairs.

A couple of days later, with the stairwell and hallways ripped down to the studs, the flooring removed to the subfloor and Cal talking with the electrician, I'm busy contemplating Phoenix's badgering about going to our dad's while tearing up the bathroom.

Phoenix's sales pitch is that we haven't given Dad a chance yet. "Doesn't everyone deserve a second chance?" he asked me the night before as we'd demolished one another in the video game.

It made me think of Max's relationships rules. Annoying, because if I was determined to follow them with her, then it should probably translate to other relationships. It had with Phoenix, but I wasn't convinced my dad deserved my forgiveness even if ten years is a long time to carry the hurt of his abandonment.

I shrugged. It was a question that only had one right answer. I couldn't exactly say "no." If I did, it meant I didn't deserve a second chance, that Phoenix didn't either, but a "yes" meant that my dad did too. Everyone who I'd written off would deserve a chance. It meant I couldn't stay sitting in my self-righteousness, even if I wanted to.

"Fine," I'd said. "I'll go."

Phoenix had slapped me on the back, grateful, but now I'm in a state of perpetual irritation working up my brain to prepare for it. I'm glad we're ripping apart a bathroom today.

My last memory of my father was the police coming to arrest him. They'd knocked at the front door. He'd run. I'd been sitting in the living room playing with a Lego set he'd given me for my birthday, knocked in the head as he'd jumped over me to get out the back. He'd run through the dining room and crashed out the sliding door, the police moving around me as they chased him. They caught him, guns out, smashed his body into the yard at the back of the house filled with a collection of rocks and overgrown weeds no one had ever taken care of. When they'd hauled him back through the house handcuffed, I'd been crying.

"It's okay, little man," he'd growled. "Big boys don't cry."

Even the policemen had said it. "There's no reason to cry, son."

Seemed like a pretty good reason at the time.

"Griffin?"

I look up from the tile I'm scraping from the floor. Cal is standing in the doorway.

"You okay? I've been talking to you for a bit."

I nod.

His eyebrows shift around on his face. "You sure?"

"Just thinking."

"I'm a pretty good listener."

Which I knew to be true even if I wasn't one to share. "My dad invited me and my brother to Christmas Eve at his place."

Cal gives me a nod; it isn't like he's agreeing but more to indicate he's listening. "You haven't talked much about your dad."

"He was in prison. He's supposedly got this set up in the city and wants us to come spend the day with him. I haven't spent any time with him since I was eight."

Cal takes a hammer and punches holes into the pink tile of the bathtub walls with the flat part of the tool. It leaves cracks and spots for him to grab hold and yank the wall out with his gloved hands. It crumbles into the reservoir of the old pink tub. "You don't want to go?"

"Not really. But my brother wants me to." I push the scraper again to dredge up some of the tile glue I missed on the floor. "I think he needs me to." I push the scraper again, and the loosened tiles clank one against another as I push them into the pile.

"Your brother?"

I nod.

Cal steps out of the tub and leans against the wall where the vanity used to be. He slips his hammer into his belt. He hums again, thinking, measuring what he wants to say. "You want some thoughts from an old man?"

"You aren't old."

"Older." He smiles, which makes the corners of his eyes curl.

"Sure."

"When I was your age, my dad and I struggled something fierce. Shit, the guy was always riding my ass to be better, to try harder, to do more, be more. Couldn't make him happy, or so it seemed. We didn't get along so great. I think the biggest disappointment of his life was when I didn't go into the military. All the men in our family had. I didn't join up partly as a rebellion at eighteen but mostly because when I looked at my grandpop, my dad, my uncles, my cousins who had, all I could see were these men, hard and angry, miserable, and hateful. They drank too much, talked about the good 'ole days and threw around insults as if they were trophies. I mean, I didn't know any better, really, but I just felt like I didn't want that for myself."

He rubs his palms together as if to wipe away whatever story he's telling. "I moved out after I turned eighteen and started apprenticing with Dell, the carpenter I told you about. Didn't talk to my dad and he didn't talk to me, either. Just went our own ways and heard about one another's lives through my mom."

He stops, and I think the story's over, but he crosses his hands over his chest and says, "But then, after I turned twenty, my dad had a heart attack. One of those nasty ones. Gone before he knew what happened, which is probably a blessing in a way, for him, but it left me reeling."

He looks down at his feet, pushes some loose grout and tile with his boots. "All those feelings I had stored up for my dad didn't go away. They just sat in the boxes I built for them here." He points at his heart and then his head. "And storing them didn't make me better. Didn't help me when I was struggling with Indigo. It certainly didn't make me better when he passed away, because now I had them stored up and didn't have a way to unpack them. You get what I'm saying?"

It's roundabout but clear enough, so I nod.

"You don't want to haul around the *what if* or the *if only*. They are heavy boxes. Better to unpack them, empty them out."

I nod again.

"Well," Cal straightens and clears his throat. "Better bang out this bathroom, otherwise Max is going to be showering with water from the stove and washcloth."

My face heats thinking about showering with her, her body, kissing her, touching her, and hearing her sounds. I look down to hide my face from Cal and push more tile up with my scraper to hide my thoughts, feeling like I might already be carting around some gigantic boxes.

By the time Max is home for break and finally agrees to share

251

our news with her dad, I'm freaking out. I'm standing at the front door on the new porch and thinking about how different everything is since the first time I stood at the doorway of the farmhouse. When the door opens, Max is there, the warmth from inside shining around her.

She steps out onto the porch, pulling the door shut behind her.

I take a deep breath as if just being near here provides me with oxygen.

She smiles and leans forward. Her hands find their way into my hair at my neck, causing adrenalin to spike and chase my nerves down my spine.

My hands are full, so I can't get as close as I'd like. Sneaking kisses between Cal's comings and goings in the house has been exhilarating and terrifying, but I need this to be real. Old me wouldn't care about sneaking about, but new me does.

She kisses me.

"What was that for?" I ask when she pulls away.

"I just couldn't contain myself." She smiles. "I missed you."

This makes me heat from the inside out. "A lot different greeting than the first time I showed up on your doorstep."

She chuckles, remembering, and opens the door, drawing me inside. "Come on. It's cold out here."

"Right."

My phone pings as we're walking into the house. I glance at it thinking it might be Phoenix, hopeful that going to our dad's for Christmas Eve the next night will be cancelled. It isn't. It's a missed call from Bella. Perplexed, I ignore it. She must have misdialed. I slide my phone back into the pocket of my coat, then take it off.

"Let me take it," she says. "Dad's in the living room." She grins and hangs the coat in a closet that Cal and I built.

I walk through the cased opening into the living room. The fireplace is bright with a fire. They put up a Christmas tree, and it gleams in the low light. Cal is seated in a chair, a cup of something in his hand. He looks up at the sound of my footsteps on the wood floor and smiles one of those soul-grabbing smiles. Now, I see where Max gets hers.

"You clean up nice. Cold out there?" Cal asks from his seat near the fire.

"Freezing." I lift the pan I'm holding. "From my mom. She's started baking. Made you some brownies."

"Does she have a 1950's mixer?" Max smiles. Dimple.

"No. Who knew you could bake without one," I say, smiling back. When I glance at Cal, he's watching us, his face passive as he sips from his cup, but I can feel the observation like the point of a nail. He knows.

"I'll get you some cider," Max says and disappears from the room.

I stand, awkward and unsure even though I've spent the last five months working with Cal, sharing meals with him on off days. He knows. He knows. I can feel it.

"Did you decide about your Dad's place?" Cal asks.

I nod stiffly, waiting for the ax to drop. I clear my throat to get words out. "Yes. Going tomorrow for Christmas Eve."

He hums a noise of approval and takes another sip.

The silence blooms again.

Max walks back through the door, carrying a cup. She hands it to me, and her eyes dance between Cal and me.

I take the cup and offer her a pleading look.

She's staring at me like I'm supposed to know what she's saying with her eyes. I don't, but I can guess. I can't think of a way through this now, no graceful way anyway.

Max grasps my hand.

Cal looks at us, down at our joined hands, then his eyes rise to connect with our faces. He looks completely unruffled. It's terrifying.

"We're dating," Max blurts. "I mean, I decided, we decided that..." her voice fades away.

I sigh. *Shit.* "I asked Max if she would let me take her on a date."

The words tumble out like someone who's tripped and can't catch their fall. "She agreed." I cringe at the awkward finish.

He hums again, taking in the information his eyes jumping between us.

"I'm sorry I didn't tell you sooner," I say, unable to meet his gaze, but then chance a look at him.

Cal sits up and forward on his chair, nonplussed. He reaches over and places his cup on the coffee table. "How long has it been going on?"

"After Thanksgiving," Max says. "A couple of weeks."

He doesn't say anything. His eyes move to the fire in the fireplace. He clears his throat and hums again, though the sound isn't approval this time, but instead like he's found the solution to a puzzle.

I look at Max, unsure what this means. I know that Cal hasn't ever been a man of many words, but I'm not sure how to interpret it in this situation.

She shrugs.

He stands up, retrieves his cup, and walks out of the room.

"Dad?" Max follows him.

I follow her. We stop at the island.

He refills his mug with apple cider, sets it on the counter, and peeks into the stove. "This is ready."

Max—now standing next to me—takes my hand. "Are you upset?"

He straightens. "Should I be? You're both adults. Why would my opinion matter?"

"It matters because I love you." Max says. "And—"

"And," I say, "I was worried about betraying your trust, sir."

He glances at us and then back at the food. "I was young once."

"You're still young," Max says.

He takes a deep breath, sets down the potholders, and turns to face us. "I respect your choices, Wells. And if Griffin is your choice, my opinion is of little import." He looks at me. "And my opinion,

254

Griffin, with respect to this situation and trust, makes for blurry lines. I feel like your job, or my role as a boss, shouldn't be about this but rather about me as Maxwell's dad. You understand what I'm saying?"

"I think so."

"That said, I trust Max. Maxwell trusts you, then I support that trust. Until I don't."

"Yes, sir."

Max squeezes my hand.

"Good. Now, let's eat."

We sit down to share our pre-Christmas dinner. The concrete in my lungs has broken up, except now that I've leveled up in the game and extended my life, there's way more at stake.

Max and Cal.

The old me operated under the reality that it was always just me. Sure, I had my bros, but my choices for the most part weren't about them. Hooking up with girls without consequences didn't impact them (or so I rationalized to myself, which I know now is a crock of shit). Those were choices I made which left me empty but didn't impact anyone I cared about (I certainly didn't care about the girls). New me, though, who's struggling to keep the more vulnerable parts of myself active, recognizes that my choices will now impact at least two very important people in my life. I'm not sure how to navigate it, feeling the pressure not to ruin it, and realizing that might be an impossibility.

3.

When I climb out of the car, I get the first honest glimpse of the apartment building where my father lives. It looks like a pile of shit with a fresh coat of blue paint. The railings are rusty and flaking black paint. I don't think it would be difficult to fix something like that, then stop myself. When had I become someone who thought about fixing things?

Phoenix leads us up the steps to the second floor and down an exterior hallway past assorted doors, keeping care not to touch the untrustworthy railing. I'm content to follow my older brother. When we reach 231, a white door with a window just to the left, we pause, but we don't have to knock because the door opens. On the other side, obviously watching for us, is our father.

"You're here." His voice is a bit too loud, full of nerves.

"Yeah." Phoenix speaks for both of us. I certainly can't find words. I just feel like backing away. "We said we would be."

"I wasn't sure if you'd change your mind." He wraps a big hand around the back of his neck. I notice the tattoo again, his fingers curled around it, and this time wonder what it is. He seems to remember he wants us inside and steps back to allow us through the entry. "Come in. Come in."

Phoenix, the braver of us, passes him across the threshold.

I follow.

I remember my father in contrasts. There is the father who would clamor around on the carpet with us. He'd walk into the house from being away for the week, tired, but happy. My brother and I would tug at his wide hands until he fell to the floor, and then roll all over him, exclaiming it was time for a wrestling match. I'd claim The Dead Man and my brother was always Stone Cold. A wrestling match would ensue, my mother leaning against the opening between the dining room and kitchen, a towel thrown over a shoulder, arms crossed, as she watched us. She never smiled, but the edges around her eyes would soften.

He'd eventually make his way across the room to her, gather her up in his arms and kiss her.

Phoenix and I would object to such a disgusting display.

Then there was the opposing image. He'd walk into the house after being away. Phoenix and I would clamor for his attention, pulling on his hands, one son holding onto each of his. He'd shut us down with a gruff word— "Stop"—the tone of his voice enough to cut our excitement at seeing him off at the knees. We'd retreat. He'd sit and watch TV.

Mom would walk in from the kitchen, the towel in her hands, and frown.

These nights they would fight, after Phoenix and I went to bed.

Jaxon Nichols wasn't a man that hurt us, not in a physical sense. He didn't raise a hand to any of us. He didn't need to. There was always something frightening about him even if he wasn't trying to be. It was as if we were always walking a razor's edge.

On the nights they fought, I would crawl into bed with Phoenix, who'd let me, but he'd turn his back on me. "Don't cry," he'd whisper sharply. "Big boys don't cry."

But I wasn't a big boy.

I realize the mystique I've assigned my father might not be accurate. He's as much a stranger to me as I am to him.

His eyes follow Phoenix first, then find me.

I look away. The naked vulnerability in them makes me uncomfortable.

The apartment is small. We walk into a living area passing over a two-by-two linoleum entry directly onto brown carpet of a living room. There's a small, fake tree with blinking-colored lights on a table next to the window in the room containing mismatched furniture. A small u-shaped kitchen with a bar and three stools a few paces from where we're standing. I notice a small hallway that disappears to the right where I'm guessing the bathroom and a bedroom are located.

"Make yourselves at home." He walks through the room and into the kitchen, where he stops at the stove and lifts a lid off the pot. "I'm not a chef or anything," he tells us. "But I've been told I make some pretty good spaghetti." He glances over his shoulder at us before returning his attention to the pot.

I look at Phoenix as I remove my coat.

He glances at me as he removes his.

We're trying for brother language, but it doesn't seem to be translating. I can't read him, maybe that isn't a shock, though. I'm barely reading my own feelings. I'm all mixed up, a series of contrasts myself. Anxious, angry, wary, insecure.

We drape our jackets over the back of the threadbare couch. It's an ugly monster with a strange shape and garish yellow upholstery. A gray sheet has partially slipped off the back and is stuck in between the cushions.

"Can I get you something to drink? I don't have anything fun. Just juice, milk, soda?"

"Water?" Phoenix asks.

"Yeah," I say. "Water is good."

My brother and I sit down on the stools at the off-white counter-top bar. The ivory cabinets are dated, with wood accents and no hardware. A strange image of us around 10 and 6 comes to mind in which we sit down at this bar. It's a made-up image because it never happened. I imagine that our dad never went to prison and instead he and Mom were just divorced. That we'd show up for visitations, and I'd grown up knowing him. But it didn't happen that way.

I press my teeth together and watch the water glass slide across the counter toward me. "Thanks." I take a sip to keep from looking at him.

"I'm really glad you're both here."

My eyes jump up to him. He's on the other side of the counter, his eyes bouncing between the both of us. He's got a short smile, tentative and hopeful.

"I wasn't sure." His eyes slide to me, and I know that he's thinking about how it went down in front of our house months ago.

I want to say, "it's more than you deserve," but I don't. There's a part of me who's looking at this man and seeing myself. It makes me angry all over, but Cal's words about carrying around heavy bags and how important it is to unpack them reminds me why I'm here.

"Why?" I ask.

Phoenix's head snaps toward me, but I can only see it out of my peripheral vision.

"Why what?" Our dad's gaze flits from me to Phoenix and back again.

"Why weren't you sure?" It wasn't the question I was going to ask. I thought it would be to ask him why he fucked around on Mom, why he was selling guns and drugs, why he threw us away, but I couldn't formulate those questions.

He runs a hand over his head. His hair has grown out some since I last saw him, still short but styled more. His hand latches on his neck, and I look at the tattoo again: letters. It's words. He opens his mouth to say something, then closes it, looks up at us, his hand still holding his neck. Then he turns to look inside the pot on the stove again. "I know I don't deserve to have you here," he finally says.

I clench my jaw to make sure I don't say anything. I'd like to tell him he's fucking got that right.

Phoenix doesn't say anything either.

Our father turns back to us. "There wasn't a day that went by that I didn't regret what happened; what I'd done to get me sent there. And I knew I deserved to lose you. I guess that's why."

"Well," Phoenix jumps in. "We're here. Now."

"You are." The way he says it almost sounds like he doesn't believe it. He opens his mouth to say something, but the front door opens.

"I'm here."

We all turn toward the voice.

A girl with her back to us shuts the door. She has dark hair, a thick braid escaping from underneath a red wool cap. When she turns, I can see she's sixteen or seventeen, her light brown skin glowing with the bite of cold on her cheeks and nose. Her hazel eyes—Nichols' eyes—are looking back at us, wide with surprise. And I know who she is: our sister.

I stand up.

She's holding a set of keys; she visits. Familiar with walking in and not knocking.

My eyes slide to my dad, then back to her. She slips the keys into her coat pocket.

"Mara," our father's voice starts, the tension in the room cracked, then reinforced by the sound. "I thought you were coming tomorrow."

My head turns to look at him. Still keeping us in neat compartments.

"Mom dropped me." Her eyes bounce between Phoenix and me.

"Well," he says. "You're here." Our father smiles a smile that's full of teeth, but it doesn't reach his eyes. He claps his hands together.

"You must be them." She looks away from Dad, and her anger takes up residence on her features, eyebrows drawn together, mouth frowning.

If I wasn't trying to recover from surprise, I might laugh.

"I didn't know I'd finally get to meet you." Her eyes settle on our dad with an angry edge I recognize.

My eyebrows rise over my eyes. I might be offended except I understand her anger, realizing we have more in common that just our father's DNA. Another Nichols family trait.

Phoenix recovers first. He steps toward her and extends his hand. "I'm Phoenix."

"So formal," she says but takes it.

"This is Mara." Dad steps past me.

I haven't said anything.

He turns and looks at me, and I get a glimpse of the tattoo. It's our names: Phoenix. Griffin. Mara. His children. He swivels his hips toward me. "This is Griffin."

I don't know how to react. I'm not ready or prepared for this and feel my protective barriers come up around me. Mara's eyes are on me. "Hey," is all I seem to be able to get out.

My phone buzzes in my pocket.

Grateful for the distraction, I hold it up. "I have to take this." I move past Mara, open the door, and escape out to the cold. When I finally look at my phone, which has stopped buzzing, I've missed a call from Bella. No message.

I stare at the phone stuck, thoughts skipping about for something to land on. The snow is patchy and dirty. Cars speed past intermittently on the roadway beyond. I wish I was with Max, wish I could talk to her about what I'm feeling, but realize that she'd tell me to find my inner strength and walk back into the apartment to get to know a sister who, until a moment ago, was an idea. Now she's a reality, a living, breathing person who is comfortable enough with our dad to walk into his apartment. The thought rattles me. How much more did he give her? Or was it something else? Maybe she visited him in prison? Maybe they wrote. And if so, where does that leave me? I don't know how to answer any of these questions, but I think about Max's rules about relationships and know I'm not following them when it comes to my dad. Not that there's much of a relationship to begin with.

I glance at the phone again, deciding I should call Bella back, in case she needed something. It's seems like the right thing to do, since two missed calls seems more like an intention than a coincidence. I press the button to return to call.

The door opens behind me, and I glance over my shoulder to see who it is. It's Phoenix, and I take a deep breath to clear the pipes. Had it been my dad, I might have walked away.

I end the call still ringing.

"You just going to stay out here all night?"

"I had a call." Not exactly a lie. He doesn't need to know I didn't get to it in time or that it was probably a misdial.

Phoenix leans against a pillar, staying clear of the railing that looks like it might crumble. He tucks his hands up under his arms for warmth. "It's cold out here."

I don't reply with the obvious or meaningless words to mirror his comment. Instead, I mirror him, leaning against a pillar and tucking my hands under my arms.

"You going to go back in?" he asks. "Or just freeze your balls off out here?"

"Did you know she'd be here?"

He shakes his head. "For what it's worth, I don't think Dad did either."

That doesn't make me feel more settled.

"She's comfortable here."

"They both live here. In the city. Probably gets to spend more time with him."

"Makes me feel like just another afterthought."

Phoenix sighs and looks out at the roadway. He doesn't say anything for a time. "Perhaps it isn't about us, you or me. Perhaps, it's just about her and him."

"I don't—" I start to say, 'I don't understand,' but Phoenix interrupts me.

"What I mean is that we shouldn't make their relationship about

262

us."

"Except, it is." I point at the door with accusation. "He cheated on mom. On us."

Phoenix nods. "That isn't her fault."

He's right, and I hate that he is, but it doesn't change the fact that when I look at her, I feel the hurt my father caused by choosing them over us. That's still how I see it.

"Would it be bad if I just wait for you in the car?" I ask.

Phoenix looks down at his feet and sort of shuffles them against the concrete.

"I don't know what to say without it coming out shitty," I add.

He pushes away from the pillar and stands. "What I think is that if you want to know our sister, then you should probably walk back inside and keep your mouth shut. If you don't, then retreating to the car is an option. But I'm thinking the only way for me to move forward is to face the shit that makes me feel uncomfortable." He studies me a moment, stalls, and seems to want to say something else.

"What?"

"I was thinking that you do a lot of running."

"What does that have to do with anything?"

"I just wondered, are you running away from something or toward something?" His eyes measure me a moment. Then he turns and disappears back into the apartment.

I hate his question. I know he isn't talking about actually running, and that observation has me feeling like I've been pegged to a peg board. Avoiding the difficult stuff is so much easier.

With a sigh, I follow him.

Inside, Mara isn't in sight. Dad is back in the kitchen at the stove. He turns when he hears us come back through the doorway, and the relief on his face is a tangible thing that affects his whole body.

"Perfect timing," he says and carries the pot around the kitchen bar, placing it in the center of a compact dinette set on which he laid out place settings.

The incongruence of this scene scrambles my brain. Father, as a criminal. Father, as an angry man. Father, as an absent dad. Now, Father, as a cook. Father, as a decorator. Father, as a family man.

He stands at the end of the table facing us. "I didn't know Mara would be here. I–" He stops, and I see his throat work as if he's trying to keep from crying. He brings his hands together again and rubs them as if to get himself under control. "I thought tonight would be about just you boys." He clears his throat. "Men. But maybe this is better?" He says it like a question, a wish, really, that maybe for the first time his two lives might intersect, creating just one.

Phoenix puts a hand on my shoulder and says, "Of course," making us a united front.

I nod.

"Please. Sit." Dad disappears down the tiny hallway, and I hear him knock on a door.

A few moments later he reappears, with Mara behind him. She's lost the hat and the jacket and is wearing one of those kinds of shirts that slip off the shoulder and leggings, mostly black. I notice she's trying to appear indifferent. I feel that look on my own face.

My heart races with anxiety and tension.

We all sit around the table. Phoenix on one side of me. Dad on the other. Mara directly across from me.

"Mind if I say a prayer?" my father asks. He holds out his hand.

I don't want to take it, hesitating.

He takes it back before I can reject him and folds his hands in front of him instead. Then he bows his head.

Mara's watching me, her gaze aloof but severe, judging me.

I bow my head, so I don't have to look at her.

"Heavenly Father," our dad starts, "thank you for your blessings. Thank you for bringing my kids tonight. Please bless the food to our bodies. In Jesus name, I pray. Amen."

I think of Cal, then. The past is the past, now I must figure the road forward. Phoenix has found a road forward; it would seem even my father has. I'm bumping along this ugly road, trying to gain traction, and maybe have, sort of, but I don't think I have the right tires or something for off-roading. It all feels slippery.

"Let's eat," Dad says.

We do. Sort of. I push the spaghetti around on my plate. My stomach is churning with discomfort. The stretches of silence between us make it worse, though I give our father an A for effort for attempting to engage us. Phoenix tries, too. More than Mara or me. We look like mirrors of one another. I think, Dad and Phoenix have a lot in common. Then I feel like a shitbag for thinking it. I keep my mouth shut; I can't imagine that anything coming out of it will be of any use to anyone. I don't feel very different than I did that night at the Quarry when I unleashed on Max, and she'd only been trying to help. Maybe it's progress that I'm not unloading.

"You run?"

My brother pokes my arm. I look at him.

"Dad asked you a question."

I look at my father. "Excuse me?"

"I didn't know you were a runner."

"Just started." I look down at the plate and force myself to take a bite, so I don't have to talk.

"Mara runs track for her school."

I look up at her.

She's watching me again with that measuring look.

"What events?" Phoenix asks, which is fitting since he was the high school athlete. I sure as fuck wasn't unless partying was a sport.

She looks away. "The 100 Meter hurdle, the 100 Meter, and the 4 by 100 relay." She doesn't look up, focused on her plate. When her eyes don't meet mine again, I wonder if she's as wary of me as I am of her. My perspective has been fixed in her being the thief, but what if she sees us the same way. The idea upends my victimhood, and I look down at the plate again.

Phoenix makes a sound to impart he's impressed. "Fast. Griffin just graduated." He's trying to build bridges. Another A for effort.

"What grade are you?" I ask her, trying to help Phoenix, even though I think I already know. So, when she says, "Junior," I knew that would be her answer. I was two when she was born. A sister. A sister I've never met until this moment. A sister I might have had.

My gaze snaps to my dad with so much anger. I suddenly realize she was never the thief. Jaxon Nichols is the fucking thief. Father, as a cheater. Father, as a liar. My eyes burn with tears I don't want, but I can't seem to keep them locked down. He stole from all of us. He stole from Mom, even Mara's mom. He stole from my brother and me. He stole from Mara. "You're such a piece of shit," I say, and one of the tears escapes down my cheek, making me even angrier. I swipe it away.

"Griffin." Phoenix reaches out a hand and sets it on my forearm.

I shrug out from under his touch, nearly upend his water, and toss my fork on the plate with a loud clank. I open my mouth to fucking unleash all the hurt I'm feeling, but my words stall. Max's rules run through my head, but I can't accept him. I can't forgive him. Instead of words, though, the tears flow, and I can't stop them. "I fucking hate you," I finally say, grasping onto the only thing I can find. Max's rule: share. That's a fucking truthful share. "I fucking hate you," I repeat and stand.

Then I walk out of the apartment to find solace in my car, but there isn't any there either.

Phoenix texts: **What happened to keeping your mouth shut?**

I don't answer him but turn on my car, so it warms up. A while later, I'm calmer and less volatile but in no way able to return to the scene of my crime. I notice a shadow move down the walkway and descend the stairs. I expect Phoenix, but it's Mara.

She hesitates at the bottom of the stairs, shoves her hands into her jacket's pockets, and turns to walk back up, but stalls. Then she straightens her spine, changes her mind, turns back around, and walks to the passenger side of the car.

I unlock it.

She opens the door. "May I?"

I nod at the seat.

She slips inside, keeping close to the door as if I'm the bad guy. I suppose after that showing, I am.

I don't say anything to her, just stare at the ugly apartment building under the glaring, yellow lights.

"I've yelled I hate him at least once a week since he got out."

"I'm behind then. I've only said it twice. Once for each time I've seen him." I trace a thread of regret that she might think she's the cause. "It isn't because of you." I grasp the steering wheel to do something with my hands.

"Really?" Her tone is unguarded a moment, surprised. "I mean, I think I've probably hated you too."

This makes me offer a short laugh that stays in my nose.

I see her relax slightly in the seat, her shoulders dropping.

"He's been a shit father," I say, and I swallow to keep new tears from invading.

"Yeah. He has." She turns to look at me. "I think he's trying though. And that isn't to excuse him or invalidate any of the feelings we have because of the shit he's done, but I do think he's trying to be better."

I turn to look at her. "Aren't you angry?"

"Fucking pissed doesn't begin to cover it." She smiles, and I see Phoenix's smile.

"I got so angry up there because I could have used a sister, you know. I could have used my brother too, but he was–" I stop, unwilling to share Phoenix's story since it isn't mine. "He wasn't around until recently."

She looks down at her hands in her lap, fingertips peeking out from her sleeves. "I don't know about the whole brother-sister thing since I've never had one, but I'd be willing to start as a friend. Griffin." She tests my name.

It's my turn to measure her with a look, to see if her offer is sincere. I don't know her well enough to assess her honesty, but I decide to take it at face value, so I nod and think *Mara* in my head.

Movement outside the car captures my attention. Phoenix crosses the parking lot toward the car.

"That's my cue," she says and opens the passenger door.

She climbs out.

"Mara?"

She bends so that she can see me.

"Thanks."

She smiles and nods, offers Phoenix a "Merry Christmas," and retraces her steps back to the apartment.

Phoenix sits down in the passenger seat, closes the door, and sits with me as we watch her, making sure she gets to the door until she disappears inside. "Well, baby bro. I'll give you credit. I didn't think you'd follow me back into the apartment, and you lasted about thirty minutes longer than I thought you would." He punches my shoulder.

I punch him back.

He rubs his arm and smiles. "Let's go home."

4.

I'm not expecting to see Bella at my front door, her body in the process of turning around to leave when I open it to leave on my way out to pick up Max for our New Year's Eve date. Bella, who's heard the door, turns, only part way, and has a strange look on her face that I'd identify as guilt but only because I've felt it a million times. On her though, the expression isn't familiar, so I could be wrong. She freezes, a strange smile that isn't really a smile, and an uncharacteristic blush stains her pale cheeks.

My engine sputters into a stall, halting at the threshold.

"I...um–" She stops and looks down at the car keys in her hands.

I reorient my own dazed expression and press my restart button. "Bella. I'm surprised to see you. Happy New Year."

She never returned my Christmas Eve call, and aside from those two stray notifications that she called but left no message, I haven't heard from her. I figured they were mistakes, like us. Discomfort wraps me in a bro side hug and smirks.

Bella, still standing on the bottom step half turned toward me, crosses her arms over her chest like she's trying to hold herself together. The pink has drained from her face, making her look paler.

I consider inviting her in, but I'm supposed to be leaving. I'm going on a date. With Max. I don't know what to do because Bella looks weird, and all I can think about is the last time she was here, about the awkwardness, and wishing it was a dream instead of a hazy memory.

She doesn't look good. Her face is strained with sharp eyebrows and a frown, the pale color now looking a little greenish gray. I'm wondering if something happened because her eyes look faded with dark circles as if she hasn't slept. I wonder if maybe she's hungover; she has that pall about her, but in all the time I've known her, I've never seen her appear unsure or tentative.

"Are you okay?" I ask.

"Why?"

Her defensiveness is sort of aggressive.

"You look–" I start and then stall to approach her with my words like I might approach a wild animal. I don't think telling her she looks awful will help me get out of the house to Max. Besides, she looks like she wants to go for my jugular, and I would hate to keep Max waiting– "upset, I guess."

She glances down at her booted feet for a split second and then back up, but she doesn't look at me. She looks past me. "Can I come in? Just for a minute?"

I look over my shoulder as if I'm about to ask permission. I'm suddenly feeling small and young. There's no one else here, and though I don't feel tempted by Bella anymore, I just feel weirded out. Then again, I reason, I should be polite. She looks atypical and maybe she just needs a friend. "Sure." I step back.

She climbs the last two steps and passes me as she enters the house.

There was a time not so long ago when all I thought I wanted was Bella. Her beauty. Her body. Her mystique. Now though, the powder scent is pungent, and I find myself comparing her to Max. Max, who's tall and strong. Max, whose smile makes me weak and strong at the same time. Max, who makes me laugh and whose arms

270

are just right. Max, who smells like cinnamon and spice. Max, who makes me feel like I'm starving.

I need to get Bella gone.

"Would you like some water?" I try politeness to figure out what's brought Bella to my door. The last time we spoke she wanted to get her life together.

She looks even paler now, like she's ill. She swallows, shakes her head, and croaks, "Bathroom?" Her eyes are gigantic with panic.

"Hallway," I say with a wave of my hand, but before I've even finished, she darts through the house, hand over her mouth, and disappears down the hall.

I follow, to see if she made it.

The door is wide open.

I stop outside.

Bella is on her knees in front of the toilet, getting sick.

"Oh. Shit. You okay, Bella? Obviously not," I ramble, rolling my eyes at myself. I back out of the room as I say, "I'll get you some water."

By the time I've walked into the kitchen and filled a glass of water, she appears at the end of the hallway looking less pale but still tentative. I set the glass on the counter and slide it across the surface like a peace offering. "Hung over?" I ask.

"I'm pregnant." She hasn't moved. Just stands like a statue at the end of the hallway.

I look at the glass on the counter and blink as I undergo a hard reset. I've gone offline, deciding I hadn't heard her correctly. What did she just say? "Hung over?" I repeat, as if to replay the last few seconds.

"It's yours."

My brain begins to spin in the opposite direction, enacting a protective force field. "What?"

"The baby. It's yours."

Now my brain hijacks the rest of me. I lean against the counter by the sink on autopilot and cross my arms. My brain is writing a list, the wheels spinning methodically to when we were together.

My birthday.

We got drunk.

We made out. Drunk.

I broke my rule.

We had sex.

No condom.

"I'm on the pill," she'd said.

I broke my rule.

"You're on the pill," I say now. I sound like a robot.

She moves from the hall and stops on the other side of the counter. "I am. I was. I don't—no. Something happened. I didn't know about the antibiotics. I didn't know." She swipes her eyes with her hand and crosses her arms over her chest again.

"Antibiotics?" I feel like my head is an empty house. The words echo inside the space, bouncing around, and I'm struggling to fit them into the right groove to put the meaning together.

"I'd been on antibiotics for—" she stops. "Why doesn't matter. It was before us—that night. It affects the pill's reliability. I didn't know." She swallows down what I assume must be guilt.

"Antibiotics," I repeat.

I look at her, trying to piece together what she's said. She looks different. Sounds different. Is dressed differently. Leggings, a long violet sweater peeking out from beneath the coat she hasn't removed. Her hair is flowing out of from under a knit, winter cap. She's pale and without the make-up she's usually wearing. This is Bella undone, and the most vulnerable I have ever seen her.

"You're sure?" I ask.

She nods, then pauses as if considering what I've asked. "Are you asking if I'm sure you're the father?"

Now that she's said it, I am. I don't want to say she's slept around, but I can't not say it either. "Are you sure?"

She shakes her head like I'm the biggest disappointment. I suppose she isn't wrong. "I knew I should have left." She turns and

272

disappears into the living room. I don't know if she means that night or earlier at the door.

My body comes online, and I move, follow her. "It's a fair question."

She flings the front door open, and it smacks the wall with a pop. "It's fucking yours, Griff." I think she'll stop there, but she doesn't. "You're the only guy I was with. And for the record, I've only been with one other guy before you, so thanks for the slut-shame." She turns away to leave.

I grasp her shoulder to keep her from storming from the house. "It's still a fair question," I say. "I wasn't trying to slut-shame you. You show up telling me you're pregnant with my kid–" my throat closes on the word– "and you didn't think I'd ask?"

She turns to the side, shaking my hand from her shoulder, and buries her face in her hands as she bursts into tears. "I was hoping it wasn't real," she sobs brokenly, her voice sounding muted as it escapes between her palms.

Not sure what to do, I stand there. One part of me wants to push her out the door and pretend the last ten minutes never happened, but another part of me figures she's scared. I fucking am, but I need to be strong. I reach out and put my hand on her shoulder again.

Still sobbing, Bella turns toward me, steps into my space, and buries her face against my chest.

Shit.

At first, I stand there with my hands out to my sides.

"I was just starting to get my life together," she says through her tears.

I put my arms around her and stand there stiffly, wishing I could teleport away.

"What are you going to do?" I ask.

"Keep it."

"Really?" It's the wrong thing to say, but I'm thinking there isn't a right thing to say. I'm struggling to swallow suddenly. A kid? Me?

I'm fucking nineteen.

She steps away from me, her eyes as hard as shiny rocks. "I don't want anything from you. I can do it by myself. I just thought you should know."

It's the wrong thing to say. I feel my gaze crystalize into rocks too, and suddenly I'm angry, so fucking pissed. Not at her. Yes, at her, but also at myself. I broke my fucking rules! I want to scream. And Max. Oh my fucking god, Max. I'd forgotten. My earlier joy crumbles when I realize—even if I already knew and told her—she doesn't deserve my shit show.

I feel sick to my stomach.

I take a step away from Bella to put more distance between us.

"Griff?" she asks.

"I think you should go," I say and am surprised by my calm. "I need to think."

She hesitates, but then turns and walks out of the house. The screen door squeals closed behind her, and I'm rooted to the floor, staring outside. I watch her get into her car. I watch her drive away. I watch the empty street, but nothing computes. I just stare until the dark finalizes outside, and I blink. I've forgotten something. I was supposed to do something, go somewhere.

A kid?

Where was I supposed to go, I wonder?

I'm going to be a dad? My father is a piece of shit.

I'm too young.

Where was I going?

I was getting my life together, I think. *It was finally feeling right.*

"With Max," I say out loud to only myself.

I sit down on the couch and stare at the TV even though it's cold and blank. I can see the outline of my shadowed reflection. It's exactly how I feel, like a shadowed version of myself. A fake. I can't face Max. She told me not to ruin it, and I'm going to blow it up.

It's been a month.

I could barely make something work for a month.

And I feel my dad seep into my bones and muscle. A family with my mom and us, the surprise of Mara. The sins of my father. I think I might throw up.

I drop my head into my hands and scrunch my fingers up into my hair. Tears slice the back of my eyes, and I'm pretty sure I'm about to bleed from my eye sockets. I can't breathe.

I can't breathe.

I can't breathe.

Suddenly, I can't sit anymore. I can't be here. I can't be in my skin. I can't be me. I stand and rush from the house; I don't even grab a coat. I get into my car and drive. I don't know where I'm going. I just drive until I'm in Tanner's driveway. And then I'm at his door. Knocking. And it opens, and Tanner's on the other side.

"Griff?" I hear him ask.

I open my mouth to say something sarcastic, to hide behind the pain and fear that's bubbling up, but I can't. Nothing comes out of my mouth, but like an idiot, burst into tears.

Men don't cry, I hear tough Griff chastise my vulnerable self, except I can't stop it.

And Tanner—because he's always been bigger and better than the way I've seen myself—wraps his arms around me and lets me.

5.

Tanner dumps all the sandwich stuff on the giant island in the kitchen of his house.

I watch him, wary, because I've just erupted my weakness everywhere, which my former best friend, who I insisted wasn't my friend anymore, just witnessed. And yet, here I am, sitting at the counter at his house where I've sat a million times. Where he's always made me a sandwich. Where we've never talked about real stuff, but I know that he's tried, and I shut him down.

I feel like a jerk.

"While I'd like to think those tears were because you missed me," he says with a smile, "I'm thinking there's more to them than that."

I watch him draw bread slices out of the plastic bag and then look down at my hands crushed between my knees. "Yeah." My eyes trace the dark grain of the light marble, and my shoulders slump forward like I'm carrying the weight of the world. I'm going to have a kid. I'm going to be a dad. I'm nineteen. I don't want to say it out loud and make it real.

Tanner picks up the packages of varied cheese. "Swiss or

cheddar?"

I don't have the heart to tell him I don't think I can eat it. Historically, we'd be getting ready to play video games, and I wish that was the reality today. I can't find a historical me, I just sit and look up at him occasionally, before returning to the veins of the marble.

Tanner hasn't said much since I got here besides offering me comfort as I cried. Now, he's focused on the sandwich. "Both," he says without waiting, nodding to himself.

I'm embarrassed but look up from a particularly dark gray vein.

He looks good. Altered somehow. I might think there was an alien wearing his skin. He's filled out too, even though he didn't have much more muscle to add. Girls always thought he was the hot one—all that construction work. I was the dark one, the mysterious bad boy with the father in prison. Skinny, wiry, and angry. I'm the same, but Tanner, even though he's concentrating on adding cheese to the bread, is emanating joy as if he found a charging station and plugs in each night. He still looks like my former best friend, but I can sense he's different.

"My dad says he saw you." He picks up the turkey and adds it to the cheese.

"Yeah."

"At his AA meeting."

"I didn't know you were talking to him again."

Tanner lays a clump of iceberg lettuce on top of thin sliced cold cuts. "Yeah." The fact we haven't talked in six months sits on that word. "Actually, we all started seeing therapists. We've gone together a bunch of times, as a family."

A shrink? The idea unnerves me, and I think about the times we both made fun of the idea. Maybe I made fun of the idea, and he just smiled.

"No. I don't feel like my balls are shrinking," he says as though heading me off before I can say it. I realize when the words leave his mouth, they sound like something I would have said before. By the sudden strain around his mouth, it bothers him.

He slathers the bread with mustard, never mayonnaise on his, because he hates it. When we were first friends, I made him a sandwich at my house, bread, bologna, and mayonnaise. He tried to eat it but kept gagging. The memory makes me smile, sort of.

I wonder if I should say "I'm sorry" now.

He slides the plate stacked with the sandwich across the counter toward me. I think about the glass of water I'd offered Bella and then shake my head to refocus on the sandwich again. I'm supposed to be taking Max to dinner. I'm supposed to be getting Max right now.

"I didn't know you were going to AA."

"I went the once. With Phoenix."

"He's back."

I nod.

"Good?"

I nod again. "Seems so."

It's his turn to nod, but then his eyes study me with too much awareness. "You look like shit."

"Thanks." I don't smile. I'd like to correct him and say *I am shit*, but I don't. It's common knowledge around these parts. I glance around, suddenly wondering what I'm doing here.

"You just going to sit there or are you going to tell me what that was all about?" He's leaning against the counter, his hands on it framing his hips.

I look at him and open my mouth to tell him I'm sorry, that I've missed him, but the words don't come out. Right behind them are the facts of what Bella just told me and the awareness that in the face of crisis the first person I'd needed, the first person I'd come to is the one I'd told wasn't my friend. Yet here I am. Here he is, accepting my weakness, making me a sandwich, and asking me what's wrong. It makes me feel terrible all over again.

He steps forward and leans on his side of the island. "I'll go first. I'm sorry about that night, in the parking lot. I shouldn't have punched you. And the night at the Quarry when I lost my cool."

He's apologizing.

I scoff.

"What?"

"Why do you always have to be so goddamn perfect?" I maybe say this harsher than I want.

His eyebrows scrunch together. "What the fuck, Griff?"

"No. Shit." I shake my head and hold up a hand. "I don't—you're just a good guy. And I'm not. I'm the one who owes you the apology. I shouldn't have said what I said about Rory. And all the things I said about you and Matthews. I was a dick. And you go and apologize first."

He sighs. "You aren't a bad guy."

I look up at him, and I feel the tears fill my eyes again. I want to cut down the kindness he's offered. I hear a lie even if he hasn't offered it as one. That's the thing about Tanner, he believes it. I swipe at a tear as it slips from my eye and dip my chin to my chest to hide it.

"What is it?"

"I'm just sorry," I say. "I wasn't thinking for a long time." I can't meet his eyes.

"We aren't together. Matthews and me."

I look at him.

He's frowning, clearly bothered by what he's shared. "So, you were right."

"I'm sorry. I don't want to be right."

"Yeah. Me too. I really like her. Check that. I love her."

My heart snags on his admission. It's so big and bold. Brave. I have to look away from how shiny he is and stare at the sandwich. "It was obvious. In retrospect."

"We still talk."

"Is that good?"

"Yeah." His dark eyebrows shift over his dark brown eyes with a new thought. "Did you just say you're sorry? Multiple times? And did you just admit you were wrong?" He pauses and looks around. "Where's the real Griff? You are an imposter."

"Fuck off," I tell him.

He laughs. "Oh. It is you."

I can't help but smile even if it's tight and doesn't chase away the dark creatures settling into my bones.

He pinches a crust on his sandwich and then looks at me. "We both messed up, but you've never stopped being my best friend, my brother, Griff. People do shitty things all the time, but I'm learning more about the idea that when I forgive them, and myself, I release the power it has over me and shit."

I want to say, "that's deep," but I bite my tongue. I recognize that comment for what it is, discomfort with his blatant vulnerability and the truth. I feel better being here right now, as frightening as it was to show up. Hadn't Phoenix said something similar? I feel better talking to my best friend again, clearing the air. Even as terrified as I am at this moment for a million reasons, listening to him and telling him "I'm sorry" feels freeing.

"You going to say something sarcastic?"

I shake my head with recognition that Tanner does know me.

"So... you going to tell me what's wrong?" He offers a kind smile, and I can see he isn't making fun of me. "You can talk to me, you know."

I just blurt it out. I don't think it's something that can be eased into. "Bella's pregnant."

His face relaxes, then opens up with surprise in increments until he swipes it with his hand, the other arm crossing over his chest and grasping onto his underarm. "Shit."

I poke at the sandwich with my finger, leaving a depression in the bread.

"Shit," he repeats, watching me. Now his arms are crossed, both holding onto his underarms. He opens his mouth to say something, but then doesn't.

I know he doesn't know what to say. I don't either, but I just tell him what I know. "She wants to keep it, and she doesn't want anything from me."

"So, you and Bella slept together? But you aren't together?"

"We hooked up once, on my birthday." He doesn't have to say it because I do: "I broke the rules." I bury my hands in my hair, elbows on the countertop. "I got too fucked up, and then I didn't use a rubber because she said she was on the pill."

"Think it matters now one way or the other how it happened? Kind of just is."

He's right, so I share what's really bothering me. "I just started seeing this other girl." I glance at him without moving my head from my hands.

Tanner leans back.

"And she's awesome."

He moves around the island and pulls his plate across the counter to where he sits down next to me. "Okay."

"And how the fuck am I supposed to drag her into this?"

"You like her?"

"Yeah."

"Love her?"

I shrug. "I don't—"

"If you like her and you think she's worth having in your life, then it isn't your choice to make for her. You have to come clean and let her decide for herself."

But how could she choose me? I've made it impossible. I wouldn't choose me. The moment I tell her some other girl is pregnant with my kid, she's going to tell me to go to hell, like she should. I warned her I'd find a way to ruin it.

My phone pings. "I'm supposed to be picking her up for a date right now." I pull the phone from my pocket.

"Griffin Nichols is going on a date?" Tanner's dark brows shift over his dark eyes, and he grins. "She must be special then."

I can't keep from smiling, thinking about Max like that, but it's subdued and difficult to hold onto; I glance at the spiderweb screen and groan.

It's Max:

> Where are you?

"Dude. What the fuck is wrong with your screen? Get that fixed. Is it her?"

I nod.

Tanner swallows the bite. "First. Why did you let me make you a sandwich? Second, get the fuck out of here."

"I don't know if I can go."

"Why? We just established you have to tell her."

It's on the tip of my tongue to say I'm scared, but that's not something I've admitted before. I don't think I have ever said those words to anyone but Max. Her rules run through my mind. Trust is the first one. I glance at Tanner, and after the last thirty minutes, I know he won't think differently of me, but my own insecurity keeps me from telling it so honestly. I skirt it. "I don't want to lose her."

"Not your choice. It's hers. But you shouldn't decide for her, Griff."

"You're right."

I text her back, *on my way*, and stand up.

"Let me know how it goes." Tanner follows me to the front door, grasping my shoulders and squeezing as if I'm on my way to the boxing ring.

"Okay." I start down the sidewalk.

"Griff?" Tanner calls after me. "I'm glad you stopped by."

"Me too."

I mean it, and feel like, maybe knowing he's got my back, I can face talking to Max. My heart is stuck under water and drowning, though I'm afraid I've just drowned this relationship, and it's DOA even before I tell her the truth.

6.

The farmhouse looks like a holiday card when I park the car and get out. The glowing Christmas lights that line the room, the tree still twinkling in the window to the right of the door. The snow glows in the moonlight. I walk to the front door, the peace of the picture doing nothing to relieve my apprehension at what I need to do. Instead, I feel worse. The beauty makes me feel like a dark stain mucking up the perfection of it all.

I stare at the evergreen wreath hanging on the front door, but I don't knock. I don't have my coat, and I know it's cold, but I also don't really feel it. I'm numb inside and out. As I stand there, I recall all the moments I've spent with Max since she's been home. The dates, the time spent with her dad, the drives. We've joked, laughed, touched, kissed. There's been the hazy reminder that I didn't deserve it with her, but new Griffin accepted it as a gift. Old Griff always knew the score. I take a step away from the door.

I pull my phone from my pocket and text Max:

> Something's come up. Can't make it.

Then I retreat for the car.

I'm to the gate when Max's voice stops me. "What's come up?"

I turn to look at her.

She's backlit by the lights they put up for Christmas, looking so pretty it hurts. She's shrugging into a coat over a black dress. Her hair is down, shining in the light. "Griffin? What is it? You've been standing out here for almost five minutes."

I swallow and take a few steps toward her.

"Where's your coat?"

I glance down at myself and picture it draped over the chair by the front door at my house where I'd set it, the moment I'd found Bella on the doorstep. I shiver. "I forgot it."

She meets me on the sidewalk, takes my hand, and leads me back to the car. "Get in. Heat on."

I follow her directions.

She gets into the passenger's side seat and turns to face me. "What's going on?"

It's not your choice. It's hers.

But I don't know how to get the truth beyond my throat. I know her rules, but I don't know how to share this. I don't even know what to think of it myself. I feel like I'm going to be sick, lean back in the seat with a groan, and close my eyes.

With a worried sound, Max leans forward and touches me, a light pressure on my arm. "Griffin? What is it? Are you okay? Your family?"

I shake my head. "No. No. I'm not okay." It comes out harsher than she deserves and not as I intended, but it doesn't change the fact that it does. "I didn't want to do this now."

"You can talk to me."

"Not about this."

She sighs. "What is it? You got some girl pregnant." She snorts at the impossibility of it.

I wince, shudder, and turn to face her.

When she sees my face, her laughter stops, and that beautiful smile—the one I love so much—fades. She retracts her touch. "That was a joke."

I feel myself crumble and collapse into a tight box. "Except that it fucking isn't. I slept with Bella, on my birthday, and didn't fucking follow my own rules. We were both drunk as fuck. I didn't use protection because she said she was on the pill. She showed up tonight and told me she's pregnant and she's keeping it. That I'm going to have a kid. I'm fucking nineteen. Is that a joke to you?"

Her eyes narrow. "The same Bella that was a bitch to you?"

"One and the same."

"No. I don't think it's a joke. You can keep your self-righteous asshole routine to yourself." Her hand comes up to cover her mouth, and I see she's trembling. Her voice quivers when she says, "You slept with the girl who said those awful things about you?"

I shrug. "She was willing."

"Right. Your rules." She turns away from me and faces forward in her seat. "Do you love her?"

I scoff. "No, I don't love her. I just fucked her." It's cold, and the perfect example of old Griff putting up armor. "I fucking told you. I told you."

"Told me what?"

"I ruin shit. See?" I pause, then say, "You should just go."

She turns to look at me, and her look terrifies me. It isn't one of anger, which I'd get. It isn't a look of disgust because that's what I feel already. It isn't a look that communicates contempt. That would be fitting. All of those would help me feel justified. Instead, it's an awful look of sadness. Her eyes have filled with tears and her chin quivers even as she tries to fight it. A few tears escape the confines of her eyes as they spill down her cheeks. She swipes them away with her fingertips, and all I want to do is gather her into my arms and hold her, tell her I'm sorry. I want to bury my face in the space between her neck and shoulder and cry too. But I don't. I don't deserve it. I don't deserve her.

"I told you that you couldn't ruin this." She pauses to gather her words again because they crack apart with her tears. When she finds a way to finish, she says, "I was wrong. Know this, Griffin, it isn't

285

because of you got some girl pregnant. It's because you didn't trust me to be on your side."

She gets out of the car, throws the door closed, and walks back into the house.

Even though every part of me stretches to go after her, I don't. Instead, I yell at the top of my lungs in the confines of my car, hit the steering wheel until it hurts, then lean forward to cry. I can't face her because I'm right—I don't deserve her—and she's right—I didn't trust her—so I drive home.

When I get there, I walk into an empty, dark house. The silence and loneliness greet me and sort of smile a dark smile, as if to remind me this is exactly what I'd accepted all those months ago. I pick up the discarded jacket on the chair. I am now alone. I walk through the hallway like a ghost. When I make it to my bedroom, I cocoon myself in the blankets on my bed, shivering, and wish for the relief of sleep so I don't have to feel anything at all.

JANUARY

1.

"Griffin?"

My mom is on the other side of my door. She's knocked several times today. This is her fourth time, and this is the fourth time I don't respond.

"Griffin? Cal called."

His name makes my stomach ache. I was supposed to help him the rest of the break with the upstairs bathroom. I haven't shown up. Partly because of Max, but a lot because of him, too. I haven't called. I'm afraid to look into his eyes having broken his daughter's heart. I hate me for it. I've fucked up all around, and there isn't anything to do to fix it. No hammers, no drywall, or the ability to call the electrician or plumber. It's just like that old wood that isn't salvageable. I'm that old wood to haul to the dump.

The door creaks open. I'm facing the blank wall where the poster once was. The paneling is rather intricate. The fake wood grain and the grayish tone. It's amazing how studying it for a while makes your brain tired and sleep easier.

"Griffin?"

The bed depresses at my feet, and I know Mom's sitting there, waiting for me to respond. Here's the thing, I figure I can outlast anyone.

"Hon? What's wrong?"

At first, I decided not to talk to anyone. Since fighting with Max a few nights ago, New Year's has come and gone. Mom and Bill, Phoenix and now even Tanner have checked in, but aside from words to keep them at bay and pacify their worry, I've insulated myself.

The semester starts next week, and I know that Cal will be putting Max on a bus today to return to campus. The thought of what's happened is like a vine of thorns tightening around me. Even if I wanted things to be different, I can't. I'll be ripped to shreds to even try.

"Griffin. I need you to talk to me."

How am I supposed to talk to her? Her one direction: *Don't you ever bring a girl home pregnant, or I will knock you into next year.* How do I come clean? It isn't because I don't want to. I could use some guidance here, but I just don't know what to say. I'll just disappoint her. I'll prove her right. I'm a fuck up and couldn't make it past the sins of my own father. Bella may have absolved me of being involved, but it doesn't feel like absolution. It feels like as much of a prison sentence as my father.

When I turned thirteen and Phoenix spilled the beans about our dad's other family, I remember vowing to never be like him. Short of drawing blood in some ritual I'd made up in my head, I'd written it somewhere. *Fuck Jaxon Nichols. I will never, ever be a shitty dad to my kids. I will be there for them. I won't cheat on my wife. I won't do drugs or go to jail. I'll do the right thing. Signed, Griffin Nichols.*

And I failed.

All around.

And Bella absolving me feels just more of the same shit.

Griff is the economy car.

Griff is a douche.

Griff doesn't need to be held accountable; he's going to prison anyway.

Griff is a low-class piece of shit.

Griff isn't worth it; he's worthless.

I don't realize I'm crying until my mom has crawled into the bed behind me and has wrapped her arms around me. She's cooing like she used to when I was eight and would wake up to nightmares after my dad had been arrested. "Baby. I'm here," she says over and over, and I cry and cry and cry. I can't seem to staunch the flow of this river of shit coming out of me.

I don't know how long she lays there.

Sleep creeps in to bring me relief and rest.

The next time I open my eyes, she's walking in again, and I wonder if it's Groundhog Day, except there's a blue tinge to the room, because the sun has gone down. Now, I'm facing the door.

"Sit up," she says.

I listen, feeling clearer. "Don't you have work?"

"I called in. Family first." She's carrying a tray, well, something flat functioning like a tray. "Make a space for this."

I flatten out my legs, and she sets what looks like a framed mirror on my lap. "Was this hanging in the living room?" I ask.

She chuckles. "Yeah. I needed something to put the soup on. Works, right?"

It makes me smile even though the rest of my face feels like I've been repeatedly punched.

There's a steaming bowl of chicken soup, a napkin, a sleeve of saltine crackers and some milk. I'm not sure I'm hungry, but it's nice. Nice to have my mom here. Nice to have someone taking care of me. "Thanks."

She sits on the bed at my feet. "It's a bribe." She offers me a grin. I've seen it on Phoenix's face, even on my own. "You've been holed up in here for days, and it's time to talk."

I pick up the spoon to the right of the bowl and slip it into the hot liquid to stir it, which helps me to keep from looking at her. I don't say anything.

She sighs. "Griffin. I have always afforded you your privacy within reason. I can tell this isn't within reason, son. I know you're

291

an adult and can make your own decisions, but just because we're old enough in the eyes of the law, doesn't mean we're ready. That's what your parents are for."

My eyes flick from the bowl and its rotating liquid back to her face. I can see her worry there, the way the corners of her eyes are weighted. The taut stretch of her mouth. But she doesn't look angry, which is her usual emotion with me. She's holding her hands in her lap, squeezing her fingers together, releasing and squeezing. Worried.

"Okay. Maybe I haven't been the best parent in the guidance department. But I'm here to be your mom. There's been so many things I've done wrong and haven't been able to be, but I'm here."

"You've always been here," I say, to pardon her of the times she's been gone.

She shakes her hand. "Not enough. I mean, it was a necessity, but it ate at me how little I could be with you and Phoenix because we had to make ends meet. Wishing doesn't change shit, but I'm here now." One of her hands wraps around my ankle.

I need to say it, as terrified as I am to say it to her. I can't hold it in anymore. "I got a girl pregnant."

Her face relaxes and takes on a neutral quality which looks weird on her, and I curl in on myself in preparation for her to unload.

"It was an accident," I add, as if it makes it okay.

She begins nodding and glancing about the room as if trying to locate something she's misplaced. "Shit. Okay. Shit. Okay." She stands, crosses her arms over her chest, and walks out of the room. It isn't a split second before she walks back in. "Okay." Her arms drop to her sides, and she returns to the end of my bed.

"Mom?"

Her gaze finally connects to mine, her eyes full of tears, but they aren't falling, just shining there. She smiles through them. "It's okay. It will be okay. Is it Cal's daughter?"

I shake my head. "No. No."

She presses a palm to her heart.

"We ended things." I'm not sure if it was officially ended or more just me disconnecting after facing her sadness, but Mom doesn't need the details.

"Who is it?"

"A girl from high school named Bella."

"And does she know what she wants to do?"

"Keep the baby."

"Okay," she repeats again and takes a giant breath as though she's trying to fill her tightening lungs with oxygen. "God. I could use a cigarette."

"You quit."

"I know." She pinches the bedspread fabric between her fingers. "And what do you want?"

A harsh breath tears through my chest. This is the first time anyone has asked me what I want. The question puts my body in suspended animation. Bella didn't. She made her choice to keep the baby, which I get is within her rights. It's her body, after all. Tanner didn't ask. Max was blindsided. I haven't even thought about what I want or that I had a choice in the matter.

I don't know what I do want, but I know what I don't want. "I don't want to be like Dad."

She tilts her head. "What does that mean?"

"Bella said she didn't want anything from me, but that isn't what I want, I don't think. I don't want to not be a dad for my kid." I think about the list I made at 13 and failed. I think of how things are with my dad. "I want to have a relationship with my kids. I want to be a real dad, not just an idea of one."

The tears in her eyes spill down her cheeks, which is strange to see because my mom doesn't cry. She swipes at the tears on her cheeks, sniffs, then smiles. "Don't hold these tears against your mom, okay?"

"Are you mad?"

She shakes her head. "No. I'm worried, but I'm proud of what you just said." She smiles again. "You need to let the girl know how you feel."

I look at the soup again. "Yeah."

She stands and swipes her hands over her thighs. "I'm glad you told me." She leaves the room but then pokes her head back in. "What are you going to do about Cal?"

About this issue, my stomach turns, and I haven't even eaten anything. I set the cracker down on the napkin and swallow my feelings. "I'll call him back," I say.

She nods and leaves me alone with my thoughts.

Calling Cal will be one of the hardest things I've ever had to do in my life. I want to avoid it at all costs. Besides hurting Max, I've broken his trust. I've let him down, and the last person besides Max I would have ever wanted to hurt would be Cal. Facing that feels like a giant mountain I have no idea how to climb.

I think of Bella standing at my door the other night. Of her hesitancy and her fear, but also of her bravery to come to see me rather than to share the news over the phone or text.

I pick up the cracker again.

As terrifying as it sounds, I need to face Cal face-to-face. It's the right thing to do. If I can't do that, how could I ever look myself in the eye again?

2.

I text Max: | I'm lost. |

She doesn't answer.

A couple of days later, I text her again:

> I've gone round and round about what happened when I went to see you.

> I'd like to tell you, but I don't know if any of it makes sense.

> I told my mom about the pregnancy. I expected her to flip out. She didn't.

> She was helpful, actually, and it made me wonder how many other times I iced her out when she could have been there for me.

> The thought made me circle back to you and what you said...

that I hadn't trusted you to be on my side...

My mom was on my side, and I told her the truth. She asked me a question no one else did: What do I want?

I know what I don't want. I don't want to be like my dad.

I want to be like Cal.

I don't want to always push people away. I don't want to be THAT version of Griffin anymore.

I've decided to tell Bella what I want.

She doesn't answer. I'm not sure I expected her to, but I miss my friend.

The next day I text her:

When Bella showed up at my door, I'd been getting ready to come and get you for our New Year's Eve date.

There she was and I freaked out because I didn't want her there. I wanted our date.

I tried to get rid of her, but then she dropped the news about the baby. I didn't do a very good job of hearing it. When am I ever very good at the emotional stuff?

She told me I didn't have to be involved just that I should know. The first place I went to was Tanner's.

Yeah. Weird huh?

From a fight—we don't talk for six months—to me showing up on his doorstep.

You know, he wasn't mad. I said I was sorry, of course, but he apologized too. I told him about the baby and about you. And you know what he said,

that I needed to tell you and trust you to know what you needed.

I thought he made sense and I planned to do that.

I stood outside your door trying to find words to tell you. Then I freaked out because none of them worked in my head.

And when you followed me, you looked so amazing—you always do—and I wasn't prepared to face you. I was prepared for the worst-case scenario in my head—you not being a part of my life—because there wasn't a best case.

There usually isn't a best-case scenario in my head, ever, so I've always made the worst case happen.

That's how I ruin things.

I don't blame you or anything for leaving. I blame myself for pushing you out the door. I don't hold you to what you said, you know, about not leaving. I made it so you didn't have a choice.

She doesn't answer.

3.

Bella lives in a little house on the opposite side of town. It's a rundown version of a little bungalow with arched windows and doors and a plaster exterior, but it lost any luster it once had. A light brown color with dark brown trim where the wood flower boxes and trim are peeling and rotted, and the plaster is flaking away, leaving exposed patches.

Those need to be fixed, I think.

Evergreen bushes dot the perimeter of the house, but their lack of shape makes them appear like dark green globs of ink leaking through a thin page. The lawn—or the weeds, since it's hard to tell which—is brown and overgrown in its drab winter coat sprinkled with mounds of intermittent snow. It's the first time I've been to Bella's, though there were many times when I'd tried to get here. Now that I am, walking up the sidewalk and into the alcove of the recessed front door, the daylight reveals a reality rather than the fantasy of what Bella once represented to me.

I knock on the door. The pounding of my knuckles against the wood matches the rhythm of my heart. My nerves are exposed and vulnerable, so I bounce on the balls of my feet while I wait. They aren't enough to make me run like I might have once done, however. I know I need to talk to Bella for me. If I keep my mouth closed and avoid the truths on my heart about this baby, I'll regret it forever. So nervous bouncing seems a good compromise.

The dark brown door with a little caged peep window opens a crack to a child's face, a little blond girl maybe nine or ten years old who reminds me of a mini-Bella. "Who are you?"

"You shouldn't open the door to strangers," I tell her.

She shuts the door.

"I'm looking for Bella. I'm Griffin. Is she home?" I say to the now closed door.

The girl yells at Bella on the other side of the door that her baby daddy is here.

After that announcement, I'm not sure Bella will even show up, but a few moments later, the door opens.

Bella steps out, shrugging into her jacket, and closes the door behind her. "What are you doing here?"

"Can we talk?"

"Oh? You're ready now?" She crosses her arms, the sound of the slick fabric of the coat hushing both of us.

I take a calming breath to wrangle my nerves, my thoughts, my patience, and catch movement in the window behind Bella. The little girl I think is probably Bella's sister is staring out at us through the glass. I refocus on Bella. "Are you upset I needed time to process?"

She zips up the coat, shoves her hands into the pockets, and shakes her head. "No. I guess not."

As much as I want to rush through this, the blue eyes pinned on me through the glass feel invasive. "Want to walk?" I nod toward the face in the window.

Bella glances behind her, then turns to look out at the street where my car is parked in front of her house. She starts down the steps to the sidewalk. I shove my hands in the pockets of my coat and follow until we're side by side. We start down the street, walking slowly as if out for a summer stroll, but the January cold tightens cords around us. From the white steam of breathing to the grays of the world around us, the world feels stripped and ready to be filled in with color.

"I probably shouldn't have surprised you like that," she eventually says.

I consider her words. "I think it would have been a surprise no matter how you told me."

We walk on, the sound of our shoes crunches the loose asphalt and reconstituted snow.

"I didn't—you know—surprise you because I wanted to pressure you or anything. I just felt like it was only right to tell you." She stops for a moment. "I meant it when I said that I don't expect anything from you."

"That's why I'm here."

"Oh?"

I stop. I need energy to formulate my words, but I can't look at her. I don't want to lose my nerve. Not because of her so much as this version of me she knows. Bella has been mean, and I didn't expect any better, more acquiescent to the idea that she is somehow better than me. My response with her has always been to find the hard shell. It's safer under there. I commit to holding onto vulnerable Griffin, the one Max saw and liked. The one Mara said she'd like to befriend. The one Tanner forgave. "You didn't ask what I wanted." I glance at her now.

"It doesn't really matter, does it? I'm the one who's pregnant." She's stopped a few paces away, facing me, but she isn't looking at me either. She's staring at something in the distance.

I study my feet. "I don't mean it like that. Like I get what you're saying, and you decided you wanted to keep the baby. That means I should get a say now, right?" I look up at her.

She finally meets my gaze and holds it. I'm not sure what I expect to see on her features, but it isn't the mixture of fear and insecurity. Bella hasn't ever seemed that kind of girl to me. Walking the halls of high school with her bevy of friends trailing her, I just always saw her as larger than life. Confident. Beautiful. Now, she looks as insecure as I feel, muted.

"I–" She stops, and her light eyebrows move about on her face as she processes what I've said. "To be honest, Griff, I didn't think you'd have an opinion. I thought by giving you an out, you'd just be relieved."

"How come?" I ask it, but I'm not sure I want to know.

She turns away and resumes walking.

I follow, but I'm content to remain behind her.

She stops, turns, and waits for me to catch up. "I thought that's what you'd want because of how you were in high school. You seemed like you didn't care about anything or anyone. Like you just wanted to party. Sleep around." She pauses and adds, "I thought you wouldn't want the responsibility."

It sucks to hear it, but it isn't knowledge about myself I haven't already faced in the last few months. That is the black hole I created. Even with all its gravity, however, I'm thinking I've got a means to escape even if it tears me apart. Maybe that's exactly what has to happen when you've made a black hole.

We keep walking in the same direction.

"What do you want?" she asks when I don't respond to her observation.

"I want to be a dad. A good one." I notice she turns her head to look at me, and I meet her gaze. She's surprised. "I need to be better than my own dad," I say. "I don't want to be hands off in my own kid's life; I want to share the responsibility."

We continue in silence.

It's her turn to stop. She turns and looks behind her, then she looks forward, and then she looks straight at me. "I don't think there's an *us*, though."

While it sucks not to be wanted, this observation doesn't hurt as much as I think it might have at one time. I can honestly assess the hurt she heaped on me, and I can honestly assess the hurt I heaped on others. My worship of the idea of Bella paired with my own damage isn't what we should be bringing a kid into anyway. "I don't think we'd work," I tell her.

This admission isn't what she's expecting because her eyebrows draw together. "Why?"

"Do you really want to get into that? I'm agreeing with you."

"Kind of."

"Were you thinking you wanted to try and have a relationship? Because I'm not sure you and I have ever had a relationship beyond alcohol and chemistry. Whatever got us to this spot wasn't because there was some great love story between us. We had sex, accidentally got pregnant, and now we're here."

She sighs and nods. "You're right. It's why I said we shouldn't be an *us*." She must recall what she'd said at the Quarry because she adds, "Not because of you, though, Griff. I didn't mean it like that."

I shrug. "Okay."

"I might understand that here," she points at her head and then replaces her hand in her pocket. "But I'm afraid to do this alone." She's tucked her chin into the collar of her jacket, her eyes downcast.

I swallow and then test out the words in my head. Then I admit them. "I'm afraid too."

Her eyes rise to meet mine. She lifts her chin. "I guess we can be afraid together then."

I offer her a small smile. "Yeah."

We turn around to walk back the way we came. The silence between us is strange as we crunch over the broken-down sidewalk and refrozen slush of dirty snow, but the hushed sounds aren't unwelcome over meaningless chatter. I'm thinking about how much better I feel having shared with her how I feel about this baby. Our baby. It's almost a feeling of elation even if it's weighted with angst.

"The ultrasound is next month," Bella says. "Would you like to come?"

I look up from the sidewalk at her. "Really?" I can hear the hope in my own voice. I feel like maybe I should be embarrassed by it, but I'm not. The hope is authentic. She smiles. A few months ago, it would have made me feel defensive because I might have assumed she was mocking my vulnerability. Now, however, I see the truth of her smile. The shine in her eyes communicates she appreciates my honesty.

We've reached my car.

"Yes. I'll text you the details," Bella says as she turns up the walkway back to the house.

"Okay," I tell her and pull my phone from my pocket to make sure I have it as if she's about to text me right then. My gaze catches on the cracks that run across the screen. I need to replace this. That's something a good dad would do, I think. He'd make sure everything was working.

I look up at Bella's house as she walks up the walk and see the work again through a different lens. My child will live here. There are things that need to be fixed. That is something I can do, I think.

Because of Cal.

My heart slams up into my ribs.

I need to talk to him.

Bella waves and disappears into the house as I get into my car.

I know I need to face Cal, but I avoid it a little longer by making one more stop. Inside one of those phone-fix-it places, I get the screen on the phone replaced. When I walk out of the store, the screen of my phone smooth and new, it's almost like I'm new, too.

I text Max after:

> I fixed my phone's screen. No more cracks.

No response.

Me to Max:

> I should have started with I'm sorry.

No response.

Me to Max:

> I miss you.

No response.

I take a deep breath, start the car, and drive to the one place where I feel like the real Griffin was excavated.

4.

Cal's rusty truck is parked outside the workshop. I knock on the front door of the farmhouse first, thinking he may be working inside. My knock goes unanswered. I turn away from the doorway and walk to the top stair of the porch, noticing there's smoke puffing from the little stovepipe chimney in the outbuilding where Cal stores his tools and supplies.

I walk across the driveway to the shop door, take a deep breath before knocking.

His footsteps thump against the wooden floor, and the door opens. He looks as he always does, calm, cool, and exactly who I want to be. "Griffin." He turns, leaving the door open. "Long time no see," he observes aloud as he disappears into the belly of the building.

I follow.

"Shut that door so the heat doesn't escape. Now, to what do I owe the honor of this visit?" He's standing at the workbench moving things about, stops and puts a hand in his back pocket as if to assess what he was doing, then moves again, lifts a giant toolbox, and sets it on the counter with a thud.

"An apology," I say. The admission sounds muted in the space, as if the acoustics have pressed in on it and held it out like a piece of artwork hanging for study.

He stops, turns, and leans against the counter's edge. He's got a cloth in one hand now and a giant metal tool he's rubbing with the cloth in the other. "About?"

I have the fleeting thought he could beat me up with that tool, kill me even, and I might even deserve it for what happened with Max and him. "Lots of things."

He cleans the tool and waits.

"For not calling. I was going through something, but I should have called you."

He continues cleaning, his eyes drifting up from his concentration on the cleaning to meet my gaze.

"And Max." I can't hang onto his scrutiny, so my eyes and my heart, trip about trying to find some place to land. "I'm sorry."

He clears his throat, then I hear him move.

When I look up, he's got his back to me again, and the now clean tool drops with a clank into its spot in the metal box.

I take a shallow breath.

"Technically, Griffin, I'm your boss. One has nothing to do with the other." I focus on the details. Those are distant from the content of this talk. His head is bowed as he looks at whatever has his attention. His red shirt stretches across his back, and I notice the way the fabric moves as he does. His hair, that dark brown color—darker than Max's—is a little long and curls against his neck.

He continues. "What happens between you and your girlfriend isn't my business unless it impacts your work. So, let's talk about the work. I should fire you," he finishes as another tool clanks into the box.

"Yes sir, and with all due respect, the second point—Max—who really should be the first, not the second—is connected to my not calling you."

He turns to look at me again. Leans again. Crosses his arms

307

instead of cleaning this time, maybe to offer me his undivided attention.

"And you're right. You should fire me. And I will accept that consequence if that's what you want, sir."

I stop. Unable to stand still under his examination, measuring my character, which I know is shit, I shift my weight back and forth from one foot to another. I cross and uncross my arms. I shove my hands into my pockets.

"I'm listening," he finally says.

"I hurt Max, not because I wanted to or anything," I add as if it will lessen the blow of what's about to drop from my mouth. "I hurt her because I didn't trust her to decide for herself what to do with some news I'd learned. It seemed too big to overcome. So, I pushed her away, thinking that was the right way to face it."

"You're talking in abstracts, Griffin."

He's right. I'm trying to talk around it. I take a deep breath, and then rush through it. "I found out that a girl I was seeing before Max is pregnant." I hang my head, ashamed.

Cal sighs.

I look up expecting to see anger, but he's setting the cloth on the workbench.

"Come on up to the house. Let's get a cup of coffee." He leads me from the workshop into the warm kitchen of the farmhouse. "Sit." I follow his instructions and sit at the island to watch him prepare a fresh pot. "So, tell me."

"Everything?"

He glances at me. "Within reason, son. I'd rather not have the details."

I smile despite myself. He sounds like Max. "I was drunk on my birthday—back in September. Hooked up with this girl who said she was on the pill. Didn't follow my own rule to use a condom and now am going to be a dad."

He closes the cap on the pot after filling the reservoir with water. "Well, I can see how that might have impacted your ability to think clearly."

"I wasn't sure how to break the news to Max. I knew I had to be honest, but–" I pause. I hadn't been. I mean, she found out, and I told her, but I'd been a coward and martyr about it. "I pushed her away."

He snaps the filter into place and pushes the start button on the coffee pot. It bubbles to life as Cal turns at the counter. He leans against it, hands folded over his chest, and crosses his legs at the ankle. "As I see it, I've got two responses." He holds up two fingers. "One as your boss, and one as Max's dad." He switches to holding up just his index finger. "First, as your boss, I can see how the stress might have impacted your ability to communicate openly and honestly with me, because you linked boss and dad together. That's reasonable and understandable. And because I think everyone deserves the opportunity for a second chance in the face of mistakes, I'd like you to return to work, since we have a house to finish."

I nod. I'm relieved, but I don't have time to process it, because he adds the second finger.

"As Max's dad, I don't have a right to make a decision for her now that she's an adult. All I've got is opinions, as she so frequently reminds me. If you want my opinion, I'm willing to share it."

"Yes, sir."

"Yes, sir, what?"

"I'd like your opinion."

The coffee pot gurgles behind him, and the scent of fresh coffee is comforting. He moves to a stool at the island perpendicular to me, sits, and then folds his hands on the counter in front of him.

"Here it is then," he begins. He takes a deep breath. "Shit happens."

I wait for him to say more, but he doesn't.

The coffee pot beeps, telling us the cycle is finished. Cal gets up and removes two cups from the hooks inside the cupboard and pours some for each of us then carries the mugs over. He sets one down in front of me and retakes his seat.

I look at it, a red mug with white writing: *Failin' means yer playin!* I rub my thumb across the writing. "That's it?" I ask.

"Pretty much." He sips from his cup and sets it down. "It's the easiest way to recognize that we can't control life. We can try, but ultimately, it happens despite our best efforts and never adheres to our best intentions. It often hijacks our plans, and we must figure out how to respond. We don't always make the best choices. I haven't. And yet, I have Max."

"Max is awesome," I say.

"Not because of me. Okay, I might have had a little influence, but Max is great because she's just that kind of person." He spins his green cup, so the handle is where he wants it. "Truth is, Griffin, life throws shit at us. We all have to dodge and weave, pivot, move forward through it. You'll mostly get hit, but sometimes you'll get lucky and dodge the big ones. Lots of times you won't. Making those mistakes is all part of the journey, and our life is defined by how we respond to them. Those are the choices we have."

"Max deserves someone better than me," I say.

"Who are you to decide that for someone?" he asks.

I shrug. "That's why she's mad."

He nods. "Yeah. That's a bullshit excuse to keep people at arm's length. It's weak."

My throat closes around that word. Weak. Everything I've tried to hide in the bluster of Griff. In the Bro Code. In the drinking. In the sex. The fear of people seeing me as weak. I glance up from the cup to look at him, hating that he's called me out on it.

Cal's staring at me with an intense look on his face.

"But she doesn't deserve to be with a guy who has a kid. She—"

"Again. Who are you to decide that for anyone? Who made you the decider?"

And he's right, again. Max is right. Tanner is right. Phoenix is right. Danny is right. I've decided for everyone, and I wonder if it has been less about them and more about me. That self-protection rather than the claim I was trying to save others. I wanted a choice

310

about the baby with Bella, but I haven't been extending choices to others. I didn't offer that choice to Max. "I see."

He nods.

"Shit happens."

Cal smiles. "Now, what are you going to do about it?"

"Come back to work."

He makes a humming noise of agreement and takes a sip of coffee. "And?"

"Apologize to Max."

He smiles. "Probably a great place to begin." He slaps my back.

"Thanks, Cal."

He smiles and nods.

Cal's kindness, generosity, and wisdom are enough to give me hope that perhaps no matter the outcome of others' choices—including Max's—and the shit life throws at me, I will still be okay.

5.

I text Max:

> I talked to two people I need to talk to, and it wasn't easy.

> The first one was Bella.

> I told her I wanted to be involved in my kid's life.

> Like co-parents or whatever they call it. I told her I didn't want to be like my dad and not be involved. She's agreed and invited me to the ultrasound next month.

> This DOESN'T mean there's a Bella and me, like a couple.

Nope.

We both agreed on that.

The second person—and the more terrifying of the two—was Cal.

I haven't gone to work, and I knew I needed to face him about stuff.

I told him about the baby. He was really helpful.

And he called me out on some of my shit, which is definitely something I needed. He always knows exactly what to say.

I still have one more person I need to talk to:

you. Max.

I need to talk to you.

No response.

FEBRUARY

I'm feeling shaky in my new skin —vulnerable—but I've found breathing helps. And talking about it, too, which is strange and adds to that messed up fear of wanting to close back up. It doesn't feel natural to share, as if I'm going against that unwritten Man Code.

But then I open the door, share, and suddenly the load doesn't feel so heavy. And those people I trusted with my truth look at me like I mean something. Who knew?

To: Griffin Nichols
123 45th Street NE
The Town, USA 67890

315

1.

I'm in my room after spending the day at Bella's working on some fix-it projects inside her house when I hear voices in the living room. Phoenix. And... Tanner? When I emerge from the hallway, Tanner is in the living room, inside the door with my brother. He turns his head toward me, acknowledges me with a head nod, and a subtle shift of his eyebrows.

"Are you enjoying it?" Tanner asks Phoenix with a smile. "Dad's a task master."

"He's cool." Phoenix's arms are crossed over his chest. "He took a chance on me."

Tanner says something about a recent project that Phoenix responds to, and I lose sense of the conversation, observing my real brother interact with my chosen brother. Tanner and Phoenix have never really known one another, and Tanner took Phoenix's place. They're so different. Tanner is taller, darker. Phoenix is a shorter version of me. He's rugged in a way that I am not, tattooed, and harder. He makes me think of the outlaws from those Westerns we used to watch, only now he's trying to go straight. Tanner is still, and will always be, the favorite sheriff.

They're both looking at me, expectant for a response.

I shake my head. "Sorry. Zoned out. I was bored."

They both swear with smiles, and Phoenix sideswipes me with an arm around my neck, as I walk deeper into the living room. We engage in a short wrestling match, just enough for Phoenix to emerge as the older-brother victor, then he leaves us for the kitchen where he's working on some new concoction, since he's taken up experimenting in the kitchen. He's been talking about going to culinary school.

"What brings you over?" I ask.

"You weren't answering my texts or my calls, so I figured I had to come over and see if you dropping by my house the other night was real. How are things going?"

I shrug.

"Want to go for a drive? There's this place I like to go when I need time to think. Maybe you'll like it."

I grab my coat and follow Tanner out to his truck.

Once we're on the road, Tanner forces the issue. "So? How did it go with the girl?"

"Which one?"

"The one you like."

"Terrible. She isn't talking to me."

"What did you do?"

"What you told me not to do."

"You're an idiot."

"Tell me something I don't know." It's rhetorical, but I say, "I told Bella I wanted to be a part of the baby's life."

I feel him glance at me as he drives us out of town. We're headed toward the Quarry. The golden hour of the sun gilds the evergreens with shimmering golden light. Even naked trees look pretty in the starkness of the winter forest. The blue orange of the sky deepens as the sun begins its descent.

"I think that's a good move. How did Bella take it?"

"She was surprised, I think. But open to it. She invited me to the ultrasound. It's next week."

He smiles. "That's really great."

His support makes me grin. "Yeah. I'm wrapping my head around it. Trying to help her out at her place. There's a bunch of shit that needs doing before the baby comes, and it's just her, her mom, and her little sister."

"Wow. Cool. Let me know if you need help. I can probably get supplies."

I take a deep breath, remembering what it feels like to have a friend. The way the world settles around you, stops spinning out of control, and becomes steady again. It makes me miss Max even more.

I watch the landscape rush past us as Tanner drives. "It's weird. Feels like now when I'm going to do something, I think is this something I should do? Maybe that makes me boring—"

Tanner contemplates what I've said, mulling it about. "I think that just means you're growing up." He turns the truck onto an access road, and we bump along an unmanaged road through the forest. "I get it," he says.

"Yeah?"

"One of the worst things—and the best things—to happen to me was when Emma ended it."

"She did it?"

"Yeah. That night we went at it in the parking lot, I showed up at her job."

"We were wasted."

"Yeah. I showed up at her workplace. Not a good look."

"Shit dude, I'm sorry."

"Not on you, Griff. I made my choices, too. And lately, after spending time working on me, staying sober, staying away from sex, I feel way clearer about stuff."

I nod. "I stopped drinking too. Started running."

"Did you know we were so messed up?" Tanner asks.

The truck emerges from the cover of trees onto a plateau at the

318

edge of the Quarry wall. Snow in various stages of decay stretches out piled up again trees, rocks, and the roadside. Tanner finds a spot to reverse the truck so that it faces the Quarry, gets out, opens the tailgate, and sits down on the edge. I join him and take a deep breath. The view is beautiful, as if it were a pretty vista trapped in a snow globe. The setting sun lights it up, so the cold seems to glisten.

"I didn't know we were messed up," I eventually say. "I think I'm still figuring it out. There are these moments when I feel clear about it—like when I'm running—and then these moments when I shut down, because I don't want to feel it. Like the other night with Max. So, then I do the same old shit."

I sit next to Tanner, mulling the truth, the shame, and the skewed way I thought it meant to be a man.

"How come you've never brought me here before?" I ask.

Tanner, hands shoved into the pockets of his jacket, stares out at the landscape, then looks at me. "I was afraid."

At first, I think maybe he means he was scared to admit his vulnerability, but I realize he was afraid of me, of how I might hurt him and this place he saw as safe. "That I'd make fun of it. Of you."

He doesn't say anything. He doesn't need to.

"You tried to talk to me, before. All those times, in different ways. I shut you down."

"Yeah. Well, I was ready, and you weren't."

"I'm sorry, bro."

"You already said it. There's no need to say it again."

"Yeah, but I feel like a piece of dirt for shitting on you."

He jumps from the tailgate and walks a few steps forward, his boots crunching through the melted snow, the debris loosened by the elements. "Honestly?" he asks.

"Yeah," I say and prepare myself for whatever he might tell me that will hurt.

Tanner bends down and picks up a rock, then launches it into the Quarry. We stare at it, losing sight of the small projectile in the infinite expanse of the Quarry. He looks around for another rock.

"I wouldn't be where I am now if it hadn't worked out that way, I think. So, whatever you did—didn't do—helped me on my path. Don't get me wrong, I was pissed at you." He reaches over and pushes me so that I nearly fall out of the truck. He grins as he does it.

I reorient my balance. "Dude!" I laugh and get out to look for rocks with him. When I find one, I let it fly. It feels satisfying, letting it go and watching it until I can't.

"The therapist asked me this one time, if I would change what happened between you and me and I was like, 'Yeah. He was my best friend,' and the therapist said, 'What if it meant you remained unchanged?' And I haven't stopped thinking about that." He throws another rock.

I toss another pebble and think about Cal's wisdom: *Shit happens.*

Tanner stops moving a moment, just stares out at the Quarry as if waiting for something. He looks up at the sky, now streaked with blue and red and orange. He looks back at me. "If we'd stayed the same, on the same trajectory we were–" He stops, and I can hear the weight in what isn't said. He's right. We'd still be trying to do what we'd always done: party, drink, drugs, fuck, learning nothing until one of us did something we couldn't recover from. Like getting a girl pregnant. Or, like Phoenix, going to prison. Or worse, dying.

"I'm glad it happened."

Cal's wisdom is right. Shit does happen. Fighting with Tanner was shit, but it was necessary because now, standing side by side at the Quarry doing something like throwing rocks over the ledge, talking about stuff that real, it's the biggest, greatest, and most infinite we've ever been. Together.

"Me too," I reply. It isn't much—those two words—but in that moment, it feels like I've spoken a universe.

2.

Pressing the video call to Danny is a step I need to take and have needed to take for some time. He never answered my text, and I know I need to clear the air with him like I have with Tanner. During my run, I got to thinking about how great it was to finally be talking to Tanner again, and after reconnecting and thanking Josh for trying to keep me connected, I realized I hadn't heard from Danny.

After stretching and regulating my breathing, I sit on the frozen concrete of the front steps to my house, the Facetime call ringing. The cold bites my ass, but it feels sort of fitting as I wait for Danny to answer. My heart snaps about in my chest like a terrified dragon, but I take a deep breath to cool his defensive fire. When I see the word *connecting*, I panic a second, then force another deep breath.

Danny's face comes into view. He looks different, his edges erased and redrawn in modified angles. His dark hair is shorter than I've ever seen it. He's lost the babyface, replaced by someone who looks like a man.

He smiles, and the feeling reaches his eyes. "Hey, Griff."
I offer him a smile back. "I wasn't sure you'd answer."
His eyebrows shift over his eyes. "How come?"

"Wasn't sure if you'd be busy or–" I pause a second and commit to being honest– "and I didn't really deserve it. I was pretty shitty. So, I wasn't sure if you'd take it."

His facial features adjust, becoming serious.

"I wanted to call you and tell you a couple things," I add.

He nods, moving from wherever he is. I hear several male voices in the background, loud and raucous.

"Is this a good time?" I ask.

"Perfect," he says and shuts a door. "Okay. I can hear you better."

"I wanted to thank you, first."

"Thank me?"

"Yes. Shit, Danny. I owe you for all the shit I've done. I took advantage of you and your kindness."

"I'm your friend, Griff."

I nod, then swallow down the unexpected tears that press against the back of my eyes. I shake my head and screw up my face a moment to fight the burn. When I'm under control, I say, "I know you are. The best, Danny. And I wasn't. I wanted to thank you for telling me that night that Tanner and I fought."

"I hardly remember what I said."

I huff a laugh through my nose. "You told me everything was my fault."

"Damn, Griffin. I'm sorry for that."

I shake my head. Tanner had this right. I'd needed Danny's anger. "No. No. Don't apologize. You were right, and I needed to hear it. I think you were probably the only one of us I would have listened to. You were always there for us, Danny—for me. Always, and when you pushed me with some tough-love shit, I finally had to look in the mirror." I pause. "So, thank you."

He isn't looking at the screen—at me—but I see him swallow and when he does finally look, he nods.

"And I already said it, but I need to make sure to say it again to you. I'm sorry, Dan. I was an awful friend, a user, and you deserved better from me. I want to be a better friend."

He smiles. "We're bros, Griff. Always."

The dragon in my heart heaves a great big puff of relief, and I stand to walk back into the house, talking with Danny some more. We catch up. I learn about basic training and his new job. I tell him about fixing things with Tanner and Josh, about Bella and the baby. The rhythm of our conversation isn't grounded in the past, however, because I'm new, and I suppose he is too. We're changing as people, which means we're reorienting with one another. The past, as heavy and difficult as it is, is the past, and now we're finding a way to move forward.

3.

Max still isn't talking to me. I've texted. I even tried calling, but my calls ring through to voicemail. The only reason I know she's alive is because Cal has mentioned small details. At the farmhouse, Cal and I are on the final stages of the bathroom renovations. Then we'll be ready to roll out with the painting and putting everything back together, just in time for Max to have a brand-new space when she gets home for spring break in March. Except Cal let it slip that he didn't think she'd be coming home, something about spring break with friends.

I'm at Bella's to install a closet system in the baby's room, but I'm in a foul mood.

She calls me out on it. "What is up with you? You're acting like a baby."

I grunt at her and use the level to mark a spot for the screw.

"I don't want your foul mood around the baby." She's beginning to show, just a tiny little swell in her lower belly. She rubs it as if protecting the baby from my mood, and I feel like a selfish jerk. "They say the baby can feel it, you know."

"Sorry," I say and drill in an anchor. "Girl trouble."

"Oh!" Bella sounds giddy and sits in a rocking chair. It creaks as she moves it back and forth. "Tell me everything. Is this the girl from the Quarry?"

I glance at her and nod.

"I don't think she liked me very much."

"Well, you didn't come across as a very nice person that night in the bathroom. What you said and all."

She reddens. "Yeah. I hate that I said it."

"Shit happens," I tell her, drawing on Cal's wisdom, holding up a bracket and screwing it into the wall. It reminds me of Tanner and my quarry-side conversation, of how sometimes you have to go through the awful stuff to get to the better, more honest stuff. But I'm not sure I'm going to get the chance with Max.

"You were with her, when we?" She stops. "Oh shit, Griff."

"No." I repeat the process for the next bracket.

"But you seemed cozy at the Quarry."

"Just friends. She didn't like what you said and was trying to help me."

The chair continues to squeak as Bella rocks, then it stops. "Griffin?"

I stop and look over my shoulder at her.

She's frozen, both hands on her belly. She looks up at me with wide eyes and smiles. "I think I just felt the baby move!" She holds out her hand.

I move to her side.

She grabs my wrist and draws me closer so I can lay my palm on her.

I don't feel anything, just notice the strange way the swell of her belly is hard rather than soft. Then suddenly, there's a light flutter, soft like the caress of eyelashes against my palm. My heartbeat quickens, a gentle quickening to match, and my eyes raise from our hands to Bella's face.

She's smiling. "Oh. Feel that?" She whispers the words as if the sound of her voice will make it go away.

I nod. "Yeah." I smile.

"She's telling us that her momma is right; she can hear us

talking."

"She?"

"Just a guess. And I like it better than saying 'it.'" She releases my hand. "So, when did you and Quarry-girl get together?"

I stand and return to the closet. I stare at the holes I've made in the drywall for a moment to register what I've just experienced, the whiplash of Bella moving through topics. I clear my throat. "Her name is Max. After Thanksgiving."

"And she ran away because of the baby?"

I shrug, not sure how to articulate it. "I think it's more complicated than that."

Bella is quiet for a while, then says, "Girls aren't any more complicated than men."

"How do you figure?" I finish the bracket and turn to look at her again.

She looks cute, more settled, and comfortable than she ever has. What I once thought was confidence was just a wall like the one I'd put up. Bella and I aren't that much different from one another. "We just want to be safe; you know? Not just physically safe, but emotionally safe. We want to know that when we need our guy, he's got our back."

"Like to fight or something?"

She laughs. "No. Like a hug or a kind word, or something romantic. A gesture."

I hum, not exactly sure how to respond to that but think about it, wondering how I could possibly find a way to extend a romantic gesture when the girl won't talk to me.

I finish the closet.

After I get home to sample some of Phoenix's grub, I low-key gag at Mom and Bill cuddling on the couch and follow that up with a shower. Once I'm in bed to sleep, I check IG and see Max has posted a story.

I'm not sure what to do, what she wants from me. I think about Bella's claim that a girl just wants to know I have her back, but if she won't talk to you, then how are you supposed to show her? I press on Max's story. It makes me want to throw my phone at the wall. She's walking into a party with Renna, her boyfriend, and that stupid shmuck from the pizza parlor. Fucking Ben.

I don't care that I've showered.

I don't care that it's as cold as the devil's balls in the Arctic Circle.

I don't care that I could slip, get lost and die in the snow that has decided to fall.

I put on my running clothes and stomp through the house.

"Where are you going?" my mom asks from the couch.

"What does it look like?" I growl. "I need a run."

"Griffin. It's too cold and dark."

"I have to go," I tell her and push through the door, close it behind me, run.

I run, the ground slick, and grueling enough to help me refocus my emotional hurt on the physical pain instead. My deep breaths freeze my lungs, hardening them into glass that comes out my mouth like ice crystals. But still I run.

I run. I run. I run.

I run from this tiny town and all its tiny expectations.

I run from the fact I'm going to be a dad.

I run from my fear and my hurt and my insecurity.

I run from my longing for a girl who doesn't want me back, and it's because I didn't trust her.

I stop running.

I didn't trust her.

I was afraid.

I take several deep breaths finding my center.

I didn't trust her.

I was afraid.

I can see the truth in it.

I didn't have her back and tried to protect my own.

When I feel the calm again, I turn around to run back.

I run toward my family.

I run toward the house where I know I'm safe.

I run toward the idea that I get to see my baby's ultrasound soon and smile thinking about the feel of it—her—moving under my hand on Bella's belly.

I run toward the realization I will be a dad soon.

I run toward the hope for Max and me but accepting it if there isn't. I have to trust her, and most importantly, I have to trust me.

4.

The white and black truck in front of my car crawls over the road. I glance at the clock on my dash and will my breathing to find calm. I'm not late—not yet— but time is short. Right after class, I jettisoned straight to my vehicle and got on the road. A trip between the clinic where Bella is getting the ultrasound and my campus in the city is about 45 minutes from door to door. I know because I timed it a few days ago. I didn't factor in a fucking, slow-moving semi.

Shit.

I tap the steering wheel to the music, but it's less to keep time and more to center my impatience. "Shit," I say aloud to no one since I'm in the car alone, then "Move!" to the truck ahead of me, not that the driver can hear me. I know there's a passing lane about a mile or so ahead, but I glance at the clock again and feel the pressure of beginning to freak out. I can't miss the ultrasound. Bella trusts me to show up. My first job as this kid's dad is to fucking show up.

When the truck finally moves into the 2nd right lane allowing faster moving vehicles to pass, I press the accelerator and speed past the truck two trailers deep thankful the roads are clear. By the time I park at the clinic, I'm five minutes late.

Shit.

I hustle through the doorway.

The waiting room is full of women whose faces swing my way. A quick scan and not one of them is Bella. *Shit. Shit. Shit.* I stop at the reception desk, a high counter that obscures a woman chatting on the line behind it. She holds up a finger, asking me to wait. Antsy, I shift my body weight from one foot to the other. I'm trying to play it cool, but I can't miss my kid's ultrasound.

I sigh.

Finally, she disconnects the call. "Can I help you, sir?"

"Uh. Yeah, I'm here for Bella Noble's appointment. We have an ultrasound today. I'm a few minutes late."

"There you are."

I spin away from the receptionist at the sound of Bella's voice. My heart drops into my gut and then climbs out, straining with the exertion and dripping with acid. "You're done already? I missed it?"

She giggles. "No. I just was in the restroom. Haven't been called back yet."

I follow Bella across the room to a pair of seats. "I'm sorry I'm late."

"You're here. Haven't gone back yet. Not late." She puts a hand on my forearm. "Relax."

"I got stuck behind a truck." I run my hands through my hair. I'm sure it's sticking up in tufts because Bella reaches up and pats it down. It's a strangely intimate gesture, but I don't feel anything but a reciprocal camaraderie that's comforting. We've found this nice place between us in the last few weeks. I've been at her place helping put things together, fixing things, getting to know her better. Like I didn't know how much she likes her beauty school stuff, which she's continued to study. She and Greta aren't friends anymore. Different paths. How she wanted to be a better example for her baby sister but feels like she failed epically. I told her she just has to pivot and be the best she can be with the way the situation presents itself.

Thanks, Cal.

"You're here." She sucks in a breath, winces, and lays a palm on her belly.

"You okay? What is it? Do you need help?" I look around like maybe I should get someone.

She shakes her head and one of her hands back and forth. "Nothing. I think I ate something that doesn't agree with me or the baby."

I sigh and lean back, finally, to catch my breath now that I'm here, and I won't miss this appointment. I'm just able to take another deep breath when the nurse enters the lobby and calls Bella into the back. I stand up after her, swipe my palms over the thighs of my jeans and follow her. I'm so nervous, though I can't figure out what I have to be nervous about. Technically, this isn't happening to me. But, by the time Bella is situated on the table, I think I might be having a panic attack.

"Griffin." Bella is staring at me, her eyes wide.

I can't answer her, but I let her catch my gaze with hers. She holds out her hand, and I take it.

"I need you to calm down. Got it?"

I nod.

"If you pass out, you're going to miss it." She offers me a smile.

I nod again and offer a short smile in return; one I have to force. I'm still trying to breathe right. I know I need to get myself together and take a deep breath.

Bella squeezes my hand. "If you can't do the ultrasound, how are you going to attend the birth?"

My eyes fly from the door and plaster themselves to hers. "You want me there?"

"Of course. Don't be ridiculous. We're doing this co-parenting thing, right?" She withdraws her hand from mine and smooths both over her belly, the knit stretching over the tiny bump of her abdomen.

"Yes. Yes!" I smile for real this time. It's a little easier.

The door opens. "Hello, Momma." The doctor enters without

even looking our way and goes directly to the computer where she logs in. "How are you feeling this month, Bella?"

"Good, except for some indigestion, I think."

I listen to Bella describe her pregnancy to the doctor who transcribes everything into the electronic chart. When they're done, the doctor finally looks our way, and she stops. "Oh. Hello. I'm Dr. Raj." She reaches out a small hand, and I take it.

"This is Griffin. The baby's father," Bella says.

Dr. Raj smiles. "Nice to meet you. How about we get a look at your baby?" She turns to the sink where she washes her hands and gloves them. "Pull up your shirt for me, Bella, just up to your bra so I can access your belly."

Bella draws it up just so it's draped across the top of her belly. The pretty skin is smooth with a gentle expanse from her navel to her hips. It makes me feel something, but it isn't something I recognize. Her body is beautiful this way, not that it wasn't before. I just didn't notice before, the way a woman's body is beyond what is sexual. I feel moved by it, but not in a way that fills me with lust, rather in a way that makes my heart move differently. Inside her is a baby, one we made—albeit accidentally—and her belly is evidence of it. It's moving, and I'm ill-equipped to process it. I swallow the emotion before it reaches my eyes.

I glance at Bella's face, and she turns her head to look at me. She smiles, and I take her hand in mine again. I don't feel panic anymore. I just feel grateful.

"Okay, now." Doctor Raj sits on a stool next to Bella and folds a paper towel into the waistband of her yoga pants, sliding it down to the pubic bone and revealing all her belly. "This goop should be nice and warm since it was in the warmer, but sometimes it's got cold spots." She squirts gel from a bottle, then uses what I figure must be the ultrasound instrument to spread it over Bella's tight skin. "Okay. We're going to take some measurements today. Check baby's organs and fluids."

She talks as she moves the wand, clicks the machine here and there. I'm looking at a glob, really, until suddenly, I'm not. The baby's profile comes into view, the head, space for eyes, a nose and mouth. I see the ladder of the spine. The doctor points everything out. My breath stalls a moment. Then the baby is gone as the doctor moves the wand to a fluttering spot on the screen.

"Ready to hear your baby's heart?" The doctor punches some buttons. A speeding rhythm like a tinny echo moves around the room and connects with the beating of my own heart.

"It's so fast," I say.

"About 150 beats per minute," Dr. Raj replies. "Perfectly healthy."

I glance at Bella. She's staring at the screen, her eyes filling with tears, but she's smiling.

Dr. Raj continues moving the wand, talking us through it, then stops. "Want to know the gender of your baby?" She looks at Bella.

Bella smiles and looks at me. "I'd like Griffin to decide."

Chills move across my skin under my clothes. I'm not cold, but in the whole of everything associated with this baby, it's the first time I've had the opportunity to make a choice. I glance at Bella, not sure if there's a right answer.

Bella smiles, waiting.

I look at Dr. Raj and nod. "Yes."

"Congratulations," she says. "You're going to have a little girl."

"See," Bella says full of confidence. "Her."

My throat constricts and emotion moves through me so quick, it's hard to tamp it back down and keep it in. I look at Bella who's staring at me, a tear slipping down her cheek.

"A little girl," she repeats, smiles, then looks back at the screen.

A little girl. Who knew those three words would ever mean so much?

5.

Me to Max:

I know you aren't talking to me. I hope it's okay to still text you to share, because the only one I wanted to share this with was you.

I got to hear the baby's heartbeat today.

I didn't know, Max.

I didn't know what it would do to me. How I would feel.

After the appointment, I got into my car and cried.

Maybe that's weird, and maybe that makes me seem weak, but hearing her heartbeat for the first time filled me with so much feeling, it was all I could do to hold it in until I could find a place it felt safe to let it go.

Oh yeah! The baby is a girl.

I'm going to have a daughter.

I never thought I would be excited to say that I'm going to be a dad, but Max, my feelings have changed since I first learned I was going to be a father.

I've been wondering if that's how my dad felt?

I wish I had my friend Max back to talk to. I miss her.

I think it's beautiful, SK. I'm sure your dad was just as excited about you.

Max

I reply:

Maybe I should go see my dad.

She doesn't respond.

6.

A few days after the ultrasound, I drive to my dad's apartment. I'm already in the city because of school, so it's an easy detour. The decision to do it is on impulse. He's been on my mind a lot.

The apartment complex looks the same, but now without the glamour of Christmas lights strung up on the dilapidated building to dress it up. As I climb the stairs, I question why I'm there. The last time I was with him, I called him names, but I walk down the second-floor walkway and knock on his door anyway. Compulsion won't let me leave even if I don't have an exact answer as to why I'm there. I might feel both relief and despondency if he isn't home.

The door opens.

My dad looks the same as he did in December, only his hair has gotten longer. He's wearing a black t-shirt and jeans, fit and handsome even in his forties. I can see the ink spilling down his arms.

"Griffin?"

My name inked on his neck.

"Is it a bad time?"

He shakes his head. "No. Never. Not for you." He widens the

door.

I walk inside.

He closes the door behind me.

The apartment looks the same, only the Christmas stuff is gone. It's neat. I'm not sure I would have ever assigned my father the quality of neatness, but then how would I have known? He wasn't around much when I was little. Then not at all.

"I'm glad you're here." He runs his hands over his pants nervously. "Sit. Sit." He holds his hand out toward the couch. "Can I get you something?"

I sit down on the edge, leaving my coat on and my keys in hand. "No. Thanks."

Dad sits down in a chair perpendicular to me. And waits.

There's music on, an older tune from when he was probably my age. A notebook and pen sitting open on the table as if that's where he'd been sitting—and writing—when I knocked. I look at him a little closer. It's strange at that moment to think of him as a young man, my age at one time, though I logically know it. A moment ago, he was in his apartment enjoying some music, just being with his own thoughts and ideas and hopes and dreams. Or so I'm imagining.

I study my car keys, unclear what I want to articulate, but acknowledging that there are feelings guiding me instead. "I'm going to have a baby," I tell him after some time.

"Phoenix mentioned it."

My gaze flicks up from the keys to his. "Wow. I'll remember to thank him for talking behind my back." Betrayal hits me. A horrible image of Phoenix and our dad talking and laughing about my circumstances flashes like a moving slideshow in my mind, but then I realize I'm lying to myself to justify the anger rather than acknowledging the hurt. It's a dangerous, slippery slope.

"It wasn't like that."

"How was it then?" Even knowing it, I struggle to turn it off. My reactions feeling more like predictable rotations and revolutions of normalcy to keep me safe.

"I ask about you. He shares what he can."

I stand up, restless suddenly. Angry. A quiet voice asks if that anger is really at my dad, but I shut it down. "Well. I thought you should know you were going to be a grandpa. Now that you know, I guess I don't need to be here." I move to the door and hear him stand up behind me.

What are you running away from?

"Griffin?"

I stop with my hand on the doorknob.

"Please, stay."

Or are you running toward something?

I look down at my hand on the brass fixture. A choice. Cal's wisdom assails my thought process. *Shit happens.* And maybe that's what I was thinking by coming here. An acknowledgment that perhaps it wasn't in my father's grand design to leave me, to be arrested, to have another kid, but it happened. Just like it wasn't in my grand design to get pregnant with Bella or lose Max.

"Was it hard leaving us," I ask.

"I didn't–"

I turn, and my look must be enough to sever the words in his mouth.

"You're right. Not the arrest. The other stuff." He sighs and walks into the kitchen where he pours himself a cup of water. "I wish I could say 'yes,' Griffin, but I was a young and stupid man then. Selfish. Unhealthy. Broken. I'm walking the line a bit better now," he says, "but I have many regrets that I'm better able to understand now."

"Like?"

"Like cheating on your mom. Like doing the shit that got me sent to jail. Like missing out on your life. And as much as I regret hurting your mom, I can't completely discount the joy I have in Mara, who wouldn't exist if I hadn't." He leans over the counter, bent at the waist. "That probably isn't what you want to hear."

"I just want the truth."

338

"Okay." He nods. "Fair enough." He stands up straight again. "The truth is, when I look in the mirror, I recognize my failure every day. It's a terrible burden, but I can't allow the self-pity that tempts me. I did it to myself. Instead, each morning when I look at my reflection, I say to myself, 'Be better today. Make better choices today. Be there for your kids today.'"

I step away from the door and turn toward him. "Getting pregnant was an accident," I admit. My words are vulnerable and full of open-ended hope. I think: *I messed up. I need some help. I need you.*

But I don't want to need him. I press my teeth together.

He doesn't say anything, just waits for me.

So, I keep going. "I thought my life was over, but–" I stop and swallow. "It is strange to say that I feel like my life is just beginning?" I don't know why I've said this, but then maybe it's because I'm so different.

He offers me a gentle smile, gentle like the man I remember playing with me when I was little, wrestling with Phoenix and me in the living room and letting us win. "I don't think that's strange."

A part of me wants to hang onto the anger I feel, and I think it's still there filtering most of how I am with him, but I also feel a hope, something different than just anger. Hope that maybe by accepting his flaws and all, that I too can be accepted, flaws and all. I say, "It's a girl."

He smiles. "Congratulations."

I nod. "Well, I just wanted you to know." I turn back to the door and twist the doorknob to open it.

He moves around the counter. "I'm glad you did."

I turn away.

"Griffin?"

I stop and turn back toward him.

"Maybe we could meet for breakfast, or you could come with Phoenix one of these days."

I take a deep breath. Another choice. I can continue down the path away from him, down the road of hating my father, of being bitter and angry. I can continue to shut him out, but I can also make a different choice. Run toward something instead. "Yeah. I'd like that," I say.

He offers me a look that can only be described as relieved joy, and when he nods, his eyes sparkle with tears.

I close the door behind me and walk away from the apartment. I think it might be the lightest I've felt in months.

7.

To Max: I went and saw my father, told him about the baby.

I'm not sure how I expected it to go.

It's always tense between us, not because of him, but because of me.

This time, I felt like I wanted it to be different, so I didn't run away which is what I've done since he got out.

My dad told me that he wants to be better, and I decided that if I want people to trust in me, I should probably do the same, right?

I keep circling back around to that night when I didn't trust you to be on my side.

I wish I'd made a different choice, but like Cal said, sometimes life kicks you in the balls and you have to figure out if you're going to lay there or get back up.

Okay, he didn't say it exactly like that. ☺

I spend nights wishing I'd made a different choice.

Replay it over and over wondering how it would be different.

I know it was my fault, Max.

I didn't trust you because I was just a coward.

Afraid you wouldn't choose me because I wouldn't choose me.

I know you've moved on, and I'm happy for you.

I just miss my friend.

I miss you too, SK.　Max

MARCH

I've discovered a magical phrase that when employed appropriately is a game changer. I'M SORRY. If I'd understood the power of these words, when utilized honestly, I might have found this place of freedom sooner.

They've lightened that heavy load on my back and helped me reorient that picture of what kind of man I want to be.

To: Griffin Nichols
123 45th Street NE
The Town, USA 67890

1.

Me to Max:

> You know you told me one time—

> that time we went to the Bend—

> that my name meant a "guardian of treasures," and you believed it.

> I loved that you did.

> It made me feel like it could be true.

> All my life I thought my name meant monster, and that's kind of how I've acted.

> Like one of those self-fulfilling prophecies or something.

The truth is, though, Max,

I didn't guard my treasure. I pushed her away.

I wish there was something I could say to fix it,

But I messed it up.

I'm sorry for that.

I heard you aren't coming home for spring break, which made me sad.

I had hoped to tell you 'I'm sorry' in person, but I get it.

You're moving on.

Maybe with the many number of Bens in your life ☺

I hope you have fun and enjoy your break.

I'm trying to follow your relationship rules, so I wanted you to know that no matter what, I want to be a better treasure guardian.

I will always treasure our friendship—

I miss that, most.

I will always treasure the lessons you taught me,

and the way you made it clear you believed in me.

I will always treasure the way you made me feel like I was the best version of myself,

and now that I know what that feels like, I can work for that on my own.

I treasure that you made me face my shit

(well, you and Cal). ☺

So, for all of that, thank you, Maxwell Wallace.

Your friend forever, Griffin.

She doesn't respond.

2.

When I go to the kitchen to get some food, Mom is sitting on the couch, wrapped up in a blanket on the couch watching late night TV.

"Hey," she says when I walk through to the kitchen.

"Where's Bill?"

"Not sure."

The way she says it sounds weird.

"Everything okay?" I walk to the opening between the rooms, lean against the wall, and study at her. It's a rare opportunity to do so. This woman who never sits, never watches TV, never idle. She doesn't have time for it. Instead, she's been a flurry of movement, of problem solving, of tough love. Now, she looks quiet and still.

She glances at me and then looks back at the TV. "I broke it off with him."

"Really?" I'm surprised and go to the couch to sit down next to her. "How come? I thought you really liked him."

We listen to the studio audience laugh at something the host says.

She mutes the TV. "I did like him. I mean, I do like him, but there was just something in my gut telling me I was having to try too hard to be content."

"But aren't relationships about work?"

"Definitely." She looks at me. "I'm no expert or anything, but it felt a lot like I was working to keep things together, and I don't want that for myself again. I want someone who's willing to work for me too." She looks at me. "Do you know what I'm saying?"

"I think so."

"You told me not to settle. And as nice as a person as Bill is, that's what I felt like I was doing. Making allowances for all the ways I was having to adjust. I don't want to be the only one making adjustments."

"I'm proud of you, Mom."

A smile blooms on her face. "Why would you say that?"

"Because you're strong. You've held us together. You've been both my mom and my dad. I think you're the best. And whoever you date should know that and treat you that way too."

She adjusts on the couch and leans against my shoulder. "Thank you for that, Griffin." She unmutes the TV a while, and we watch the jokes and then the interviews.

I get up and make us some microwave popcorn which we share.

We laugh at a stupid monologue and silly commercials. Eventually, Mom mutes the TV again and says, "You know? If no one comes along, I'm okay with that, too."

I look at her a nod. Strangely, having gone through what I've experienced with Bella, and even with Max, I understand what she means. At one time, I remember hiding from being alone, but now, having faced it and found comfort in my own skin, I'm not afraid to face it anymore.

"Let's catch the popcorn," I tell her and take a popped kernel, throw it up and try to catch it with my mouth. It hits me on the chin.

Mom laughs. "No, thanks." She snuggles in closer, and we watch a black and white movie until sleep makes it impossible to watch anymore.

I'm alone at the farmhouse the next day, earbuds in my ears, listening to the playlist I made Max for our road trip. One of my favorite songs is in the midst of a guitar solo, and there's a nice beat that makes spreading paint on the walls easier. Otherwise, I'd be bored out of my mind, especially since Cal isn't here for company. Not that he talks all that much, but there's something nice about just being around someone and the comfort of knowing they're there.

The key, I decide, is being content either way.

My phone pings through my headphones. I wrap an arm around the extended pole of the paint roller and hold it against my side to check who's texted, figuring it's Tanner and hoping it's not Bella. He left for California a couple of days ago on some big adventure to offer a grand gesture to Emma. He's staying with Josh, and going to watch our former classmate, Atticus Baker, in his basketball game. It sounds like fun, but I'm content to be here, where I can be close to Bella, who called me yesterday after the appointment and said her blood pressure was a little high. "No big deal," she reassured me. "The baby is fine."

The text is from Tanner:

Dude. Cali is crazy. Tanner

Me Why?

Hard to explain. I thought the city was big. San Fran is giant. So many people. And the PACIFIC OCEAN!

Pretty?

Well… When you can see it through the fog, yeah.

Pics? How's Josh?

> Same. He says 'S'up'.

> Yo! How's Emma?

> Haven't seen her yet. Tomorrow.

> Nervous?

> Fuck yeah. She can skewer me with a word.

> I don't think she would have said yes if she wasn't interested. What did Josh say?

> Same.

> You're good. Use the Tanner swagger. Got to go. Some people have to work.

I replace the phone in my pocket with a smile and rewet the roller with the same gray shade Max picked out for downstairs, continued in the upstairs landing hallway. I'm so grateful my friends are back in my life. I wonder if Max is having fun on her spring break trip with Ben. Shit. No. Her friends, but in my head, I've worked it up to be with Ben and wishing she was with me. I just miss her.

My phone pings again. "Freaking Tanner," I say out loud and rest the painting pole in a one-armed hug again to balance it against my shoulder.

It isn't Tanner. Max has initiated a text.

> Hey.

I hesitate, heart pounding. There's a lot riding on my response. I text:

> Hey.

And roll my eyes at myself. *Idiot.*

> Is my dad home?

It's a weird question. I glance about, even though it's a dumb response, since I know he isn't.

> No. Out on a job. Why?

There's a thump downstairs. I turn off the music, hear the door close, and text her again:

> Wait. I think he just got back. Need me to tell him something?

"Cal?" I call down the stairs, but he doesn't answer. I lean the paint poll against the wall, knowing I'm going to have to fix it after and hop down the stairs. "Cal? Need some help–" But I stall on the bottom step. "What the–"

Max is standing just this side of the closed door, a bag on the floor near her feet. She looks good, so good. Perfect. Beautiful, and I know what she feels like against my hands. I tamp down my longing to kiss her. She isn't smiling and looks worried. Unsure. This isn't how I think of Max, whose tenacity sat with me, a stranger, outside of a convenience store, who asked me if I was a serial killer while she laughed.

I take the final step down, my chest tight with concern. "Are you okay? What happened? You're supposed to be—not here."

She nods, then her mouth skews sideways like she's trying to hold in her emotions.

I shove my hands into my pockets and fist them to keep myself steady. But my muscles seem to decide to pulse with adrenaline, nerves twitching, so I withdraw my hands and cross my arms tightly.

She scrunches up her nose like she needs to sneeze. Her eyes are shiny. She closes them. "You're painting."

I nod and look up the stairwell. "Finishing upstairs. Working on the punch list to finish it out." When I return my gaze to her, she's looking up the stairs past me. "What are you doing here?"

She chews on her upper lip, then says, "I didn't go."

"I see that."

She smiles, but it's subdued and at the floor, not at me. "Right. Let me fix that." She looks up with a nod, as if she's come to a decision, and meets my gaze. Her eyes crash into mine, and the longing in them tugs at my belly as the tightening reaches around to my back. "I didn't want to go," she says. "I thought I did, but the closer it got, the more I thought about home."

I swallow and struggle because my mouth is dry. Her eyes are telling me one thing, but I'm trying to line it up with her words and actions, which aren't clear. "Your dad will be happy."

"Yeah. Um. He will be." She crosses her arms and takes a step forward. "But he isn't the reason I came home." She pauses and takes another step. "I wanted to see you, Griffin, and I miss you, and–"

But I don't let her finish. I close the distance between us in two steps, take her face between my hands and kiss her. God, I kiss her, like every fiber of my being is fused with hers. It's like getting a deep drink of water after walking through the desert. "I'm sorry." I kiss her with the worship I feel moving through me. When I draw away from her, I say, "I'm sorry. I should have asked."

She smiles, and her shiny eyes spill over with tears. She reaches up and pushes some of my hair off my forehead. "I was hoping it wasn't too late."

I wrap my arms around her. "I'm sorry, Max. So sorry. You were right."

She clings to my back, my t-shirt bunched up in her hands, the cool air in the house biting at the skin of my back. "I should have stayed and fought with you. For you. I shouldn't have walked away. I'm sorry, too. I didn't follow my rules."

I kiss her forehead, her temple, her cheek. I swipe at the tears on her cheeks with my thumbs. "You're here now. Do we still need to fight about it?" I ask and smile against her lips. "I could muster some fighting words if you give me a moment, I'm sure."

She shakes her head with a growing smile under my lips and tugs my body closer to hers. The kiss she gives me is sweet, until it isn't. Her mouth begins to take, and I give, her want like mine, deep and insistent. My stomach clenches, and my heart trips up as I shiver, the heat turning up a few notches in my chest. When her breathing becomes heavy and she whispers my name into my mouth, it's nearly my undoing.

"Max. Max," I say against her skin, pulling away.

I'm at work.

I'm at work.

"I'm at work," I finally say. "And I have to not get fired, because your dad will have my head if I mess up again."

"Again?"

"Yeah, I can't let him down."

Her fingers graze my face. "I'll help." She smiles. "Help me with my bags?"

I nod and follow her up the stairs, wondering how I'm going to finish the work with her beside me when all I want to do is keep her in my arms.

It turns out, however, that moving through the punch list isn't so bad when we check off the items together. The painting, the outlet covers, caulking goes quickly because we talk, which I'm pretty sure is probably more important between us at the moment than the physical stuff.

"Was Renna upset you didn't go with them?"

"Maybe, but she understood."

"And Ben?" I ask.

"Worried about all the Bens in my life?"

"Just one."

"Ben and I went out for coffee."

"Yeah?"

"Yeah."

"You're here," I say.

"I am. He isn't you."

I set the putty down and lean against the counter next to her.

"I read and reread your texts. I loved them."

"I just...I needed to talk to you. I missed you and I didn't know how else to figure out what was happening." I pause, drawing a breath, examining my open palms, not looking at her. "You didn't text back."

"I wanted to. I just didn't know what to say."

I meet her gaze.

"I wrote you a letter; I just never sent it."

"What did it say?"

"About how I was feeling, and how much you mean to me and about how for the first time in my life, you made me feel like I was just right."

"You are."

"I was—am—insecure about Bella. I don't want to be, but I am."

"Bella and I aren't like that. Even with one night, we weren't ever anything, you know. Drunk. We're just partners for the baby." I pause, knowing what I need to say and a little tentative because I know it could be what ends things. But it's her choice. I can't decide for her. "That's really important to me, Max."

Max reaches out and plucks something from my t-shirt on my arm. The touch burns through to my skin and into my bloodstream.

I move to stand in front of her. With a finger curled under her chin, I lift her face to look at me and wait until she does. "Plus, there's a big problem with Bella."

355

Her eyes search mine. "And what's that?"

"She isn't you."

Max smiles. That dimple.

I lean down. "I mean it." I press my lips against that little divot just to the left of her mouth.

She pulls me against her and turns her head, so our lips connect. I groan. "Max."

She hums, tilting her head so the kiss deepens.

I reach down and lift her so she's sitting on the counter, then step in between her legs. "I'm supposed to be working."

She smiles against my mouth. "But isn't this more fun."

My heart skydives in my chest. "Yes. Stop." I run my fingers through her hair and straighten. "Max?"

"Yeah?" She tilts her head closer to my hand.

"Are you really okay with the idea of me being a dad? I understand, Max, if you aren't. It's big. I'm having a kid."

Her eyes flutter open, and she measures my face with her gaze. "I'm not scared of that."

"I can't promise it won't be complicated, but Max, if you'll have me, I'm all in."

She grins. "All in, huh?" Her eyes flick up to mine.

"Are you being naughty?"

She wiggles my hips using my belt loops and grins. "Yes."

"I'm at work."

"Fine. Where's the paint brush." She gives me a quick kiss. "I'll follow you."

She does.

We spend the rest of the afternoon talking, stealing kisses and touches, and finishing the punch list. I think about Mom and her decision to break-up with Bill, her feeling like she was making all of the allowances. I don't feel like that with Max, and maybe we're being naïve to think we can work through a baby that's going to take up a huge part of my life, but right now, whatever this is, I feel seen. I feel heard. I feel respected. And I look at her and feel the same. I see her. I hear her. I respect her. Maybe that's all we can strive for in any relationship.

3.

The lake sparkles through the trees when I park the car in the space in front of Josh's family cabin. It's a bright blue-green sparkling in the spring sunshine. Remnants of snow are spread thin or in piles clinging to the landscape, but this isn't a trip to frolic in the sunshine. When I climb out of the car, my nerves are exposed and compressed with anticipation. I glance at Max as she gets out of the passenger's side. We spent most of the two-hour drive talking with ease, but the reality of finally being alone hovers like the cold mountain air.

After nearly a week of making out in my car, dodging Cal, and putting off Max who seems okay with having sex in the backseat, but I've refused—I want our first time to be memorable and special—I've finally reached out to my friends for advice. Awkward, but kind of perfect for a new bro code we're creating, Tanner brings it up to Josh (they are still in California together, Tanner's grand gesture a success), and Josh suggests his family's cabin which is free and clear for a private, weekend getaway before she returns to school for her final term.

"This is beautiful," she says.

I wait a beat before saying, "I'll make sure the key works before we unload."

She nods and stretches.

The three stairs up onto the covered deck are packed with a cycle of snow that has melted a few times over. I notice that I'm focusing on the details of things, as if to calm my insides from the anticipation, the fear, the hope wrapped up in being with Max. Holding the screen door with my body, the key slips into the lock, and the door opens with a slight shove to loosen it from the swollen frame. It's dark and cold inside.

Her footsteps thud against the wood of the porch, then I feel her warmth behind me. She leans and looks over my shoulder. "It's cute." She walks past me into the main room and turns. "I'll open it up and air it out a bit."

A few trips between the car and the cabin later, I stand at the front door with a bag slung over my shoulder.

Max has opened the curtains so the light filters in through the large windows. She's also opened windows, and the musty smell that met me has already waned. The cabin is a comfortable space, not large like Josh's house, but cabin cozy. A small family room in an open living space decorated in reds and greens, includes a table large enough for six people. The main room connects to a kitchen and a hallway that leads to the back of the house. There's a cold fireplace, waiting to be lit to warm the whole place, and an open stairwell leading to an upper level.

Max is in the kitchen, unloading a weekend menu into the small refrigerator and looks up when she hears me. "You planning on coming inside or just taking up space in the doorway?"

I look down at my shoes, the toes at the threshold, then back at her.

She walks across the room to me and stops just close enough that I could just lean to kiss her.

"I want you to know," I start, "I don't have, like, expectations. I mean, I have hopes, but I don't want you to feel—"

She puts her fingers against my lips. "Stop," she says gently.

"Griffin." My name is quiet, and she takes my hand. "This is about us, whatever that means. Let's not worry, okay?"

I nod and smile under her hand.

"One moment at a time." She smiles and then rubs her arms. "Would you build a fire?" Her smile and eyebrows shift with the innuendo.

I step across the threshold into the cabin and kiss her cheek. "Yes. I'll do that for you." While she finishes the job she started in the kitchen, I start a literal fire.

We explore the cabin. A bathroom, bedroom, and sun porch down the hallway from the kitchen. Up the stairs, another bedroom with bunk beds, a third bedroom with a queen and a bathroom.

"This one?" she asks me with a smile.

"Unless you want the one with the bunk beds. I get the bottom if you do," I say.

She takes the bag she's carrying and drops it in the room with the queen, then takes my bag and sets it next to hers. "Technically," she says and turns to look at me. "We've already slept together. Several times."

My heart speeds up, and I step into the room with an urgent need to kiss her. "True."

"And showered together."

I swallow, recalling that memory, and nod.

She takes a step closer to me. "I need this out of my system, or I'm going to be a nervous wreck." She reaches for me.

I feel a tingle and the weight of her fingertips against my shoulder blades. I reach out and smooth her silky hair that doesn't need it. I just want to feel her, reassure myself she's here. "Are you sure this is what you want?"

She nods and meets my gaze. "Yes." She leans forward and kisses me. "You?"

"God, yes."

Kissing her is like coming home. Like comfort food and joy. It's like feelings wrapped up in a box for Christmas and tied with a ribbon. I kiss her, wanting her to know that, because in all the times I've kissed and been kissed, it hasn't ever felt like this. So important, and in that moment, I realize it's because I love her. I love Max Wallace, and maybe I've loved her for a long time and didn't understand it until just now.

The thought terrifies me.

I told Tanner one time that loving a girl was just a way to let her have power over you, to be pussy whipped and to lose your independence. When I think about it, however, it doesn't feel like that with Max, and maybe my claim was just wrapped up in misconception and ideology I didn't really understand. Kissing her, talking with her, being with her feels like a missing piece of a puzzle being discovered. Understanding that makes my heart expand in my chest, and I kiss her more deeply.

Our kisses become hot and burdened. We unburden one another. Max removes my sweatshirt. I help her with her sweater. She helps pull the t-shirt over my head. What started slow begins to move with frenzy. There are words, names, breathy sounds, moans, and hands. Everywhere. Skin to skin as we shed the rest of our clothing.

"Max. You're so beautiful," I tell her, my hands skimming over her skin, touching her, stroking her. She writhes under me, and I'm wound up. I can feel it under my skin. "I'm not going to last, Max," I tell her even as I'm putting on the condom.

"Please, Griffin. I want you," she says, grasps my hips, and draws me into her.

And my body both tightens and releases.

Done. Too fast.

"Oh shit," I breathe and drop my head forward onto her shoulder. "I'm sorry, Max. I'm so fucking sorry." I'm embarrassed and feel the protective walls come up. I know how it should be to be better than that. It was bad for her, and I'm pretty sure she's going to be so disappointed. I'm fucking disappointed. She's going to think being with me is horrible. The economy car.

I slip off her and onto my belly next to her. "I'm sorry, Max."

"Sorry about what? What is it?" She rolls toward me.

"It felt like my first time." I press my face into my arm to hide. She giggles.

I turn my head, annoyed, and look at her with one eye. "Please don't laugh."

She tries to straighten her face but fights with her smile. "I'm not laughing AT you," she says. "I promise. It's the situation."

I sigh and shake my head, returning to hide in the darkness against my arm. "You make me crazy."

"In a good way, I hope."

I grunt at her. "Sometimes."

She pinches my arm. "Hey."

I emerge from my hiding place and peek at her. "I feel bad, okay? And stupid. So please don't make fun. Now, we'll only remember our first time wasn't good."

She scrunches up her eyes and nose. "What are you talking about? That was fun, and I distinctly remember our first time being together was in my dorm room. We did a lot in my dorm room." She wiggles her eyebrows. "And that was pretty awesome."

I can't help but grin at her and the memory. I look away, my chin resting on my arm.

"We may not have done the whole penetration stuff, but isn't that still sex?" Her fingers are in my hair, and she twirls the locks.

"Yeah. I just—" I clamp my mouth shut. I don't know what to say. I'm afraid to tell her what's on my mind. Like letting go so soon, what will she think of me? "I wanted it to be special."

"Every time I'm with you feels special." She scoots closer, her gorgeous boob presses against my arm, and her leg drapes over my backside. She tugs me against her. "Talk to me, Griffin."

I lean up onto my elbows. Staring at the headboard feels safer. "You make me feel stuff, and I haven't felt like this before, so I just got wound up. All those make out sessions. Fuck, Max." I finally look at her. She's watching me. Waiting. "I'm crazy about you, and

362

now, I'm afraid you'll think I'll always be that bad."

"First, it wasn't bad. It was just…quick." She giggles.

I roll my eyes and scoff.

"Second, I'm figuring that wasn't the last time, so we'll get another go at it." She smiles.

"I sure hope so." I smile, and look down at the light, green pillowcase.

She runs a hand down my spine, skimming my skin and sending a warm message to my nerve endings. "And three, feel what?"

With my chin on my shoulder, I study her. Telling her how I feel is a risk, but I think about all the ways I've insulated myself all these years and where it got me. What I told Tanner was a lie because it was meant to be tough and in control, but it isn't a truth. I think about what happened the last time I didn't trust her with my feelings and how that pushed her away, and this is one of those things that I will have to trust her with even if it means I could hurt. "I'm not sure how to say it."

"You're making me nervous," she says. Her hand continues its repetitive journey back and forth over my skin. "Just say it."

I turn toward her and reach out, exposing my heart, putting my hand on the swell of her hip, and pulling her closer. "I love you. There. I love you."

That beautiful smile I love so much, the one with the dimple, graces her face. She moves, pressing my back onto the bed, and climbs on top of me. "You do?" She kisses my mouth, then pulls away. "Because I love you, Griffin. I've wanted to tell you for so long, but I didn't want to scare you away." She kisses me on the mouth, then pulls away again. "You love me. You love me," she sings, and it makes my heart sing along with her. *She loves me. She loves me.*

"Let's go get something to eat." She climbs from the bed, shrugs into my sweatshirt.

"Now?" I ask.

"Yeah." She grins at me. "We've got time." She leans forward

363

and kisses me again. "No need to rush." Then she holds out her hand to help me up.

I slip back into my jeans and t-shirt and follow her down the stairs.

The fire has warmed the cabin, and it's cozy. Being there with her is domestic and hints at the way we are together, at least in the magic of our newness, and I wonder if that fades. It did for Mom and Bill, but then Mom said she'd felt it in her gut long before she ended it. I don't feel like that with Max at all and decide not to worry about it now. I choose to be present and not to let what happened earlier hover around me. I want just to be here.

We make a sandwich and share it.

We laugh.

We dream.

We sit on the couch by the fire.

We talk.

Max has decided that she wants to major in business.

I tell her that after giving school a chance, I don't like it, but I love working for Cal. I love building and think that's what I want to do.

We talk about parenthood, and I share my fears about fatherhood.

We make plans that include one another.

I feel full of her, of the moment, of us.

"You think it's dangerous to be too happy?" I ask her.

"Why?"

I shrug. "I'm not used to feeling like this." I get up and add another log to the fire. "I'm used to doubt, hurt, and anger."

She watches me and tucks her bare legs under her. "Maybe we train ourselves how to feel."

"What do you mean?"

"Like if you're used to being angry, that's the norm, so that's how you usually feel. Or sad."

"Or happy?" I ponder it. "Maybe. But when something goes

wrong, you aren't happy."

"No. No one is happy when something goes wrong."

"Like when we got in our fight."

She looks at me. "Yeah. Like then. But that doesn't mean you can't find it again."

I return to the couch and sit next to her. "Do you feel happy?"

"Everyday." She unfolds her body and leans toward me. "But I don't think I've ever been this happy."

"I think we would make people gag at how happy we are." I smile at her and lean forward to kiss her.

She laughs under my mouth. "Definitely."

We kiss, the fire is warm, but the heat between us, warmer.

"I'm so happy to be here," she says into my mouth.

I smile, laughing. "Me too. Me too. Me too." With each repetition, I kiss her until she's on her back on the couch, and my hips are now sheltered between her legs.

"I guess that means you won't be able to get rid of me." She smiles.

"I don't want to," I say, grasping her hips and settling in deeper. I kiss her.

She returns the kiss.

When the kissing and touching becomes more focused and desperate, when we've shed our skin of all the layers between us, I use my body to speak to her exactly as I need it to. Her body answers fluently. Together. And this time, it's perfect.

APRIL

I can't go backward, even if it feels safer there.

It isn't.

To: Griffin Nichols
123 45th Street NE
The Town, USA 67890

1.

"She's pretty," Cal says from the doorway of the workshop. His back to me, he's got one hand in the pocket of his jeans and the other wrapped around a coffee mug. It's a crisp April morning, a Saturday. The sun isn't high yet, and the frost is still sparkling on things trying to turn green.

I stand up straight, after placing some stray tools in the container, then join him.

He's staring at the house.

He's right.

Nine months ago, the house looked like the wind was going to blow it over. Now it looks brand new. New wood. New wiring and plumbing. New drywall and flooring. Kitchens and bathrooms redone. New windows. New siding. New paint. New roof. All that new mixed with the old bones and sinew of a house built to hold onto new memories. All those months ago, it had just been a broken-down house. Now, it's a home. His and Max's.

He sips his coffee. "I'm never going to recuperate that money." He sighs and looks at me, barely turning his head.

"Maybe it isn't about the money, though."

He sips from his cup. "Of course it isn't. I've just spent a lot of years flipping houses, Griffin." He looks at me. "It's always been about the money."

I nod at the house. "But this one isn't a flip. You built Max a home."

He hums and stares at the house again. Then he nods and turns away from the doorway, smiling as his steps echo against the old wood. "We built it. She's happy we're staying."

"She is." And I am too, but I keep this to myself.

"Ready to help me redo this building?"

"Yep," I tell him and continue going through things. We've just started working on the workshop, using nights and weekends when I'm here and not with Max. We've both been busy with other projects. With the house done and Cal deciding to make it his and Max's home, he's shifted from being an on-call fix-it guy to taking on clients wanting their own fixer uppers. I've agreed to help him, so he can keep teaching me, but for a steady income I took a job with Tanner's dad.

"How do you like working for that James fella?" Cal asks.

"It's good. He's fair."

"He called me. Needs an experienced finished carpenter. Seems someone might have told him about me."

I just smile. "You going to take it?"

"I'll bid to him like a subcontractor."

I nod and watch him crouch down to look at some junk we pulled from the rafter space in the workshop.

"I'm proud of you, Griffin," he says and picks up a nice board. He looks at the grain. "This is a keeper," he says and sets it in the pile we've started for the stuff to keep and store while we renovate. He returns to the pile.

"Sir?"

"That day you showed up for the job." He chuckles. "I thought I'd lose you after that first hard day, when I had you pulling down that porch. You looked ready to run. No tools. No gloves." He laughs now. "Wasn't sure you'd last."

I smile and shake my head, embarrassed. It's difficult to hear and

369

accept positive things when the negative ones are easier to believe. I'm working on it.

"But you stuck it out. Says a lot about you. When I can afford it, I'm going to steal you away from that James outfit." He offers me a smile. "Put you on the payroll. You're a hard worker."

Happy with his approval, I return to my task.

My phone vibrates in my pocket. I hope it's Max. Since she's been back at school, I miss her and look forward to our check ins. We've been making the distance work. This weekend she had a big project—finals are soon—so I stayed home.

Plus, it's time to start thinking about those final projects around Bella's house that Tanner and Phoenix are going to help me with before the baby arrives. She's seven months along, almost eight.

Bella's name is in my notification.

I swipe to open my phone:

> Something's wrong. Going to the hospital.

My heart suspends as the rest of me free falls. I text her back:

> What's wrong?

But she doesn't answer.

I dial her, and it rings through to her voice mail. I hang up.

"Cal," I say. I can hear the worry in my voice, but I take a deep breath, willing myself not to freak out. I wave the phone at him. "Bella texted. She's on her way to the hospital. She thinks something might be wrong."

"Go. Go." He swipes his hands in a motion toward the door, follows me out, and watches me from the driveway as I drive away.

The moment I rush into the emergency waiting room, Bella's little sister, CeCe jumps up. "Griffin." She rushes into my arms, trembling. The little girl clings to my waist; I pat her back and crouch down to be able to see her. "Bella was crying. And there was blood."

She whispers the last word, traumatized. Her eyes are wide with panic. "Is she going to be okay?"

My heart, which has been beating in my throat, tightens with terror.

I glance around looking for Bella's mom. She isn't there, but a lady is with CeCe I've never met. She introduces herself as Aunt Tina. The information isn't sticking. My brain and body are in emergency mode.

"Can I go back?" I ask, still holding onto Bella's little sister. I lean to look at her. "I'm going to check on Bella, okay?"

The aunt draws CeCe from me and back to the seats in the waiting area.

I find the phone near the heavy, wide doors separating the waiting room from the emergency room and call beyond them. Someone answers it: "ER Nurse's Station."

"I'm here for Bella Noble."

"Are you family?"

"No."

"I'm sorry, but—"

"I'm the baby's father," I say, cutting off whoever is on the other line. "She contacted me."

"Are you her legal spouse?"

"No."

"Hold on, please."

There's a click, and the line goes dead.

I hang up the phone but lean against the wall near it.

If I'd been trying to hold myself together, now I'm panicked. Adrenaline rushes through me, and I cross my arms over my chest, wishing I'd grabbed a sweatshirt from the backseat of my car.

I pace. Every second feels like an eternity.

I pick up the phone again. I'm told to wait again. "I want to come back," I say.

"Sir. I need you to hang on. We need to figure out what's happening, then someone will come find you."

I don't know how long I stand near that phone in front of those doors. Long enough to watch them open and straighten in anticipation that whoever is coming out of them represents news and a ticket back. Long enough to watch several people come and go. Long enough to lean against the wall because my legs have grown tired, arms crossed tightly over my chest. I could go get a sweatshirt, but I don't want to leave in case someone comes for me. I don't know what's happening. I don't want to worry anyone, but the longer I'm there, the more worried I become. The more alone I feel.

I draw my phone from my pocket to check the time again and think about calling my mom. I wish she were here with me. The doors open with a hissing sound of the hydraulics. I straighten, and my heart seizes when Bella's mom walks out.

She doesn't see me at first. Dazed and pale.

"Minny," I say and catch her eyes.

She does a double take of me. "Oh my god, Griffin. They rushed her back."

"Back where?"

"Surgery. Oh my god." She grabs a hold of me, the strong smell of old cigarettes clinging to her, and she squeezes me as she cries.

I'm okay to be a wall for the moment, a foundation to hold her up, but my heart races. "Why?"

She can't put words together yet.

CeCe comes around the corner at the sound of her mom's voice. She hustles through the wide hallway and wraps her tiny arms around her mother's waist. Minny lets go of me, reaches down, and lifts CeCe into her arms, cooing as she walks away.

I'm left near the door, unsure, feeling useless and powerless. "What's happening?" My throat tightens. It's bad. "Is Bella okay?"

Minny, CeCe in her arms, turns and looks at me, and I have never felt so separate from something that directly impacts me. From the end of the alcove she says, "I don't know. She started bleeding. And contractions. And it just got worse and worse. Then

Bell's blood pressure was dropping." She stops and shakes her head. Her breath gets caught on the inside of her lungs a moment, but she gathers it to get her tears under control. "They took her to surgery." She opens her mouth to say more, then closes it; she can't seem to speak around the tears anymore. She shakes her head.

"What is it?" I ask even though every part of me doesn't want to ask it. I know that whatever is on the other side of the question isn't good. I reach back for the wall behind me, palm flat against the smooth surface, for support.

She shakes her head. "They couldn't find the baby's heartbeat." She squeezes CeCe tighter and walks away, leaving me alone in the hallway near the emergency room door.

I drop into a crouch and shove my hands into my hair. My eyes scan the speckles in the linoleum of the floor as if there might be an answer to whatever is happening in the key of the pattern there. With a shaky breath and shaking hands, I call my mom.

"Mom."

"Hey." She sounds happy.

Tears leak from my eyes. "I'm at the hospital. It's Bella and the baby. Are you here?"

"No. Home. Shit. I'm on my way. What happened?" I can hear her moving, thumps and creaks against the housing of the phone.

"Mom... they can't find the baby's heartbeat." My throat closes around the last word and tears flow more freely. I can't even swipe them from my eyes.

"Griffin. Oh my god. I'll be there."

"Emergency."

She cuts the line.

I sit on the floor, outside those giant doors curled into myself. My butt on the cold floor, my knees drawn up to my chest, my arms crossed tightly over the top of them. I've dried my face, but I feel the tears cutting up the back of my throat.

I don't know how long I sit there. I'm a statue.

Ten seconds.

Ten days.

Time isn't working. I'm frozen. Numb.

I see feet move past me. Wheelchairs. Gurneys. There are faces and voices, words that are presumably clear and understandable, but I'm not holding onto details. Rather, I'm detached from reality. I lay my head on my arms, resting on my knees.

Waiting.

"Griffin?" My mom's voice.

I look up. She's crouched in front of me, her hands on my arms. Then she's drawing me against her, her arms around me. She becomes the wall I need. My hands cling to her, and I let the tears come because I'm afraid. I'm so goddamn afraid. "They can't find the heartbeat," I repeat over and over through my tears. My mom— the wall— is replaced by Phoenix. Then Tanner. They're both dressed in work clothes. They take up sentry duty around me.

Ten thousand million hours later. Or maybe it's an hour—I can't tell—the door opens again. Someone dressed in scrubs emerges from the giant doors.

I scramble off the floor. It's the billionth time I've done this, hopeful for news.

The doctor—like everyone before her—glances at me but her eyes bounce away. She isn't looking for me. I follow her to see who she's looking for as she moves deeper into the waiting room. When the doctor stops in front of Minny, I hustle across the room.

"…she's not lucid right now and might be in recovery for a while. She lost a lot of blood, but we were able to stabilize her. She's been admitted. I'll send someone back when they move her to her room so you can be with her."

Tears stream down Bella's mom's face.

"And the baby?" I ask.

The doctor looks at me, then at Bella's mom who nods. The doctor shakes her head. "I'm sorry."

"Sorry for what?" I ask, thinking perhaps she's referring to Bella.

Someone pulls at my sleeve, but I yank away.

374

"Sorry for what? What about the baby?" I ask.

"We did everything we could, but this happens sometimes."

"What happens?" I ask again.

"A placental abruption. The baby didn't make it. I'm sorry."

I back away from the doctor and shake my head. "I want to see Bella," I say because the doctor is lying. And if I just see Bella, she'll be able to show me that everything is okay.

I bump into someone and turn. It's Phoenix. I turn the other direction, and Tanner flanks my other side. Their faces are drawn and worried. Mom's crying just a step behind them, her hand covering her mouth, a tissue exploding from under her hand. "They won't let me see Bella and my baby," I tell them.

Phoenix puts a hand on my shoulder. "Let's sit for a minute."

I shake him off. "I don't want to fucking sit. I want to fucking see Bella and the baby."

"Griff," Tanner says, and his eyes fill. "Griffin." He plucks at the sleeve of my t-shirt.

"Get the fuck off me," I yell. People around me jump, and the security guard walks into the room. Phoenix holds out his hand. I feel like punching Tanner when he steps closer. I shake my head. "She fucking made it!" My eyes are filled with tears, and I can't see. I swipe at them with my fingertips so I can see Tanner to hit him.

He steps closer and this time wraps his arms around me, tight. "Griffin. I'm so sorry."

"Fuck you," I sob, but there isn't any fight in my words or my body now. I bury my face in his shoulder and cling to him, my hands grasping onto the back of his shirt. He holds me up because I feel like I might fall. "She's not gone."

"I'm sorry. So sorry," he repeats. "I've got you."

I push him away. "No. No. No." I back away, shaking my head, then turn, escaping them. Voices call after me as I disappear through the sliding doors out into the sparkling golden sunlight. I rush through the parking lot and into my car. Then I drive. Away. Tears stream down my face with my heart coming out of my mouth.

2.

Car slides over pavement like lightning in the sky.

Flashes of concrete spaces ruled by abstract thought: move forward and away.

Don't ponder. Deny. Deny. Deny.

Move away.

It's not real. Deny. Deny.

The black road stretches and disappears around the bend.

The tires rumble against the asphalt, a welcome white noise.

The car is warm.

I feel tired.

Move forward and away.

Deny.

Alone.

Breath catches on hooks in my lungs. I can't get it moving again. Breathe.

I can't deny it, so I say out loud: "This isn't real." My voice is a stranger's.

I swipe at the tears in my eyes, so I can see the road.

Unhook another breath. Breathe.

I can't focus. I hurtle through space and time in my metal spaceship as the real world blurs around me. I swipe moisture from my eyes to stay clear.

Where am I? There's nowhere to go. Nowhere to hide from—

"This isn't happening." Shake my head. Try to deny.

I can't unhook another breath, and panic finds a place to sit inside me; I'm possessed.

"This isn't-" I start to yell it, but it catches on the hooks, remains suspended and swinging like slaughtered meat. Can't deny it. Can't.

A brain voice talks to me (it has my mother's voice): *It is real. It is. There's no denying it. This is happening.*

I hit the steering wheel with my hand. The car shakes, veers, reorients, rocking back into its lane.

My voice bellows rage, my spaceship has become a cave; I can't get away from myself.

Squeeze the steering wheel until my hands lose feeling.

Spit sharp shards from my eyes, slicing feelings and shredding coherence. Swipe the glass on my cheeks with frustrated sounds.

Drive.

A glance in the rearview mirror. The road is empty behind me, but—

If I just turn around and go back, maybe—

If I can just—

—fix this. The doctor was wrong. There's been a mistake. I can fix this.

Fix it.

Fix it!

Breath catches on the hooks.

I can't breathe. Oh my god. I can't breathe. I can't breathe.

Stop.

Find your breath. "This is real."

Stop.

I park the vehicle and bust out of the metal prison, sucking breaths. Hands to knees, I think I might be sick. Only air moves through my mouth. Tears through my eyes.

Then I run.

Run.

Feet pounding the ground, reverberating through my body, so I can feel the pain of something tangible.

Run.

Feel.

Run.

Feel.

When I finally stop running, I'm at the edge of the ghost town at The Bend. The abandoned buildings stretch out like shadows as darkness chases the sun. My lungs stretch for breath, aching with the exertion, but it's a physical pain preferable to the emotional pain moving through me. I shuffle through the street, hands on my head, walking without direction. I stop at the saloon and climb the steps to look inside. Even though it's getting dark, I can still make out the emptiness within, the forgotten place, and discarded things, waiting for someone who will never come to claim them.

I turn away and sit down, my back to the saloon's wall as if I'm waiting for the owner to open so I can get the first drink.

The ghost town's shadows stretch around me. It's cold now, since the light has faded, and I shiver, but I don't get up to go.

I'm alone.

My phone vibrates in my pocket. I leave it and wrap my arms around my middle, holding my insides in and fold over.

I'm not sure why I drove here. The emotions crashing about inside me seemed to make the choice. The denial, the bargaining, and the anger.

I watch the sun sink and the inky shadows deepen, reaching toward me like fingers. I wonder if maybe they'll snatch my soul. "You should take me instead," I yell out into the night. *You should take me instead* echoes back.

"Why?" I ask to no one.

"Why?" I ask a little louder.

"Why?" I yell and the question echoes back at me, *Why?*

Maybe I'm hoping for an answer, but there isn't one. Only the question bouncing around in the shadows around me.

My phone chirps again. I let it.

My throat is raw from yelling and crying.

My baby died.

My baby died.

My baby died.

I test the words in my head, first, then say them to the darkness. "My baby died."

I hadn't wanted her at first. I remember feeling sorry for myself because I was just nineteen. Too young to be a dad. I'm too young to be a dad with a daughter who died.

My phone vibrates again. I ignore it.

I keep replaying the scene at the hospital. The doctor's words. Bella's mom. Her sister and aunt. Phoenix and Tanner—my brothers—trying to support me. My mom. It makes my stomach ache, rolling it all around in my head, trying to make sense of what has happened.

I don't want it to be real.

"My daughter died." I yell it out. The words bounce back. *My daughter died.*

Being here—alone—seemed right, a private place to be in pain, but now that I'm here, I'm feeling the depth of the shadows. I've been here before, in the shadows. I've remained in them most of my life, safe but stuck.

My phone rings again.

This time I look at it and see all the notifications: Mom, Phoenix, Tanner, Max, Josh, Cal, Danny. My dad.

I can choose to stay here—alone—in the dark, shadowy ghost town of my own making. Stuck, like in my dreams. Or I can choose to face the pain. With those I love to help me. A choice. I stand up and look around and walk back the way I came, leaving the dark ghost town behind.

When I finally make it home, I climb the steps and the door opens, yellow light from inside, bursting out.

"Oh, Griffin." My mom's arms are around me.

I bury my face in her shoulder, but instead of crying, I just cling to her like a child needing her comfort.

She makes sounds and constructs words, though they aren't hitting the mark. It's her arms and her presence that are. She draws me into the house.

I stall. It's full.

Mom. Phoenix. Dad. Tanner. Cal. Max.

"You're here," I tell them all, but my gaze stops at Max.

Max takes the steps to close the distance between us and takes my hand in hers. "I came as soon as I heard." She wraps me in her arms. "I'm so sorry, Griffin."

I lean forward and rest my forehead against her shoulder. "She died," I whisper.

Max cries with me.

There is comfort in being in the light with people who chase shadows. I'm not used to allowing in the light, but Max has taught me how. I must extend trust. These candles warm me. My mom and Phoenix. Tanner. Cal and Max.

Then my dad draws me into his arms. "I'm here, son," he says as he cries with me.

I let him. Content to cling to the strength of others because I don't have any myself.

Time has stopped.

I exist.

There must be sleep. I wake in my bed, Max curled around me.

Phoenix has coffee made by the time I wander into the kitchen. He sets a cup on the counter, so I don't have to move any more than necessary.

He and Mom drive me to the hospital to visit Bella.

I find my way through the maze of hallways to the door with the number Bella's mom gave me.

I knock on the wall to the side of the door. I can't see inside the room, a rose-colored curtain pulled to offer privacy to the patient.

"Come in." Bella's voice is reed thin.

Uncomfortable, I slip through the opening near the wall, trying not to disrupt the curtain.

Bella, sallow and broken, is curled in the hospital bed. A white blanket covers her to her shoulders. She's wearing a blue hospital gown with strange green shapes, IV needle tubing attached to her somewhere, monitor of some sort keeping track of her pulse. When she sees me, she bursts into tears, and covers her face with her hands.

I fight tears and make my way to the empty chair at her bedside. When I sit, I put my hands in my lap, afraid to touch her, unsure of the right thing to do is.

She holds out a hand to me.

I take hers. Her skin is cool and dry.

"I'm so sorry," she says through her tears.

"Me, too," I tell her.

She shakes her head. "No. I mean. I must have done something wrong." Her throat closes around the words.

I shake my head and squeeze her hand. "No. No. Bella. Don't. You aren't to blame."

She continues to cry. I hold her hand, my thumb moving over her skin, offering comfort I don't feel but wanting to offer something anyway.

"I keep thinking if I'd just done something different," she says. "Then I feel guilty because I hadn't wanted her at first." She sobs each word, her body shaking with the effort.

I shake my head again, but I don't offer words to combat her thinking. I've been there in other situations, including this one. If only I'd worn a condom. If only I'd said "no" instead of going through with it. And that thinking spirals into more *if onlys* and tangential *what ifs*. Our baby wouldn't have been. We wouldn't be going through this now. It's a slippery slope, I think, and one that doesn't take us anywhere good. "Don't. Okay. It isn't your fault."

We sit together in silence, her hand in mine.

I'm not sure how long, but it's long enough for Bella's crying to subside.

"Can we name her?" she asks. Her voice lacks substance and echoes exactly how I feel.

My eyes fly from our joined hands to her tear-streaked face. I nod, unable to form words.

"I've been calling her April."

"That's pretty," I tell her. It makes me think of flowers and springtime.

"It means 'to open,'" she tells me. "I looked it up."

I open my mouth to tell her that's the perfect name for our girl, but my throat closes around the words, so I just nod again and allow the tears that are gut punching me to flow.

Bella squeezes my hand this time, offering comfort.

We sit together until Bella finally sleeps.

I leave when her mom arrives.

MAY

I'm going to be tested. I get that now. The question, I guess, is if I've learned what I need in order to pass them, or if I'll fail. Sometimes it feels like the light at the end of the tunnel is a moving target.

I take the steps to make it out, but for some reason, the tunnel keeps stretching out in front of me. "Keep walking forward," I'm told. So, I do, but it isn't easy.

To: Griffin Nichols
123 4 5th Street NE
The Town, USA 67890

1.

I tighten the black tie. It's stark against the white shirt. These meaningless details attach themselves to the underside of my skin, as if hanging onto them will make all the rest of what's happened hurt less. They don't, but then at least I can think about those things rather than the fact we're having a funeral service for my daughter today.

"You want to wear it or take it?" Max asks, holding up the black suit jacket I bought. She arrived this morning to help, early enough to crawl into my twin bed with me and offer me the comfort of her presence.

"I'll put it on at the church." I stare at my reflection. Old. When I'm old, I wonder if I'll recognize myself. If I'll stare at my reflection and think: *Hey. We met fifty-three years ago.*

Max walks up behind me and wraps her arms around me from behind, laying her cheek between my shoulder blades. She doesn't say anything, and I appreciate it. There is nothing to be said. Her arms constrict as though she's trying to offer me her strength. It's nice to have her back since the end of her term.

I cover her hand with mine, draw it up over my heart, take a deep breath, and let my chin fall to the top of the tie. "I don't know if I can do this," I tell her.

She takes a deep breath, waits, then says, "Words. Words. Words. More words. Words. Words." She peeks round my shoulder at me in the mirror and offers me a dim smile. "Did that help?"

I give her a slight smile and turn in her embrace to hold her. "You, being here, helps," I say against her neck.

Later, at the grave site, I sit next to Mom and Phoenix. Bella is with her mom and sister. We are all faded roses, somehow. I think we must be beautiful in our grief, but broken and withered too, folded in on ourselves. The pastor says the words over the tiny casket. When it's time, he calls April's parents forward. I stand and offer Bella my hand. She takes it, and we stand together, side by side one more time. One time, really the only time, we'll ever have something to do as parents together. Behind us, the plethora of people whose collective love and generosity helped us have this opportunity to say goodbye.

As empty as my heart feels, it feels expansive in that emptiness.

Bella cries next to me, her head bent forward, a handkerchief pressed to her face.

I wrap an arm around her shoulders.

She leans against me and reaches out to touch the casket. "I'm sorry," she whispers. Only I can hear it. We set our flowers down and move to allow others the opportunity to come forward. People have already offered sympathies at the church service. Now, it's a private moment before April is buried. Bella and I wait at the edge of the harness holding the casket above ground.

People make their way up to drape the casket in flowers. Each of them is here for us, Bella and me. They never knew April, and yet here they are here to express their love and sympathy for us. It's humbling. My family is here including my dad and Mara. Cal and Max. Tanner is here, and Emma is with him. Josh. Atticus. Danny. Friends of Bella's. So many people here, to offer their support during our tragedy.

A year ago, we were getting ready to graduate. I sat with Tanner at graduation practice and needled him into partying. I figured that was all there was moving forward. The thought makes me look at the casket holding my girl. It's heavy. I remembered thinking then that my life was defined by the parties, the sex, my friends. Now, it feels defined by the moment when I lost someone I hadn't known I would want until she wasn't there anymore.

I glance at my father. He said something like that to me a while ago. The awareness that he'd been young and stupid in his youth, and it wasn't until everything was stripped from him that he understood what it meant to face regret.

I squeeze Bella's hand.

She lays her head on my shoulder.

And together we watch as our daughter's casket is piled with flowers to say goodbye.

2.

Our house is filled with people, and I wish they were gone. I'm tired of being polite. My mom offered to host the luncheon after the funeral, and I'm grateful for her, for her generosity, but I'm bone tired.

I leave the confines of the overly full living room and walk out to the backyard to lean against the shed all the way in the back. The tears are gone, but the anger isn't, though it isn't as acute now that time as passed. I'm not angry at anyone specifically, just pissed. The levity of rage feels better than the weight of sadness.

Bella walks across the yard toward me. She stops a few paces away and holds out a silver flask.

I shake my head. Today might be a day I would drink enough to just float away when I know I need to be present.

She takes a sip and scrunches her nose with the burn. "The last time we drank this, we didn't make the best decisions." She moves to lean against the shed next to me.

Silence takes over. I'm pretty sure she's remembering that our bad decisions made April. I'm in pain now, and I will be forever at this loss, but I can't honestly say that I regret what happened because it would be negating the importance of my baby in my life, even if I didn't get to meet her.

I got to see April on the monitor.

I got to hear her heartbeat.

I got to feel her move inside Bella's body.

I got to fall in love with a daughter I never met.

I got to fix a closet for her, build a crib, help Bella prepare for her arrival.

I got to make a friend in Bella.

I got to begin to feel a little like a father.

I got to become a better version of myself.

Sure, losing April, this aftermath, is hell on earth, but calling that night a mistake would somehow take away from the way she impacted my life. I wouldn't trade that for anything.

Just like Tanner said.

"We weren't numbing our feelings for the right reason then," I say.

She gives me a wry look and holds out the flask again.

I take it and hold it up. "To April." I sip, then hand it back to Bella, content to feel this pain rather than numb it.

"You think she's scared?" Bella asks. "In the dark?"

Before, I didn't think much about the afterlife. If it exists. Now though, I can't think about anything so hopeless. It only fills me with more anger, thinking at the unfairness of it all. Instead of hurting Bella with my philosophical meanderings, I just take hold of her hand and squeeze. "I don't think she's in the dark. I think she's with angels. It's bright and happy there."

Bella nods, and I release her hand. "I like that." She leans her head back against the building and helps me continue holding it up.

Eventually, Max walks out.

"Hi," I tell her when she gets closer after working her way across the lawn that Phoenix and I mowed the day before. It smells fresh and green, like life, and on such a dark day. Max looks beautiful—like life—and I want to touch her.

"Hi." She smiles at me. I'm so grateful she's still smiling at me even with as much of a shit as I am. "Hi, Bella."

Bella smiles at Max, greets her. "I'm going to go find Minny." She gives me a teary smile and walks back to the house.

I hold my hand out to Max.

She takes it.

I draw her against me and drop my head into the space between her neck and shoulder.

"Is that whiskey I smell?"

I nod. "Yeah."

"Drunk?"

I shake my head. "The thought did cross my mind."

"And?"

"And my judgement is never very good when I go there. Probably better not to." I kiss her neck again. "Is it really bad that what I want to do right now is have sex with you?" I kiss her neck.

"Is that the whiskey talking or you?"

"Just me." I smile at her and then nip at her neck.

She offers a sweet sound like laughter held in a pretty jar. "Is it bad that I'm super insecure about you and Bella? Even though I totally don't want to be."

I lift my head and search her face. "Really?"

Max reaches up and swipes a lock of my hair away from my face, trapping it in her fingers. She nods. "I hate it, but it's there in all of its ugliness. And on such a day, too. It makes me feel like a petty bitch." She offers a wan smile.

I use both arms to squeeze her close. "I think we should organize a mud wrestling match. Two beautiful women fighting over me—Griffin Nichols. That would be a first." I smile.

She swats my chest. "You are sexist."

I continue smiling. "Except, two conditions aren't being met to make it a worthy contest."

Her eyebrow shifts over her eye, and her mouth thins out with that look of irritation. "Which are?"

"The first is that both girls would need to want said guy, and at last count only one inexplicably does."

"And the second?"

"The said guy would need to be interested in seeing who the victor would be, but this guy is already standing here holding her." It's my turn to touch her hair, skimming it over her skin and hooking it behind her ear. "She won his heart a long time ago."

Max smiles, a blush staining her cheeks. "When did you become such a quasi-romantic?" she asks.

"You, Maxwell Wallace, bring that out in me."

She kisses me on the mouth, fully, draws back, and says, "Is it really bad that I would like to have sex with you right now?" She smiles.

I grin at her. "Let's sneak away," I whisper in her ear. "Your house is empty."

But before we can make it a reality, Tanner walks over with Emma, Josh, Danny, and Atticus. Max straightens up, smoothing out her black dress.

"Thanks for being here," I tell my friends, looking at each of them. My eyes stall on Emma. She and I haven't ever been friends. I was a jerk to her, but she offers a kind look, then glances at Tanner. They're holding hands. I understand now, with Max's hand in mine, what he was trying to hold onto. They look right together. I resolve that I need to take time to apologize to Emma.

Each of them talks at the same time.

"Of course."

"Are you kidding?"

"What are friends for?"

They situate themselves in a semicircle around Max and me and talk. It isn't about deep stuff like life and death, but rather the simple joys of experience and memory. The laughs and jokes of a year spent apart. I pull Max closer, and listen, not in a mental space to share. Grief is like a black hole sucking everything in and nothing gets out of its gravity. But I am content to be surrounded by people I know that I can say I love.

JUNE

1.

A year ago, at Senior Send-Off, my friends and I were at the Quarry, partying, facing graduation. After the norm of jumping from the rock, I'd gotten so drunk, I'd woken up in a lawn chair at Bella's camp freezing my balls off in the cold. The campfire was barely embers, and my head pounded with a raging hangover. I'd thought that was living. Back then, I'd thought Tanner was being a jerk, pulling away from his bros. Now, sitting and watching the campfire, I know the asshole wasn't him. It had always been me.

We've returned to the Quarry, no longer seniors but a year removed from it. The vibe at the current Senior Send-Off isn't different. The music of the various parties, the sound of people jumping from the rock, the singing and laughter from distant campsites remains much the same. It's a rite of passage between the end of something and the beginning of something else—if you're lucky to recognize it. The vibe around our campfire now reminds me of that year of experience stretched behind me, and how different I feel now.

My old friends made new are here: Tanner, Josh, and Danny. They have been here since the funeral, though Danny has been back and forth between his post, he was able to get leave again to be with us this weekend. There are also new relationships: Max, Emma, Atticus, and Ginny. Their friend, Liam, Facetimed in from New York where he couldn't get away from an internship. A year ago, I wouldn't have associated with people like Max, or Emma and her friends. I would have used people like Atticus and did use my own friends to get what I wanted. A year ago, I was looking for my next party and my next lay and murdering the vulnerable part of myself to stop feeling weak.

I see the truth, now: being vulnerable is strength.

It's hard to take my eyes away from the flames of the campfire. It moves in the darkness like it's doing a dance. Sparks shoot off into the sky like fireworks, adding to the din of the voices of my friends, talking around me. I glance away from the flames to find Max, suddenly needing to see her, to reassure myself that she's real and there, and remind myself I'm not the same Griffin I once was.

She's on the other side of the fire, talking with Emma. Smiling. The good one, though it isn't quite the same as the one she gives to me, and that makes me feel special. She tells me I am every day without ever saying a word. She believes in me, and her love has made me believe in me too.

She draws a lock of her straight honey hair with her finger and hooks it around her ear, then tilts her head and leans forward a touch as if to hear Emma better. She's taller than Emma who's also leaning toward her, talking as if they're telling secrets.

I don't know why this makes my heart race.

I suppose Emma could be telling Max what a dick I was—am— was. Maybe her stories could scare Max away from me forever. I would deserve that.

My heartbeat isn't fearful though. Instead, the rhythm is rooted in something different, like contentment and joy. Feelings Max has inspired in me to grasp and keep. Feelings I've discovered grow when nurtured.

Max turns and looks at me as if she can feel my stare. She smiles. The good one.

My heart speeds up even more with the physical and emotional connection I have with her.

She says something to Emma, then walks around the fire to me and perches on my lap, leaning forward to press her mouth to my jaw. "I missed you."

"I'm right here," I tell her.

She leans back and studies my face as if memorizing it. "I know." She sweeps a lock of my hair off my forehead. Her touch ignites sparks that explode like fireworks in my chest, like the spark of the fire a moment ago. "You were just too far away."

I squeeze her with my arms.

"Would you like to roast some marshmallows?" she asks.

I chuckle. "Do you?"

She grins. "Yes."

I kiss her dimple. "Okay."

"Would you find me a stick?"

"I'll do you one better," I tell her. "I brought roasting sticks. But you're going to have to let me get up."

She smacks me with a quick kiss, stands, then holds out her hands to help me up from the chair. She smacks my ass and giggles as I walk away.

When I make it to the table, I look around the items. Packages of chips and cookies, hot dog buns, coolers, paper products.

"Griffin?"

I glance away from the stuff on the table.

Emma is standing next to me.

I straighten. "Oh. Hi, Emma." I glance at the campfire to look for Max, feeling like perhaps I've been set up. She's sitting in the chair I'd occupied, listening to something Danny is telling her. She nods, focused on his words.

I swallow and look back at Emma.

Her head tilts up to study me with her big eyes and a neutral expression. I can't tell if she still hates me, and I wouldn't blame her. I was awful to her about Tanner. I used my words to hurt her and my actions to sabotage their relationship. I know I need to apologize to her for how I treated her, if not just for her and Tanner, but because like Phoenix said, making amends is important to getting better for myself. "I'm glad you're here," I say and want to cringe. It sounds stupid.

"Before you say anything," she says and looks down at her feet. "I want to apologize."

Wait. "What? That's—" I pause and physically take a step away from her. I shake my head. What's with her and Tanner?

"Hear me out," she says, then meets my gaze.

"I'm the one who needs to be saying sorry."

She gives me a tentative smile and holds up her hand. "I judged you. Unfairly. And I'm sorry for that because I've come to know you better since I've been back. I wrote you off. I'm so sorry."

I open my mouth, and nothing comes out. I'm not sure what to say to that so instead of thinking about it, I say, "I deserved it, Matthews. I wasn't very nice to you. Before."

"Well, I knew better than to judge someone else," she says and moves some packages on the table, rearranging them. "I did it anyway."

"You weren't the only one. And—" I say before she can interrupt me— "I never made it easy on anyone not to judge me. I wanted to apologize to you. I said some messed up things." I don't tell her I was afraid of her. Afraid of what she meant and that I was losing Tanner. I glance across the campsite to find him. He's roasting a marshmallow, trying to get it what he calls *golden-perfection*. He doesn't like them burnt. I didn't lose him. Or Josh, who's talking with Atticus and Ginny. Or Danny, who's laughing with Max. My friends are here. I'm here.

I look at Emma again. "I'm sorry for that."

She nods. "I accept it." She glances at the campfire, then back at me. "Can you forgive me?"

I smile then but can't quite look at her. "Of course, Matthews."

"I'd like us to maybe try to be friends too." She holds out her hand.

I take it. "Me too."

"That's for me," she says, "but it's also because I really like Max. She's great, and mostly because I love Tanner so darned much, and he loves you."

I like the way Emma's thoughts sort of run together like she's thinking aloud. I grin and feel the glow of warmth at her declaration of feelings for Tanner, as if making an announcement like that is common and easy. I suppose declarations of love should be, expressing the truth of what stitches together your heart.

So I clear my throat and draw the parts of me together so that there's only one of me. "I love him too, so I think that's a good idea."

Before I know it, Emma's arms are around me in a hug. She laughs. "I'm so relieved." She pulls away, looking away as if she's nervous.

I follow her gaze to Tanner.

"I've got it!" he says to us and holds up his marshmallow stick. "Golden perfection, Matthews! Get over here."

Emma grabs a pack of marshmallows from the table. "We'll need more of these."

I watch her walk away, then turn back for the sticks. I find them stuck between two coolers. When I straighten, I look across the campsite filtered in firelight and study friends, my chosen family. My heart fills up with the firelight glow to overflowing.

I remember when there were too many holes in my heart to hold onto the joy or the hope. I used patches of sarcasm and anger to hold myself together, to patch up the leaking parts of my torn heart. The parts of me keeping me protected, or so I believed. Now, though, having been through the valley of heartache and starting the climb out, I realize I don't need the disconnected parts of me anymore. I don't need the gentle Griffin hiding in the prison of his broken heart. I don't need the sarcastic Griffin to hold the emotions back. I don't need douchey Griffin to chase people away and keep them at arm's length. I don't need angry and unapproachable Griffin to keep the rest of him sheltered and protected from possible heartache. There is no honor in denying that there is pain and hurt, because in denying it, it's like saying it didn't happen.

The fight with Tanner happened. So did the healing.

The loss of my friends happened. So did the reunion.

Having unprotected sex with Bella with real consequences happened. So did the idea of impending fatherhood.

April happened.

Her death happened.

But it goes back and back...

My father's arrest and imprisonment. So did the tentative way we've found to be in one another's lives.

His secret family. So did a new sister.

My brother's leaving. So did his return.

Every moment, every hurt can't be ignored, but neither can the joys that were born from them. Like now.

I walk across the campsite toward the dancing fire, to Max who has taken my heart and helped me stitch it together so that I am no longer a Griffin stuck in a ghost town he made, or a Griffin in monster parts, but instead, just Griffin, whole, Guardian of Treasures.

Max looks at me when I reach her and gives me the smile I love so much.

I smile back.

Note to self . . .

Don't forget: Shit happens.

And when it inevitably does, I don't have to face the challenge alone. I've got friends and family to help me. This life stuff is about the choices I make in the face of challenges.

So don't be a dick.

Don't be an ass to Max. Talk to her. Always. And Tanner, Danny and Josh. They've got my back.

Be nice to Phoenix and Mom. They love me. Remember that Dad is trying but he won't always get it right.

Text Mara.

Notes & Further Reading

The most obvious of the obvious, I am not a man, and yet, here's a book (plus a half of one with *The Stories Stars Tell*) exploring male culture. What could I possibly know and understand about manhood besides my life married to one, my childhood raised with many, a professional life working with teen males, and being the mother of a teenage son? Not a whole lot beyond what is observable and personally anecdotal. Therefore, besides talking to a plethora of dudes, I consulted the written word to get a sense about the male culture I was attempting to write.

These are a list of books I read on the topic in case you might be interested in exploring the topic of masculine culture further:

Boys and Sex: Young Men on Hookups, Love, Porn, Consent, and Navigating the New Masculinity by Peggy Orenstein

The Man They Wanted Me to Be by Jared Yates Sexton

A Better Man: A (Mostly) Serious Letter to My Son by Michael Ian Black

Masterminds and Wingmen: helping Our Boys Cope with Schoolyard Power, Locker-room Tests, Girlfriends, and the New Rules of Boy World by Rosalind Wiseman

Raising Cain: Protecting the Emotional Life of Boys by Dan Kindlon, Ph.D., and Michael Thompson, Ph.D.

In the Echo of this Ghost Town Playlist

Music always plays such an important role to my creative process in growing with the characters as I write them.

Ghost Town by Vancouver Sleep Clinic
Inside Out by Mokita
Dogcatcher by Elliot Moss
Everybody But Me by Nick Wilson
Wild by Hailaker
Be Slow by Harrison Storm
Necessary Friend by namara
Half-Saved by Luca Fogale
Obvious by UTAH & CHPTERS
Maybe Don't by Maisie Peters & JP Saxe
Again by Sasha Sloan
A Little Bit Yours by JP Saxe
More Than Friends Mokita
Maple by Jome
I Never Wanted Anything More Than I Wanted You by Kina Grannis
you were good to me by Jeremy Zucker & Chelsea Cutler
Don't Wait by EXES & Dashboard Confessional
Always by By the Coast
Golf on TV by Lennon Stella & JP Saxe

Songs without lyrics:

Who We Want to Be by Tom Day (Featured in the book trailer. Thank you, Mr. Day!)
Precipice by The Flashbulb
The Proposal by AK & Mapps

I didn't include every song on the list. If you're interested in more music, look for the "In the Echo of this Ghost Town" playlist on Spotify. The playlist Griffin made for Max is also on Spotify titled: "Griffin's Road Trip Playlist." Please consider purchasing songs if you are able to support these talented artists, many of them also independent, just like indie authors.

Acknowledgements

As I was writing *The Stories Stars Tell*, an incredible human and early reader, Lavinia Ungureanu, shared with me how much the fight between Tanner and Griffin left her wanting to know more. She mentioned a moment in the story when Tanner went to talk to Griffin, and just before Tanner left the house, there was a brief glimpse of Griffin's vulnerability and insecurity. That moment, she said, when paired with the fight, made her wonder what happened to Griffin. I couldn't shake Lavinia's question, eventually writing the fight from Griffin's perspective. After writing that scene, I knew I had to tell Griffin's story. So, Lavinia, thank you for asking that question. You are directly responsible for Griffin's story.

After that first draft was done, I had a lot of help reading this story and Max's version *When the Echo Answers*. Thanks is owed to a plethora of people: Rayna York, Stephanie Keesy-Phelan, Becky Clark, Misty Wagner, Maggie Freidanne, Janine Caroline, and of course, Lavinia. Thank you to my Salon Crew who listened to me vent about Griffin and is idiotic choices. Thank you to Katherine Lamoureaux. You are an angel who wears an editor's wings and works so hard to make sure things are in their rightful place. Thank you to authors Rob Rufus and Brandann Hill-Mann for being willing to read and offer your perspective. Writing a book really can't be done without the village. Thank you all.

Thank you to Sara Oliver who over the last seven books has used art to make my books look like spun gold. Thank you for your hard work and the willingness to work with me (including but not limited to my random thoughts about symbolism and character's clothing).

Thank you to my family. You are always willing to listen to my rants and the strange meanderings of my mind. You put up with moods, and my shapeshifting throughout my creative process—most times in unattractive ways. I'm so appreciative of you. To my friends who walk into bookstores and talk about me to the proprietors because you believe in me (thank you, Kori). I can't begin to tell you how much it means.

To all the readers, thank you. Your delight in these characters makes the journey to tell their stories so meaningful. It's a treasure to sit down and push through the draft, the rewrite, the revision, and the edit along with the rest of the publishing process because I know it's for you. THAT is the *sparkley* part. Thank you so much for your support, your reviews, and sharing your love of the work with others.

Each singular thread of my gratitude is tied to the tapestry of my faith journey and my heavenly Father, through whom all blessings flow. I humbly walk through this life in honor and service to glorify my savior, Jesus Christ. Though I admit my extreme flaws as a human being and rest in the understanding that I'm accepted by that Grace. A gorgeous human, Misty Wagner, once remarked, "I love that you love Jesus but swear like a sailor." I laughed with her completely content in the awareness that I am accepted flaws and all—just like Griffin.

EXCERPT

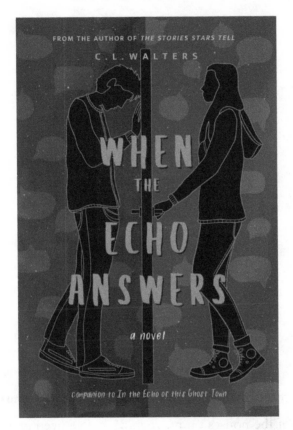

Max's story available now.

1

"Dad." I breath the word like a prayer when the house comes into view through the pickup's window. I should be used to the condition of the houses on move-in day—I've lived in so many of them—but this one might be one of the worst I've ever seen. Besides the anemic-looking siding, the wrap around porch resembles broken bones held up with weak crutches while the ghost of its foundation sits in the middle of a field in dire need of surgery. I think, perhaps my dad has lost his mind.

"I know it looks a fright," Dad says as he turns our rusty pickup into the drive.

A fright is an understatement. The house looks like a strong wind will blow it over after the ghosts finish their century-old party in it.

"Dad," I repeat. I'm not sure why I'm surprised. Not really. Over the last eighteen years of my life, we've moved ten times, and with each move, the house has always looked like a dump, maybe with the exception of house three. "There's no way you're flipping this before I leave for school."

We bounce along a driveway that needs repaving—or our truck needs new shocks. It's hard to decide which. Maybe both.

The sun wanes in the afternoon sky, lighting everything in beautiful hues of gold, but it doesn't seem to help the dilapidated building I'm about to call a temporary home look any better. I can't look anymore and turn away from the house, thinking about the plan he shared with me on the drive: fix this one up in a hurry—before I leave for college—flip it to help pay for school expenses not covered by my scholarship, and move onto the next one closer to school. It isn't going to happen. Eight weeks isn't enough time.

"I know it looks bad. I know." He puts the truck in park. We sit next to one another in Rust Bucket, facing a front door that's cracked up the center. Silence stretches a few extra beats, then my father adds, "But, I'm going to hire someone to help with this one."

"Dad." I shake my head this time as the air leaves my lungs. He's never hired anyone before, aside from tradesmen who help with stuff he doesn't do. Taking on a hire sounds like a lot of extra cash. "For real?" I ask.

"Sure," he says and taps the steering wheel, as if offering himself reinforcement to make it so. He looks at me and smiles. "When we sell this baby—for sure."

"Dad–" I can't seem to find another word.

"No. No." He shakes his head and looks at the house. "It's got amazing bones," he says—just like he always does—and so far, in my eighteen years on this planet, he hasn't been wrong. We've always had a roof over our head, even if sometimes there are holes in it until he fixes them. And we've always had food to eat, even if we don't always have a place for a table. He's always made sure I had clothes and shoes, even if we've had to shop at thrift stores. Truthfully, I haven't ever wanted for much, even if I'm not one of those kinds of people who wants much.

"Come on," he says. "Let me show you." He climbs out of the truck, the door squealing as he pushes it open.

I follow him but leave my bag inside the cab.

He high steps through the grass and looks over his shoulder at me. "Wait. I'll make a path for you."

I watch my dad push down the grass with his feet. That's my dad, my knight in shining armor, willing to brave the grasses with his boots so that I'll be comfortable. I'm wearing shorts, and I shouldn't have. I know better. First night in a flip is always about jeans, long sleeves, and hard-soled shoes. Sometimes I think Hazmat suits have probably been in order like house number five when we had to go get a hotel room for a couple weeks.

I hadn't thought my clothing choices through this morning, annoyed that we were doing this yet again. It might be early July, but summer months don't matter to a house that's falling apart. The rodents don't care either. Or squatters. Or whatever kinds of other items we might find inside I don't want to consider.

When it's clear the stubborn reeds aren't going to lie flat, he walks back to me and offers his wide back.

"Hop on, Max-in-a-million."

"Dad. I'm a little old for this."

"Aw. Humor your old man."

I jump up and let him piggyback me to the porch, which I can see needs to be completely redone. I'm factoring cost. The crack in the front door looks like the crack in Amy's wall in the first episode of the eleventh iteration of Doctor Who. Shit. Replacement. Cha-ching. Rodents guaranteed.

"Don't worry. We'll patch it up until we get the replacement."

As if the front door is the only thing needs replacing, I think but don't say it.

When Dad sets me down, he climbs the steps that buckle under his weight with creaks and groans but thankfully don't snap. He looks over his shoulder at me with one of those excited twinkles in his stormy-sea-colored eyes which are striking in contrast to the rich, sun-kissed hue of his face. "You ready to see this masterpiece?"

"As ready as I'll ever be."

The front door opens.

And it's a dump, just like I thought.

He has to push the door open through a pile of dirt, and, upon closer inspection, leaves, which makes me think there must be a broken window. The stairwell is intact, but a few of the stairs are cracked like chipped teeth. There's a musty odor of decomposing wood. The condition of the house is terrible, and I look at my dad with wide eyes.

"Remember, Max—" Dad turns to me, hands on his jean clad hips—he obviously knew how to dress, though in my whole life, I can't remember my dad ever wearing anything different— "you have to look at the place as it can be, not how it is. See through the damage to all the ways we'll fix it to—"

"—make it new," I finish for him. "Yes. I know, Dad. But—"

"No 'buts,'" he says, holding up a hand. "Just look."

I sigh and nod.

It's an old farmhouse, but under the grime, age, and harsh reality of time, I can see little treasures. The hardwood floor is mostly intact for some spots, though I'm wondering about that subfloor that creaks as our steps echo through the empty rooms. There are gorgeous, stained-glass windows still intact, set in the framed doorways between rooms. The kitchen needs a complete gut, and it makes me hear alarm bells of all the cash about to bleed out into the remodel. The shiplap looks shot, but the fireplace in the living room is beautiful with what looks like original river rock.

"Well?" Dad's voice is hopeful.

I follow him up the stairs. "I can see why you like it."

He flashes me a grin, which is infectious. It always is.

I share a smile with him. My reciprocation seems to relieve some of his tension when his shoulders droop to normal position.

At the top of the stairs, the walkway splits and the spindles of the banister forms a U around the stairwell. Closed doors outline the space. I follow my dad to the left. "I think this could be your room, but you can choose."

He pushes open a door.

I have to give my father credit. Even though the house is a dump—and looks like it might be haunted—the bones of this room are magical. The steeply pitched ceiling, dormered windows with places to sit though they look like they might have nests of something. The walls are bleeding old wallpaper, but I can imagine a new pattern, a beautiful room. "It's got potential," I tell him with a grin.

His eyes twinkle again. "Let me show you the rest."

After the tour, I can see the promise of the house, but I don't see how he's going to get it done in eight weeks—even with help. This will take months, which makes me look sideways at him again. My dad is a smart man. He's been doing this a long time, and while his timing isn't always perfect, he must know this is going to take the better part of a year to finish even with help. Looking around, I know he knows it, and I wonder why he's adamant about the timeline.

"I'll order us some pizza for dinner?" he asks. A tradition on the first night of each of our moves.

"Perfect," I say and wipe my hands over the back of my shorts, then realize I've probably wiped grime on my ass. I glance over my shoulder and twist to check, though I'm not sure why I'd care.

"It could be our last one." I look up at him and notice his gaze flick away. He swallows, then with a dip of his head says, "I'll start moving stuff in."

"I'll sweep up the sleeping spaces for the mattresses and lay the tarps. Don't move mattresses without me."

He nods. "Wouldn't dream of it."

I move out the front door, down the porch, and through the tall grass to the pickup to get my change of clothes. As I open the truck door, I look back at the house as Dad emerges from the doorway to grab the first boxes we'll need to settle for the night. My heart expands in my chest, already missing him, though I haven't left yet. With my leaving-for-college deadline impending—eight weeks away—Dad's strange timeline coincides. I wonder if it has more to do with me leaving rather than the actual completion of the house. Maybe it's his way of trying to make me feel better, or himself.

The thing is it doesn't make me feel better.

I change my clothes and get started on my assigned move-in day tasks. By the time the pizza arrives, I've swept the bedrooms and laid the tarps for the mattresses; Dad and I have moved our mattresses and important boxes from the trailer hitched to the back of the truck. We'll have the rest to unload in the morning. The sun has gone down, and without electricity, we're living by lantern light.

"Dad, you have definitely underestimated how long this house is going to take," I say, drawing a piece of pepperoni from the box. "I mean, Holmes Street was about this size but didn't have as much work. We were there for two years."

"True," Dad says and takes a sip of his cola he just opened. "But it also had a basement that I finished, and I had that full-time job." He takes a bite and finishes it. "Remember Misten Avenue? That one was terrible, and we were there for less than a year."

I'd forgotten about that. "Give me that." I take his soda and hand him his water bottle. "You can't drink that."

He gives me one of his looks, his mouth tensing with impatience. He shakes his head. "I didn't hire anyone to help at Holmes or Misten. And I like soda."

"Soda is diabetes juice, and you're predisposed."

He chuckles. "Look at this temple." He flexes, which makes me laugh because he always uses the same lines. "It wasn't too long ago I was a linebacker–"

"–averaging two and a half sacks, a game. Yeah. Yeah. Drink the water, Dad."

We eat in silence a moment.

"What's the rush, Dad?" I ask, plucking at a piece of pepperoni.

"You're leaving for school," he says as if he's announced the date of my birth, just matter of fact.

"What does that have to do with it?"

He looks up at me, and I see a look I don't recognize on his face, but it burns out just as quickly when he covers it with a smile. "Just seems like a natural point to shoot for. Look for a new place closer

413

to the college so you don't have to travel so far to visit."

"It's only three or so hours from here. An easy bus ride," I point out.

He maintains the smile, but I see it's not in his eyes. Maybe that's the lack of light cast by the lantern. He nods and takes another bite of his pizza. "What am I going to do without you to keep me on track? I might go off budget."

I swallow and take a bite of my pizza, feeling guilty. It's always been us. Dad and Max-in-a-million against the world. "Aw, Dad. I won't be far," I remind him. This is why he'd relented on this place. Besides being a steal—which he loves for the eventual bottom line of the flip—the school I got accepted to was just a few hours away by car. "We have phones. Goodness. And eight weeks to flip this dump." I wonder if the reason he's adamant about his unrealistic timeline is because he's as scared to be on his own as I am to be on mine. I haven't considered the impact of my leaving on him. I haven't allowed myself to ponder it. It's complex and stitched together with a complicated history I know I can't unravel.

He gives me a chuckle. "Don't you worry your head. Your old dad's got it."

"Can we afford help?" I ask.

He sniffs and knuckle itches a spot on his nose, which makes me wonder if he's coming up with a lie. It wouldn't be the first time he's given me just enough truth mixed with a version of optimism riding the line of a lie to keep me complacent. "I'll have to dip into savings."

My eyebrows rise with a question. "Dad. I need the truth."

He raises his hands. "For real. I have a few side gigs lined up already—legit—and I'll offset it with some savings so we can get started right away."

I nod. "And while you're working the side gigs? How is this house—which is generous identification by the way—getting done?"

"The hire."

I give him a side eye.

"You and me plus one more. I think we could knock this out in no time." He smiles around his bite, and I have the sense he's telling himself this story as much as he's telling me. "Have I ever steered us wrong?"

I shake my head. He's taken us into some pretty horrible houses, but he's always made it out of them just like he's said even if his timelines haven't always been accurate. There are always unforeseen complications, and I'm one hundred percent sure this house is full of them.

"Dad?"

"Yes, daughter?"

"Aren't you tired of fixing houses for other people? Don't you ever want to find a place of your own?" This is a question I've asked him before, but his answers have been as shifty as the houses we've lived in, taking on characteristics of whatever house it was at the time. I'm expecting him to say something metaphorical about the stained-glass inserts, but he doesn't.

He clears his throat.

"Dad?"

"Home is where you are."

And I'm leaving.

I don't think he understands that this answer makes me feel like I'm carrying the world on my shoulders, like I've got to hold it up for both of us. I swallow the bite. "What about when I leave for school?"

He doesn't respond.

"Dad?"

"I messed this up, didn't I?"

"What?"

"Being your dad?"

I set my pizza on the paper plate. "What are you talking about?"

He looks at me, his gaze connecting with mine. "I just—I thought it would be an adventure after–" He stops. I know he was going to say, "after your mom left," but can't bring himself to say it. His regret is written on his face even after thirteen years. This isn't because I think he's still in love with her, but her abandonment left both of us as ghostly as the houses we inhabit.

When I was younger, I used to resent the moving, but now that I'm eighteen, I can understand it. I scoot closer to him and lay my head on his shoulder. "Our adventures have been the best," I say, and I'm being honest because they've been with him, even if there's resentment mixed in. I want him to know I love him, but I can't—won't—be a heartbreak, too. "I'm just worried about you when I go to school. You being alone."

This is the first and thickest thread wrapped around my heart. Dad has chosen me every day. He's lived for me. He's been my number one, and now I'm leaving him alone. If I thought too long and hard about it, my breath turns to steel in my lungs. I'd consider not leaving. Dad wouldn't allow it. Going to college feels a bit like abandoning him—like mom. Worse yet, I want to leave so bad, and I'm afraid it makes me just like her.

"What's this?" He wraps a strong arm around me. "Last I checked, I'm the dad. Don't you worry. If all goes well, I'll be right behind you looking for the next place."

Thing is, I can't help worrying about him.

I was five when my mom left us. Indigo Denby—in as much as I can piece together between what my dad has said and what I remember—was a free if unstable spirit unable to be saddled with a husband and a child. A hippie wrapped up the privilege of growing up wealthy, she disappeared, and after a search, was found strung out on drugs (not the first time) and incoherent. Her parents—grandparents who I've had very little interaction with—admitted her to a rehab facility. The divorce papers were delivered to Dad shortly after, and he was given complete custody, her rights as my mother signed away. We haven't heard from her—or my grandparents—since. These are fragile threads I don't understand as clearly since I was only five at the time, but threads that stitch together my experience, nonetheless.

Later, after Dad and I have cleaned up dinner and escaped into our own spaces to get some rest, I wait for the quiet to steal around the house. In the dark of the new room, my lantern glows in the horribly stark space with new shadows and new sounds. I eventually sneak from my bedroom, taking great care to keep my steps from creaking as I move to the stairs. A strange noise reverberates through the belly of the old farmhouse, and I freeze at the top of the stairs, wondering if I should have braved the window and the tree. I hold my breath.

I wait.

My dad clears his throat.

When the silence settles again, I take a step down the stairs. It squeaks. There's a moment when my heart speeds up with fear, thinking maybe I'm going to alert my dad, but I don't hear any movement from his space in the house. I keep going, moving slowly until I'm on the ground floor and out the cracked front door now covered with a plank of plywood.

As much as pizza is a first day move in tradition with my dad, sneaking out that first night is wholly mine. My ritual started at house five. Up to then, my dad and I bunked it in the same room, and his presence gave me bravery. When I turned twelve, there was a shift in me wanting to be brave and independent, to prove I could sleep in my own room by myself. My fear of the new places and my imagination, which conjured all sorts of terrifying creatures stretching in the shadows, did a number on my confidence. Instead of going to my dad, I snuck out into the dark where it felt safer. That night, I found a way to claim some power. After that, I continued to sneak out every first bedtime in a new place. Disappearing into the darkness of a strange place isn't because I want to sneak around. Rather, it feels like one of the only things in this pattern of living over which I have control. Tonight is the last time, I figure, because it's my last move with my dad and is more about the nostalgia of the routine of things rather than the compulsion to control something.

House nine, he caught me sneaking back in.

He was pissed. "Do you understand how dangerous it is?" The panic was clear in his eyes. "Why didn't you just ask? I would have taken you somewhere."

I recognized the disappointment, and I hated disappointing him.

"Why?" he'd asked.

I just shrugged. I didn't know how to put into words the why, not without hurting him. I was being dragged all over the country to fixer uppers by a loving dad, running from the ghost of a drugged-out mom who was too broken to choose us. I had this awful truth of being an outsider—always an outsider—to face the trepidation that pressed in against us every time we started over. I'd been seventeen then, and the sneaking out felt more like a sticking middle finger at the world. A loud "fuck you" to the universe, to every kid that had made fun of me, to my mom, and even my dad on some level.

I didn't think he'd get it, and I refused to hurt him because even if it was a small rebellion, I knew he didn't deserve it.

As I walk down the driveway, I consider that part of the reason I think my dad was so panicked that night he caught me wasn't just because he was scared for me. There is this part of him that probably thought about my mom. The way she walked out into the night and never returned to us, and how he couldn't fix that. My dad can fix anything. Seriously. He's made nine houses look like custom homes. Any problem I've brought home—cuts, scrapes, and bruises both physical and emotional—he's been both Dad and Mom to restore me to normal working order. He couldn't fix my mom, and I'm pretty sure, knowing my dad like I do, he gave it his best go.

As I walk out into the darkness beyond the farmhouse, I wonder if I hide my first night sneak-out from him because I don't want to hurt him like my mother did. I've thought about what it would feel like to just keep walking. The idea took root when I was fifteen— house eight—I thought about just going, finding a place to settle down for good. I was smart enough to know it didn't work like that, which brought me home. It made me wonder if Mom had found it easy to leave us. To leave me. I'd gotten caught up in how much that would hurt Dad, which I knew I couldn't ever do to him, and I wondered how it couldn't have been a part of my mom's thinking. I don't specifically remember the leaving. She was there one day and gone the next. Each time I walk out into the night, I wonder if she weighed us in her decision, and I can't think she did.

When I was younger and asked my dad why she left, he'd just say, "Indigo was a free spirit."

Back then, I imagined her like a bird needing to fly. Now, as I walk toward the streetlights ahead, I don't think of anything so romantic as a bird needing freedom. I just think she was selfish, and maybe—I worry—I'm exactly like her.

I've got eight weeks in this dump since college races toward me. I can hear the sadness and the fear in my dad's voice when he talks about it, but his fears don't change the fact that I'm leaving. It's always been us, and when I look ahead to that eight-week deadline, what I feel is the impending anticipation of freedom weighted with a heavy cost: leaving my dad behind and alone. I finally get to make choices for me. I finally get to make friends. I finally get to stay somewhere—four years—in one place and grow some roots even if my dad jumps around business as usual. As much as I love my dad, I'm looking forward to leaving this vagabond lifestyle for something that's mine, of creating a permanent home. As much as I want my dad to settle somewhere, I don't know that he ever will. The thought makes me bitter, tired, and sad all at the same time. What it boils down to is I'm leaving him and no matter how I try to dress that up, I know I'm just stepping into my mother's skin. And I'm cognizant of how selfish that makes me.

COMING SOON!

A New Cantos Novel

Fall 2022

 BOOKS

Also by CL Walters

Available Now!

EXCERPT

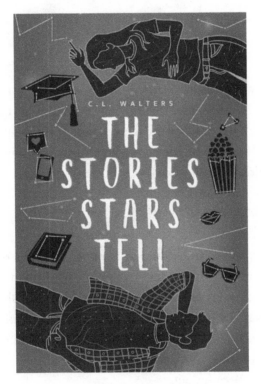

Available Now!

senior year

(14 days to graduation)

emma

I squeeze my eyes shut, terrified I'm about to screw this up. Three deep breaths. Slow. Steady. In. Out. The sound of my breath echoes in my head like the rush of the wind through the tree leaves in my backyard, and the fear of failure, which always sits in the front of my brain, drips down through my body into my stomach.

I could forget my part.

I could ruin everything.

I could be sick.

I picture Cameron, standing in front of his dad's red Ferrari in his khaki pants and suspenders over his dark brown shirt ranting about conquering his fear right before he kicks the shit out of his dad's car. Okay. He's a fictional character from one of my favorite movies of all time, *Ferris Bueller's Day Off*, but still. I'm going to kick the shit out of this, like, speech-Ferrari.

Breathe in. Breathe out.

"Emma?"

The sound of my name, as though it's being called through a tunnel, draws me back. I open my eyes and look into the familiar bright blue eyes of my best friend, Liam.

"Emma? It's almost time. You're doing your breathing thing?"

He's dressed in a business suit, charcoal gray and red tie with those chic pants and shoes that make him seem like he's stepped out of a male fashion magazine. Far more fashionable than most males in these competitions who look like they're wearing their father's Sunday suits. He is beautiful. Dark haired, thin and fit, handsome and not into me at all (I'm not into him either). We've been best friends since third grade in Mrs. Hale's class.

My insides shimmy, but I nod. "Cameron. Remember Cameron."

"What?" He adjusts his black-framed, hipster glasses which he pulls off to perfection.

"Just channeling Cameron." I tug on the bottom of my matching charcoal gray jacket.

Liam reaches out, fixes my collar, and then takes both of my hands in his. Leaning forward, he presses his forehead to mine. He smells like wintergreen mint, familiar and comforting. "We've got this. We've practiced this. We know it. We. Know. It."

I close my eyes. "We do," I repeat, and my heartbeat slows to the rhythm of his words. Liam. My best friend. "Our last time in duo," I whisper. Tears threaten to fall. "What am I going to do without you?"

He pulls back but keeps hold of my hands. "Do. Not. Cry." Hand squeeze. "You have to keep your make-up looking good. Game faces. Let's kick the shit out of this speech, like Cameron did the car."

I smile, because he knows me, and I nod. "Let's do it."

Our names are called. We walk from the wings out onto the stage and take our marks.

We slay it. Of course we do, because that's who we are.

Later, Liam and I are at my house for our usual Saturday night John Hughes movie of the week. It's what we always do on a Saturday night, except for that one Saturday junior year when I went off the rails. The popcorn is made, drinks are chilling, and *Pretty in Pink* is cued up. While we wait for Ginny — our other bestie — to arrive, we both scroll through Instagram.

"Look at this one," Liam says. He's on the floor with his back against the couch. His legs — fit in cotton twill — are stretched out in front of him, crossed at the ankles. He holds up his phone.

"What is that?" I ask.

"It's Baker's house."

"Baker? As in Atticus Baker?"

He nods. "Party there tonight." He continues to examine his phone, and I watch him.

Instead of scrolling through the feed, he stops and scrutinizes Atticus Baker's page. Picture after picture, even reading the comments. It strikes me, because Liam hasn't ever expressed an interest in anyone specific (he's kind of private like that). As he looks through Atticus Baker's feed, it dawns on me how much of a risk Liam took to tell his truth. How lonely it might be in our small, conservative town. Lately, with graduation impending, I've thought about what kind of risks I've taken in my life (that one time junior year notwithstanding), and the answer has been none.

"I see you, Liam. You think Atticus is hot," I say with a giggle.

"Who doesn't? He's gorgeous."

He continues to study every single picture Atticus has posted, and I recognize familiarity in his actions. I've done it. My own phone, at the moment, is open to Tanner James's IG feed, as per usual. I press on his story and watch a video of him walking into Baker's party, but I don't show Liam. He doesn't approve of my infatuation with one of the biggest f-boys at school. I don't blame him; it's suspect.

Instead, I reach out and ruffle Liam's hair, which I know he hates. "But you like him like him."

"Stop!" He lurches forward to get out from under the destructive force of my hand and adjusts his hair back into place, not that I could have done much to those product-laced locks. "And shut up. I don't." His ears turn red.

"You are so lying." I grin and search for Atticus's IG feed on my phone. "He is really handsome," I say when I find it.

I select a gorgeous picture of Atticus and turn my phone to show him. Liam glances at it but looks away, aloof and noncommittal. Even I can't detach from the beauty. Atticus is gorgeous: tall, black, stylish, fit. He's a basketball player at our high school and got a full ride to St. Mary's in California. All of his pictures have this low-key, I'm-so-casual vibe in a matching filter, so there's no way it's casual. But, damn. "Liam. He's so hot, you have my approval," I tell him, even though I know how horrible and objectifying it sounds. Not that Liam needs my approval.

He groans. "Stop, Emma. For real. Atticus is like–" He pauses and turns his shoulders so he's facing me. "Look–"

"Mr. Liam, sir, I don't much feel like one of your lectures," I interrupt in my best patronizing student voice, because Liam is always lecturing me. Mansplaining. The jerk.

"Atticus is like — out of my league. And that's *if* he's gay." He looks down at his phone again. "I mean, I think I got some vibes, but my vibes are inexperienced. I have no idea what I'm doing. Besides, how many openly gay men do you think there are in this backwater, hick-horrible town?" He offers an old man grunt of disgust and readjusts himself with his back against the couch's seat again. "I can't wait to get out of here."

I understand his sentiment, though my prison is of a different kind: Christian family, striving for perfection where nothing real ever happens. Okay, maybe that's not fair, but it's how I feel sometimes. I can't wait to leave and distance myself from stifling expectations to experience my own version of freedom.

I try to give Liam a pep talk anyway. "None of us know what we're doing. We're all faking it. Ferris is the only one who seems to have it all figured out, and he's a fictional character. No one is like that."

"Has what figured out?" Ginny asks from behind us. Liam and I turn and watch her walk into the finished basement from the stairs. "Your dad said to come down, and he'll bring us some fresh cookies when they're out of the oven."

The third of our Bueller troop flops onto the couch next to me

427

with her fresh-coated vanilla scent. She's been on a new kick to live as a 1970's hippie in order to explore the ideology of antidisestablishmentarianism, mostly to annoy her dad and stepmom. The outfit today: tie-dye cotton maxi-skirt she made herself and a black shirt without a bra (which is very noticeable because of her gorgeous boobs and high beams she's been very proud of since she got them). The whole no bra thing has really pushed the buttons of her stepmom which Ginny loves to do more than anything. She lays her head on my shoulder and threads her arm through mine.

"Life," I say, in answer to her original question.

"Our parents don't even have life figured out. Obviously," Ginny replies. "Case in point: my dad and step-monster. How could we — mere eighteen-year-olds? I take that back. We might have it more together."

"Something new?" I ask. The last installment of *The Life and Times of Ginny Donnelly* had her stepmother forcing her to paint her bedroom since she's leaving for college soon. Her stepmom is determined to convert Ginny's room into a fitness haven and has been taking measurements for her equipment.

"Besides Operation Kick Ginny Out of Her Room? Nothing new. I don't want to talk about them, or the fact that she made me go through my closet to consolidate everything into boxes for storage."

"Sorry, Gin." I squeeze her arm with mine. "On a happier note, we were discussing something intriguing. Specifically, Liam's crush on Atticus Baker."

He turns his back to us and resumes his stylish leaning against the couch, looking like a modern James Dean. He's got it all: the hair, the glasses, the pout.

Ginny sits up. "Atticus Baker? Man, he's hot."

"That's what I said."

"Is he gay?"

"We could run a new operation: Find out if Atticus Baker is

Gay," I offer. "We could all slide into his DM, and see?"

"Emma." Liam's voice is threaded with a warning, like a brother who has reached the threshold of annoyance.

I smile. "I'm sorry, Liam. Am I hurting your feelings?" I lean toward him and nuzzle his ear.

He moves to get away from me again. "No." He swats at me. "And no offense, but we know how the last operation you planned went."

I glance at Ginny, who raises her eyebrows and tilts her head. "He has a point."

I know they're referring to the junior year debacle. To be fair, if I was going to sneak out and go to a party, I was going to go all in. Especially if getting caught by my parents was a risk. I hadn't gotten caught, but I had gotten what I'd been after: a kiss — a gorgeously memorable hot kiss that I hadn't been able to forget. From Tanner James. "Everything turned out okay. We didn't get into trouble. Really, when you list out the successes against the failures, that was a win-win."

Liam looks at me like I'm delusional, and perhaps I am. "Emma, if you think you won in that situation, you're wrong. You haven't stopped infatuating about the school's biggest douchebag since. And for someone who claims to be a feminist, that's some contradictory bullshit."

I look to Ginny for backup, which I don't get. "He's right." She shrugs and flops against the couch. "It's been over a year, and you're still struggling with it."

They're both right. I sigh because I *am* infatuated with Tanner James, and I know better. "It doesn't matter. Graduation is two weeks away. We're going to kick ass, say our smarty-pants speeches, and leave for college. Which I will cry about later. Tanner James will be old news. My infatuation with him will be spent as I walk onto a college campus as a co-ed surrounded by beautiful men and women and a playground of sexual awakening."

Ginny and Liam glance at one another with saucer-shaped eyes and then collapse with laughter.

"Emma! I can't believe you just said that." Liam laughs even harder.

"Sexual Awakening. Emma." Ginny shrieks, falling away from me at her waist.

"Wow. You're giving me a complex."

When their laughter subsides, Liam climbs up onto the couch.

With me in between them, sulking, my arms crossed over my chest, I say, "You make me sound like a prude."

"That's not what we mean." Liam pats my leg. "I'm sorry if I hurt your feelings. I just–" He pauses and looks at me over the top of his glasses, reminding me of his dad. "Emma, you're pretty conservative when it comes to stuff like that. And scared about, like everything."

"What? Sex?" I say, still pouting but knowing he's right. I haven't done much in my eighteen years besides masturbate. I'm not ignorant about sex. I may have been raised with Christian parents, but they have been open and frank about sex. While the discussions have moved around the naturalness of the act, the underlying message has been an expectation to wait until marriage. Besides the junior year operation, I'd kissed a couple of other guys. Add to that my date for junior prom, Chris Keller, who tried to pressure me into sex and went so far as to grope me in the limo. I'd slapped him (so much for uncomplicated). Without a doubt, I'm curious and interested in sex, but it's clear my wiring leads to the red wire, not meaningless romps in the back of limos.

"Yeah, sex," Ginny says. "You overthink everything. Sex, like, isn't a thinking endeavor. It's all feeling."

I stand up to get away from them and their words, which I recognize as true but don't want to. "I'm not scared of sex."

Liam stands and mirrors me. "Emma — you're Claire." He points at the TV screen where *Pretty in Pink* waits for us.

I narrow my eyes at him. "I'm not Claire, who's in *The Breakfast Club*, by the way. I'm not a stuck-up, snobby, princess, tease."

"No. Not like that part. Like the sexually repressed part," Ginny says. "The one who secretly likes the bad boy but won't act on it."

"Except–" I hold up a finger for emphasis– "I went into the closet with bad boy John Bender just like she did, only it was junior year with Tanner James." I want to lash out at Liam who's checking out a guy but is too scared to find out if he's gay. And Ginny, who slept with her last boyfriend because she wanted to "get over" her virginity. With my hands on my hips, ready to deflect, I pause and bite my tongue. It's petty and mean, and I love them too much.

"Emma." Ginny's chin falls against her chest, and she stares at me under her lashes. "You had to be drunk to do it."

She's right. *Operation Kiss Tanner James* required me to be drunk, because I couldn't muster up the courage to be bold. But then when had I ever? If it wasn't about church, or school, or duo with Liam — things that I could control — when had I ever been brave?

"Fresh cookies, hot from the oven." My dad with plate in hand maneuvers down the steps into the basement. He looks up with a smile when he reaches the bottom and pauses a moment, assessing the tension in the room. "Everything alright?"

"Perfect." I cross my arms over my chest.

"Those cookies smell delicious, Mr. Matthews," Liam says, turning on the couch to face my father.

Kiss ass.

"How many times have I said it's okay to call me Mo?"

Liam snags a cookie from the plate as my dad sets it on the table between the couch and the TV. "Thanks, Mo."

Dad straightens, walks over to me, and gives me a side hug.

"Thanks, Dad."

"*Pretty in Pink* night?" His eyes bounce from me to Liam to Ginny. He lingers and clears his throat. "Not many of these left, huh?"

We all mumble affirmations at him. I'm sure none of us are truly ready to come to terms with that fact yet, even if we say we're ready to leave.

"I'll leave you to it, then." He squeezes me against his side once more and then disappears back up the stairs.

After he's gone, I look at my friends feeling hurt and vulnerable. They might as well have just said I was the most boring person on the planet — and they'd probably be right.

Ginny pats the couch cushion next to her and holds her arms out to me.

I walk into them, flop forward, and lay against her awkwardly.

"Your Emma-think isn't a bad thing. It's an Emma thing. You're awesome. When you're ready — you'll know," she says. "In fact, because you're you, you'll probably have the best first experience of us all. All that thinking and analysis to make sure."

I move off of her to sit.

"And," Ginny says, "believe me. You don't want a Dean on your hands." Each of us snorts in reference to her first, the aftermath of just trying to "get over it." She shudders and takes my hand in hers. "Maybe it will be like a sexual awakening in college next year, or maybe it will be a hot someone this summer. Perhaps it will be in four years, or maybe it will be on your wedding night. It doesn't matter. What matters is YOU get to decide that for yourself, and that will make it perfect."

Liam sits down on the other side of me and takes my hand. "And I'll be there cheering you on for your first encounter with the D, or the V — whichever you prefer."

"I don't know why this suddenly became about me."

"Here. We can make it about me," Liam says. "I'm still a virgin."

"A status you'd like to change with Atticus Baker." I wiggle my eyebrows at him.

He smacks my shoulder. "Shut it, bitch." Then he chuckles.

"Let's get this John Hughes night moving already. Turn on the movie. Wait, Pretty in Pink? Maybe we should switch it to The Breakfast Club." Ginny lets me go and leans forward for popcorn. "We've got some analysis to do on that dialogue between Allison and Claire tonight, I think."

After an argument about sticking with our planned movie schedule, we watch *Pretty in Pink*. Ginny relents because Andie needs analysis of her attitudes about men: douchebags versus the best-friend. I point out one of my best friends is gay and the other one isn't; it's not an option in all circumstances. We're all in agreement that Andie should have ended up with Duckie (cue giant eye rolls), but as the movie plays, I'm distracted. I attempt to stay in it with my friends since our John Hughes movie nights are dwindling down to a handful. My mind keeps turning back to junior year. I think about how I'd played that night and the aftermath and wish I'd been braver.

About the Author

CL Walters writes in Hawai'i where she lives with her husband, two children, and acts as a pet butler to two pampered fur-babies. She's the author of the YA Contemporary series, *The Cantos Chronicles* (*Swimming Sideways*, *The Ugly Truth* and *The Bones of Who We Are*), the YA/NA Contemporary romance *The Stories Stars Tell* as well as the adult romance, *The Letters She Left Behind*. *In the Echo of this Ghost Town* and *When the Echo Answers* are her sixth and seventh YA/NA Contemporary novels. For up-to-date news, sign up for her monthly newsletter on her website at www.clwalters.net as well as follow her writer's journey on Instagram @cl.walters.